SPECIAL MESSAGE TO READERS

THE ULVERSCROFT FOUNDATION
(registered UK charity number 264873)
was established in 1972 to provide funds for
research, diagnosis and treatment of eye diseases.
Examples of major projects funded by
the Ulverscroft Foundation are:-

- The Children's Eye Unit at Moorfields Eye Hospital, London
- The Ulverscroft Children's Eye Unit at Great Ormond Street Hospital for Sick Children
- Funding research into eye diseases and treatment at the Department of Ophthalmology, University of Leicester
- The Ulverscroft Vision Research Group, Institute of Child Health
- Twin operating theatres at the Western Ophthalmic Hospital, London
- The Chair of Ophthalmology at the Royal Australian College of Ophthalmologists

You can help further the work of the Foundation
by making a donation or leaving a legacy.
Every contribution is gratefully received. If you
would like to help support the Foundation or
require further information, please contact:

THE ULVERSCROFT FOUNDATION
The Green, Bradgate Road, Anstey
Leicester LE7 7FU, England
Tel: (0116) 236 4325

website: www.foundation.ulverscroft.com

Kathleen McGurl lives near the sea in Bournemouth with her husband and elderly tabby cat. She has two sons who are now grown up and have left home. She began her writing career creating short stories, and sold dozens to women's magazines in the UK and Australia. Then she got sidetracked onto family history research, which led eventually to writing novels with genealogy themes. She has always been fascinated by the past, and the ways in which it can influence the present, and enjoys these links in her novels.

You can discover more about the author at http://kathleenmcgurl.com

THE FORGOTTEN SECRET

It's the summer of 1919, and Ellen O'Brien has her whole life ahead of her. Young, in love, and leaving home for her first job, the future seems full of shining possibility. But war is brewing, and before long, Ellen and everyone around her are swept up by it. As Ireland is torn apart by the turmoil, Ellen finds herself facing the ultimate test of love and loyalty . . . A hundred years later, Clare Farrell has inherited a dilapidated old farmhouse in County Meath. Seizing the chance to escape her unhappy marriage, she strikes out on her own, hoping the old building might also tell her something about her family's shadowy history. And when she stumbles across a long-forgotten hiding place, she discovers a clue to a secret that has lain buried for decades . . .

Books by Kathleen McGurl
Published by Ulverscroft:

THE GIRL FROM BALLYMOR
THE DROWNED VILLAGE

KATHLEEN McGURL

THE FORGOTTEN SECRET

Complete and Unabridged

CHARNWOOD
Leicester

First published in Great Britain in 2019 by
HQ
An imprint of HarperCollins*Publishers* Ltd.
London

First Charnwood Edition
published 2020
by arrangement with
HarperCollins*Publishers* Ltd
London

A catalogue record for this book is available
from the British Library.

ISBN 978–1–4448–4392–7

To all my Irish in-laws
— this one's for you

Historical Note

If you were educated in Ireland you'll probably know all this already, in which case feel free to skip this section. Everyone else — please read on. I hope this will help provide some context for the novel. I'll keep it as short as possible!

By the early twentieth century, Ireland had been ruled by England since Norman times. Over the years there had been various uprisings: notably Wolfe Tone's United Irishmen rebellion of 1798. In response to this, the British Parliament passed the *Acts of Union* in 1800, formalising Ireland's status as part of the United Kingdom of Great Britain and Ireland.

Many Irish were still unhappy under British rule. Harsh penal laws against Catholics and the aftermath of the Great Famine of the 1840s led to ever greater hostility against English landlords. In the late 1800s and early 1900s there was much discussion in parliament about the possibility of 'Home Rule' for Ireland. By 1914 a Government of Ireland bill was making its way through the British parliament system when the First World War broke out. It was put on hold.

But Irish nationalists weren't prepared to wait for the end of the war for discussion to resume. At Easter 1916 various Irish nationalist forces combined in an uprising, taking control of parts of Dublin. The Proclamation of the Republic was read out from the steps of the General Post

Office, declaring Ireland's independence. British troops soon quashed the uprising, and most of its leaders were executed.

In the parliamentary elections of 1918 just after the end of the war, Ireland's primary nationalist party Sinn Fein won a large majority of the Irish seats in parliament. However, they refused to swear the required oath of allegiance to the King, and instead set up the first Dáil Éireann(Irish Council), declaring Ireland to be an independent nation. Thus, Ireland slid into war against Britain. (One Sinn Fein MP was Constance Markievicz, the first woman to be elected to the UK Parliament. She was in jail at the time, for her part in the 1916 uprising. Constance was also the founder of the Fianna Éireann, 'Warriors of Ireland', a kind of military boy scouts, whose alumni went on to join the Republican army.)

In the cities, British troops kept control but in provincial areas it was the paramilitary police force — the Royal Irish Constabulary — that was left fighting against the nationalist Irish Volunteers. The RIC was reinforced by the undisciplined Black and Tans, named for their mismatched ex-army and police uniforms.

The War of Independence was largely a guerrilla war, with atrocities committed by both sides. It was characterised by attacks and counter-attacks, shootings and reprisal actions, often against civilians. Towns were looted, homes and businesses were burned, and people executed.

In 1921 the British prime minister offered a truce: the terms of which divided Ireland, forming the Irish Free State but with six counties of

Ulster remaining part of the United Kingdom. The Irish leadership were split over whether to agree, but eventually signed the treaty. This disagreement led inevitably to civil war, between those who were pro- and anti-treaty, that lasted from 1922 until a ceasefire in spring 1923.

During World War II Ireland remained neutral, and it was after 'the Emergency' (as it was termed in Ireland) that the Republic of Ireland was formally inaugurated in 1948.

The anti-treaty nationalist forces combined as the Irish Republican Army, and remained active on and off throughout the decades, fighting for Ireland to be once more united. Their campaigns escalated during the 1970s and 80s, a period known as 'the Troubles', and only came to an end with the signing of the Good Friday Agreement of 1998.

In this novel, the historical chapters start in 1919, just as the War of Independence was escalating in intensity. I've referred to Irish nationalist forces during the War of Independence as 'Volunteers' throughout, though there were various groups involved. Volunteers from this period are often known now as the 'old IRA'. Blackstown is a fictional place.

1

Clare, February 2016

We rounded a corner, turned off the narrow country lane and onto a gravel track, drove past a little copse of birch trees and there it was. Clonamurty Farm, County Meath, Ireland. Old, tired, dilapidated and in urgent need of repair. But it was mine. All mine, and *only* mine, or soon would be. A little shudder of excitement ran through me, and I turned my face away so that Paul, my husband, would not see the smile that had crept onto my face.

I think it was in that moment that I first realised my life could change, for the better. If only I was brave enough to seize the day.

'What a godforsaken mess of a place. Good job this is a hire car. That track'll be trashing the tyres,' Paul grumbled, as he parked the car beside a rusty old piece of farm machinery that had waist-high thistles growing up through it.

'I expect it could be renovated, with a bit of money and a lot of effort,' I said. Already I could see its potential. With the weeds cleared, the stonework repointed, the rotten windowsills replaced and painted, and a new porch built around the front door it would be beautiful. A lazy Labrador sunning himself in the yard and a couple of cats nonchalantly strolling around owning the place would complete the picture.

As if I'd conjured them up, two tabbies appeared around the corner, mewing loudly, tails held high, coming to see who we were and whether we had any food for them, I suspected. I smiled to see them, and bent down, hand outstretched, to make their acquaintance.

'Clare, for God's sake don't touch them. They'll be ridden with fleas and Lord knows what else.'

'Aw, they're fine. Aren't you, my pretties? Who's been looking after you then, since your daddy died?' I felt a pang of worry for these poor, beautiful creatures. Though they weren't especially thin, and their coats seemed in good condition.

'Their *daddy*. Oh grow up, will you?' Paul stomped away from me, towards the front door, and fished in his pocket for the key we'd picked up from the solicitor in nearby Blackstown. Actually the solicitor, Mr Greve, had handed the key to me. It was my uncle Pádraig who'd left me the farm in his will, after all. But Paul had reached out and snatched the key before I'd had the chance to take it. The farm wasn't quite mine yet. I needed to wait for probate to be completed, but we'd had the chance to come over to Ireland for a weekend to view the property and make a decision about what to do with it.

I followed Paul across the weed-infested gravel to the peeling, blue-painted front door, and watched as he wrestled with the lock. 'Damn key doesn't fit. That idiot solicitor's given us the wrong one.'

I peered through a filthy window beside the front door. 'Paul, there are boxes and stuff leaning against this door. I reckon Uncle Pádraig didn't use it. Maybe that key's for another door, round the back, perhaps?'

'The solicitor would have told us if it was,' Paul said, continuing to try to force the key into the lock. I left him to it and walked around the side of the house to the back of the building. There was a door at the side, which looked well used. A pair of wellington boots, filled with rain water, stood beside the step. I called Paul, and he came around the house, his lips pinched thin. He never liked to be proved wrong.

The key fitted this door and we entered the house. It smelled musty and unaired. It had been last decorated at some point in the 1970s, I'd say. I tried to bring to mind my memories of the house, from visits to Uncle Pádraig and Aunt Lily when I was a child, but it was a long time ago and I'd been very young then. My maternal grandmother — Granny Irish as I called her — lived here too in those days. I have clear memories of one of my cousins: David (or Daithí as he renamed himself after he became a committed Republican), hazy memories of his two older brothers but only vague impressions of a large rambling house. I have better memories of the barn where I used to love playing hide-and-seek with David among the bales of straw. Sadly, David and his brothers had all died young, which was why the farmhouse had been passed down to me.

The door led into a corridor, with a grubby

7

kitchen off to the right and a boot-room to the left. Straight ahead a wedged-open door led to the main hallway, which in turn led to the blocked-off front door, the sitting room and dining room. This area looked familiar. There'd been a grandfather clock — I looked around and yes, it was still there! — standing in the hallway. A memory surfaced of listening to it chiming the hour when I was supposed to be asleep upstairs. I'd count the chimes, willing it to chime thirteen like the clock in my favourite book — *Tom's Midnight Garden* — and was always disappointed when it stopped at twelve.

We peered into each room. Upstairs there were four bedrooms, a box-room and a bathroom. All felt a little damp, as though it had been months since they'd been aired or heated. As with the downstairs rooms, the decor was horribly dated. I expected Paul to make sneering comments about the state of the place — and to be fair, it was in a total mess — but he surprised me by commenting favourably on the layout, the size of the rooms, the amount of light that flooded through the large front windows. 'It could be quite a house, this,' he said.

'It certainly could,' I replied. 'And we could come for holidays, let the boys use it and perhaps rent it as a holiday home in between, after we've done it up.' I could see it now. Long, lazy weeks, using this house as a base to explore this part of Ireland. It was within easy reach of Dublin and the east coast, and the surrounding countryside of rolling farmland was peacefully attractive.

'Don't be ridiculous. We can't do this place

up. We live in London. And why on earth would anyone want to come here for a holiday? There's nothing to do. No. Like I said earlier, we'll sell it to, some developer or other, and I have plans for what to do with the money.'

'Can we at least discuss it?' I couldn't believe he was dismissing the idea of keeping the farm, just like that.

'What's to discuss? I've made up my mind. As soon as probate comes through, I'll put it on the market. We can find suitable estate agents to handle it for us while we're here.' He smiled at me — a smile that did not reach his eyes but which told me the matter was closed. 'Come on. Let's go and find somewhere we can have a cup of tea. I've got to get out of this depressing house.' Paul turned and walked along the passage towards the back door. Somewhere upstairs a door banged, as though the farmhouse was voicing its own disapproval of his words.

As I followed Paul out, knowing there was no point arguing with him when he was in this kind of mood, I realised that he would not be able to do anything without my say-so. The house and all its outbuildings, Uncle Pádraig's entire estate, had been left to me. Not to Paul, just to me. So if I wanted, I could refuse to sell it, and there'd be nothing Paul could do about it. Except to moan and snipe and make my life a misery, of course.

It hadn't always been like this. We'd been married twenty-five years. He swept me off my feet when I first met him. I was fresh out of university with a degree in textile design but not enough talent to make it as a designer, and was working in a shoe shop by day and a pub by night to make ends meet. It was not what I'd dreamed of for myself.

Then one day, the best-looking man I'd ever set eyes on came into the pub and ordered himself a gin and tonic, and 'whatever you're having, love'. Usually I turned down these offers — the bar staff were not allowed to drink alcohol while on shift although we were allowed to accept soft drinks from customers. But this time, something about his sparkly eyes that seemed to look deep into the heart of me, something about his melodious voice and cultivated manner, something about his sharp suit and immaculate shirt made me accept, and then spend the rest of the evening between customers (it was a quiet night) leaning on the bar chatting to him.

He was in the area for a work conference, staying in a hotel just up the road, but couldn't stand the company of his colleagues another moment so had escaped from the hotel bar and into the nearest pub. By the end of the evening we'd swapped phone numbers and agreed to meet up the following day when I wasn't working, for a drink. He turned up that second night with a gift of the best box of chocolates I'd ever had, and a perfect single stem red rose in a plastic tube. My previous boyfriends had all been impoverished arts students. No one had ever treated me like that before.

He used to sing that Human League song to me — you know the one: 'Don't You Want Me, Baby'. I wasn't exactly working as a waitress in a cocktail bar when he met me, but pretty close. And he liked to tell people he'd pulled me up, out of the gutter. 'Who knows where she'd have ended up without me, eh?' he'd say, patting my arm while I grimaced and tried not to wonder the same thing.

Paul had been kind in those early days. Thoughtful, considerate, and nothing was too much trouble for him. He was always planning extravagant little treats for me — a surprise picnic on the banks of the Thames, a hamper complete with bright white linen napkins all packed and ready in his car; tickets to Wimbledon centre court on the ladies' final day; a night away in the Manoir aux Quat'Saisons. All would be sprung on me as a surprise.

It was exciting, but looking back, perhaps slightly unnerving in the way that it left me with no control over my life. I'd have to cancel any plans I had made myself, to go along with his surprises. And any twinge of resentment I felt would turn quickly into guilt — how could I resent him doing such lovely things for me? When I told my friends of his latest surprise treat, they'd all sigh and tell me how lucky I was, and ask could I clone him for them.

Gradually I'd stopped making my own plans, at least not without checking with Paul that it'd be all right for me to see my parents, or spend a day shopping with a girlfriend, in case he had something up his sleeve for us. And so as Paul and I became closer, my old friends had drifted away as I'd rarely seemed to have time to see them and had cancelled on them too many times.

★ ★ ★

We left the farm in silence, and got back in the car to return to Blackstown in search of a café. I spent the journey wondering what plans Paul had made for the money if we sold the farm. Perhaps he'd surprise me, the way he so often used to, and present me with round-the-world cruise tickets, or keys to a luxury holiday home in Tuscany.

It was the sort of thing he might have done in the early days of our relationship. He'd stopped the surprises after the boys were born — it wasn't so easy to swan off on weekends away with toddlers in tow. But the boys were in their twenties now and had left home — Matt had a job and Jon was a student. Perhaps Paul did want to rekindle the spirit of our early relationship. I resolved to try to keep an open mind about the farm, but I would certainly want to know his plans before I agreed to sell it.

★ ★ ★

There's something funny about being at my stage of life. OK, spare the jokes about the big change, but being 49 and having the big five-oh looming on the horizon does make you re-evaluate who you are, what your life is like, and whether you've achieved your life's dreams or not. Ever since my last birthday I'd been doing a lot of navel-gazing. What had I done with my life? I'd brought up two wonderful sons. That had to count as my greatest achievement.

I say 'I' had brought them up although of course it was both of us. Paul wasn't as hands-on as I was — it was always me who took them to Scouts, attended school sports day, sat with them overnight when they were ill. But then, Paul would always say his role was to be the breadwinner, mine was to be the mother and homemaker.

I've tried to list more achievements beyond being the mother of well-adjusted, fabulous young men, but frankly I can't think of any. We have a beautiful house — that's down to me. Maybe that can count? I decorated it from top to bottom, made all the curtains, renovated beautiful old furniture for it. I did several years of upholstery evening classes and have reupholstered chairs, sofas and a chaise longue. But all this doesn't feel like something that could go on my gravestone, does it? *Here lies Clare Farrell, mourned by husband, sons and several overstuffed armchairs.*

*   *   *

We arrived in Blackstown, and Paul reversed the car into a parking space outside a cosy-looking tea shop. I shook myself out of my thoughts. They were only making me bitter. Who knew, perhaps he did have plans for the proceeds of the sale of the farm that would help rekindle our relationship. Surely a marriage of over twenty-five years was worth fighting for? I should give him a chance.

'Well? Does this place look OK to you?' he

asked, as he unclipped his seatbelt.

I smiled back as we entered the café. 'Perfect. I fancy tea and a cake. That chocolate fudge cake looks to die for.' Huge slices, thick and gooey, just how I liked it. I was salivating already.

'Not watching your figure then? You used to be so slim,' Paul replied. He approached the counter and ordered two teas and one slice of carrot cake — his favourite, but something I can't stand. 'No, love, that's all,' he said, when the waitress asked if he wanted anything else. 'The wife's on a diet.'

I opened my mouth to protest but Paul gave me a warning look. I realised if I said anything he'd grab me by the arm and drag me back to the car, where we'd have a row followed by stony silence for the rest of the day. And I wouldn't get my cup of tea. Easier, as on so many other occasions, to stay quiet, accept the tea and put up with the lack of cake.

It was so often like this. Once more I wondered whether I'd ever have the courage to leave him. But was this kind of treatment grounds enough for a separation? It sounded so trivial, didn't it — *I'm leaving him because he won't let me eat cake and I've had enough of it.* Well, today wasn't the day I'd be leaving him, that was for certain, so I smiled sweetly, sat at a table by the window, meekly drank my cup of tea and watched Paul eat his carrot cake with a fork, commenting occasionally on how good it was.

2

Ellen, July 1919

Three good things had happened that day, Ellen O'Brien thought, as she walked home to the cottage she shared with her father. Firstly, she'd found a sixpence on the road leading out of Blackstown. Sixpence was the perfect amount of money to find. A penny wouldn't buy much, and a shilling or more she'd feel obliged to hand in somewhere, or give it to Da to buy food. But a sixpence she felt she could keep. It hadn't lasted long though, as she'd called in at O'Flanaghan's sweetshop and bought a bag of barley-drops. She'd always had a sweet tooth and even though she was now a grown woman of eighteen she still could not resist the velvety feel of melting sugar in her mouth.

The second good thing was the one that most people would say was the most important of the three. She'd got herself a job, as upstairs maid for Mrs Emily Carlton, in the big house. Da had been nagging her to get a job and bring in some money to help. There was only the two of them now in the cottage since one by one her brothers had gone across the seas to America, Canada and England. Da was getting old and appeared less able (or less willing, as Ellen sometimes thought, uncharitably) to work, and had said he needed Ellen to start earning. She'd been keeping house for him for five years now, since Mammy had died during that long, cold winter when the whole of Europe had been at war.

But it was the third good thing to happen that Ellen rated as the best and most exciting; the event she'd been looking forward to for months. It was the news that at long last Jimmy Gallagher was home from school. For good, this time. He was the same age as her, just two months older, and had been away at a boarding school for years, coming home only for the long summer holidays.

It was Mrs O'Flanaghan at the sweetshop who'd told her the news. The old woman remembered how Ellen and Jimmy would call in for a pennyworth of sweets on a Friday after school, back in those long-ago childhood days when they both attended the National School and had been best friends. Jimmy had passed his exams now, and finished high school. 'Set to become a lawyer, if he goes off to university and studies some more, so he is,' said Mrs O'Flanaghan. 'But first he'll help his daddy with the harvest. And maybe he'll decide to stay on and become a farmer. Those Gallaghers have such high hopes for him, but I'm after thinking he's a simple soul at heart, and will be content to stay here in Blackstown now.'

Ellen certainly hoped so. She calculated when would be the soonest that she could go over to Clonamurty Farm to see Jimmy. Not today — it was already late for her to be getting home to cook the tea. Tomorrow, then. Sunday, after church, if she didn't see him in church. She was

16

not due to start at Mrs Carlton's until Monday.

Ellen rounded the corner and turned off the lane, up the rutted track that led to her home. It was looking more and more dilapidated, she thought, sadly. Back when Mammy was alive, Da would never have let the thatch get into such a state, sagging in the middle and letting water in over the kitchen. The gate was hanging off its hinges, and the front door was waterlogged and swollen, its paint long since peeled away.

'Hello, boy,' Ellen said to Digger, the elderly wolfhound who had hauled himself to his feet, wagging his tail at her approach. She fondled his ears. 'Daddy in, is he? I've news for him, so I have.'

Digger pushed his muzzle into her hand, and she remembered the pack of barley sugars. She gave him one, which he ate with a crunch, and then she pushed open the door to the cottage.

'Da? I'm back.' Mr O'Brien was sitting in his worn-out armchair beside the kitchen range, his head lolling back, mouth open, snoring loudly.

'I'll make you a cup of tea, will I?' Ellen didn't wait for an answer, but began setting the kettle to boil, clattering around a little so as to wake him naturally.

It worked. 'Eh, what?' he said, sitting upright and blinking to focus on her. 'Ah, tis you, Mary-Ellen. Late, aren't you?'

'Not really. I have good news, Da. I'm after getting myself a job, up at Carlton House. I'm to start on Monday. Ten shillings a week.'

'Ah, that's grand, lass. Keep two yourself and the rest towards the housekeeping. You'll be back

17

each day to cook for me?'

Ellen shook her head. 'The job's live-in, Da. I'll get a day off every Sunday and will come home then.'

Her father pursed his lips. 'Who'll cook for me, then?'

Ellen was silent for a moment. 'I'll make you pies on Sunday that'll last the week.'

'And what of potatoes? I'll have to cook my own, will I?'

'Da, you wanted me to find a job. And now I have. You'll be grand.'

Seamus O'Brien grunted. 'Cooking me own tea. Women's work, that is.'

Ellen ignored him. She was used to his grumps, and knew he was more than capable of boiling a few potatoes. She poured water into the teapot. Should she tell Da about Jimmy being home? A smile played about her lips as she thought of Jimmy, and imagined meeting up with him tomorrow.

'What's that you're so pleased about, girl? Your new job?'

'Aye, that, and the fact that Jimmy Gallagher's home, so I heard.' The words slipped out unbidden.

'Michael Gallagher's lad, from Clonamurty?'

'That's him, Da. I was at the National with him, remember?'

Seamus O'Brien shook his head. 'Don't be getting ideas. Them Gallaghers are too good for the likes of us. They'll be looking for a lass with money for their Jimmy. Not a kitchen maid, like you.'

18

'Upstairs maid,' Ellen said quietly. But her father's words stung. Was she really too lowly for Jimmy? Not that she thought of him as a potential suitor, or at least, she tried not to. These last few years they'd only seen each other a half-dozen times each summer and Christmas, when he'd come home for school holidays. She'd thought their friendship was strong, and that Jimmy liked her company as much as she liked his, but what now? Now they were both grown, both adults, would he still like her? Or was she just a childhood friend, someone to think back on fondly?

She didn't know. She wouldn't know until she saw him again and had the chance to judge his reaction on seeing her. She hoped if nothing else they would still be friends, still share a few easy-going, laughter-filled days together like they always had. One day, she supposed, he would find himself a sweetheart and that would be hard for Ellen to deal with, but she would smile and wish him well. Occasionally she had dared fantasise that she would become his sweetheart, but her father was probably right. His parents would want someone better for him, and who could blame them?

He'd almost certainly be at Mass tomorrow. She'd find out then, for better or for worse, whether his last year at school had changed him or not.

* * *

Jimmy was indeed at Mass. She saw him walk in with his parents and younger brother, so tall now, so handsome! His dark-blond hair, too long across his forehead so that he had to keep flicking it back. A smattering of freckles across his nose — faded now compared to what he'd had as a child. His broad chest and long, elegant hands. She felt a flutter in her stomach. Would he want to know her any more? She tried to catch his eye, carefully, as she didn't want her father to see her doing it. But he didn't notice her, or if he did, he made no sign.

The service, led by Father O'Riordan, was interminably long. The priest was getting on in years, and Ellen often thought he was simply going through the motions rather than truly finding joy in the presence of God. His sermon, as it did so often, rambled on, touching on several topics but not fully exploring any. Ten seconds after it was over Ellen could not have said what it was about. The only thing for certain was that she had learned nothing from it, despite listening intently.

When she went up to receive the Holy Sacrament, she once more tried to catch Jimmy's eye, but he was at the far end of a pew on the other side of church, and did not go up for communion. That was odd. To be in church and not receive communion? He must have something on his mind he wished to confess to the priest, and had not had the chance to do so before Mass, she thought.

At last the service was over. She walked out with her father, feeling a strange mixture of delight at having seen Jimmy again but disappointment that he had not acknowledged her in any way. At the door of the church her father stopped to say a few words to the priest, and she caught sight of Jimmy once more, over the priest's shoulder, standing a little way off.

He was looking right at her, smiling slightly, and making a surreptitious hand signal, fingers splayed then closed, not raising his hand at all. Anyone watching would have thought he was just stretching his finger joints.

But Ellen knew different, and the sight of that gesture filled her with joy. It was part of their old childhood sign language — a set of signs they'd made up so they could signal to each other in class without the teacher realising. There were signs for 'see you after school by the old oak', 'watch out, the teacher's coming', 'I have sweets, want to share them?' Jimmy had made the sign for 'see you after school'. She was puzzled for a moment but quickly realised he must mean 'after church'. She signalled back 'yes' (a waggling thumb) and had to suppress a snort of laughter when he replied with the sign for 'want to share my sweets?' accompanied by a lopsided cheeky grin.

As soon as her father had finished speaking to the priest, she made some excuse about having left something in the church. 'I'll see you back at home, Da,' she said. 'Couple of things I need to do, then I'll be back to cook the Sunday dinner.'

'Aye, well, don't be long, girl,' he replied, his mouth downturned as it so often was these days. He walked off, not looking back, and as soon as he'd turned the corner and was out of sight Ellen darted off through the churchyard in the opposite direction, to the old oak that stood on the edge of a field beside the river. It was near the National School, and had been the place where she and Jimmy always met up after school when they were children.

He was there now, waiting for her. 'Well! Here we are, then,' he said, smiling broadly. She was not sure whether to hug him, kiss his cheek, or shake his hand. In the past she'd have thrown herself at him, arms round his neck, legs around his waist if her skirts were loose enough and she was sure he could take her weight. But they were grown-up now, and surely that wasn't seemly behaviour? She was still dithering when he resolved the issue for her — holding out his arms and taking her two hands in his. 'Well,' he said again, 'you're all grown-up now, Mary-Ellen, so you are!'

'Still just Ellen, to you, though,' she replied. There were altogether too many Marys around the place without adding to them by using her full name.

'The lovely Ellen,' Jimmy said, bringing a blush to her cheek. 'You've changed.'

'How?'

'More beautiful than ever,' he said, so quietly she wondered if perhaps she hadn't heard him properly. When she didn't reply, he let go of her hands, took her arm and began walking through the park. 'Aren't you going to ask me how my last year in school was?'

'How was it?'

'Boring as all hell.'

Ellen gasped to hear him use such a word, and

Jimmy laughed. 'The teachers taught me nothing. Nothing at all. But I studied enough to pass my exams, so the old man's pleased with me. Now I've the whole summer at home to help with the harvest and decide whether I want to go on to university and become a lawyer, or stay here and become a farmer. Wildly different choices, aren't they?'

Ellen nodded, willing him to say he wanted to stay in Blackstown. 'What will you do?'

'Ah, my sweet Ellen. Sometimes fate has a way of deciding things for us. Sometimes something becomes so important to a person that they actually have no choice. They just have to follow where their heart leads them, no matter what.' He gazed at her as he said these last words. For a moment she thought he was going to pull her into his arms and kiss her, right there, in the middle of the park, where other folk were strolling and might see, and might recognise them and tell her father! But she'd take that risk. Her heart surged. Surely he was saying that she was the most important thing in his life, the thing his heart would insist he follow?

But his next words changed everything. 'Ellen, let me tell you what happened this year at school. The teachers taught me nothing but I learned plenty, anyway. One of the old boys organised a club, called the Dunnersby Debaters. But we weren't a debating society. We were there to learn Irish history, the real history, not the English version the masters taught. We learned the Irish language. We heard all about Wolfe Tone, and the 1798 rebellion, and all the other attempts to rise up against our oppressors. We learned exactly what happened in the 1916 Easter uprising, and why we must not let those efforts die in vain. Ireland *must have* home rule. One way or another, we must find a way to achieve it. I joined the Fianna Éireann too, and learned to shoot, so when the time comes I'll be ready.'

His eyes were blazing as he made this speech. She could see the passion surging through him like wildfire. They'd spoken before, a year or two ago, about the prospect of Irish independence, but had mostly been repeating what they'd heard their parents say. Ellen had never been sure whether it would be good for Ireland or not — would the country not be worse off if it threw off its connections to its powerful, wealthy neighbour and branched out on its own? Was it not better to be a little part of a bigger nation, than a small, poor nation that was independent?

But clearly Jimmy had made up his mind the other way. What would that mean for him? What would it mean for her, and the future she hardly dared dream about, a future with Jimmy at her side?

3

Clare, February 2016

'So, how was the house, Mum?' my son Matt asked, when I met up with him for our regular weekly coffee a few days after coming back from Ireland. Matt had graduated from university a couple of years ago, and now worked for an IT consultancy based in London, which meant we could easily meet up.

I sipped my Americano before answering, trying to decide how best to describe Clonamurty Farm. 'Hmm, Dilapidated,' was the word I picked in the end.

'But with potential?' Matt was studying me carefully. 'Mum, there's a twinkle in your eye. You can't disguise it.'

I smiled. He probably knew me better than anyone, Paul included. 'Yes, it certainly has potential.'

'So?'

'So what?'

'So are you going to move there, do it up, get in touch with your Irish heritage and all that?'

'Your dad doesn't want to. He wants to sell it to a developer as soon as possible.'

Matt frowned. 'It's not his to sell though, is it? What do *you* want to do with it?'

I picked up a teaspoon and stirred my coffee, which didn't need stirring, before answering.

When I looked up Matt was still frowning slightly. I wanted to tell him to stop before the lines became permanent. I wanted to rub my thumb between his eyes to smooth them out. 'Well. How do I answer that?' I said, still playing for time.

'Truthfully? Come on, Mum. You can tell me anything — you know that. I won't tell Dad.'

'OK. The truth is, I don't really know what I want. Part of me says yes, your dad is right, we should sell it, take the money, invest it for the future, give some to you and Jon.'

'And the other part?'

I took a deep breath. 'Says I should move to Ireland, no matter what.'

'With or without Dad?'

'It'd probably be . . . without him, I think. He wouldn't want to look for a new job in Ireland. Perhaps he'd come over at weekends, or . . . '

' . . . or you'd use this as a chance to leave him?'

There they were. The words. Out there, in the wild. Matt had said it, not me, but I needed to answer. It felt like the point of no return. I took yet another deep breath, this one shuddering. 'Ye-es. I suppose so.'

I don't know what reaction I expected from him. But it wasn't this. He leapt up, grinning, came round the table and leaned over me to hug me. 'Oh, Mum. At last! You're doing the right thing. You know you are. It's time for you to have a life of your own, not dictated by Dad. He's always putting you down and trying to stop you doing anything for yourself. I know you stayed

26

together for me and Jon, which is lovely of you, but we're grown-up now and if you two separate, we won't mind at all. It won't hurt us. Jon feels the same — I know because we've discussed it.'

I picked up a napkin and dabbed at my eyes, which had sprung a leak. It was a weird feeling, knowing our two sons had discussed their parents' relationship and come to the conclusion I should leave my husband. Very weird. 'We've been married twenty-five years, Matt. It's a lot to throw away and I need to think it through carefully before doing anything.'

'You're not throwing anything away. You're just moving on to a new phase in your life. It's the perfect opportunity, Mum. You'll have somewhere to live and money of your own, so you won't be dependent on him or any divorce settlement. You'll be far enough from Dad to stop him interfering. Because you know he'll try to.'

I nodded. Yes, he would try to interfere. He'd try to stop me. 'But I'd also be far from you and Jon.'

'Ryanair fly to Dublin for about fifty quid return. We could come over to see you for weekends every couple of months. I'd love to see my great-grandparents' farm.' Matt sat down again opposite me, but kept hold of my hand across the table. I loved that my sons were so tactile and affectionate.

I felt a tear form in the corner of my eye. 'Can't help but wonder what your grandparents would have thought, if they'd still been here. Marriage is supposed to be for life.'

Matt smiled. 'They'd feel the same way Jon and I do, I'm sure. They'd want what's best for you, and it's been obvious for ages that staying with Dad isn't doing you any good. You know, Grandma used to pull me to one side and ask me on the quiet if I thought you were happy with Dad. I used to say yes of course you were, as I didn't want to worry her, not when she was so ill at the end.'

'Oh, sweetheart.' I had to wipe away another tear at that. Mum had been in such pain in her final days as the cancer ate away at her. She'd been in a hospice, in a private room, with Dad at her bedside and the boys and me visiting as often as we could. I went every day at the end. Paul only came once, stayed five minutes then announced he had too much to do. I'd told myself it wasn't his mum, and he was feeling uncomfortable not being part of her direct family. But the truth was he had never really wanted much to do with my parents. Dad had died only a year after Mum. But before he'd gone, he'd gifted me his car — a three-year-old Ford Mondeo that Paul had immediately appropriated as his own, trading in our elderly BMW. Until Uncle Pádraig's legacy, the car was the only thing I owned outright, under my own name.

'So, you going to do it, Mum?' Matt said, dragging me back into the present.

'I don't know yet. I'm going to have a good long think about it.'

'You do that.' He was thoughtful for a moment, then looked at me with a smile. 'Do you remember that poem Grandma used to quote? *I will arise and go now, and go to Innisfree.* That's what you should do.'

'Go to Innisfree?' I said.

'Or whatever the farm in Ireland is called. Arise and go now. That's my point.' He pulled out his wallet to pay for our coffees. 'This one's on me. And don't forget you can ring me any time if you want to discuss it more. Jon and I will do all we can to help you.'

'Not if it puts your dad against you. I don't want you to ruin your relationship with him on account of me.'

'Mum, I don't have much of a relationship with him anyway. Don't think Jon does either. It was always you, when we were kids. You were the one who walked us to school, took us to swimming lessons, helped us with homework, played endless games of Monopoly with us on rainy days and all the rest of it. A proper parent. Dad was just a shadowy figure in the background.'

'On holidays though, he played with you then?'

'Did he? I don't remember. When I think of family holidays, I picture you digging sandcastles or helping us fly kites. I suppose Dad was there, but he just doesn't figure in my memories.'

Matt got up to pay our bill. Those last words had made me kind of sad and lost in my reminiscences again. I'd always thought that our family holidays were the best times, when Paul had been a proper dad for once.

★　★　★

29

We hadn't been married long when I became pregnant with Matt. Paul was delighted when I showed him the blue line on the pregnancy test, and immediately took me out to a swanky restaurant for dinner. Bit wasted on me though, as I had developed an odd metallic taste in my mouth (which continued for the whole first trimester) and nothing tasted right. But I was happy that he was happy, and excited about the prospect of motherhood.

Paul insisted I gave up working in the shoe shop when I was six months gone. 'You can't be bending down over people's feet with that huge bump,' he'd reasoned.

'But what about maternity pay?' I'd said. 'I need to work a bit longer to qualify.'

'You won't be going back to work after the baby's born, Clare,' he'd said. 'You wouldn't want someone else bringing up our child, would you? Anyway, a decent nanny would cost us more than you earn anyway.'

There'd been no arguing with him, and while I was sad to give up having my own little bit of income, he was right about the cost of childcare. I could always find something part-time later on, when our child or children reached school age.

It was an easy pregnancy. I spent the last three months getting a nursery ready for the baby, decorating the room in palest yellow with a stencilled frieze of farm animals around the walls, painting an old chest of drawers and adding more animals to it, making curtains and a matching floor cushion, and re-covering a fireside chair that would be my seat for night-time feeds. That was the first chair I re-covered, and I enjoyed it so much I vowed to learn how to do upholstery properly.

When Matt was born, Paul showered me with gifts. Flowers, chocolates, champagne, pretty white shawls to wrap the baby in, a gorgeous bracelet with a baby charm. No expense spared. I felt like a queen. I felt loved and cherished.

Paul proved to be a hands-off dad. I don't think he changed a single nappy. I told myself he worked hard all day and deserved a break in the evenings and at weekends, and baby-minding was my job, but to tell the truth, I would have appreciated a bit of help now and again, and maybe a few lie-ins. It would have helped Paul bond with Matt.

I tried to encourage him to do more. But he'd just sigh and say some things were best left to women. I told myself that once we were out of the baby stage, he'd be more interested. When he could take Matt to the park, kick a football, ride bikes — that's when Paul would come into his own as a father.

Little Jon came along when Matt was nearly three, and here, I thought, was the opportunity for Paul to do more with Matt, leaving me free to look after Jon. Matt was potty trained and a very biddable child, easy to handle. But there was no change. Paul kept a distance from both boys. He'd occasionally accompany us on a trip to the park or the swimming pool, to the boys' delight. Family holidays were fun too, when Paul would act like a real dad for once, being relaxed and playful, the way I remember my own dad being all the time. I always put it down to Paul's stressful job in telecom sales, and assumed he could only properly relax when he was away from it all on holiday. At least that's how I remembered it, but Matt seemed to have different recollections.

It was probably the holidays and the way the boys worshipped him when he did spend time with them, that kept me with Paul all those years. Looking back, I'd probably fallen out of love with him by the time Jon was a year old. I just told myself everyone found the baby and toddler years hard. And he still bought me surprise gifts and treats every now and again. I knew he must love me. I was just being ungrateful and somehow dissatisfied with life. I had a husband who from the outside appeared to dote on me, two gorgeous little boys, a lovely house. What more did I want?

Now, as I left the café with Matt, I realised that after so many years I was at last beginning to work out what I wanted. A little bit of independence and the freedom to make my own decisions, such as whether I wanted cake with my cuppa or not.

★   ★   ★

I had a phone call that night from Jon. He rang at eight p.m. — the time when Paul goes out to his regular twice-a-week gym class. Whenever the boys ring at this time it's because they know they can talk to me without their dad listening in.

'Hey, Mum. I had a call from Matt. He told

me what you and he were talking about today. Just wanted to let you know that if you decide to go for it, and leave Dad, that's all right by me. Actually, more than all right. I think it'd be great for you.'

'Aw, Jon.' I felt tears well up again. Maybe it was the menopause coming on, or maybe just the stresses of making such a big decision, but I seemed to be constantly weepy.

'Hope you don't mind that he told me,' Jon said, sounding a little unsure.

'Of course not. I know you two are close and tell each other everything.'

'Ahem, not quite everything. He doesn't know about my dangerous liaison with the fire-eating circus acrobat who tied my legs in knots during a three-day tantric sex session . . . '

'Jon!'

'Joking! Course he knows about that!'

You never knew with Jon, when he was being serious and when not. But he never failed to lighten the mood and make me smile. My tears were gone already.

⋆   ⋆   ⋆

It took a few weeks more, and a lot of soul-searching, and some long chats with Matt and Jon, before I finally came to a decision. Yes, I would do it. I would leave Paul. I would *arise and go now*. Perhaps I should have done it years ago, but it would be easier now — less messy as I could simply move to Ireland and leave him the UK house. I just needed to wait for probate to

33

be completed so that the inheritance was mine, and then I could go. Oh, and I needed to tell Paul, of course. How, I wasn't sure. I decided to wait for the right moment. Whenever that would be.

Uncle Pádraig's solicitor, Mr Greve, called me one day, while Paul was at work and I was in the middle of going through my wardrobe, throwing out clothes I knew I'd never wear again and wouldn't want in Ireland. I was in the habit of doing this once a year anyway, so it wouldn't rouse Paul's suspicions.

'Mrs Farrell? I have good news for you. Probate is almost complete. I need your bank account details to pay the money into.'

'Money? I thought there was just the farm in Ireland.'

'Ah no. There's a fair amount of money in the estate as well. Not a huge fortune mind, but enough. So I need your bank name, account number and sort code. Do you have them to hand?'

I felt a wave of panic wash over me. The only bank account I had access to was a joint account. If the money was paid into that, Paul would be able to get at it. He'd notice it immediately — he got alerts on his phone whenever there was any activity on his account — and he'd quite possibly move it out and invest it somewhere else where I couldn't touch it. He might be my husband of twenty-five years, but I couldn't trust him with this. It was *my* money.

'Er, no. Sorry, I don't have them right here.

Can I call you back later with them?'

'Yes of course, but the sooner the better so we can get this all neatly tied up. You have my number, I think.'

'I do, yes.'

'Good. I'll wait to hear.' Mr Greve hung up. He'd sounded vaguely irritated that I wasn't the sort of organised woman who had bank details to hand.

I grabbed a jacket and my handbag, and rushed out of the house. Paul had the car at work, but it was only a forty-minute walk into the town centre and if I hurried I could get there, see to my business and get home again in time to cook Paul's tea. Yes, I was the type of housewife who always had her husband's dinner on the table when he came home from work. A throwback to the 1950s. Sometimes I despised myself for it. Though not for much longer.

There were three banks with branches in our small town, and I nipped into the first one I came across — Nationwide.

'I need to open a bank account,' I told the clerk, slightly breathless from my fast walk to town.

'All right, what kind of account did you want? And do you already have any accounts with us?' she asked.

'Just a regular account. And no, I don't.'

'OK. Wait there, I'll see if someone's available to talk you through the options.'

I was lucky. Someone was available and I was ushered to a desk behind a partition, where a smart young man with 'Dan' on his name badge sat opposite me with a pile of leaflets. I was blushing with embarrassment that a woman of my age — almost 50 — did not have her own bank account, and did not know the difference between a SIPP and an ISA, a current account and a savings account. I'd had my own account before Paul, of course, but I'd closed it on his advice when I stopped working when Matt came along, and had just used our joint account for the twenty-four years since then. Dan was patient and gentle with me, but I could tell he thought I was an oddity.

'Well, Mrs Farrell, as you're wanting to pay in an inheritance but still have instant access to the money, I would recommend our Flexclusive Saver account. Decent interest rates yet fully flexible. We can open that now for you, if you have some proof of ID and proof of address.'

I hadn't for a moment thought I'd need anything like that. I'd been so far removed from all this sort of thing — Paul of course handled all our finances and paid all the bills. But thankfully I had my driving licence on me, and at the bottom of my handbag was a water bill with a shopping list scribbled on the back. Dan accepted those.

Twenty minutes later I left, grinning like a cat with cream, clutching a piece of paper with my bank account numbers on it. A card would arrive by post in a couple of days, Dan said. Our post arrived around midday so I'd be able to pick it up before Paul saw it.

Back home I called Mr Greve, passed on the bank details, and made myself some tea in an attempt to calm myself down a little. I'd done it. I'd taken the first step towards independence.

Next step, tell Paul.

4

Ellen, July 1919

Ellen set off to start work at her new job the next day with a spring in her step. She'd packed a few things in a holdall — even though Mrs Carlton's big house was only a couple of miles away from her father's cottage, her job was live-in as she had to be up at six to set the fires in the bedrooms, bring hot water upstairs in ewers and then fetch the mistress's breakfast, which she always took in her room.

She was looking forward to starting the job, a new life away from her increasingly morose father. She felt a pang of guilt that he'd have to fend for himself during the week, but she'd baked two large mutton pies the previous day and stored them in the pantry, and she'd made enough soda bread for a few days, and a fruit cake, and stocked up on general groceries. He'd manage, she told herself.

And Jimmy was home. Jimmy was home! When they'd parted the day before, he'd promised to meet her this morning to walk with her as far as the gates to Carlton House. She had to pass his home, Clonamurty Farm, on her way anyway.

Sure enough, there he was, leaning against the gate post as she approached. The low morning sun was behind him, shining like a halo around his floppy blond hair. Such a contrast to her own dark curls. Ellen smiled as he greeted her and began walking alongside her.

'So, all ready for your new job?' he asked.

'Yes, all ready. I've my things packed in this bag. They'll give me a maid's uniform up at the house. My room will be right up in the attic. I hope there's a window with a view.'

'Maybe a view back to Clonamurty, and if you're unhappy you can signal me from the window. One lit candle means all's well, two means come and rescue me.' There was a mischievous glint in Jimmy's eyes as he said this.

Ellen giggled, but a little part of her wondered whether Jimmy would really 'rescue' her if she was in need. It was an enticing thought. She felt herself blushing so turned her face away.

They chatted and bantered as they walked the short distance to Carlton House. Jimmy did not say anything more about his political beliefs or his desire for an independent Ireland, for which Ellen was grateful. Their time together would be all too limited now that she was working six days a week, plus cooking for her father on the seventh, and she did not want to spend time talking politics.

At the end of the long drive lined with elegant poplar trees that led up to the big house, Jimmy stopped. 'You probably oughtn't to be seen walking with me on your first day, so I'll leave you here. Good luck!'

'Will I see you on Sunday?' Ellen asked, turning to face him. 'It's my day off. I'll be at Mass, of course, and have to see Da, but . . . '

'I'll meet you here and walk you home. Then I can see you after church if you've time, and walk you back here in the evening. If you like.'

Her eyes shone. 'Yes. Yes, all that would be lovely, so it would.' Something to look forward to, all week. Six days until she'd see him again.

'I'll be away, then. Hope all goes well. They'll love you, sure they will.'

He took a step towards her and for a moment she thought he was going to take her in his arms and kiss her goodbye, but he just picked a loose hair off her shoulder and then raised his hand to wave farewell.

She watched him walk back the way they'd come for a moment, then turned and began making her way up the long gravel driveway towards the big house. She'd only been there once before — the previous week when she'd attended an interview with Mrs Carlton. She'd expected to meet a housekeeper, but it was the lady of the house herself who conducted the interview. There'd been an odd question about Ellen's family background, and she'd found herself talking about her great-grandfather who'd fought alongside Wolfe Tone in the old rebellion. Mrs Carlton had pronounced herself pleased, and asked Ellen to begin work.

★ ★ ★

And now it was time to start her new life. When she'd reached the house, she went around to the kitchen door, knocked, and was shown in by a scowling housemaid.

40

'You'll be the new maid, then,' the girl said. It was a statement not a question. 'I was after wanting that job upstairs. Easier than down-stairs. Don't know why the mistress didn't give it to me.'

Maybe because you're so grumpy, Ellen thought, but she smiled sweetly and held out her hand. 'I'm sorry if I got the job you wanted. I hope it won't stop us being friends. My name's Mary-Ellen, but everyone calls me Ellen.'

'I'm Siobhan,' the other girl said, 'and you'll be sharing my bedroom.' She did not shake Ellen's hand.

Siobhan took her through the kitchen and along a corridor to an office, where Mrs Carlton was sitting doing the household accounts.

'Ah, Ellen. Thank you, Siobhan. You may return to your duties. I'll show Ellen where her bedroom is and what her tasks are to be.'

Siobhan bobbed a curtsey and left the room, but not before she'd thrown another scowl in Ellen's direction. Ellen suppressed a sigh. She'd hoped she'd make friends here at the Hall, not enemies. And she'd be sharing a room with Siobhan. She resolved to work harder at being friendly towards the other girl. Siobhan was probably just jealous, but it wasn't Ellen's fault she'd got the job.

'I really should employ a housekeeper,' Mrs Carlton said, as she led Ellen upstairs, along a corridor and up a second flight to the attic rooms. 'I suppose I just enjoy retaining control of the household too much. Anyway, here's your room. That's Siobhan's bed, so you have this one

41

under the window.' She opened the door onto a small room, with a dormer window that looked out across gently rolling farmland. In the distance was a ribbon of silver — the Boyne. Ellen crossed to the window and peered out. Yes, she could just about make out a farmhouse not far from the river. Clonamurty Farm, and in it, Jimmy.

'This is perfect, thank you, ma'am,' she said, placing her holdall on the bed. 'Should I change now or get straight to work?'

'Ah, your uniform. Just a moment, I'll call Siobhan to fetch it. Oh, and call me Madame. Not ma'am, and not Mrs. Those forms of address are just too . . . English, I suppose.' She smiled. 'Just my little idiosyncrasy.' And then she left the room.

Ellen took the opportunity while she was alone to have a look around. Besides the two narrow beds there was a washstand, basin and ewer, a chest with four drawers, two bentwood chairs and a small mirror hanging on the wall. There was a neat little fireplace with a bucket of sweet-smelling turf to burn beside it.

A worn-out hearthrug was on the floor, and a sampler hung over the fireplace with the words *'Many suffer so that some day all Irish people may know justice and peace — Wolfe Tone'* embroidered upon it, signed with the initials E.C. Mrs Carlton's first name was Emily, Ellen knew. Was it Mrs, sorry, *Madame* Carlton herself who'd embroidered the sampler? The words were so patriotic, so Irish, and yet Madame Carlton was English — at least, she was one of the Anglo-Irish aristocracy. She was a widow, but her husband had been a Member of Parliament, spending most of his time in London.

Ellen had always thought the desire for Irish independence was something only the poor wanted and fought for: the downtrodden, those whose ancestors had perished during the Great Famine, those who had nothing to lose and everything to gain. But here was the widow of a British MP, embroidering quotes like that and hanging them in her servants' rooms, and asking not to be called Mrs because it was too English-sounding.

She was still standing in front of the fireplace pondering this when Madame Carlton arrived back in the room, carrying a neat black dress, white apron and cap. 'Your uniform, Ellen. I have guessed at the size, but it should be about right.' Her gaze followed Ellen's to the sampler. 'And are you a patriot, my dear?'

Ellen gaped for a moment, not sure how to answer or what she was expected to say. Madame watched her for a moment and then her eyes softened. 'I am sorry. That was wrong of me to ask such a thing on your first day, when I barely know you. Suffice to say that all here are Fenians and true Irish patriots. I would employ none other. We believe in the Cause. Irish independence must be won at all costs. I know something of your family, Ellen, and feel that you will fit in perfectly.'

She handed Ellen the uniform. 'So, put this on, and report downstairs to me. You'll find me in the housekeeper's office.'

Madame Carlton left the room, closing the door behind her, to allow Ellen to get changed. She did so, quickly, her mind reviewing all that she had heard. Between Jimmy's declaration of support for the Cause and now her employer's, she seemed to be surrounded by people who wanted a free and independent Ireland. But her own thoughts on the matter were still unresolved.

★ ★ ★

The week passed quickly. Although she was an upstairs maid, with easier work than the downstairs and scullery maids had, she found it exhausting and crawled into bed each night aching all over. She was on her feet from six a.m., running up and down stairs, setting the fires, fetching fuel, jugs of warm water to wash, bringing breakfast trays up and clearing them away after. Later she had to make the beds, change sheets, clean bedrooms, sweep the stairs and landings, clear out grates and set the fires ready for the evening.

Besides Madame Carlton there was a succession of visitors using the many guest rooms on the first floor. Ellen rarely glimpsed the guests, and was often instructed to leave their breakfast trays outside the door. Madame seemed endlessly busy, running her household, entertaining her guests and conducting serious-looking meetings either in the library or the dining room. When these were in progress, the servants were instructed to keep well out of sight at all times. Madame herself would emerge to fetch a tray of refreshments if needed.

Siobhan had softened towards her a little, as Ellen had displayed relentless friendliness towards the other girl. She'd got the impression Siobhan was most miffed about having to share a bedroom, so Ellen had tried to be as easy-going a room-mate as possible. They'd begun chatting for a few minutes at bedtime, exchanging little stories about their work, speculating on who Madame's latest visitors had been.

'Something to do with the fight for independence,' Siobhan said one night. 'Our Madame's really tied up in all that, you know. She'll suck us into it as well, if we're not careful, so.'

'Do you want to be part of the fight?' Ellen asked.

Siobhan was quiet, as though she was mulling over her answer. 'Not sure. What about you?'

'I'm not sure either,' Ellen had whispered in reply. Even as she said the words, she wondered how she'd have answered if it had been Jimmy asking her. She knew she'd do anything for him.

⋆ ⋆ ⋆

At last it was Saturday evening, and Ellen was free to leave Carlton House for twenty-four hours. She'd arranged to meet Jimmy at the end of the drive, and had time to go for a walk with him before returning to her father.

She walked down the drive carrying half a ham wrapped in muslin that the cook had given her. 'The mistress said to give it to the dogs but it's still perfectly good, so you take it home for

45

your daddy, now,' the cook had said, handing it to Ellen with a smile. She had so much to tell Jimmy. Not least her growing realisation that Madame Carlton seemed to be deeply involved with the fight for independence.

Jimmy was leaning against the gate post, hands in pockets and a thoughtful expression on his face.

'All right, Jimmy?' Ellen said as she approached, and Jimmy hauled himself upright with a shrug.

'Yes, sure I am. How're you? How was your first week?'

They fell into step, walking down the lane towards Clonamurty Farm. Ellen told him of her duties, of her room-mate Siobhan and her less-than-friendly welcome, of the other staff.

'And your mistress, Mrs Carlton? How do you get on with her?' Jimmy asked. There was an odd tone to his voice.

'She seems very nice,' Ellen said, guardedly. She still wasn't sure whether she should voice her suspicions about Mrs Carlton. Even to Jimmy.

'Just nice?'

'There's something odd. She wants to be called Madame and not Mrs. I think she's . . . well, I think she's involved with the Irish Volunteers, so I do.' There. It was out in the open. 'Jimmy, you won't say it to anyone, will you? I'd hate for her to get in any trouble because of me.'

To her surprise Jimmy laughed, and then flung an arm about her shoulders. 'Ah, my sweet Ellen. Of course she is involved! She runs a branch of the Cumann na mBan. You've heard of that, haven't you?'

She had. It was the Irishwomen's Council — an auxiliary branch of the Irish Volunteers, fighting for Irish independence. 'So you know what she does? There are always people coming and going, having meetings and all sorts.'

'Yes, there would be. She's quite senior in the organisation. She's important to the Cause.' Jimmy nodded knowledgeably.

Ellen wanted to ask how he knew so much about it, but Jimmy had withdrawn into himself again, with that serious, thoughtful expression he'd had when they met. She wanted to snatch away his hat, run off with it, have him chase her, laughing, the way they used to when they were children. But something told her it wouldn't work now; he'd just be annoyed at her. They were adults now, and Jimmy clearly had something serious on his mind.

'What are you thinking about?' she asked, quietly, after they'd walked in silence for a few minutes. They weren't far now from his parents' farm, and he might leave her there, and they'd have no more chance to talk until after Mass tomorrow.

He smiled at her, and stopped walking. There was a wooden fence lining the road, and he pulled her over to sit with him on the top rail.

'I'm thinking about my future. And Ireland's future. And how the two are intertwined.'

She frowned. 'Of course they are, since you live in Ireland.'

He shook his head. 'I mean in a more profound way than that. I've made my decision, Ellen, about what I'm going to do now that I've

47

left school. I've been thinking long and hard about it this week, and I realise now what's the most important thing to me.'

She watched him, a little spark of hope in her heart that he would tell her the most important thing in his life was her, and that he had decided he wanted to be with her, now and always. But as soon as the thoughts crossed her mind, she dismissed them. Something in his expression, in his distant gaze across the fields, told her he cared more for something else. 'What is it?' she whispered, hardly wanting to hear the answer. It would change everything — she knew it.

'Ireland, Ellen. Ireland's future, Ireland's freedom. Ireland's independence. That's it, Ellen. That's the most important thing, the thing my heart says I must follow, no matter what. I've joined up. I'm a Volunteer. The Cause, Ireland's independence, that's what's calling to me. I'll be neither a lawyer nor a farmer. I'll be a soldier for Ireland, till the day I die or the day Ireland is free, whichever comes first.'

He jumped down from the fence as he made this speech, and wheeled around to face her. She'd never heard so much passion in his voice. Tears sprung to her eyes as she realised two things simultaneously — first that she loved him with all her heart and would never love anyone else as much, and second that she was losing him.

'Ah, Ellen, what has you crying?' His expression was softer now, the fire in his eyes dimmer but still there, smouldering.

'The thought of you fighting and maybe dying

for the Cause. Surely it's not worth it?' She dashed the tears away with the back of her hand.

'It is worth it. One man's life is a small sacrifice to make for a country's future. I love my country, Ellen. I have to do this. I have to fight the British. You are not to worry. I'll be all right. I'll do my part, but I'm young and fit, canny and clever, and I'll not get caught and I'll not be killed. You wait and see! You'll be proud of me yet, and we'll be able to tell our grandchildren that I fought for their future.'

Ellen was once again left speechless, still trying to process what she'd heard about grandchildren, when Jimmy grabbed her suddenly, pulling her off her perch on the fence. He squeezed her against him and landed a huge, passionate kiss on her lips. It wasn't quite how she'd imagined their first kiss would be — she'd pictured a more tender moment — but it was still a kiss and it was intense.

'Ah, Ellen,' Jimmy said, holding her tightly and burying his face in her hair. 'It has me all fired up. And you, my love — believe me, you mean just as much to me as Ireland does.' He kissed her again, gently this time, his lips warm against hers, the fire within him spreading into her and with it the certain knowledge that he loved her. And she loved him, and together they would build a future.

If the Cause didn't claim Jimmy first.

5

Clare, April 2016

In the end I waited till probate was complete, the money was in my account and Clonamurty Farm was in my name. I didn't mean to wait that long to tell Paul; I was just weak and couldn't seem to find the right moment. Or the courage.

He'd had his dinner — fish pie, and a glass of Sauvignon Blanc. I'd eaten almost none of mine, having made up my mind that tonight was the night we'd have the conversation. My stomach was churning. 'Not eating?' he'd asked, and I'd grunted and shrugged, then forced down a mouthful or two.

I'd cleared up. He'd gone to the sitting room and put the TV on in the background while he read a magazine. Something to do with cars, I noted. Well he'd need to read up on car recommendations. 'Our' car was actually my car — Dad had given it to me when he gave up driving, and I was going to use it to take my stuff to Ireland.

I stood in the doorway of the sitting room, breathing deeply and summoning up the courage to speak. Paul looked up and frowned. 'Well, either come in or go out. Don't stand there like some kind of zombie.'

'Sorry. I'm coming in. Just — we need to talk.' I took a few steps forward. I could feel my heart pounding.

'Hmm? What about?' Paul had returned his attention to his magazine.

I took a deep breath. 'Probate on Uncle Pádraig's will is complete. The money's in my bank account.'

'Ah, right. That's good. I'll get online and invest it later. Got my eye on a couple of safe retail bonds.'

'Er, no. I mean it's in *my* bank account. My private one, not our joint one.'

He put down his magazine and looked at me over the top of his reading glasses. 'You don't have a bank account.'

'I do now.' Oh why could I not just come out and say it? *Paul, I'm leaving you.*

'Why is the money in there? I can't access it if it's only in your name.'

That's the point, I wanted to say, but stopped myself. 'Paul, the money's in there because it's mine, not yours. And the farm is mine.'

'But we decided to sell it, didn't we? What are you getting at, Clare?'

This was it. This was the moment. 'I've decided to keep the farm. I want to live there.'

'What? But it's uninhabitable!'

'Just a bit dirty. I'll soon sort it out.'

'Clare, you are mad. It's revolting. It'll take more than a bit of Vim and a quick hoover round, you know. Not something you can do in a few weekend visits.'

'I'll have longer than that. I'm going to live there permanently.'

'Well I'm bloody not!' He stood up and crossed the room, towering over me.

51

'No. I'm not expecting you to. Paul, I think . . . I want . . . I think we should separate.' There. Said it. The words were out there and there was no clawing them back. To give myself strength I imagined Matt and Jon standing at my side, holding my hands and lending me support. And Mum, behind me, whispering in my ear, *arise and go now*.

'Separate? What? Why? Don't be ridiculous. Aren't you happy? You have this beautiful house, all the time in the world to get your hair done or whatever it is you do with your days. Get this stupid notion about the farm out of your head, Clare. I don't want to hear any more of it. We'll get it on the market as soon as possible, and use some of the money to go on a cruise. How does that sound?'

'I don't want to go on a cruise. I want to live at the farm in Ireland. On my own. I'm sorry, Paul, but this is it. No, I'm not happy. I need things to change.'

'You're menopausal, aren't you? That's what this is about. Your hormones. Can't you see a doctor and get some tablets or something?'

That did it. 'I'm not fucking menopausal, Paul. You're not listening to me. I'm saying I want to leave you. I have had enough of you controlling everything and telling me what to do. I want to be independent, to be in control of my own life, and now I have the money to do it. I'll be gone in a few days' time, and till then I'll sleep in Matt's old room.'

'Is this about Angie?'

I stared at Paul. Angie was a woman he'd

worked with for a while. He'd invited her round for dinner once or twice, and she'd brought a different date each time. He'd slept with her at a conference, I'd found out. He'd apologised and swore it'd never happen again. And I'd believed him and stayed with him. For the sake of the boys, who'd been under 10 at the time.

'Angie?'

'Because if it is, remember that all happened ages ago. Been over for years and there's been no one else since.'

'No, it's not about Angie,' I said, coldly. 'As you say, that's all in the past.' To tell the truth, I'd pretty much forgotten about it.

He shrugged. 'What *is* it about, then?'

'Me. It's about me, and what *I* want, for a change. And what I want is to be far away from you right now.'

I turned to leave the room but Paul caught my arm. 'Not so fast. How can you want to throw away twenty-five years of marriage just like that? I thought we had a good, strong marriage!'

'It was good in parts, Paul. I'm not throwing the past away. I'm just moving on. It feels like the right thing to do. For me.'

'Not bloody right for me though, is it? Who'll cook my dinner if you're not here? Who'll clean the house?'

'Buy ready-meals and employ a cleaner,' I replied, yanking my arm out of his grasp. That confirmed it. All he wanted me to stay for was to be his housekeeper. The sooner I left the better. I ran out of the room and upstairs, and began moving my things into the spare room. Paul

53

hollered up the stairs after me, something about I'd regret it and come back with my tail between my legs, but I ignored it.

In the spare room I sat on the bed and let the tears come for a while. Paul did not come upstairs. I heard the TV being turned up. After a while I pulled myself together, took out my phone and texted the boys — *It's done. Told him. He's not happy.*

Jon texted back within minutes — *Well done. Xxx. Love you.*

And Matt rang me. 'You OK?'

I sniffed. 'Yes, I suppose so. I'll be moving to Ireland as soon as I can.'

'You can stay with me if you need to. I can sleep on my sofa.'

'It's OK. I need to be here to pack anyway.'

'Here if you need me,' he said, and once more I rejoiced in my strong, supportive and loving sons.

★　★　★

Next day I booked a car-ferry crossing from Holyhead to Dublin for Friday morning, then spent the rest of the day packing. Paul had been silent in the morning before work, barely acknowledging my presence. I knew it had been a shock for him, and I understood that he was hurting, but I had to do this. It'd be better for both of us in the long run. He'd find another Angie, sooner or later. As I thought this, I realised I didn't care if he did. In fact, if it helped him let me go, it'd be better if he did take up with someone new quickly.

I came upstairs in the evening with a basket of clean washing, and caught Paul standing at the door to the spare room, looking at the half-packed boxes and suitcases I had strewn all over the floor.

'You're really doing this, then?' he said, his voice flat and tight.

'Yes.'

'Hmm. You'll come running back to me within a month, I'll bet.' He turned and pushed past me, downstairs, and a moment later I heard the front door slam. I breathed a sigh of relief and got on with sorting out the washing. Much of it was mine, but some was Paul's and I folded it neatly and put it away, just as I had done for the past twenty-five years. Who would do this after I'd gone? I'd never known Paul put anything away. To him, cupboards were for taking things out of.

★ ★ ★

At last Friday arrived. It had always been my day to have the car for shopping, and Paul took the bus to work. I had told Paul I would leave on Friday, and he'd rolled his eyes but said nothing. I don't think he really believed I was going.

After he'd left for work, I loaded the boxes and cases I'd packed into the car, washed up the breakfast things, wrote Paul a note, had a last look around the house I'd furnished and decorated and lived in for twenty years, and left. On a whim, that I wondered if I might come to regret, I posted my keys back through the letter box. It would show Paul I was serious if nothing else. The house was in his name only, after all. I wanted, and needed, nothing more of it.

It was a long and tedious drive to Holyhead, but I put the radio on loudly and sang along to any tunes I knew, to take my mind off what I was actually doing. It was a big step. A huge one. I wasn't sure yet that I would be able to cope on my own. The car had Bluetooth capability, and both sons called me while I was driving to wish me well. Their encouragement lent me strength, and despite having to wipe a few tears away if I thought too deeply about what I was doing, I felt strangely elated. This was it. The start of a new adventure. Whether it turned out well or not remained to be seen.

It wasn't till I was on the ferry that I realised I'd never told Paul I was taking the car. My car, I reminded myself.

It was a smooth crossing, and I amused myself with a puzzle book until we passed Ireland's Eye. Then I spent the rest of the time on deck, gazing at the land that was to be my new home. It was a bright April day, the sun glinting off the waves and the hills of Howth resplendent in green and purple heather. I smiled. Perfect weather for starting a new life.

Once docked in Dublin, it was less than an hour's drive out of the city and north-east into County Meath and on to Blackstown. We'd done this journey many times when I was a child, but that was before the motorways were built, before the Irish building boom of the Nineties and early

Noughties. Nothing looked familiar to me, until I turned off the motorway and onto the smaller roads into Blackstown, which I'd driven with Paul in the hire car when we came to view the farm. As I passed a signpost I noted the Irish form of the town's name — *Baile Dubh*. Maybe I'd try to learn some Irish, although I knew that the *Gaeltacht* areas, where Irish is the predominant language, were all further west.

I'd arranged to collect the keys from the solicitor, Mr Greve, and once they were in my handbag, I decided to call in at the coffee shop I'd been to with Paul. This time I ordered a large piece of chocolate fudge cake with cream. No one to stop me now! So this was freedom. Boy, did I enjoy it! I noticed the waitress grinning at me, clearly delighted I was enjoying my cake so much.

As I left the café I noticed a bookshop opposite, the type that sells a mixture of second-hand and new books. A man of around 50 or so, with a sweep of grey hair across his forehead, was just leaving and locking up. I made a mental note to check it out next time I was in town. Hours rummaging around second-hand bookshops was one of my favourite pastimes. Needless to say, it wasn't something I got the chance to do very often when out with Paul.

I remember once coming home from a rare Saturday out with friends, to find he'd 'thinned out' (his words) my bookshelves. All my favourite novels had been thrown out, and the empty shelves filled with piles of car and computer magazines that had previously been stacked on the floor in Paul's home office. I felt a wave of contentment wash over me as I realised that now I could rebuild my book collection, in my own home, and no one could stop me. A visit to Blackstown bookshop was high on my list of things to do.

★ ★ ★

As is so often the case in Ireland, the bright clear day didn't last long. By the time I reached Clonamurty Farm the sky had clouded over and the first spots of rain had begun to fall. I dashed round to the back door, unlocked it and fell inside before it got too heavy. It was gloomy inside so I reached for the light switch, but it didn't work. I tried another. Nothing. No electricity.

I felt an irrational wave of panic rise up, but quickly squashed it down. Must be just that the house had been unoccupied and the electricity company had cut off the supply. It'd only need a phone call to get reconnected. But who should I call? I realised I didn't even know the name of any Irish electricity companies. I could look it up online, I supposed, or phone Matt and ask him to look it up for me. Yes, that would be easier.

I pulled out my phone to call him and discovered it was out of charge. Out of charge and no electric in the house. That wave of panic rose up in me again. Was there a call box anywhere near? Or should I drive back to Blackstown and ask at the café — maybe the waitress would let me borrow her phone.

I glanced at my watch. It was gone six-thirty so the café would be closed. I considered my options. I could drive back to Blackstown, try to find a public phone, or perhaps even find a hotel or B&B to stay in just for tonight. I'd be able to charge my phone and call Matt, or ask the B&B owners how to get electricity reconnected. But it was growing dark and I didn't fancy driving the unfamiliar narrow lanes in the dark. I wasn't a confident driver at the best of times. Paul usually did all the driving.

The alternative was to stick it out here at the farm. Find a torch or some candles. Manage without electricity for the first night, then go into Blackstown and get things sorted out in the morning. This option didn't appeal — I fancied the idea of a B&B more — but then I imagined Paul's sneering laugh if he heard about it. 'Couldn't even manage one night alone,' he'd say. 'You're nothing without me, Clare.'

Funnily, that thought, and his voice sounding so clear in my head, made up my mind for me. I *was* something without him. I'd prove it. I'd deal with this somehow. I went through to the kitchen and rummaged through cupboards and drawers while there was still a little grey light creeping in at the windows. In a dresser drawer I found some matches. And in another cupboard was a box of cheap white candles.

'We have light,' I said to the empty room. And the oven ran off bottled gas so at least I'd be able to cook and boil water. I hadn't brought anything to cook, but another search through the cupboards turned up half a pack of Barry's teabags and an assortment of tinned food, some of which was still in date. I first cursed myself for not thinking to do some shopping in Blackstown before coming here, and then smiled as I realised I could make a meal of sorts with a tin of boiled new potatoes, a tin of corned beef and a tin of beans. It'd do.

I dug out the least burned and battered saucepan I could find in the kitchen, filled it with water and put it on the hob to boil. There was a collection of chipped mugs in a cupboard (and my favourite 'World's Best Mum' one in the car, but it was bucketing down now so fetching that would have to wait) so I made myself a cup of tea. No milk, but black tea was better than no tea.

It was odd but as soon as I had a cup of tea in my hand and a candle lit and placed on the kitchen table, I felt better. I had light, I had a hot drink and I would be able to make myself a meal later. But first, before it was fully dark, I wanted to explore my new home.

It was a strange feeling, going round it this time. Last time, with Paul, had been all about my memories of the past as I recalled visiting here as a child. This time was all about the future, as I tried to envisage how I would clean up, decorate and use each room. It would be a big job. Poor old Uncle Pádraig had clearly not spent any money on the place for years. Seventies' brown floral carpets clashed with Eighties' cheap black ash-effect furniture. There was woodchip wallpaper painted peach on most walls.

Upstairs, ancient candlewick bedspreads covered lumpy mattresses. One bedroom was filled with boxes of old paperwork. I wondered if any of it would be interesting, or if it was just old bills and bank statements. One day I'd have to go through it all.

I chose the least damp-smelling room for my own, and set about making the bed with the best of the bedding available, making yet another note to buy new bed linen as soon as possible. Why hadn't I brought some from home? We had far too many sets, and Paul would not even have noticed if some disappeared. I left a couple of candles on the bedside table for use later. The box of matches was in my jeans pocket.

The living room was the most habitable room. A worn-out armchair sat near the fireplace, angled so that the occupant had a view through the window across the fields. I sat down and contemplated the view as the rain stopped and the clouds parted to reveal the very last of a dusky sunset.

'Well, this is nice,' I told myself. And it was. It was mine. My chair, my house, my view. I could make it something special, somewhere the boys would want to come to visit. Somewhere I could bring friends to. Somewhere I could feel safe as I gradually cut ties to Paul and gained my independence. Arise and go now. I'd done it.

Sitting there, in that old armchair looking out at the view brought back memories of my childhood, when I'd visited Clonamurty Farm several times while Granny Irish was still alive. She was my mum's mum, and lived with Uncle

Pádraig in the farm that had been hers and Granddad's. Pádraig had taken it over, and then Granddad had died when I was 3 so I don't remember him.

I do remember Granny Irish though. So unlike Dad's mum, who I called Nanna. Where Nanna was round, smiley and plump and always feeding me sweets and chocolate whenever my parents looked the other way, Granny Irish was tall, thin and rarely smiled. She would have been a good-looking woman in her youth, with her high cheekbones and startling blue eyes, but as an old woman she appeared (to me as a child, at least) forbidding and austere.

She habitually wore a long black dress, almost to her ankles, and a hand-knitted shawl in a nondescript shade of beige. Her hair was pinned up in a bun. She was an old-fashioned woman — even in the 1970s she was old-fashioned. Mum tried to buy her new, brightly coloured clothes and persuade her to have her hair done differently, but Granny Irish wouldn't have it. 'What was good enough for my mammy is good enough for me,' she'd say, her County Meath accent so strong I could hardly understand her.

I think her looks, her manner, her strong accent and her belief that children should be tamed and kept out of sight were what made her seem such a distant, forbidding figure. As a young woman she'd worked as a maid in a big house not far from Clonamurty Farm. She would never talk of those days, though, no matter how much we children would pester her.

There were family legends about her that I'd

heard later, mostly from my cousin David, of how she'd played a part in Ireland's War of Independence. Near the end of the war, she'd been some sort of spy, he said, feeding information on movements of the British run paramilitary Royal Irish Constabulary back to the Irish Volunteers who were fighting for independence. David had spoken of her actions in reverent tones, as he did any Republican.

Granny Irish died when I was 11, and we came over for the funeral. I remember my cousin David telling me then that he'd always been a little fearful of her, even though he'd grown up having her around. 'It was always so hard to please her,' he'd said. 'Hard to make her smile, or get her to talk. But I always wanted to hear her stories of the war, and write them down before they were all forgotten.'

★ ★ ★

I shuffled in my chair, and felt an ominous bulge in the seat beneath me, suggesting a spring had worked loose of its ties. And the fabric on the arms was worn with the stuffing poking through. Well then, maybe stripping it back and reupholstering it from the woodwork up could be a good first project for me. As soon as I'd sorted out the utilities and cleaned the place up, of course. And now that I was here in Ireland, in my grandmother's old house, I thought I'd like to find out more about my ancestry as well. Maybe some of those papers upstairs could have belonged to Granny Irish. It'd be good to find out more about her.

I should have asked Mum and Uncle Pádraig more about her, while they were still around. Why was it always the case that you left these things too late? All those memories, buried with the last generation.

6

Ellen, October 1919

As the weeks passed, Ellen fell into a routine of work during the week, meeting Jimmy on Saturday evenings, and spending Sundays at home with her father and Digger before returning to Carlton House. Digger at least was always pleased to see her, even if Da would grumble about having to cook his own meals.

Ellen was enjoying her job, now that Siobhan was acting a little more friendly towards her. They'd established a habit of chatting for half an hour or so every night at bedtime, and Ellen felt a tentative friendship towards the other girl. Madame Carlton was a good person to work for, and Ellen was growing used to the idea that the house was used by the Irish Republicans, with men arriving for clandestine meetings that took place after dark. Occasionally rooms were designated out-of-bounds to all staff, for reasons Ellen could only guess at.

On Saturday evenings Jimmy would meet Ellen at the end of Carlton Drive and they'd walk hand in hand back towards Clonamurty Farm. Ellen knew his parents and brother well by now and thankfully she'd been accepted into the family as Jimmy's sweetheart, despite her father's misgivings that they would look down on her.

'Always thought you two would get together,'

Mrs Gallagher had said, as Jimmy and Ellen stood side by side in the kitchen at Clonamurty Farm. 'Even right back then, when you were knee-high to a leprechaun.' She'd smiled. 'You make my lad happy. Thank you.'

Ellen wasn't happy about Jimmy's involvement with the Volunteers even though she didn't know too much about what he did. He'd sometimes say something vague about planning an ambush, moving 'supplies' (by which she assumed he meant weapons and ammunition) across the country, hiding from the enemy. She worried constantly that he'd put himself in danger, though this war seemed unlike any other she'd heard of or read about. There were no troops marching along the roads, no battles, no trenches, no cavalry charges. Just occasional reports of someone shot in a remote spot, or a raid by the Royal Irish Constabulary on a house or pub where Volunteers were thought to be hiding, or ambushes by Republicans on motor vehicles carrying British troops.

Since September, the conflict had stepped up a gear. Thankfully the action seemed far away with very little happening in the county of Meath or at least not near Blackstown, a fact for which she was very grateful. Even Carlton House seemed far removed from the acts of war, despite Madame's involvement.

★　★　★

One fine, bright Saturday in early October Ellen was given the full day off work, in addition to her usual Sunday day off. She was allowed to leave immediately after completing her morning chores, although she had to return to Carlton House by six o'clock that evening. Jimmy was free, and they'd arranged a day out, with a picnic provided by Jimmy's mother.

Jimmy met her at the end of Carlton House drive. He was holding a basket containing the picnic, with a rug draped over the top of it for them to sit on. It was a cold day but there was no wind and the sky was a glorious blue. They walked towards Blackstown where Jimmy led them to a bus stop.

'No better place than the Hill of Tara on a day like this,' he said, as they boarded the charabanc that would take them past the foot of the hill. Ellen smiled happily. She didn't mind where they went, on such a beautiful day. It was enough that they could spend the day together. She'd been to Tara before, on an outing with her family while her mother was still alive. It had rained that day, and she could remember only wet grass, a ruined picnic, and huddling in the nearby church when the rain fell harder.

When the bus was about halfway to Tara it stopped to take on passengers, and two men dressed in tan uniforms got on and walked down the aisle of the bus, peering at all the passengers.

Jimmy made a quiet sound, and without warning caught hold of Ellen and pulled her towards him, kissing her soundly on the mouth. He'd tugged his cap low over his eyes.

'Ha, look at these two!' laughed one of the men in uniform.

Ellen tried to pull away, embarrassed to be caught kissing in public, but Jimmy was holding her too tightly, still kissing as though his life depended on it.

The men passed on down the bus, taking a seat at the back, and finally Jimmy let her go. He slid down in his seat so his head barely showed over the back of the seat. 'Sorry about that,' he whispered. 'Don't want to show my face to any of those thugs.'

Ellen began turning to look at the men, but Jimmy caught her arm and stopped her. 'They're Black and Tans,' he explained. 'They don't know my face, and that's the way I need it to stay. Ours is the next stop, thank the Lord.'

When the bus stopped again they got off, and Jimmy bent over the basket as if checking its contents, his back to the road, until the bus moved on.

'Come on. Let's get going.' He took Ellen's hand. They crossed the narrow lane and set off up a track beside a church that Ellen recognised from her visit here as a child.

'Jimmy?' Ellen said, when they were part way up, 'what would have happened if the men on the bus had seen your face?'

In response he put his arm around her and pulled her close. 'Nothing, my sweet. Nothing at all. I'm not known to the Black and Tans. But it would be wise for me to keep it that way. Can't be too careful.'

'Who are they?'

'Auxiliaries, brought in to supplement the RIC while the conflict is on.' He sniffed. 'I've heard that most of them fellas were in prison in England, and were asked if they'd rather come over here and shoot Paddies instead of serving out their time. Of course, they jumped at the chance. Thugs, the lot of them.'

She shivered. 'Keep safe, promise me.'

'I will.'

They'd reached the top of the hill. The view in all directions was spectacular. Ellen spun around, gazing over the fields and hills and farms that were spread beneath her. 'It's as though you can see right across Ireland from here,' she said. 'When I came before it was too misty and wet a day to see anything. Now I can see why the ancient kings built their forts up here.'

'They'd be able to see enemies coming from a long way off,' Jimmy agreed. He led Ellen over to the mounds of earth that marked where the Iron Age fort had stood, and together they walked around it. A few sheep were up there, grazing contentedly on the short grass. 'When the old kings had their seat here, Ireland was independent, mistress of her own destiny,' he said, wistfully. 'She was beholden to no one, least of all England. Did you know Ireland is the only country in Western Europe that was never part of the Roman Empire? We were free and proud. And so we shall be again.'

'Come on. Let's sit and have our picnic,' Ellen urged him. It scared her when he spoke with such fervour. Although she knew and understood that this was a crucial part of who he was, she found it hard to accept that he would lay down his life for his country, if it was required of him. Would he lay down his life for her? She would never ask it of him, though she knew she would sacrifice herself for him, without hesitation. Was that the difference between men and women? That women loved their man and men loved their country best? How then, did women like Madame Carlton fit in? As a widow perhaps she was free to care more for her country and its future.

They spread the picnic rug on one of the ridges of earth that had once formed part of the Iron Age fortifications, sat down and opened the basket Jimmy's mother had packed for them. Bottles of beer, hard boiled eggs, cold boiled potatoes, a jar of chutney, slices of ham and thick chunks of soda bread were all neatly wrapped in paper. There were two plates, knives and forks nestled at the bottom of the basket.

'This looks wonderful, so it does,' Ellen said. 'You must thank your mother for me.' Her own father had muttered in disapproval when she'd told him she was going out with Jimmy for the day. But she was a grown woman, who worked hard all week, and it was up to her how she spent her day off. These days, when they were young and free and able to spend time together, were so precious. Who knew how many of them there would be?

With luck the conflict would end soon, and Jimmy would marry her. Maybe it would drag on for years, keeping them apart, keeping Jimmy in danger. She shook the thought out of her head. Live in the moment, Mary-Ellen, she told herself. Tis all you can do, and tis the best place and time to be.

On impulse she reached for Jimmy and pulled him towards her, kissing him, just as he had done to her on the bus. The kiss was long and deep, and she felt herself melting into him as he pressed himself against her. She wanted him, she realised. They weren't married, it was wrong, but it felt so right! She'd give herself to him, if that's what he wanted. She was ready to take such a step. And maybe it'd keep him close if they became lovers. It'd help him realise how much was at stake, and perhaps persuade him to put her first . . .

But after a while he pulled away, flushed and panting slightly.

'Oh, my love,' he said. 'There'll come a time for us, you'll see. When you and I can be together, properly, and for all time. It's not here and now though. I . . . I love you. But we have to keep apart, do things properly, wait until the time is right.'

'Jimmy, when will that be?' she whispered, knowing how he'd answer.

He sighed and looked away from her, leaning back against the earthen mounds. 'When the war is over. When Ireland is free. I cannot commit to you before then. I am sorry, but you must understand — this is who I am. This is why I've been put on God's earth — to take part in this struggle, to do my bit. Please, you must let me.'

Her eyes filled with tears, but she nodded. 'Of course. I will wait for you. Just . . . '

He smiled. 'I know. Just keep safe. I will.' He leaned over and gave her a chaste kiss on the cheek, then lay back on the rug, looking up at

71

the sky that was now streaked with high wispy clouds. 'Listen, let me tell you about a mission some of my Volunteer comrades were on last week.'

She shook her head. 'No, don't tell me. The less I know, the better.'

'It's not like that. It'll amuse you, honest it will. And no one was hurt.'

'Go on, then.' She lay beside him, her head on his shoulder, to listen.

He cleared his throat. 'So, a company of Volunteers, a few fellas among them I know, had been tasked with transporting some weapons across the county. Too far to carry them, too far for a horse and cart, and they had no other transport, but the guns were sorely needed for . . . well . . . for another campaign.'

Ellen pressed her lips together. She did not want to think about what the guns were to be used for.

'Anyway, one of the lads had a bright idea. He went to the telegraph office, and sent a telegram to the local doctor, an Englishman named Doctor Johnston who was known to drive a large motorcar, telling him that a woman who lived in a remote farm was in desperate need of his attendance, and he was to come at once.

'The doctor set off, but on the way, on a bridge, he met with the company of Volunteers. They stopped him and commandeered his motorcar. He protested of course, telling them he was on an urgent call — at which they came clean and told him it was a hoax. He waved his travel permit at them — issued by the Black and

Tans — but that didn't cut the mustard either. Finally, as he looked about to explode with fury, they gave him a receipt for his car.'

'A receipt?'

'Well, they just scribbled something on a piece of paper and handed it to him.'

'He'll get his motorcar back though, won't he?'

'Aye. When the war is over. That's what it said on the receipt.'

Ellen smiled. 'That could be years!'

'It could indeed.'

She laughed. It was a comical image — a blustering English doctor being forced to give up his car to the Irish Volunteers, and being given a meaningless paper receipt for it. Well, if this was the sort of mission Jimmy was involved in, she had little to worry about. It all sounded rather good-natured, on the whole.

★ ★ ★

As the day wore on the sky clouded over and temperatures dipped. Ellen began to shiver. Her shawl was not warm enough for an autumn day without the sun shining. Jimmy packed up the basket while she folded the picnic blanket, and they descended the hill back to the lane to catch a bus to Blackstown. They journeyed home in companionable silence. Thankfully no Black and Tans got on the bus this time and the journey was a peaceful one.

It had been a day to remember, she thought. One to look back on, in the dark days to come.

She shivered a little, in Jimmy's arms, wondering why that thought had appeared in her mind. Who knew what was to come?

★ ★ ★

That evening, she lay in her narrow bed recounting the events of the day to Siobhan.

'I'm after having the day off too,' Siobhan said. 'Madame wanted the house empty for more of her ridiculous cloak-and-dagger stuff.' She sighed. 'I wish she wouldn't do it. Puts us all in danger, so it does. I've a mind to look for a job elsewhere, but this kind of work isn't easy to find, while the war's on. You were lucky, you know. Walking into it, the way you did. Becoming Madame's favourite in the first five minutes.'

'Ah, sure I'm not her favourite,' Ellen protested, but Siobhan had turned her back to go to sleep, signalling the end of the conversation.

7

Clare, April 2016

I woke in the morning wondering for a moment where I was, gazing around at the unfamiliar floral wallpaper and faded curtains through which weak sunlight was streaming, and then remembered. I recalled too the search for candles, the milk-less tea and makeshift supper. I'd made it through the first night. I'd coped. I hadn't given up and run away to a B&B. And today I'd get the electricity reconnected and buy some food. I smiled, feeling pleased at having proved I had a tiny bit of independence hidden deep within me.

Breakfast was just another cup of black tea. I warmed some water on the stove for a wash and then drove into Blackstown where my first stop was the café for a coffee and proper breakfast, and to plug my phone in to charge while I ate it.

The waitress, recognising me from last night, smiled and introduced herself. 'Hi. I'm Janice. Saw you here last night. On holiday, are you?' She looked to be in her mid-thirties, with a round smiley face surrounded by a mass of unruly curls.

I shook my head. 'Not on holiday no. Actually I've just moved here, to my uncle's old farm that I've inherited. I'm Clare.'

'Pleased to meet you, Clare. Which farm

would that be, then?'

'Clonamurty.'

She frowned. 'Can't say I know that one. Who was your uncle?'

'Pádraig Kennedy. The farm's a few miles out of town.'

'Towards Bettystown?'

I wasn't sure of the geography. 'East-ish.'

She nodded. 'I know where you mean. Sorry to hear of the loss of your uncle. I knew him a little. Knew of him anyways. Everyone knows everyone in this town, so they do.'

'It was years since I last saw him. His sons all died young so he'd named his sister — that's my mum — or her descendants in his will. Mum died a couple of years ago, so it's all come to me.'

'That's so sad. About your cousins and your mum, I mean. And you're going to live here?'

I nodded, but said nothing. I didn't feel quite ready to tell her I'd left my husband yesterday.

'Ah that's grand. Well, will I get you a coffee?'

I laughed, realising I had not yet given her an order and a few more people had come in while we chatted. 'Yes, thanks — there's nothing in the house yet. Coffee and scrambled eggs on toast would be wonderful.'

'Sure,' she replied, patting my shoulder as she passed on her way back to the counter. I had a feeling Janice and I could become good friends, in time. I certainly intended visiting this café frequently, if that cake I had yesterday was at all indicative of the quality of food.

★　★　★

Mentioning my cousins to Janice set me off on another trawl through my memories while I waited for my order. Uncle Pádraig had three sons. Brian, the eldest, was ten years older than me, and when we went visiting he was always far too interested in his latest car, or latest girlfriend, to pay his little cousin much attention. He was the glamorous one, in my eyes. The one with smart clothes, long slicked-back hair and a glint in his eye. He was a charmer, and on the odd occasion he did notice me, ruffle my hair, or pick me up to spin me around, I'd be delighted. I hung off his every word. We'd go back to England and Mum would get fed up of me saying, 'Brian said this; Brian thinks that.'

'Ah, enough of what your cousin Brian thinks,' Mum would say. 'That one's too flashy for his own good.'

He married three times, each wife taller and more blonde than the last, and died in a horrific car crash in his Porsche on the Route des Crêtes in the South of France. 'Typical of Brian,' Mum had said, between her tears at the funeral. 'Lived fast, died young, in such a clichéd fashion.'

My second cousin, Dwayne, couldn't have been more different. Where Brian was good-looking and flashy, Dwayne was plain and quiet, though when he smiled he could light up a room. He was always tucked away in his bedroom, reading books of sermons, fingering his rosary, praying in front of his little glass case that he said contained a hair of St Catherine of Siena. I liked him, but never quite knew how to handle his deep religiosity. We, the English

77

branch of the family, were lapsed Catholics.

Dwayne joined the Christian Brothers, and trained as a teacher in a boys' school. He sent Christmas and Easter cards every year, and a dutiful letter to my mum on her birthday, which always ended with the words, 'Pray every day and you'll not go far wrong.'

Dwayne died just four years ago, aged 53, of cancer. Uncle Pádraig phoned Mum, who was at that time dying of cancer herself, although we didn't know it at the time. He was the last of Pádraig's three sons to die. Mum went over to Ireland for the funeral, came back looking ill and exhausted, and full of news that Pádraig was insisting on changing his will in her favour, now that all his sons were gone and he had no grandchildren. Mum had argued it with him, saying what would *she* do with a farm in Ireland? But Pádraig had insisted, and said it could all come to me if I outlived Mum.

Mum had told me this on the quiet, when Paul was not around. I think she knew then she was dying but had not told me or Dad yet. I think she also knew I was unhappy with Paul, and could see that an inheritance, in time, from my uncle might be my escape route. She was a wise woman, my mum.

And then there was David, Pádraig's third son and the one closest to me in age, being only two years older. But I don't think it was just our proximity in age that drew us together. We shared a lot of interests (he lent me the entire set of Enid Blyton Mystery books) and we often went out cycling together along the country lanes surrounding the farm. It was David who first took me to the Hill of Tara (on a long day's cycle ride when we were in our teens), and told me the legends of the ancient kings of Ireland. He knew so much about his country's history. He was, of all of them, the most Irish, the most proud. The most Republican.

He was arrested for the first time when he was 20, on suspicion of involvement in planning an ambush of British troops on the border near Blacklion. There was not enough evidence to convict him, although one of his friends was imprisoned. It was after this that David announced by letter he wanted to be called Daithí, the Irish form of his name.

Mum had shrugged, taught me how to pronounce it (Doh-hee, more or less) and written back, urging him to 'be careful, stay out of trouble'. I asked what she meant. Why did she think he could be in trouble? 'Oh that boy,' she'd replied. 'There's only one way he's headed, with beliefs as strong as he has. Your granny has a lot to answer for, putting ideas in his head.' I wasn't sure what she meant, and she refused to elaborate. David was her favourite nephew, I knew, but also the one most likely to exasperate her. I only heard the reason for his arrest many years later.

The second time Daithí was arrested he ended up imprisoned in Long Kesh, where he died a couple of years later, of pneumonia, or so we were told. ('Pneumonia, my arse,' said my mother, through her tears at his funeral.) I was 22 at the time. It was hard to equate the smiling, Enid-Blyton-reading, cycling, Irish-history-loving boy

I'd known as a child with a convicted terrorist. Even now it's hard for me to get my head around.

Morbid thoughts. And yet today was the first day of the rest of my life. Time to shake off the past and look to the future.

★   ★   ★

A decent breakfast and the excellent coffee Janice served made me feel a lot more positive. When I'd finished eating and the café was quiet, she sat with me and told me where the supermarket was, and how to get my electricity reconnected. In turn, I ended up telling her a little about Paul. She regarded me with sympathy and then patted my shoulder in solidarity. 'Sounds to me like you've done the right thing, making a clean break. Your good old uncle, eh, providing you with an escape route!'

'That's what I thought,' I replied, gathering up my things. It was time I got going. My phone was fully charged but I was reluctant to turn it on while I was still in the café. There'd be messages from Paul, I was sure of it. I wasn't ready to face them just yet, although I knew I'd have to, soon.

'Use the café's phone to call Electric Ireland,' Janice said, as though she could mind-read. 'Go on. It'll only take a moment and the sooner you call them the sooner they can get working on it.'

So I called them and they promised to have the electricity reconnected by the end of the day. Another problem solved, and I could put off switching my phone on for a little while longer.

I left the café promising to be back again

tomorrow, taking with me a slice of chocolate fudge cake wrapped in a napkin, which Janice had insisted I have. 'It's the last slice and a bit too crumbly to serve to a paying customer,' she'd said. 'I'll be making more today.'

⋆　⋆　⋆

Food shopping was high on the list of things to do next. As was poking around Blackstown. There was that bookshop I'd spotted opposite the café, and as Uncle Pádraig had left no reading material in the house other than a few volumes of Padre Pio sermons (probably left over from my cousin Dwayne) and those boxes of old papers and letters, I was keen to buy myself a few novels.

But before all that, I realised I should ring or at least text the boys. That meant turning my phone on. There was a small park — just a patch of green really — at the end of the high street, surrounding a spreading oak tree with a bench underneath. I sat there, pulled out my phone, took a deep breath and turned it on. Once it was registered on Vodafone Ireland the notifications began coming through. Texts from both boys asking if everything was OK and if I'd arrived safely. Texts saying I had seven voicemail messages. A text telling me that there were no roaming charges as I was in a 'roam-free' destination. And a series of texts from Paul.

Why aren't you at home?

Where's the car?

Why aren't you answering your phone?

Are you serious about leaving? You'll never cope on your own.

I called Matt. He said you'd gone to Ireland. Is that right?

If you're in fucking Ireland where's the car?

If you've taken the car, how the fuck am I going to get to work?

It was clear he hadn't believed me when I'd told him I was leaving. He'd dismissed everything I'd said as worthless, and had only believed I'd left him when Matt confirmed it. And he seemed more upset about the car than anything else.

My first reaction was anger when I read those texts, and then I calmed myself down, read them again, and realised they were almost comical. I realised too that I didn't care.

Next, while I still had that 'don't care' feeling, I listened to the voicemails. There were two from Matt — a 'hope all's OK' one and another warning me Paul had rung him; and the other five were from Paul, saying much the same as the texts but in increasingly belligerent tones. The last asked what he was supposed to have for dinner. I laughed out loud at that one, and pictured him heating up a few tins as I'd done. More likely he'd have phoned for a takeaway curry, despite the freezer full of good food, and several ready-meals in the fridge. I'd stocked it up for him before I left.

So there were three phone calls to make.

I called Matt first.

'Hey, sweetie. Just letting you know I got here safely. All's good.'

'Mum, that's great! I mean, really. Well done. You took the car, right?'

'I did. Your granddad gave it to me, after all.'

'Yeah. Um, Dad's furious about that. Has he called you?'

'He's tried to and left messages. My phone was out of charge and there was no electric at the farm last night. It's being connected today.'

'Were you OK? No lights or anything?'

'I was fine. I found some candles and the oven runs off gas.'

'Wow. Well done.'

'What for?'

He hesitated before answering and I pictured him scrabbling around for the right words. 'For doing it, Mum. For putting yourself first. For getting yourself over there and beginning to get things sorted out. It's a big, brave step. I'm so bloody proud of you.'

There was a catch in his voice at the end, and I felt my own eyes begin to well up. Time to change the subject. I didn't want to sit here, in the middle of Blackstown, blubbing. 'Thanks, love. Well I'd better phone Jon, and then work out how to respond to your dad's messages.'

'Ignore them. Block his number.'

'No, love. I need to talk to him. It'll be all right. We're grown-ups, after all.'

'Hmm, is he? Well good luck then.'

I'd need it, I thought, as I said goodbye and hung up. All very well me sounding cool and grown-up about it when talking to Matt but inside I was quaking. I called Jon next, for more moral support, before tackling Paul. It would not

83

be an easy conversation.

It wasn't. There was ranting, from him, and crying, from me, despite my best efforts to stay calm. He'd thrown out the ready-meals I left for him in a fit of pique. He'd eaten nothing last night other than a tin of beans on toast and tonight he'd call for a pizza and he expected me home tomorrow. 'You'll be fed up of your little adventure by then,' he said, the sneer in his voice loud and clear. 'Something will go wrong and you won't know how to get it fixed, and you'll be on the next boat home.'

'I've already got some things fixed and sorted,' I said, not able to resist. 'The electricity's being reconnected. The oven works. I'll be home soon — sure — my new home of Clonamurty Farm.'

There was more ranting about the car. I pointed out (again) that it was mine, my name was on the registration certificate, and that if Paul needed a car he could easily afford to buy himself one.

The conversation was going nowhere. I could feel myself beginning to want to make excuses, to apologise, to find solutions for his problems. This was not how it should be. I'd left him. I did not want to go back. I'd loved him once, at the beginning, loved all that he'd done for me. But over the years he'd begun more and more to control every aspect of my life. I'd become dependent, and stifled, and it was time for me to go. I realised I had to get off the phone before I caved in, before he set me back a few steps.

I interrupted him in mid-flow as he ranted about how there'd be no one in when the postman called and what if there was a letter or parcel that needed signing for? Had I thought of that when I'd done my flit and left him all alone?

'Paul,' I said, 'I'm not coming back. You need to understand that. I know we need to talk about this, but not now. I've things to do. Goodbye.'

And I hung up on him. I'd never done that before to anyone. It felt strangely liberating, that I could simply press a button and switch him off like that. *Arise and go now*, I told myself. It was becoming a bit of a mantra.

But the phone rang again almost instantly, the display showing it was Paul. I pressed the red button to decline the call. Another first. And then I switched my phone off. Perhaps I should block Paul's number, but for now, I decided the best thing to do was to control the times he could contact me, and only switch the phone on when I felt prepared to talk to him. Or rather, prepared to listen to his tirades.

★   ★   ★

I sat on the bench for a few moments longer to gather my thoughts. It was a blowy day; changing from bright April sunshine one minute to dreary grey the next. Above me, the oak was only just coming into bud. A nearby ash tree was in full leaf, vibrant green against the grey stone buildings behind. I tried to remember the old rhyme — *oak before ash, in for a splash; ash before oak, in for a soak.* Hmm. It'd be a wet first summer in Ireland for me, then. But from what I knew of Irish weather the summers were always wet. You'd get occasional sunny days, which if they fell at the weekend would have everyone rushing off to the nearest beach. Bettystown.

A memory surfaced of a long-ago trip to that beach, with Uncle Pádraig, Aunt Lily and the boys, and my parents and me. I'd have been about 10 years old. Dad had wanted a game of cricket on the wide, flat sand, but Uncle Pádraig had brought hurley sticks and we ended up playing some sort of made-up game, a cross between hurling and hockey, as I could only manage to hit the ball when it was on the ground. David had promised to teach me to play properly.

I remembered how later that day he'd given me a little talk on how the Gaelic games, Hurling and Gaelic football, had become a kind of symbol of Ireland's independence from Britain. They played soccer and rugby too, but it was the traditional Irish games, played nowhere else, that drew the biggest crowds and evoked the most national pride.

It cheered me up, thinking about those times. I resolved to drive to Bettystown beach on the first decent day, and see if it was still how I remembered it.

I walked back up the high street, past the café where I waved at Janice. Opposite was the bookshop I'd noticed yesterday evening. It was open, and I decided to spend a few minutes browsing and perhaps buy a few books before I headed off to the supermarket. I smiled to myself as I crossed the road. How that would annoy

Paul, if he was here — me prioritising reading over cooking and eating! But he wasn't here, and this was my life, and if I wanted to buy books and go hungry I could do just that.

Inside, the shop was one of those wonderful little bookshops where you could spend hours. The front half was new books, with a corner for children equipped with a carpet and some bean bag seats. The adult section was enticingly laid out with the books displayed on pale wooden shelving. At the back of the shop, older, dark wood shelves held second-hand books, organised roughly by subject with hand-written labels sellotaped to the shelf edges. The shop had expanded into a few separate rooms at the back, and I was delighted to discover a cubby hole of books on Irish history. Something I knew not enough about.

There were posters up in the shop celebrating the 100-year anniversary of the Easter uprising, 1916. I remembered my mother and Daithí going misty-eyed whenever they talked about Pádraig Pearse, James Connolly and the declaration of the Republic on the steps of the General Post Office. Now that I was planning to make my home in Ireland, I wanted to understand more about the country's history.

I picked up a couple of second-hand Maeve Binchy novels, and a new one by Barbara Erskine, and a worthy-looking overview of Irish history, and took them all to the cash desk at the front of the shop. The silver-haired man I'd seen locking up yesterday was there, sorting through a box of second-hand books and writing prices on their inside covers. He was younger than I'd thought, I realised, as he pushed his piles of books to one side to make room for my purchases. Probably around my own age.

'Good morning!' he said, as he punched the prices into an antiquated till. 'That'll be thirteen euros ninety. I'll knock off the ninety as a discount, as you're buying four books at once.'

'Oh, thanks!' I dug out my purse and realised with horror I only had a ten-euro note. I'd spent the rest of my cash over at Janice's café. 'Do you take credit cards?'

He shook his head. 'Sorry, no. But you can pay me later. I'll make a note of your name and the amount. It's no bother.'

'Really? Or if there's a cash point nearby I could go there?'

'There is, but it's out of order, or it was about two hours ago when I was trying to get some cash out myself.' He put my books into a bag, handed it to me and opened a notebook. 'Thirteen euro, then, and if you could tell me your name?'

'Clare Farrell. I'm new to the area but I'll be back here tomorrow with the cash, I promise.'

He wrote down my name then held out a hand to shake. 'Pleased to meet you, Clare Farrell. I'm Ryan McKilty.' He smiled as he spoke, making his eyes crinkle up at the corners. He had a pleasant, open face and I liked him instantly.

'Good to meet you, too. Must admit I was delighted to find a bookshop in the town.'

'Ah yes, I cling on to business. The supermarket sells a small selection of best sellers, but if you want a wider choice or nonfiction there's only me, unless you go to the Easons over at Navan. You said you were new to the area? Moved to Blackstown, then?'

'Nearby. Clonamurty Farm.' I explained for the second time that morning my inheritance. Ryan had passed the farm but had not known Uncle Pádraig. It didn't surprise me — there were so few books left in the house it was clear Uncle Pádraig had not been much of a reader.

'Well, you're very welcome. Good to see a new face in town. And I hope to see you in here again soon.'

'Of course, I owe you some money, don't I?'

'Ah, you do, so. I'd forgotten already.' We both laughed, and I turned to leave.

'See you soon, then.'

'Aye, I'll look forward to it,' he replied, holding the door open for me.

★ ★ ★

I was in a fabulously positive mood by the time I returned to the farm. I'd made two friends — Janice and Ryan — stocked up on food and reading material, and even better, Electric Ireland had done their stuff and the power was back on.

'A pretty good first day, all round,' I told myself, as I settled with a cup of tea (with milk this time) on the battered old armchair in the sitting room. That broken spring dug into my bum again, and I shifted position to try to get more comfortable. It was no good.

'I'm going to have to do something about you, aren't I?' I said, to the chair, then shook my head. It was only the second day living alone, but I was already talking to the furniture. I stood up, put my tea on the mantelpiece, and knelt down to take a close look at the chair. It was old — probably late Victorian, and had an old nylon stretch cover over some other layers of upholstery. Definitely a great project for me, to strip it back, fix that spring, and reupholster it, assuming the woodwork was sound. I'd left all my upholstery tools in England, of course, but there was a barn outside with a workshop at one end.

No time like the present, I thought, and I went out to the barn. Those tabby cats I'd seen on my first visit with Paul were hanging around in the yard, and came scampering over to greet me as I walked across to the barn. There was another house a couple of fields away — I guessed they came from there, or at least went there for their food.

The barn looked as though it had once been a cowshed, but the stalls had been removed. In Uncle Pádraig's time it had been used to store farm implements, and a rusty old plough still stood in one corner. He'd sold his tractors long ago when he sold the land and gave up farming. At one end was a workbench, with a battered old chest of drawers beneath and some tools hanging from nails on a board above the bench. There'd be no specialist upholstery tools here of course, but I'd be able to make do until I could order new ones online.

Sure enough I found a sturdy wide-tipped screwdriver that would do as a ripping chisel, a short-handled hammer and a pair of pliers. Enough to start stripping back the chair. I took them inside, gulped down my cooling cup of tea, and set to work.

First I removed the hideous nylon cover. Underneath was ill-fitting brown velour that had been stapled on. Probably some amateur attempt at upholstery. I wondered if Uncle Pádraig or Aunt Lily might have done it, as I prised the staples loose and pulled them out with the pliers. And under that layer was a well-worn corded cotton in a swirling floral design. Possibly the original. This was properly tacked on, with a layer of calico beneath, and I knew under that would be the stuffing, probably horsehair. It was a dusty job and I began to regret doing it inside. I should have taken the whole thing out to the barn.

It was as I removed the cover on the left wing that I discovered the hole. It went in behind the fabric of the back, deep into the chair between the frame and the stuffing. Some tacks had come away leaving a gap you could slip your hand inside. I couldn't resist — and although the thought crossed my mind there could be decades-old dead spiders in there — I pushed my hand in and felt around. It'd be a marvellous hiding place. Perhaps there'd be a wodge of old bank notes inside?

I felt a flutter of excitement when my fingers brushed against paper — there was definitely something in the hole. It could, of course, be simply newspaper stuffed in to pack a gap. But even old newspapers could be interesting. I gripped the paper between two fingers and gently drew my hand back out. There was something solid folded into the paper as well. Carefully I extracted the little bundle from the hole and took it to the table to inspect it in better light.

Definitely more interesting than old newspaper — the paper was a birth certificate dated Christmas Day, 1920. Folded inside was some sort of medallion, with an inscription on the back: *James Gallagher, 1910*. I'd seen something like it before. My cousins had had them. It was a communion medallion, given to a child when they made their first Holy Communion. Who was James Gallagher? And why was his medallion tucked inside a chair along with a birth certificate for someone else?

My grandparents had married in 1926 and, as far as I knew, moved into Clonamurty Farm around the same time. So these items in the chair were from before their time. What was their story?

8

Ellen, October 1919

In late October, a few weeks after their visit to Tara, Ellen found Jimmy in a humour as grey as the moody autumn skies, when she met him at the end of the drive. He greeted her with a kiss as usual, but then didn't take her hand as they walked along the lane. She tried to engage him in conversation as usual, but he seemed taciturn and unwilling to give more than single-word answers.

Eventually, as they approached Clonamurty Farm, she could bear it no longer. 'Jimmy, what's wrong? Have I done something to upset you?'

'What? No, sure you haven't.' He stopped walking and turned away from her, gazing across the fields.

'What, then? You seem different today. Is something on your mind?'

He sighed. 'I was at a funeral today.'

She gasped. 'Oh! I'm sorry. Whose was it?'

He shook his head. 'No one you know. A member of the Volunteers.'

'What happened?' she asked, quietly.

He hesitated a moment before answering, and, she noticed, would not look her in the eye. 'He was shot by the Black and Tans. They had evidence he was planning an ambush out on the Dublin road, and they raided his home. They found some weapons, took him outside and shot him. Right there, in his own yard.'

'Jesus, Mary and Joseph,' she said, crossing herself. 'That's terrible, so it is.'

'Thanks be to God his wife was out at the market with their baby. Another Volunteer was able to find them and get them away to a safe place.'

'Why? Surely the Black and Tans would not have hurt a woman or child?'

Jimmy shook his head sadly. 'They have done so, before now. They're a bunch of thugs, nothing more. They should have arrested Gerry, taken him for questioning and given him a fair trial. But they just executed him on his own doorstep.'

'I'm so sorry. Did you know him well?'

'He was a good man.'

Ellen bit her lip as Jimmy fell quiet, still gazing into the middle distance. Then, suddenly, she made a decision. 'Take me to see his grave, please.'

He turned to look at her, frowning. 'Why?'

'He died for his beliefs. For our country. I'd like to pay my respects.'

He regarded her for a moment, seriously, and then nodded. 'Very well. We have time now. Gerry is buried in Blackstown cemetery. Not so far for us to walk.' He reached out and took her hand and they resumed walking. Jimmy remained silent but something about him seemed more relaxed now, as if he was pleased she wanted to visit the grave.

★ ★ ★

Gerry's grave was at the furthest edge of the cemetery, beyond the rows of older graves that included Ellen's mother and grandparents. There was no headstone yet, and the gravediggers had only just finished shovelling the soil on top of the coffin. The grass around the grave was muddy, trampled no doubt by dozens of feet of patriotic Irishmen a few hours earlier.

Ellen stood a few feet away from the as yet unlevelled mound of earth, her head bowed, as she considered what a sacrifice this unknown-to-her man had made, in pursuit of freedom for their country. She found her thoughts straying to his wife and baby. What would become of them now? This Gerry had put them at risk by his actions, for his beliefs. Did his widow share those beliefs? Or was she now wishing she'd been able to stop him getting involved, to keep him safe somehow?

She glanced across at Jimmy. Was this to be his fate too? Buried six feet under, while she stood and wept at the graveside? She shuddered at the thought.

Jimmy was speaking, quietly, as though only to himself. She moved a step closer to hear his words. It sounded like he was praying, and if he was, she'd join in. But the words were not any she had heard before.

' . . . the fools, the fools, they've left us our Fenian dead. While Ireland holds these graves, Ireland unfree shall never be at peace.'

'Jimmy? What are you after saying?'

He looked at her and she was shocked to see tears in his eyes. 'Tis the words Patrick Pearse spoke at the grave of O'Donovan Rossa, founder of the Irish Republican Brotherhood, back in 1915. I read them in an article in *An Phoblacht* and have never forgotten them. They are the truth. Unfree, we shall never be at peace. We must fight, Ellen, fight on. Mourn our dead but never give up. Gerry must not have died for nothing. We must not allow him to have died for nothing!'

He turned to her and grabbed hold of both her hands. 'You must not fear for me, Ellen. If I die for this Cause, I die for something I believe in and long for with all my heart. I can think of no better end than to be buried alongside Gerry here, if I have in some small way moved Ireland closer to her independence.'

His eyes were shining again, with that same fire she'd seen when he'd told her of his decision to join the Volunteers. This was him, this was her Jimmy, this was the path he had chosen in life. All she could do was support him, pray for his safety, and pray that the conflict would be over soon and that Ireland would somehow gain her freedom. For no other outcome would guarantee Jimmy's safety, she knew that now.

★   ★   ★

Later that day, Ellen was sitting in the living room at Clonamurty Farm, drinking tea while Mrs Gallagher asked her about her work up at the big house.

'Is it true,' the older woman whispered, 'what they say about Mrs Carlton? That she, you know, is *involved*?' She mouthed the last word.

'Er . . . um . . . ' Ellen was at a loss as to how to answer. Mrs Gallagher didn't know about Jimmy's involvement, as she put it, either. Thankfully Jimmy re-entered the room at that moment, carrying a plate of biscuits his mother had asked him to fetch from the kitchen.

'Mammy! Don't go asking things like that! If Ellen knew anything she'd be wise not to tell you, or anyone else.'

'I'd be worried, I would, if I thought she was working somewhere where the people are involved. I'd fear for her safety. I fear for you too, Jimmy. I pray every night that you won't get yourself caught up in it all. I mean, we all want an independent Ireland, but can't we just leave it for others to fight for it?'

'Mammy, if everyone thought like that no one would fight and the Cause would never be won,' Jimmy pointed out, quietly and reasonably. 'Someone has to rise up and fight for it.'

Ellen fidgeted uncomfortably in her chair, the old armchair that always sat by the fireside, and heard an ominous rustle from within it. Jimmy must be hiding something in his secret place. She sat still, hoping Mrs Gallagher hadn't heard the rustle.

★   ★   ★

They'd been about 10 years old when Jimmy first showed Ellen his hiding place. It was after school. They'd walked home together from the National School as they always did, passing

97

Jimmy's home at Clonamurty Farm first.

'Come in, have a drink of milk,' Jimmy had said. 'Mammy won't mind. She likes you, so she does.'

So Ellen had gone inside to the Gallaghers' large yet cosy kitchen, and waited while Jimmy filled a mug with fresh milk from a large jug that sat covered with a muslin square. The milk was creamy and still slightly warm from the cow. There was no better drink, Ellen thought, as she gulped it down. She wished her family owned a cow, but they were too poor. Her father worked on other people's farms, only tending a small plot himself. They kept chickens and sometimes a pig. Her mother took in laundry to add a little to the household income.

'Come on, I want to show you something,' Jimmy said, when she'd finished her milk. He grabbed her hand and led her through to the family's sitting room.

Ellen hesitated on the threshold. She'd been to Clonamurty Farm many times before, but usually just to play in the hay barns, or visit the latest batch of kittens. She'd been in the kitchen a few times but never into the 'good' rooms.

'It's all right, there's no one in here, and Mammy's away at Blackstown market,' Jimmy said. 'Come on in.'

She crept inside and looked around. It was a bright, comfortable room with windows that looked out over a garden and beyond, to the fields she knew so well that dropped away towards the River Boyne. There were full-length curtains at the windows, a sofa and armchairs arranged around the fireplace, and several pictures hanging on the wall. So different to her own cottage, with its single room that functioned as both kitchen and living room, its hard wooden settle, battered table and bentwood chairs. At home their only picture on the wall was a faded depiction of Jesus, his heart exposed and shining. This room looked so much more comfortable and homely.

'Over here, look.' Jimmy was crouching beside one of the well-stuffed fireside chairs. Ellen knelt beside him, and he took her hand and pushed it into the chair, between the wing and the back. There was a slit in the fabric there, where some stitching must have come undone. 'Feel around inside,' Jimmy instructed her.

She did as he said. She could feel a wooden strut, part of the frame of the chair, and some rough horsehair stuffing. 'What's in here?'

'Reach in deeper,' he said. 'It's my special hiding place, that I use when I have something I don't want Mickey to find. Small brothers are so annoying. But you, you're my best friend, so you can know about it.'

She was a little nervous. Was he playing some sort of trick? Would her hand close around a dead mouse or something equally horrid? But this was Jimmy, not one of her brothers, and Jimmy didn't play tricks on her. She trusted Jimmy. Eventually she found it — a small net bag filled with something hard, round . . .

'Pull it out,' Jimmy said, grinning.

She did. It was a bag of glass marbles. Beautiful, swirling colours ran through their middles. 'Oh, they're grand!' Ellen exclaimed.

'They were a birthday gift from an uncle. A late one,' Jimmy explained. 'Let's share them.'

'Oh, no, I couldn't . . . they're yours!'

'But it's more fun if we have some each. We can play marbles and try to win them off each other.' Jimmy pulled open the net bag. 'You pick first.'

★ ★ ★

He'd always been like that — sharing everything with her, doing whatever was best for everyone rather than just best for himself. It was one of the things Ellen loved most about him. The only thing he didn't share, now, was details of his activities with the Volunteers.

Jimmy used the hiding place in the chair now, to store any papers he wanted kept away from prying eyes. 'You can't be too careful, so,' he'd said. 'I trust my parents, of course, but if anyone else was visiting the house and came across any letters from members of the Irish Volunteers, it could mean trouble. There's information I wouldn't want to get into the wrong hands.'

Ellen didn't like to think what might be hidden there now, what those rustling papers might contain. If Jimmy was suspected of being a Republican and the farm raided, as had happened to that poor man, Gerry, she didn't know how she'd be able to go on with life.

9

Clare, April 2016

I gathered up the covers I'd ripped off the chair, stuffed them into a bin bag and dumped that out in the barn. The next stage would be messier — removing the calico to expose the stuffing and then the underlying springs, webbing and hessian. Some of it would have rotted into dust. The place to continue working on this chair was in the barn, but first that would have to be cleared, and that was too big a job for today. It was still only my first full day in my new home, after all.

I laughed at myself for having started an upholstery project when I had not even put away my food shopping. Talk about getting my priorities wrong. I shuddered to think what comment Paul would have made if he was here. But hey, it was my house, my life, and if I wanted to strip chairs ahead of putting food in the fridge then I would.

But some food was perishable and now the electricity was working I needed to get it put away. The fridge, of course, was ancient and also dirty, with what might once have been a tomato rotting in a back corner, and several jars of jam and chutney in varying stages of decomposition. 'A new job everywhere I turn,' I told myself, and set myself to cleaning it out before I put my food in.

That's when I realised I needed to be organised and make myself a list of jobs, prioritising those I needed to do quickly to make the house habitable, and those I could put on the long finger, as Uncle Pádraig might have said, leaving them till a later date.

A couple of hours later I'd had a sandwich as a very late lunch, cleaned and stocked the fridge, and written a long list of jobs. I felt tired and a little overwhelmed by all that would need doing, and was ashamed to find tears springing to my eyes. Was I really capable of building this new life, all by myself? The house needed huge amounts of work — water from the taps was brown so it probably needed re-plumbing; it definitely needed rewiring; there were damp patches in many rooms; the bathroom suite was old and stained; cupboard doors were hanging off in the kitchen and the lino was curling up at the edges; the carpets stank of dogs and were dated and worn; all the furniture was long past its best; and that was only the interior of the house.

To my untrained eye it looked as though the brickwork needed repointing; some of the wooden window frames were rotten; the front door stuck and there were a few roof tiles missing. And then there were the outbuildings — that barn and two small cottages that might once have housed farm workers.

Where would I start? How did I ever think I'd be able to do this alone? Maybe I should have listened to Paul and sold it. I could have used the proceeds to buy a small modern house for myself. Why did I want to take on this great big, rambling, rundown farmhouse? Just because it held some childhood memories for me, and could put me in touch with my Irish ancestry? Or just because it was the quickest way for me to get out and leave Paul? If I'd waited to sell it and buy somewhere else, it could have taken months. Years, even, to find a buyer for Clonamurty Farm.

Besides, I'd wanted a challenge, hadn't I? Lord knows why. It was enough of a challenge to be starting a new life without Paul. I was certain, I thought, that I'd done the right thing there, at least.

I was still sitting at the kitchen table, sniffing back tears and feeling sorry for myself, when I heard a knock at the back door, that led into the corridor beside the kitchen. 'Hello, anybody home?' came a call, and I recognised Janice's voice.

'Yes, in here,' I called back, and she came in, followed by her four children.

'Just popped by to see how you were getting on. Did you get the electric fixed? Do you need any shopping — we're just off to Tesco now. Anything I can do for you?'

I smiled. 'I think I'm all right. Yes, the electric's back on, and I went shopping. I was just making a list of what needs doing in the house. It's all a bit daunting. Cup of tea? I'm afraid I've nothing for the kids.'

'Ah they're grand. Yes please to tea. Sit down there and do your homework.' This last was directed to the kids, who all immediately took a seat at the kitchen table and pulled out books. None of them actually opened the books, however; they were all too busy gazing round at my kitchen, giggling, poking, and shushing each other.

I put the kettle on. 'So, do you want a tour of the place? It's all a bit of a mess.'

'I'd love to! Kids, sit there, don't move, behave.' We set off upstairs, where she commented on the good size of the rooms and what potential they had. In the sitting room she patted the chair I'd begun work on. 'Needs to go in a skip, I'd say.'

'Absolutely not! The frame's sound. I'm going to strip it right back and rebuild it.'

She widened her eyes at me. 'You can do that?'

'I did upholstery evening classes for a few years. I've done several of this kind of chair. Hopefully I'll be able to do a decent job on this one. I fancied a project.'

She laughed. 'Like the house is not enough of a project?'

'Ha! I know. But I do like renovations. Soft furnishings, upholstery — those are my areas.'

'Curtains?' Janice said, fingering the moth-eaten faded mustard-yellow velvet that graced the French windows.

'Definitely.'

'I need some new ones. I can't make them though, and they don't do ready-mades in the right size. You could go into business doing soft furnishings around here. We've no one in Blackstown doing it.'

It was a thought, and a pleasing one, that I could perhaps spend my days doing what I loved best and making money from it. 'Better get my own house in order first though.'

'Sure. Well, later in the year if you have time and fancy it, I'd love some new sitting-room curtains. I'd pay you, mind. I could be your first customer.'

'OK, you're on!'

Janice walked across the room, heading back towards the kitchen where her children were ominously quiet. She spotted the birth certificate and medallion I'd found in the chair, and touched them, her face puzzled.

'What are these?'

'I found them tucked inside the chair, between the cover and the calico,' I explained. 'I've no idea whose they are. Not my uncle or his family, anyway.'

'James Gallagher. James O'Brien. Never heard of either name. But they're old. These people would be long dead.'

'Must be someone who lived here before my uncle's family,' I said. 'My grandparents moved here in the mid-1920s as far as I know. So it's before their time. I don't recognise those names. It'd be great to find out who they were. Is that a communion medallion, do you think?'

'Looks like it, sure. You're given them as a child when you make your first Holy Communion. You're supposed to treasure them for ever. I've no idea where mine got to!' Janice threw back her head and laughed.

I laughed too. 'I guess James Gallagher never knew where his got to, either. Unless he's the person who tucked it into the chair. But why would it be with a birth certificate?'

'Are they related to each other?'

'Different surname, so I guess not. Ah well. I suppose we'll never know.'

'You should ask Ryan. The fellow who runs the bookshop opposite my café. He's into genealogy and local history. He'd be able to look up these guys and find out more about them. I'll introduce you to him, next time you come by the café.'

I smiled. 'Actually I've already met him. I was in there this morning buying myself some books.'

'Oh yes?' Janice put her hands on her hips and tilted her head to one side. 'And what did you think of our local silver fox?'

'He seemed nice,' I said. Why my cheeks felt flushed was a mystery.

'You like him!'

'I only said half a dozen words to him. And, Janice, I only left my husband yesterday. Give me a chance!'

Janice had the grace to look mortified. 'Ah, I'm sorry. Me and my big mouth. He is a nice fellow, though. He'll definitely be interested in your little mystery, if you ask him. I'll stay well out of it. Kids! Come on, we must be off and leave poor Clare in peace!'

'It's all right, you don't need to rush off.' I was more amused than offended by Janice's match-making. 'Good idea though, I will ask Ryan about how I could find out more about these people, or anyone who lived here before my family. I want to research my own genealogy too. It'd be a nice little project.'

Janice laughed aloud once more. 'As if you haven't enough to do! Ah, but we must be getting on anyway. Ciara's got her Irish dancing lessons, and Donny's going to a sleepover for his friend's birthday. So I'll be one down tonight. Come on, gang. Say goodbye to Clare.'

They mumbled 'bye' as they traipsed out. 'Come again. I'll make sure I've some Coke and biscuits next time. Or one of your mother's chocolate cakes from the café.'

The oldest girl who I guessed was Ciara pulled a face. 'We get all Mammy's leftover cakes. I prefer shop-bought.'

Janice rolled her eyes as she ushered them outside. 'There's no pleasing some people. Come on or you'll be late, so you will.'

⋆ ⋆ ⋆

The house seemed doubly quiet after they'd gone. I made myself some dinner, then sat on the grimy old sofa in the sitting room with a glass of wine. It had been a long day, but I felt good at what I'd achieved. Janice's visit had really helped. I could do this. With the support of my sons and some local mates, I could do this. And although it was only day two, I felt I'd made a start at forming some new friendships.

⋆ ⋆ ⋆

In the early days of our marriage, my friends all thought Paul was wonderful, whisking me away on surprise weekends in spa hotels or city breaks.

Prague, Paris, Lisbon, Florence — we've been all over and stayed in some lovely places.

Call me ungrateful, but at times I resented the 'surprise' aspect of these trips away. I think I'd have liked them more if I'd been involved in choosing where we went; if I'd been allowed to find guidebooks and read up on the places before the trip; if I'd had the anticipation as well as the event. Sometimes the way Paul sprung the surprise on me left me feeling unsettled and disorientated. I'd have things planned for the weekend, but then Paul's surprise trip would mean my plans had to be cancelled.

I know, I know, what a hardship — having to rearrange a shopping trip and do the gardening some other time so as to make time for a weekend strolling along the banks of the Seine and browsing the art in the Louvre. But there was one weekend in particular that might explain why I came to resent these surprise weekends away.

I'd hardly seen my old school friends since we married. There was a group of four of us, and we'd done everything together when we were at school. After school we made a point of meeting up several times a year. As we got older this dwindled to a once-a-year shindig — we'd book rooms in a cheap hotel somewhere we could all get to easily and have a great night catching up and reminiscing. Lots of wine would be drunk and lots of giggling accomplished.

One by one we'd got married and had all attended each other's weddings. Babies were born and our weekends away were harder to manage but children have two parents, and apart from in the very early months babies can be left with their fathers.

Crunch time for me came after our eldest, Matt, was born. He was nine months old and already weaned when the girls' weekend came round. It was just one night away, and only twenty miles from our home, and it had been written in our house diary for months. In the week leading up to it I had gone through Matt's feeding routines with Paul, and made sure he knew how to mix up formula and heat up baby food. He'd listened and nodded and everything seemed to be lined up ready for me to have a great couple of days with my old mates.

Until the Friday morning, the day before I was due to go to meet them. Paul was up early, even before Matt was awake, and he brought me breakfast in bed — a tray laid with tea, toast, a boiled egg. He was smiling broadly as he brought it in.

'Surprise!'

'Ooh, this is lovely,' I said, sitting up and arranging a pillow behind my back so I could put the tray on my knees. 'What's the occasion?'

'Look under the napkin.'

I lifted the napkin, and there was an envelope. Inside were two tickets for the Moulin Rouge for the next day.

'You've always said you'd like to go.' He sat down on the bed and took my hand. 'Excited? Your parents have agreed to take Matt for a couple of days. They'll be here in an hour to collect him. Our flight's at twelve.'

I couldn't answer for a moment. I just sat there holding the tickets, trying to remember if I'd ever said I wanted to go to the Moulin Rouge.

'But what about my weekend away?' I managed in the end, my voice emerging as a squeak.

'This is your weekend away, darling! Properly away, in Paris, with me. Better than staying in that old Travelodge up the road.' He was still grinning and holding my hand.

'But why did you book it for this weekend, Paul? When you knew I had made plans?'

'Ah, pfft. Your plans are easy enough to change. See your friends some other time. When I'm at work, maybe. You've got all week to see them, rather than spoil my precious weekends by leaving me with the baby.'

'The baby? *Our son*, you mean.' I felt my eyes fill with tears. I'd been so looking forward to seeing my friends. 'And it took us ages to get this weekend sorted. It's not easy to find time when all four of us can meet. Sarah and Lynne both work full-time. Jess has been living in the Far East for a year and only just came back. Paul, you knew about this weekend. It's been booked for ages!'

'So have those tickets. There's a long waiting list for the Moulin Rouge, you know. Honestly, Clare, you're so ungrateful. We're booked into a gorgeous boutique hotel up in Montmartre, too. The tickets include dinner before the show. It'll be amazing!'

'I'm sure it will, but . . . ' A tear escaped and slid down my cheek. I'd been longing to see Jess and hear all her tales of ex-pat life in Bangkok,

110

and show them all photos of baby Matt.

'It will. Anyway, you're coming with me. I have a case for you half packed — you might want to check you're happy with the dress I put in for you to wear tomorrow night. Come on. Eat up your breakfast. And stop crying. You don't want your parents to see you looking all miserable when you've got such a treat ahead of you!' He patted my hand, stood and left the room.

So, I had to call Jess, explain and apologise, and ask her to pass the message on to the others. She sounded a bit cold with me on the phone. I wasn't surprised. The weekend had been picked to fit with her return from Bangkok. 'Next year, then,' she said. 'If you can manage it.'

'Oh, I'll be there next year, don't you worry,' I said.

But I wasn't. Every year there was some reason why it was impossible for me to go. One year I was heavily pregnant with Jon and Paul said it was too dangerous to be away from home in case I went into labour. Another year he was sick, contracting food poisoning the day before. Another time his mother arrived for an extended visit. And then there were no more girlie weekends booked.

I thought the meet-ups had naturally come to an end, with everyone finding it harder now they had husbands and children to work around. But I heard on the grapevine much later that the other three had continued to meet, and just stopped inviting me as they thought I didn't want to see them any more.

'Friendships naturally come to an end,' Paul

had said. 'You can't expect to still get on with people you met when you were 10, when you are 30, or 40.'

But I had got on with them. And I missed them so much. Paul had driven a wedge between us.

What made the whole Moulin Rouge episode worse is that when we arrived at the airport Paul pulled out an envelope from the travel agent's with the tickets in. I caught a glimpse of the covering letter, and it was dated just two days earlier. So he hadn't planned this before I planned my girls' weekend as he'd said, but had booked it only a couple of days before.

★   ★   ★

Now, as I sat in my own house, away from Paul, I wondered if I'd be able to rekindle that friendship with Jess and the others. It'd be worth a try. I could send them all an email, tell them my news, and maybe even suggest a reunion weekend, perhaps in Dublin. It had been a long time, but there was nothing to lose.

10

Ellen, October 1919

When Ellen returned to Carlton House on Sunday afternoon, the day after she'd stood with Jimmy at his friend Gerry's graveside, all was in uproar. The servants were running to and fro, carrying towels, sheets, bowls of water and bundles of rags, up and down the stairs.

'What's happening?' Ellen asked Siobhan, who was running down the stairs with an empty water jug, her cap askew and her apron untied.

Siobhan shook her head. 'I don't know. The mistress is after wanting this and that, the messages are coming thick and fast and my feet are worn off. Here, you're the upstairs maid, you can take over now you're back.' She thrust the jug at Ellen. 'Madame wants this filled with water, and ice from the ice-house, and take it up to the green bedroom. Leave it on the little table outside the room and knock three times, then wait. Madame will come out for it and to give you the next order. I'm fair worn out, so I am. Time for me to have a sit-down in the kitchen.' She didn't wait for an answer.

Ellen sighed and carried the jug to the scullery where she left it on a bench, then took off her coat and hat and left them with her overnight bag just inside the housekeeper's office. If Madame Carlton was upstairs then she wouldn't notice the office being used as a temporary cloakroom. Ellen could quickly run up to her second-floor room with her things later on.

She retrieved the jug and went outside to the ice-house, where she chipped away at the ice until the jug was half full, then went back inside to fill it with water from the scullery tap. She looked down at herself — she was still wearing her weekend dress. What would Madame Carlton say? But then, it was not yet five o'clock, not yet the time she was due back at work in any case.

Ellen hurried up the stairs to the room Siobhan had mentioned, and knocked three times on the door as instructed. Madame Carlton must have one of her mysterious Volunteer guests in there, she supposed. The door was answered almost immediately by the mistress herself.

'Ah, Ellen. I am glad you are back. Wait here a moment.' She took the jug, passed it to an unseen person inside, and then stepped out into the corridor closing the door behind her.

'Madame, I am sorry, I am only just returned and have not had time to change yet. I'll do so now, really quickly, so I will.' Ellen bobbed a curtsey and turned to go, but the mistress caught at her arm.

'No, wait. It's good that you are in your own clothes. I have an errand for you. I need you to go to Drumlane and fetch Doctor O'Mahony. Tell him it's urgent, a brother is injured.'

Ellen opened her eyes wide. 'But, ma'am, what about Doctor Morris, in Blackstown? That's so much closer and I can run there in twenty

114

minutes . . . ' It would take her over an hour to walk to Drumlane, she knew.

'I know Doctor Morris. But he is not, shall we say, as *sympathetic* as Doctor O'Mahony. I am sorry, I know it's a long way and I would send one of the men from the stables, but he would be stopped and questioned. You are much less likely to be questioned, and if you are, say you are fetching the doctor for your father.'

'Madame, who will question me?'

Madame Carlton caught hold of her hands and paused a moment before answering. 'Ellen, I'm afraid the Black and Tans have set up a roadblock between here and Drumlane. You are a young girl and they will let you through without any problems, I am sure of it. Hurry now. It's important the doctor gets here as soon as he can.'

'Won't he be stopped by the roadblock too?'

'He will have a pass. Don't worry about the doctor, just yourself. Can you do this for me?'

She nodded and curtseyed again. 'Yes, Madame.'

Madame Carlton smiled. 'Good girl. And, Ellen? You are doing this for your country, as well.'

Ellen stared at her, but the mistress turned and went back into the green bedroom. Ellen took a deep breath and hurried back down the stairs and through to the housekeeper's room to retrieve her coat and hat. It was a bitterly cold day, and she had a long walk ahead.

'What is it she wants this time?' Siobhan appeared from the kitchen. 'Why are you not yet in uniform?'

115

'I've to go out on an errand,' Ellen replied, buttoning her coat.

'Glad it's you and not me, so I am,' Siobhan said, returning to the kitchen.

Yes, Ellen thought, it would be nice to be able to go and sit in a warm kitchen now, sipping a cup of hot chocolate. But a doctor was needed — a sympathetic doctor, Madame had said, and somehow Ellen knew the mistress wasn't referring to his bedside manner — and someone had to fetch him. She left the house through the servants' entrance at the back, and set off down the drive, walking at a brisk pace that she hoped she'd be able to keep up all the way. She was doing this for her country, just like Jimmy. That thought sent a thrill of pride rushing through her.

Her route took her through Blackstown, along the high street and out the other side of town, past a cluster of houses and then along a country road that led to Drumlane. She had not been this way since the war began.

The roadblock was set up just outside the town. A farm cart had been placed blocking half the width of the road, and four men dressed in their mismatched black and tan uniforms and armed with rifles, guarded the open side. Ellen could see them as soon as she rounded a corner, and for an instant she faltered, unsure whether to go on or try to find a way past them through the fields.

But they had rifles, and if they were suspicious, might they not just shoot at her? Better, she decided, to raise her head, act confident and innocent. For she was innocent, wasn't she? She was only fetching a doctor. For her father, who was sick. Coughing, with blood in his phlegm, she decided, remembering how her mother was before she died. And if they asked why she did not go to Doctor Morris she'd reply that she had tried the Morris's house but the doctor was not at home, and her father was so very sick she'd decided to go on to Drumlane for the other doctor. Her sister was left nursing their father.

Yes, that was a plausible story. Feeling more confident now that she'd worked it all out, she quickened her pace and walked directly towards the roadblock.

'What's your business, miss?' one of the men asked as she neared them. His voice was rough-sounding, with an English accent. Jimmy had said the Black and Tans were mostly hardened criminals, given the choice to fight the Irish rather than serve out their jail terms.

'Fetching a doctor,' she replied, hoping her voice was trembling less than her knees.

'Right pretty lass you are. Wouldn't mind seeing you again when you come back this way,' the man replied, with a leer.

She hesitated, not sure if that meant she could pass or not.

'Well, go on with you,' he said, waving his rifle as if to push her past with it. She scurried past, trying not to run, scared they'd shout out and stop her after all, terrified she'd feel the sudden searing pain of a bullet in her back.

No, Mary-Ellen, she told herself, you've done

nothing wrong and even the Black and Tans wouldn't shoot an innocent girl in the back.

But how innocent was she really, now that she was involved with the Cause, albeit in a very minor way? She was fetching a doctor, presumably to tend to an injured Volunteer. Who he was or how he'd come by his injuries she might never know, but it may well have been in an attack against the very men she'd just passed.

She reached the doctor's house and passed on the message. Doctor O'Mahony, a man in his thirties with an impressive moustache, regarded her solemnly as she repeated what Madame Carlton had told her to say.

'Thank you, young colleen. You've done a great service today. I'll ride over to Carlton House immediately. I'm sorry I cannot offer you a lift.'

'That's all right. But, sir, there are Black and Tans on the Blackstown road . . . '

He smiled. 'I know. But they will let me through. Now, go inside where my wife will give you some tea and soda bread to nourish you for your journey back. Rest as long as you need to.' He waved her through to his kitchen, while he went round to the stables.

* * *

Ellen was very grateful to get back to Carlton House that night. It had become dark as she walked home, and despite the sustenance the doctor's wife had given her she was starving. Her feet were sore too, from the long walk. And she still had her regular Sunday evening chores to do before she could collapse into bed. Perhaps Siobhan would help her out a little. But it wasn't to be. Siobhan stayed in the kitchen all evening, apparently hard at work polishing cutlery, while Ellen ran around the house attending to her usual chores as well as more fetching and carrying for the doctor and Madame Carlton, who both remained in the green bedroom for hours.

The next day Ellen rose at six o'clock as usual to start her morning chores, including setting the fires in all the bedrooms currently in use. She knew better than to go into the green room, however; although she was curious who was inside.

Madame was still in bed, but woke as Ellen crouched beside the fire, arranging turf and kindling.

'Ellen, is that you?'

'Yes, Madame, sorry to disturb you. Will I light the fire now for you?'

'Yes please. I must get up and see to our patient, and relieve Doctor O'Mahony who's been with him overnight. Ellen, you did a good job yesterday fetching the doctor so promptly. You may have saved a good man's life. Thank you. As a reward you may have the afternoon off tomorrow.'

'But I just had a day off, so I did!' Ellen blurted out.

'Yes, and you deserve more time. You may leave after lunch and return by six o'clock. Just rest on your bed if you don't want to go out anywhere.'

'Thank you, Madame.' Ellen smiled and

119

curtseyed, then lit the fire and left the room. She was lucky to have such a thoughtful employer. She could go and see Jimmy again, at the farm. Maybe he'd know something about who was in the green bedroom. She could tell him her own small part in the war, and he'd be proud, and his eyes would shine as he gazed at her, and he'd pull her close and kiss her long and deep . . .

★ ★ ★

The day passed much as usual, with Ellen catching up on her chores, still wondering who was in the green bedroom, and looking forward to her extra afternoon off tomorrow.

'Are you recovered after your long walk yesterday?' Madame asked, as Ellen collected a tray from the green room in the afternoon. 'We could not telegraph Doctor O'Mahony, you understand. The telegraph office is watched and telegrams intercepted. I could not risk the other side finding out about our guest. I am glad we could trust you to take on this mission.'

'It's no problem, Madame. Whatever you ask.'

Madame regarded her as though weighing something up. 'You're a good girl, Ellen, and one I can trust. May I ask you, do you have any experience of nursing?'

'Not much, ma'am, though I did help look after my mammy at the end of her life.'

'And are you afraid of nursing? Of tending to the sick or wounded, clearing up their mess, dressing their wounds?'

'No, Madame, not at all.' People were people,

and surely there was no more worthwhile job than helping someone get better.

Mrs Carlton smiled. 'Good. I should like you to help with some nursing duties. As you are aware, we have a patient in the green bedroom and he is requiring round-the-clock care at the present time. You may leave your chores for this evening, as I would like you to sit with him for the next few hours to allow me to have a little rest. I shall return and take over from you by ten o'clock. Your evening meal will be brought to you. Now, follow me and I shall introduce you to your patient.'

'But, Madame . . . ' Ellen looked at the tray she was still holding.

Mrs Carlton smiled, took it from her and placed it on a side table in the corridor. 'I'll take that back downstairs later. Now come on.'

Ellen followed her into the bedroom. The curtains were drawn and the room was gloomy. In the bed she could just make out a man, propped up against several pillows, with one shoulder and arm heavily bandaged. Another bandage was around his head, and he had one black eye. It was hard to be sure of his age, but Ellen judged him to be no more than 30.

'Captain Cunningham? May I introduce Ellen, who is going to help nurse you. She will sit with you for the next few hours and I will return to cover the night shift. Is there anything you need?'

The man's good eye roved over Ellen, and he gave a half-smile. 'Water, if you would, please.' His voice was cracked and forced, as though talking was a huge effort.

Ellen stepped forward and poured a glass of water from a jug that stood on a side table, and at a nod from Mrs Carlton, approached the bed. She put a hand behind Captain Cunningham's head to steady him and held the glass to his lips while he took a sip. When he'd finished he leaned back and closed his eyes.

Ellen replaced the glass on the side table and looked at Madame, who nodded her approval.

'Keep an eye on that head wound. If the blood soaks through the bandage you will need to change the dressing. There are clean bandages and absorbent pads in that basket on the chair. At seven o'clock he should have another dose of his painkiller — two teaspoons of that medicine. He'll probably sleep after that. Make sure he drinks as much as possible. Are you hungry, Captain Cunningham?'

The man shook his head weakly, keeping his eyes closed.

Mrs Carlton sighed. 'We've been unable to tempt him to eat but he needs to keep up his strength. I'll have some scrambled egg sent up. Even if he only eats a tiny amount the doctor said it would do him good. See if you can persuade him. Is everything clear?'

'Yes, Madame.' Ellen began tidying and straightening the bedclothes as Mrs Carlton left the room. A little later she returned herself with the egg, and Ellen managed to coax the patient to eat three spoonfuls before he collapsed back onto his pillow, exhausted by the effort.

A few minutes later, gentle snores told her Captain Cunningham had nodded off, so when everything was in order she pulled a chair within reach of the bed and settled down. There was a book on the table beside the water jug — an edition of Charles Dickens's *A Tale of Two Cities*. She was not sure if she was allowed to read it, but there seemed to be nothing else to do for the time being, so she picked it up and began reading, staying alert to her patient in case he woke or needed anything.

It was a long evening, but eventually Mrs Carlton returned, looking refreshed from her sleep.

'Thank you, Ellen. You have done a good job.'

'I've done nothing, Madame. Captain Cunningham stayed asleep almost the whole time. If you want me to sit longer . . . '

'No, you can go now. Perhaps you can take over for a bit in the morning, after your morning chores are done, and before you have your afternoon off.'

'Yes, Madame, of course.' Ellen curtseyed and left the room, noticing Mrs Carlton pick up the book and sit in the same chair Ellen had been in.

★   ★   ★

That night when they were in bed, Siobhan asked her where'd she'd been all evening. Ellen hesitated to tell her, but realised it was no secret that an injured man was in the house. All the staff had seen the doctor arrive.

'I was nursing,' she said.

'A Volunteer?' Siobhan asked.

'Mmm.' Ellen tried to be non-committal with her answer.

'Do you think they'll win?'

It was dark so Ellen couldn't see her face, but there was something odd about her tone. 'I don't know,' she replied.

'Do you want them to?'

'Of course. Don't you?'

'Ah, yes, I suppose so, in the end. Can I tell you a secret? It's killing me, keeping it. I'll explode, so I will. But you can't tell anyone. Not a soul. I'd lose my job.'

Ellen was quiet for a moment. They'd become sort-of friends, but not so close that she felt she wanted to know Siobhan's darkest secrets.

'Please, Ellen? It's nothing bad, honest to God. But I just want someone to know.'

'Go on, then.'

Siobhan took a deep breath. 'It's this. My brother's after joining the RIC. Above in Leitrim, not here in Meath. He's on the other side, now, and I don't know who to support. Who's right and who's wrong.'

Ellen's eyes widened at this, and she thought carefully about how to answer. 'Siobhan, I won't tell a soul, sure I won't. But while you live in this house, you must support the Volunteers. If you don't, you must leave, or you'll put us all in danger.'

'I won't do anything. Madame's been good to me. Thanks, Ellen. I feel better for having told someone. It felt like a heavy secret, you know?'

Ellen did know. It felt heavy on her, too.

11

Clare, May 2016

One morning I woke up, in my fresh new sheets bought from Dunnes Stores, and realised I'd been in Ireland a week.

And then it was ten days, and then two weeks. Time was speeding up.

I'd spent the days organising the house. I'd hired a skip, which stood across the yard opposite the unused front door. In it I'd tossed anything that was unsalvageable and unusable. Anything I didn't want but which was serviceable had been free-cycled or given to charity. I'd kept upholstered furniture and anything sound made of wood. Those could be restored and given a new lease of life. The house was half empty now, but it would make renovations much easier having less junk to move around.

I'd also gone through the boxes of paperwork Uncle Pádraig had left stored in one of the bedrooms. It was mostly old bills, some correspondence from decades ago, and ancient back issues of farming magazines.

But tucked deep in one box were a set of cheap exercise books, and on the front of them I recognised the teenage David's handwriting. *A History of Ireland's Fight for Independence by David Kennedy.* I flicked one open and read a little. It looked like he'd written up everything he'd learned from school, and drawn maps and diagrams to illustrate it. I smiled at the thought of him doing all this extra-curricular homework — not something his brother Brian would have considered for a moment.

A few pages further on it became a little more interesting, and I settled myself down, sitting on the floor leaning against a pile of boxes to read on. He'd interviewed Granny Irish. She'd been notoriously difficult to talk to as I recall, and had rarely wanted to say much about her part in the War of Independence. But David had managed to get her to talk, and had written it all down. It was strange, reading my grandmother's stories like this, told in my cousin's words. Both of them long gone. Both of them committed Republicans, who'd fought for their country's freedom in different ways.

I asked Granny if she was proud of everything she did in the war, David had written.

Her answer surprised me. 'There was one thing I shouldn't have done. One thing I wished I hadn't done.'

But she wouldn't tell me what it was, no matter how often I asked. In the end she got cross with me and I had to stop asking.

I smiled, reading that, imagining teenage David pestering our rather cold and distant grandmother. Well, whatever it was she regretted, she'd presumably taken the secret to her grave.

★   ★   ★

Paul had called me every day. I'd kept my phone switched off most of the time and only switched it on when I felt up to listening to his messages — always rants, accusing me of taking things that were his, going on about the car and how hard it was without one. (Although Matt told me he'd bought himself a second-hand Ford Focus two days after I'd left. I didn't let on that I knew this.) In the end I'd bought myself a cheap new phone with a pay-as-you-go SIM from Vodafone. I'd told the boys and my new local friends the number and kept it switched on. Only Paul ever called the old number now.

The boys were both planning to come to stay in a couple of weeks' time, for my birthday.

'Must help you celebrate the big five-oh,' Matt had said. 'Can't believe my mum's going to be 50.' I couldn't believe it either. Such a milestone. I'd been putting off thinking about it. Half a century!

'It's only the number of times you've been round the sun,' Jon said, on the phone one evening. 'Nothing special, even if the number is *astronomical*.' Trust him to make a joke of it. If I'd been in the same room, he'd have had a gentle slap for that one.

I had a vague idea I'd take them out for a meal somewhere. Or perhaps I'd have a small party in the farmhouse. I could invite Janice and her kids, Ryan, and . . . Who else did I know well enough to invite? Mr Greve the solicitor perhaps? Hmm. Perhaps not. To be frank, I didn't really know Ryan well enough. I tried to imagine calling in at the bookshop and inviting him to a party, but just thinking about it made my cheeks burn with embarrassment and my hands feel clammy. I was too shy to do such a thing.

★ ★ ★

Bit by bit I was building my life here. I went to Janice's café at least three times a week, and she'd called on me on the way home from school with assorted children in tow twice more. After that first time I'd made sure I always had biscuits and juice or pop to offer them. They referred to me as Aunty Clare, which made me smile.

I'd been back to the bookshop too, to pay my debt, but had not had the chance to ask Ryan about researching my genealogy or the names on the communion medallion and birth certificate. Whenever I went in he seemed to be busy with other customers, phone orders or with unpacking new stock. I'd end up buying something, exchanging a few words and leaving, feeling vaguely disappointed.

It was Sunday morning, and I'd had a lazy start. All the local people would be at Mass. I wondered if I should start going — there was a large grey-brick church dedicated to St Barnabas in the centre of Blackstown. Mum had been brought up a Catholic and had attended Mass every week until she came to England. She'd been unable to find a Catholic church within walking distance of her first digs, and had quickly become a lapsed Catholic.

When I'd asked her about it she'd shrugged and said I should form my own opinion. I guessed that she'd never been particularly devout, or else she'd have tried harder to keep going to church in England. When I was growing up there was a Catholic church on my way home from school. I only ever set foot in there when my Irish grandparents were visiting. I was baptised Catholic but that's as far as it went. Never did First Communion or anything else. Dad was an atheist and I'd never really given it much thought.

But here, in this country where everyone went to church and all children took classes in school to prepare them for First Communion, where the priest was an important member of the community, I felt perhaps I should try to join in a little. If nothing else I might get to know some more people.

My job for the day was to begin making more space in the barn, so I could get on with some furniture restoration and upholstery projects out there. That old armchair I'd enthusiastically begun stripping back on my first day was still sitting in its calico underwear in the front room, feeling sorry for itself. I dressed in my oldest jeans and a ripped sweatshirt I'd found in one of the wardrobes upstairs. A part of me hoped it had been Daithí's, rather than Uncle Pádraig's or anyone else's. But that was unlikely. Daithí had died so very long ago, way back in the 1980s.

I headed out to the barn with a cup of coffee, to assess what needed to be done. It was one of those grey days, no wind, no rain, no sun. Just right for getting on with the job and not feeling I should be somewhere else, doing something else.

Firstly there was some rubbish to clear. There was space in the skip, so I set down my coffee on the old workbench and began gathering up the soggy, mouldy cardboard boxes that were piled along one side of the barn. All were empty, or contained only more, smaller, empty boxes. Who knew why Uncle Pádraig had kept them. But they were easy to clear and soon in the skip.

In the back corner was some rusty farm machinery. Some sort of plough, which looked as though it would have attached to a tractor. And some other rake-type attachment. They were too heavy to move on my own. I'd need to wait until Matt and Jon came.

I gazed around. The workbench I could tackle on my own — I could go through the tools, keep what was usable, throw out the tins of rusty screws. And the end wall — there were old pieces of furniture and more boxes piled up higgledy-piggledy. I ought to be able to go through that lot by myself. But it was hard work. I finished my coffee and sighed. Maybe I should have waited till one or other of the boys was here to help. It'd be more fun with someone else.

It's spooky, but it was right as I was thinking that, that a battered old estate car drew up outside, and out climbed Ryan.

'Hey!' he called, raising a hand in greeting as he crossed the yard towards me. 'I hoped this was the right place. Janice told me where you lived. Hope I'm not disturbing you, but I thought I'd call in and see how things are going. Whenever you've been in the shop I've been too tied up to spend long chatting.'

I smiled. It was good to see him. 'No, you're not disturbing me. I was about ready for a rest and a cuppa. Tea?'

'That'd be grand.' He followed me inside and sat at the kitchen table while I put the kettle on.

'Sorry about the state of me. I've been trying to clear some junk out of the barn.'

'So I saw. I can give you a hand when we've had our tea, if you like.'

'Are you sure? It would help; there are some heavy things I can't shift on my own. Old farm stuff. And I don't know what to do with the metal implements — don't think they should go in the skip.'

He shook his head. 'No, but I know a fella who deals in scrap metal. I'll give him a call and he'll come by and collect it. Might even give you a few euros for it.'

'I don't want money. I'll just be grateful for it to be gone.' I handed Ryan his tea. It'd be wonderful having his help for a while in the barn. I wondered how long he might stay. 'Oh, before I forget, Janice said you might be able to help me with tracing who lived here before my grandparents. I found something . . . ' I nipped through to the sitting room and retrieved the communion medallion and birth certificate from the mantelpiece where they had been since I found them. 'Look, I found these tucked inside an old chair.'

Ryan raised his eyebrows as he took them from me and peered at them. 'This child was born during the Anglo-Irish war, the fight for independence. And the medallion's even older. Yes, I can help try to find these people. What a wonderful little mystery!' He pulled out his phone and took close-up photos of both items. 'Well, I'll see what I can find for you.'

'I want to research my own ancestors, too. There are family legends about my own grandmother being some sort of spy for the Volunteers during the War of Independence. I'd love to find out more about her.' I pulled a face. 'Wish I'd asked my mum while she was still alive.'

Ryan gave me a sympathetic look. 'Always the way. When we're young we're more interested in the future than the past.'

We chatted about how I was settling in and my plans for the farmhouse and barn while we drank our tea. I found him to be good company and easy to talk to.

A little later, out in the barn, Ryan helped me drag the plough and the other thing (a harrow, Ryan told me) out to a corner of the yard. 'If we pile up any other unwanted metal over there, Lenny can drop by and pick it up any time he's in the area,' Ryan said.

In the corner where the machinery had stood there was a rotting piece of carpet, almost obscured by piles of leaves and rubbish that had blown in over the years and got caught among the machinery. I fetched a sack and we scooped up the rubbish, then rolled up the ancient carpet and threw it into the almost-full skip. Poor Ryan was covered in dirt already.

'Ah, it's no matter,' he said, brushing

ineffectually at his T-shirt. 'There's nothing that won't wash out. Hmm, what's this?' He was looking at the flooring we'd just revealed. There was some sort of wooden trapdoor there, set into the concrete. There was no ring or handle or any way of pulling it up.

'There's a crowbar here somewhere,' I said, rummaging around in the tools on the work-bench. I brought it over and handed it to Ryan.

'You want to see what's under here?' he asked, looking up at me from where he knelt on the filthy floor.

I felt a pang of excitement and nerves. Too right I wanted to see! It could be a cellar, or a buried box of treasure, or an entrance to a secret tunnel . . . I realised I had probably read too many Enid Blyton books in my childhood, but then again, who wouldn't be excited uncovering a concealed trapdoor? 'Of course I do!' I said to Ryan, failing to keep my tone cool and nonchalant.

He forced the crowbar between the wood and the concrete floor, and levered it up. The wood began to split, revealing hinges. He moved the crowbar to the opposite edge from the hinges and tried again. This time the trapdoor lifted. I leaned over him to peer beneath.

There was a shallow hole, dug into the floor beneath the barn. Inside was a wooden crate.

'Ah, I bet I know what's in there,' Ryan said, as he reached in to open the crate. But it was nailed shut. 'Can you give me a hand to haul this out? I expect it'll be quite heavy.'

'Sure,' I said, and got into position. I was

dying to ask him what he thought would be inside. God, I hoped it wouldn't be bones!

Together, on our knees, we reached down and got hold of one end each of the crate, and lifted it out. As Ryan had predicted, it was heavy, and it was all I could do to stop myself toppling forward on top of it. We dropped it on top of the open trapdoor, and Ryan picked up the crowbar again to lever off the lid.

Whatever was inside was covered with a piece of dirty sackcloth. 'It's like pass the parcel — yet another layer before we find out what's in there,' I said, as Ryan pulled back the cloth. Underneath were more pieces of sackcloth, but this time each piece was clearly wrapped around something long and narrow. I was beginning to guess myself what they might be. Ryan took out the top one, placed it on the floor and began to carefully unwrap it.

Inside was a rifle. It had a wooden stock, rusty muzzle and the trigger mechanism looked like brass. 'Ha, as I thought,' Ryan muttered, half to himself. He pulled out another package, and unwrapped a handgun, and then another. In all there were six rifles and seven handguns in the crate.

'Oh my God,' I kept saying, as each one was uncovered. 'What on earth was Uncle Pádraig doing with a stash of weapons under his barn?' Even as I said it, thoughts of Daithí and his involvement with the IRA crossed my mind. I'd never known exactly what he did and what he was imprisoned for, or the truth about his death in prison. I opened my mouth to say something but decided against it. Some things, my mother always said, are best kept within the family.

'He may not have known about them. These date from before his lifetime. I'd say they were from the War of Independence, or perhaps the civil war. The early 1920s, either way,' Ryan said, as he turned one of the rifles over in his hands. 'It's not uncommon, you know. Guns were hidden during the War of Independence. And after the civil war, which followed immediately after, the Republican forces were supposed to hand in their weapons. Some did, but many kept them hidden. This is not the first time I've heard of guns being found underneath a cowshed. Or in a cellar, or under the stairs.'

'Are you sure they're that old?'

'Pretty much. The rifles look like Lee-Enfields. Not that I'm an expert.' He pulled out his phone and took pictures of them. 'I'll do a spot of googling, and try to confirm that.'

'But . . . what do I do with them? I don't want them here. Do I report them to the police or something? Would a museum want them?' I had no idea what to do with them.

'Yes, I think we should inform the Gardaí. Not sure whether a museum would want them. Most have got stacks of the things already, but you never know. If not, the Guards will dispose of them, I'm sure. Want to take a closer look?' Ryan was holding the rifle out to me, laid across his flattened palms.

I shuddered. I'd always had a horror of guns. Something so easy to use that could kill a person at a distance scared me. 'No thanks. Put them back in the box. I'll need to find somewhere safe for them until the police come and take them away. Wouldn't want anyone breaking in and stealing one.'

'They probably wouldn't fire now. I suspect the mechanisms are too rusty,' Ryan said, looking closely at the rifle he was holding. He pointed it down at the floor, away from where we were sitting, and put his finger experimentally on the trigger.

'Don't!' I squealed, not able to help myself. Guns scare me.

Ryan looked at me in alarm and put the gun down, wrapping it back in its sack cloth. 'Sorry. I'll pack them up. Where do you want them put until we know what to do with them?'

'There's a cupboard in the hallway. I think they're better off in the house.' Although I hated the idea of having them anywhere near me. These things probably killed people, in their day. But leaving them in the barn where anyone could walk in and take them didn't seem right. Had Granny Irish known about them? Had she had anything to do with them?

Ryan stood up, replaced the lid of the crate and hauled it up. 'Show me where, then.' He followed me inside and I pointed out the large hall cupboard I'd cleared out a few days earlier. There was space on the floor for the crate. Once it was stowed I closed the door firmly.

'More tea, Ryan?'

'Yes, please.'

As I put the kettle on again I asked him more about the Irish War of Independence, realising I

136

only knew the roughest outline of what happened. Ryan gave me a brief overview, from the rebellion of Wolfe Tone and his United Irishmen in 1798; the 1916 Easter uprising when the Republic was first proclaimed; through to the 1919–21 Anglo-Irish war, which culminated in the treaty with Britain that led to the formation of the Irish Free State and partition, the creation of Northern Ireland.

The civil war followed almost immediately, between those who were pro- and anti-treaty, with the pro-treaty side winning. The anti-treaty side — the Irish Republican Army — had never accepted partition, and of course, I knew all about their campaigns of the 1970s and '80s, before the Good Friday Agreement finally brought peace.

'I've a number of books on twentieth-century Irish history in the shop,' Ryan said. 'I'll dig out the best of them for you to take a look at next time you come by.'

'Thanks, I'd like that,' I said, smiling over my tea mug at him. It had been an interesting and enjoyable morning, all the better for having Ryan's company. He was nice, Janice had been right about that. And he was attractive, in a silver fox kind of way. But I wasn't in the market for a new man.

★ ★ ★

After Ryan had gone, I was left pondering those guns and what they stood for. Growing up half-Irish in England in the 1970s had been an

137

interesting experience. On the one hand there were the newspapers, my teachers, the BBC — all telling me that the IRA had 'murdered' British soldiers, while the soldiers had 'shot dead' the terrorists. And then there was my mother, urging me to remember there were two sides to every story, and that every news source would be biased one way or the other.

'Watch for the use of language,' she said, 'and remember that one man's 'terrorist' is another man's 'freedom fighter'.' Years later, when I understood more of Daithí's involvement (though I never knew the full story) I would remember those words, and try to tell myself that Daithí did what he did because he believed it was right with all his heart.

But those beliefs killed him, in the end. After an explosion at a military barracks somewhere in County Armagh in which six British soldiers lost their lives, Daithí was arrested and this time there was enough evidence to put him away. He was sentenced to life and sent to Long Kesh. Daithí only lasted three years in prison.

Mum was devastated by Daithí's loss. He'd been her favourite nephew. She'd never say it out loud, being married to an Englishman and a long-time resident in the UK, but I knew in her heart of hearts she would have liked Ireland to be united once more, and was secretly proud of Daithí for having the courage of his convictions, even if she was at the same time appalled by the consequences of his actions. It was a tricky balance, being an Irish Republican back in those days of the Troubles.

12

Ellen, October 1919

It was raining when Ellen left Carlton House for her unexpected free afternoon, and set off for Clonamurty Farm. No Jimmy to meet her at the end of the drive today, as he had no idea she'd be coming. She hoped he'd be at home. If not, she was sure his mother would give her a cup of tea and let her sit and chat for a while in the kitchen. Or she could go home and surprise her father. But if she did that, no doubt her father would give her jobs to do, and it was supposed to be a rest after her exertions yesterday.

She half-ran to the farm, trying to keep under the shelter of overhanging trees where possible, but even so she was soaked to the skin by the time she got there. And the blisters on her left foot, from the long walk yesterday, felt very sore. She ducked in through the gates of the farm and ran straight across to the kitchen door. She tapped on it and then entered, not waiting for a response. Mrs Gallagher had always told her to come straight in, every time.

There was no one in the kitchen. She stood on the back doormat and shook the worst of the wet from her coat and hair, and went down the passageway to look into the sitting room. No one there either.

'Jimmy? Mrs Gallagher?' she called, but there was no response.

There'd been someone outside, she recalled, having caught a glimpse of someone near one of the barns. She'd had her head down against the relentless rain when she'd arrived. Maybe it was Jimmy working out there. She turned the collar of her coat up, and went out again through the kitchen door and across the yard to the barn.

The barn door stood part open, but as she approached she hesitated. Jimmy was in there — she could hear his voice, and his father with him, but there were also two other men.

'They'll be safe here. No one would suspect us.' That was Mr Gallagher.

'They'd better be. We need them guns. We'll be back for them soon, when things are a bit quieter. You mind they're kept covered.' Ellen did not recognise this voice.

Mr Gallagher spoke again. 'Aye. Close the trapdoor, and I'll spread the straw around a bit. They'll be well hidden. And none here will breathe a word.'

There was the sound of a creaking trapdoor being lowered, and straw being brushed across a floor. Then footsteps. Ellen ducked back behind the door and ran back towards the kitchen door. Whatever she'd heard she wasn't supposed to have heard. His father knew Jimmy was in the Volunteers but not his mother, and Jimmy had urged Ellen not to let on that she knew.

She twisted round, smiling, as Jimmy and the others emerged from the barn, trying to look as though she'd only just arrived. The two men she didn't know scowled at her, but she ignored them and ran into Jimmy's arms.

'Hello! I'm after getting a half-day off. Madame Carlton said I could.' She hoped the mention of Madame might reassure the men that she was on the right side.

'We'll be off, Gallagher,' said one of them, and Jimmy's father grunted in response. The two strangers set off in the direction of Blackstown.

'I've work to do,' Mr Gallagher said, as he picked up a bag of tools and trudged off into one of his other barns.

'Come inside, out of the rain,' Jimmy urged, leading her towards the kitchen door. 'Mammy's gone to market. I expect she's waiting till the rain stops before she comes back.'

Once inside the dry kitchen and divested of her coat, Ellen turned to Jimmy. 'I overheard something as I approached. I shouldn't have, but couldn't help it. Something hidden in the barn?'

Jimmy nodded. 'A stash of guns. Forget you heard anything. Say nothing to anyone. If the Black and Tans found out we were storing them they'd . . . well . . . there's no telling what they might do.'

'I met some Black and Tans yesterday,' Ellen said. She was bursting to tell Jimmy of her small part in this war. He listened intently as she related the tale of her mission to fetch the doctor, and her nursing duties.

'He's a good man, Doctor O'Mahony. You did well.'

'Do you know Captain Cunningham?' Ellen couldn't help but ask.

Jimmy nodded. 'A good man. One of the best. He was involved in an ambush on the RIC barracks on the Dublin road that went wrong. One Volunteer escaped, two were shot, and the man your mistress is helping was shot and left for dead. The man who escaped fetched help and went back to rescue him. Thankfully by then the Black and Tans had moved on.'

Ellen was horrified. She looked at her feet for a moment, then raised tear-filled eyes to Jimmy. 'Tell me, my love, is this the sort of mission you are asked to carry out, as well? Could it be you one day, brought back to Carlton House bleeding and dying?' The last word emerged as a broken whisper.

He took her hands in his across the kitchen table. 'I'm careful, always cautious. I take no unnecessary risks. But I must do what I am asked to do by my superiors. For the good of our country. Ireland needs me.'

'So do I,' she whispered, and he took her face in his hands and kissed her, long and deep, until she melted into him and forgot all her concerns. Jimmy would be safe on his missions. He had to be. The alternative was unthinkable.

★   ★   ★

Ellen's mind was still on the cache of guns hidden under Mr Gallagher's barn as she walked back to Carlton House. She was terrified she would somehow let slip what she'd seen and heard, and bring trouble to Clonamurty Farm and its inhabitants. She'd never been good at

142

keeping secrets as a child, but these days she was getting plenty of practice. She supposed it became a way of life in the end, this not trusting, keeping quiet, holding secrets. It had all been so much easier when she and Jimmy were children, when life was fun and innocent, and the only secret they kept was where they'd found a blackbird's nest.

★ ★ ★

It was in the afternoon of the next day that the news came. Ellen was on duty in Captain Cunningham's room. She'd just finished changing the dressing on his head, and was wondering whether to do the one on his shoulder too. She wanted to know what could have caused such an injury, but knew better than to ask him outright.

Her patient had been awake for part of the day, and they had chatted about inconsequential things — the fineness of the bedroom's decor, whether green was the best colour for a bedroom or was blue more restful, how good the weather had been over the summer and whether the winter would be a cold one, whether Ellen was enjoying the Dickens book. But neither had said anything of importance. Ellen guessed that perhaps Captain Cunningham was not sure whether she could be trusted, not sure what she'd been told about him. And Ellen felt that the less she knew the less likely she'd ever let anything slip. Her greatest fear was that some day the RIC, or even worse, the Black and Tans, might question her and she'd inadvertently blurt

143

out something incriminating.

Madame Carlton came rushing in to the green bedroom in the mid-afternoon with the news. She looked flustered and upset, wringing her hands.

'Oh, Jack. It's horrible. I hardly want to pass on the news but you must be told . . . '

'Madame, should I go?' Ellen hated to interrupt but did not want to stay to hear something she shouldn't.

'No, Ellen, you stay. I am only here to pass on some news and then I need you to stay with Captain Cunningham a little longer. You will hear the news by other means in any case.'

'What is it, Emily?' said the man in the bed.

'Those . . . ruffians, those thugs . . . the Black and Tans — they have attacked Blackstown. They've gone on the rampage. Shops and pubs looted, people turned out of their homes, many buildings still burning.'

The Captain cursed under his breath before asking, 'What triggered that?'

'A gang of them were drunk, ran out of money, said they were 'requisitioning' whiskey and ale from one of the pubs. The landlord tried to limit how much they took but then it all turned nasty.'

Captain Cunningham shook his head sadly, as Ellen tried to stifle a gasp. 'Anyone hurt?'

'Some injuries. The pub landlord was badly beaten. A few people suffering from burns. No reports of deaths, thank the Lord. The injured have been taken to hospital in Navan.'

'Please God they'll be all right.' The Captain

144

crossed himself and Ellen mirrored the movement. So this was the type of thing the Black and Tans did, that Jimmy had been afraid of! Why were they so undisciplined? Setting fire to civilian houses was hardly an acceptable act of war, was it?

'There's more,' Madame Carlton said, quietly.

There was silence in the room as both Ellen and Cunningham waited to hear what else she had to say. She paused for so long that Ellen began to move towards the door, thinking that perhaps it was not for her ears, but before she reached it Madame spoke again.

'They're saying, in the town, that if only the Volunteers had not attacked the RIC barracks then this would not have happened. They're blaming the Volunteers. We're losing support, Jack. After all we've done. All you've sacrificed.'

Captain Cunningham sighed and shook his head, then looked up at Madame Carlton sadly. 'We're playing the long game, Emily. There are bound to be setbacks. There have to be sacrifices for us to achieve our aim. I'm sorry, of course I am, if innocent people have been hurt in the attacks. That was never our intention. But in the long run . . . '

'In the long run, if more innocents are hurt or killed, will we be able to hold up our heads when we tell the tale of the struggle to our grandchildren?' Madame spoke quietly and there was a break in her voice.

Captain Cunningham paused for a long while before he answered, and once again Ellen wondered if he was waiting for her to leave. But she somehow seemed rooted to the spot. He'd tell her to go, or Madame would, if she was supposed to, surely. Finally he did answer, his voice quiet but firm, full of conviction.

'As long as we can be sure we have done everything in our power to secure the independence of this nation, then yes, we will be able to hold up our heads. The crime is to do nothing, and let our fates continue to be determined by a distant government. As the great Parnell once said, *we must each one of us resolve in our own hearts that we shall at all times do everything that within us lies, to obtain for Ireland the fullest measure of her rights.*'

Madame Carlton regarded him for a moment and then nodded. 'Well, I shall leave you to rest now. Ellen, could you close the curtains please, and ensure Captain Cunningham is comfortable. I shall be back to take over in a couple of hours.'

She left the room, and Ellen did as she was bid, closing the curtains, plumping up the pillows and straightening the bedclothes.

'You're Jimmy Gallagher's young lady, aren't you?' Captain Cunningham said suddenly.

Ellen blushed and startled. 'I am, sir. Do you know him?'

'A good lad. In my company. He was one of the ones who got me here, after I was shot.'

'I'm glad, sir. He never said.'

'Ah, secrets. He's sworn to say nothing to anyone, and I'm afraid that includes you. But you're in on this now, one of us. Speak to Mrs Carlton about joining the Cumann na mBan. We could do with more girls of your calibre.'

'Sir? What do they do?'

'Carry messages, scout locations, nurse the injured Volunteers.' He laughed, then clutched his shoulder as though in pain. 'You've been doing all that already though, haven't you? It was you who fetched Doctor O'Mahony the other day, Emily told me.'

'Yes, sir, it was.'

'Then I must thank you. Along with your young man, you've saved my life.' He caught her hand and squeezed it. Ellen felt a rush of pride. Madame Carlton's words about grandchildren ran around her head. Would there be a future in which Ireland was free, and in which she had children and grandchildren, and would be able to openly talk about her small part in this war? Would Jimmy be by her side in this future? She hoped so, more than anything. The idea of sharing the future with anyone else was intolerable.

13

Clare, May 2016

It was three days after Ryan and I discovered the guns when I finally plucked up the courage to call the Gardaí about them. I had no idea what they would do. The guns were clearly old as Ryan had said, but presumably could still be used if cleaned up. I hated having them in the house and every time I'd walked past that cupboard I had glared at it and shivered a little. And I can't say how many times I'd opened the cupboard to check they were still there.

It was ridiculous. All I had to do was make a single phone call. Finally, on Wednesday afternoon, I did it. I found the number for the Blackstown Guards station and called them direct, rather than use the emergency number.

'We'll send someone round,' said the woman who'd picked up the phone. 'They do sound like they're from the 1920s. We've experts who will know. Meanwhile, don't touch them or move them, will you?'

I promised I wouldn't, blushing at the memory of Ryan unwrapping them and then carrying the crate inside. I should have left them under the floor in the barn I realised, covered by the old carpet. What were we thinking?

The Guards arrived an hour later. There were two: a young man in his twenties and a woman I judged to be around 40. I showed them the crate in the cupboard.

'Is this where you found them?' asked the female Guard.

'Er, no. They were under the floor in the barn. I'm clearing the old barn to use as a workshop. I do upholstery, and need the space.' I realised I was gabbling, as the Guard stared at me.

'You brought them out and in here by yourself? Must weigh a lot, that box.'

'There was someone else here. He carried them in. I thought they'd be safer inside, less likely to . . . fall into the wrong hands, as it were.'

'When did you find them, Mrs Farrell?' asked the young Guard.

'Er, Sunday. Meant to call you before, but, well, you know how it is, time runs away with you, ha-ha.' Oh God. I sounded like such an idiot.

They questioned me for an hour, taking copious notes. I'd thought they would just pick up the crate and take it away and that would be it, but apparently they needed to know how long I'd lived there, how long Uncle Pádraig and my grandmother had lived there, did I know who'd lived there before. Not yet, I wanted to say, but I plan to find out. Thankfully I stopped myself from blabbering on about the medallion and the birth certificate . . . and my cousin's involve-ment in the IRA back in the 1980s. Some things are best kept quiet, though they no doubt had Daithí on their records anyway.

Finally they left, taking the guns with them. I was glad to get the guns out of the house, although as intrigued as ever about how they

149

came to be buried under the barn. Hopefully Ryan would be able to shed some light, or give me some pointers as to how I could research who'd lived here before my family. I had a feeling the guns were somehow connected with the medallion and birth certificate. If nothing else, they dated from the same era.

Could they have anything to do with Granny Irish? There'd been no mention of guns being buried in Daithi's notebooks, but I guessed if she had told him about them, he'd have gone looking for them.

⋆　⋆　⋆

A couple of days later Ryan called me. 'I've dug out some Irish history books for you,' he said. 'I've got someone else covering the shop today and was going to bring them round to you, but my car's in the garage. Needs a new battery. And tyres. And brake discs. And there's a strange knocking sound coming from the engine.'

'Oh dear, sounds expensive,' I replied. 'Well, I could drive down to town and collect them. It's very kind of you.'

'Not at all. I'm cross about my car, though. I was going to offer to take you on a bit of a tour of the area — to Trim Castle, the Hill of Tara, to the site of the Battle of the Boyne — places where you can feel Ireland's history all around you. It'll have to be some other time.'

'I could drive,' I said, tentatively. Some men don't like being driven by women. Paul never did.

'But then you wouldn't have the chance to

look out at the countryside,' Ryan replied.

'I don't mind. I'd see enough. Maybe we could just go to one place today, leave the others until your car is fixed?' I must admit, I loved the idea of getting out and about for a day. The sun was shining and I'd spent far too long shifting dusty old furniture and bric-a-brac around the house over the last couple of weeks. It was the perfect day to drive around the countryside and I couldn't think of anyone better to go with than Ryan.

'All right, you're on. Pick me up at home, whenever you're ready. I have the books here for you.' He gave me his address, and I promised to be there within the hour.

Just time for a shower, a coffee, and an agonising fifteen minutes trying to decide what, out of my meagre wardrobe, would be appropriate to wear. I ended up in jeans and a long colourful top, with my trusty leather jacket over the top.

I couldn't help but smile to myself as I got ready. I was enjoying this new life I was building here in Ireland.

★ ★ ★

Ryan lived in a newish house, in an estate on the edge of Blackstown. I don't know why but I was surprised at this when I arrived at his address. I'd imagined him in an old stone-built cottage with resident ghosts from the time of the Great Famine. He was clearly so interested in history it was odd to find him living in such a modern house.

151

'Less maintenance, better location closer to town,' he said with a shrug, when I commented on it. 'I may run a second-hand bookshop but underneath it all I'm a practical kind of guy.' He smiled, his eyes warm and friendly.

We decided to drive out to the Hill of Tara. 'A site of ancient Irish history,' Ryan said. 'It's an old Iron Age hill fort, but legend has it that the old kings of Ireland had their seat here. On a day like today you can see for miles from the top of the hill.' He'd prepared a flask of coffee and had a Dunnes Stores carrier bag with a few packets of biscuits in. 'Not quite a picnic but perhaps better than nothing,' he said, smiling again.

'Lovely idea,' I said, as we climbed into my car. Ryan threw the books he'd picked out for me onto the back seat. We set off, with Ryan navigating along a series of narrow, winding roads, bordered by high hedges, surrounded by lush farmland. It was a beautiful day, all blue sky and sunshine but quite chilly due to a strong breeze that sent kapok clouds skipping across the sky. The kind of day when you feel good simply being alive, and find yourself counting your blessings. I'd taken the big step and left Paul, and so far it was all working out. I had my gorgeous sons, both of whom were due to visit in a few days' time for my birthday. I had new friends and had made a great start in getting the house ready for renovations. And I was sitting beside a good-looking bloke whose company I enjoyed.

I must have sighed with pleasure involuntarily. Ryan looked across at me and grinned.

152

'Gorgeous day, isn't it? Gets into your soul and raises it up, I find.'

'It does indeed.'

We were soon at Tara. There was a small car park beside a nineteenth-century church that I remembered from my visit here with Daithí all those years ago. Behind the church a path led uphill, through the graveyard then through an iron gate onto the hill itself. I couldn't help but peer at a few of the headstones on the way past. I loved old graveyards; the way they pull you into the past as you read the names and dates of those who've gone before. Here, there were a few from 1919 and 1920. I wondered if any were soldiers or victims of the War of Independence.

'So, here we are,' said Ryan, as we reached the top of the hill. 'You can follow the lines of the Iron Age fort that was here quite easily. Over there's a Neolithic tomb they've excavated. And this' — he put his hand on a standing stone — 'is the Stone of Destiny. It's where the ancient kings of Ireland were crowned.'

I stood and gazed around. There were a few sheep up there, grazing the thick green grass. The ditches and mounds of the hill fort were easy to pick out. It was a magical place. You could almost feel the air buzzing with the weight of its history — so much must have happened right here through the ages, it was as though it seeped through to the present. And the view, across rolling green fields and low hills, with occasional villages and farms tucked in the hollows, was magnificent.

'Magical, isn't it?' Ryan said.

'That's exactly the word I would use. All that ancient history bubbling just beneath the surface.'

'Lovely way to put it. And some not so ancient history too — there was a battle here in 1798 between the United Irishmen and British troops. An early attempt to gain independence for Ireland. That Celtic cross over there marks the site of the battle. And then the great statesman Daniel O'Connell held a rally here, campaigning for repeal of the *Acts of Union* that bound Ireland to Britain. So this place played its part in the fight for Irish independence as well.'

I looked around again and walked over to the Celtic cross, trying to imagine a bloody eighteenth-century battle raging around me, and a Victorian statesman making an impassioned speech. It had all happened, right here. It made me shiver — not with cold but with awe.

Ryan had walked over to stand beside me. 'Coffee time?' He spread a picnic rug on the ground, on one of the Iron Age ramparts, and poured coffee from the flask into two small plastic cups, handing me one. I sat beside him on the slope and sipped it slowly, still soaking up the atmosphere of this extraordinary place.

'In the nineteenth century,' Ryan said, 'Ireland was like a battered wife to Britain's domineering husband. The 1916 uprising was Ireland saying, 'I've had enough. I want to be out of this marriage.' And then the War of Independence was the long and bitter fight for separation, ending only when an exhausted Britain agreed to divorce, but only if it could keep the house.'

'The house?' I asked.

'Northern Ireland.'

I smiled. 'Nice analogy.' In my own divorce proceedings, I'd be happy for Paul to keep the house, now that I had my own.

We stayed at the Hill of Tara for an hour, enjoying the coffee and biscuits, wandering around the ramparts and looking at the view in all directions. Eventually the chill wind made us decide to head back down. There was a small gift shop just along the road, selling Irish souvenirs and with a decent selection of books on Irish history. I didn't buy any as there were enough in the back seat of the car to keep me going, but I bought a Hill of Tara tea towel and postcards to send to the boys.

'It's been a lovely morning,' I said, as we walked back to my car. To be truthful, I didn't want it to end.

'Fancy lunch out? There's a good pub not too far from here,' Ryan said, sounding almost shy as he asked.

'That sounds perfect,' I said, overwhelmingly glad that he too did not want our outing to come to an end just yet.

★ ★ ★

Lunch was lovely. I remember nothing about the food, only that throughout our meal we swapped life stories, laughed, joked, discussed everything from ancient history to modern politics, and ended up feeling as though we'd known each other for a lifetime. At least, that's how I felt, and as Ryan smiled at me when we left the pub I was pretty sure he felt the same way. For some reason I felt suddenly shy and fumbled in my handbag for my car keys to avoid looking him in the eye.

But the day had to come to an end. Ryan had an evening appointment with a book dealer and I'd promised Janice I'd babysit for her for a couple of hours while she went to Ciara's school parents' evening. I dropped Ryan off at his house, with a cheery, 'must do this again some time', by which I meant 'tomorrow if possible', and set off towards Clonamurty Farm (or 'home' as I was beginning to think of it) with a stupid grin on my face and a head spinning with memories of the day and dreams of the future.

Spinning too fast, as it transpired. I was only half a mile from home, on the narrow lane that leads up to the farm, when it happened. My attention was elsewhere — to be precise, it was lying on Ryan's picnic rug alongside him on the Hill of Tara. I was probably going just a little bit too fast, around a bend, and there it was. A cow, in the middle of the lane, chewing contentedly on the narrow grass verge between the lane and the hedge. It must, I discovered later, have squeezed through a gap in the hedge a bit further up.

'Shit!' I screamed, slamming on my brakes but at the same moment realising I would not be able to stop in time. I had to choose, left hedge or right hedge or straight into a wall of beef? I chose left, careered over the verge and smashed the car into the hedge, praying as it went in that there'd be no solid tree trunks in the middle and perhaps the car would just crash through and out the other side in the field. I think I even envisaged driving on through the field and back onto the lane at the next gateway. I felt a massive surge of relief that I had managed to miss the cow. Funny what goes through your mind at a time like this, when everything seems to be happening in slow motion.

I don't know what I hit in that hedge, but whatever it was flipped the car over, and the next thing I knew down was up and up was down, and I was hanging by my seatbelt with spent airbags deflating all around me. '*Shit!*' I screamed again, as the car slithered to a halt on its roof in the field.

'Dad's going to kill me,' was my next useless thought, as I realised I was not hurt. Followed by, 'but Dad's dead, so it'll be Paul who kills me,' before I remembered that I'd left Paul and the car was mine.

And then I took a few deep breaths and realised I should get myself out of the car. It wasn't easy, but I managed to unclip the seatbelt, wriggle myself upright and force open a back door. Neither of the front doors would open. I reached back to the dash and switched off the engine, then tugged my handbag free from where it had caught around the passenger seat and crawled out. Ryan's books were scattered all around the car, and I spent a moment gathering them up, my hands shaking so much I could barely hold them.

Why rescuing the books seemed so important while my car was clearly a write-off I don't know.

157

I sat on the muddy ground in that ploughed field, with the books on one side of me and my trashed car on the other, and sobbed. It was a few minutes before I was able to pull myself together, get my phone out of my handbag, and call the emergency services.

★ ★ ★

I was taken to hospital — the county hospital in Navan — for a check-up and then discharged. No injuries other than a few scratches and bruises, though they warned me I'd be stiff for a few days and gave me some painkillers anyway. I'd called Janice and had to apologise that I couldn't babysit, and I took a taxi back home. Janice was in her car sitting outside in my yard when I arrived. She got out as soon as the taxi pulled up and ran over to hug me gently.

'God, Clare! What a thing to happen! Are you OK? It's all right, I found someone else to mind the kids, and I can see Ciara's teachers another time. I'm here to cook you some dinner and make sure you're all right. You can stay at mine tonight if you don't want to be alone. God, you poor thing! A cow, was it?'

She took my arm and led me inside, fussing over me as she put the kettle on. And of course, I did that typical female thing — I'd been pretty calm and collected and in control since I called the emergency services but as soon as I was offered tea and sympathy I cracked. Tears streamed down my face and my shoulders began heaving with sobs.

'Oh, you poor thing. It's the shock, so it is. Come on, cry on my shoulder; let it all out, now.' Janice pulled up a chair beside me and wrapped her arms around me. I clung to her as if I was drowning and bawled my eyes out. It was the realisation the crash could have killed me. It was the way a perfect day had ended so horribly. It was the thought that I could so easily have hit and killed that cow. It was the knowledge that now I had no car, and although the insurance would no doubt pay out, the insurance was in Paul's name, not mine, and that meant I'd have to tell him what happened.

14

Ellen, March 1920

It was the middle of March before a day of fine weather finally coincided with one of Ellen's days off. Over winter she'd had so many cold and wet walks to Clonamurty Farm, and to her father's cottage. Not to mention the increasing number of times she'd been sent by Madame Carlton carrying messages here and there. Ellen was a sworn-up member of the Cumann na mBan now, and proud of it. Siobhan wasn't, and seemed to resent the fact. Knowing Siobhan's secret about her brother's involvement with the RIC played on Ellen's mind — should she break her promise to Siobhan and tell Madame? But Siobhan had declared that her sincerest wish was for an independent Ireland. She wanted the same as the rest of them. It wasn't her fault that her brother thought differently.

Ellen had been given a new daily task, back in December, of taking a couple of empty milk cans from Carlton House, via the track that led past the stables and out onto a lane, along the lane for half a mile and into a farmyard. There she would hand them over to a man, who was dressed in green tweeds and who never spoke a word to her. He'd take them into an outbuilding, which she assumed was the dairy but in which she never saw any dairymaids, and pass her a pair of full cans to take back, hung from a yoke across her shoulders, the old-fashioned way.

When she was first asked to deliver the cans, by Madame Carlton herself, she frowned. Wasn't there a pony and cart, or even the tractor with its trailer, which could more easily transport heavy milk cans?

'There is, Ellen dear, but there are also RIC roadblocks in place. They search every vehicle that passes. But they won't search a girl carrying milk cans. Not when they've seen that girl every day, returning empty cans and collecting full ones.'

'What else will I be carrying, Madame?' Ellen was fearful. Who was to say that one day the RIC mightn't search her anyway? Or that one day the roadblock might be manned by the more thuggish Black and Tans, who'd have no qualms about searching her, and worse.

Madame Carlton smiled. 'Only the milk cans, Ellen. But they won't always be empty on your way out. I think that is all you need to know. Smile at the RIC officers. They will doff their caps and let you pass; certainly after a few days when they are used to you, they will.'

The winter was cold and damp, and it was often raining or drizzling when Ellen made her walk over to the farm. Even so, if the roadblock was in place she'd force herself to smile cheerfully at them as she passed, and indeed she was never questioned, never searched.

'Here she is, the little milkmaid,' one of them would say, and the others would grin and joke and make deep bows or josh each other as she passed.

On the return trip, if the milk cans were equally heavy, full of milk, she felt more relaxed. But sometimes one of them would be lighter than the other, weighing only about the same as an empty one, and then she'd be on edge again as she passed the soldiers.

'Messages,' Jimmy had told her, 'that's what you're carrying. Madame Carlton must suspect her mail is being intercepted. This is her only way to keep in touch with the Volunteers.' He'd kissed her. 'I'm proud of you, so I am. Every little act for Ireland's sake, is an act worth making.'

Once, and thankfully only once, she'd had a near escape. There'd been a different set of RIC guards at the roadblock. The new commander, a hard-faced man with a scar across his face, had stopped her after the others had let her through.

'Lads, we search *everyone* who passes,' he said, gruffly.

'She's a girl — we aren't allowed to search girls,' protested one of the men.

'Not allowed to search their person, but we can search what they are carrying. Get on with it, men.'

'Sir, tis only empty milk cans,' Ellen said, but they made her put down her load and step back while they unscrewed the tops of the cans and peered inside. She clasped her hands together tightly to stop them shaking, feeling sweat run down her back despite the chill day. She prayed silently that there would be no message inside the cans today. What would she say if one was found? Would she deny all knowledge of it, and try to save herself at the expense of whoever had written the note — possibly Madame Carlton herself? Or would she take responsibility, and try to deflect attention away from those at Carlton House?

It could only have been a minute or two, but it was the longest minute in Ellen's life. At last the soldiers replaced the tops of the cans. 'Nothing here, Sergeant,' they said, and helped her lift the yoke back on to her shoulders. She forced a bright smile to her face and thanked them as she continued on her way. With luck, that would mean this particular company of RIC officers would not stop her again.

She'd reported the incident back to Madame Carlton, of course. Madame had listened gravely to her story. 'The milk cans will be empty for the next week at least, in case they decide to search you again. Let me know what happens as you pass the roadblock.'

The week had passed without incident. About ten days after being searched, Madame Carlton came to see her off on her regular milk run. She'd laid a hand on Ellen's shoulder, but said nothing. Ellen had guessed that today she was carrying a message, and felt the familiar pang of fear as she approached the roadblock, but thankfully she was waved through as usual.

* * *

Captain Cunningham had recovered, and after a fortnight of nursing had left Carlton House late one night. There had been no other wounded

Volunteers brought in since. Ellen had plucked up the courage to ask Madame Carlton why not. She'd enjoyed her nursing duties and helping Captain Cunningham get gradually better. She'd enjoyed too, chatting to him and learning about the background to the war and his hopes for Ireland's future.

Madame Carlton had answered with a sigh. 'We are being watched. The RIC suspect Carlton House of being a Volunteers' headquarters. We must be very careful not to draw any more attention to what goes on here.'

It was on the tip of Ellen's tongue to tell Madame what she knew of Siobhan's brother. Was it possible Siobhan was passing information to the RIC? She'd sworn loyalty to the Cause, but was she truly loyal? What would happen to her if the Volunteers suspected her because of her brother's involvement with the RIC? They'd question her — beat her, no doubt. No. Ellen could not betray her friend. She trusted Siobhan.

Ellen had also noticed fewer comings and goings of serious-looking men at odd hours of the day or night. In her first few months of employment there seemed to be endless meetings and all sorts of people in or around the house, often staying for a few days. Now the house was much quieter. Madame Carlton went out often, but there were rarely any visitors. Less work for her and Siobhan to do in the house, but then her new responsibility of taking the milk cans with their hidden messages to the farmyard took up more time.

One fine day in late March, on her day off,

Ellen was in high spirits as she left Carlton House to meet Jimmy. He wasn't at the end of the driveway where he usually waited for her. But as she knew the house was under observation by the RIC she guessed that would be the reason why, and she pushed on to Clonamurty Farm. He'd be there, no doubt, waiting for her. His mother would have made soda bread, and she'd have a slice of it, still warm from the oven, with a thick spreading of butter and a cup of tea, while Jimmy told her his news from the past week.

She enjoyed her walk to the farm. Lovely to be out in the sunshine, on such a glorious day, without the burden of the milk cans and yoke across her shoulders. Birds were singing, there were daffodils still in bloom along the verges, and blackthorn blossomed in the hedgerows. On the hillsides lambs were bleating for their mothers, while the flatter fields had been ploughed and sowed with wheat and barley. This was rich farming country, and at this time of year there was a feeling of expectancy in the air, as though the earth couldn't wait to get on with growing the next crop.

At the farm, Mr Gallagher was in the yard, stacking a wood pile. He grunted at her in welcome. His face was red, his lips pursed together, and he was flinging the logs onto the pile, cursing if they rolled off. He was angry about something. Ellen didn't dare ask what was wrong, and neither did she ask him where Jimmy was. She went to the kitchen door, tapped and entered. In the kitchen, Mrs Gallagher was sitting at the table, a cold cup of tea in front of her, staring at nothing. Her eyes were red as though she'd been crying.

'Mrs Gallagher? Is something wrong?' Ellen asked. Oh God, let it not be Jimmy, she thought.

Mrs Gallagher raised her head, sniffed and wiped her eyes on her apron. 'Jimmy's upstairs. Go up to him. He'll tell you what's up.'

Ellen didn't waste a minute but rushed out to the stairs. Coming down was Jimmy's younger brother, Mickey.

'He's in his room, so,' Mickey said. 'They're upset because he's off to blow up a barracks or some such. Won't tell me, he won't. Maybe he'll tell you and you can tell me. Ma didn't even know he was a Volunteer. She's furious with him. I'm going to sign up too, soon as I'm old enough. I'd've joined the Fianna Éireann if there'd been a group near enough, so I would. Parents won't send me to Jimmy's school. They say it put ideas in his head.'

He stepped close to Ellen. Mickey was as tall as her now, even though he was only 13. He whispered the next bit. 'Same ideas are in my head, Ellen. Jimmy's doing what's right for Ireland. They don't see it, the old man and the ma. They just think it's dangerous. But if something's worth having, like freedom, it's worth really fighting for. I'm right, aren't I?'

She smiled at his fervour. Now that she too was part of the struggle, seeing him champing at the bit to be allowed to play his part made her feel old. 'Sure, Mickey, I think you are right. Let me past, now. I need to talk to Jimmy.'

166

'Get him to tell you his mission. Then you can tell me. Don't forget, now. I can keep secrets, sure I can.' Mickey stood aside to let her past, and she hurried up the stairs and across the landing to Jimmy's room. She had not been up here since she was a child. Now that they were sweethearts it seemed wrong to go to his bedroom, especially if his parents were downstairs or in the yard.

She tapped on Jimmy's door. 'Jimmy? It's me. Your mammy said I should come up to you.'

He did not reply, and she was about to tap again, when suddenly the door swung open and Jimmy caught her wrist and pulled her inside. There was a fire burning in his eyes, like Mickey's but oh so much brighter and fiercer! 'You're here. I'm sorry I couldn't meet you today. I've only a short time before I have to go . . . '

She noticed then that a kit bag was on the bed, and items of clothing were strewn across the floor.

'Go where?' she whispered.

He pulled her across to the bed and gently pushed her down to sit on it, shoving the kit bag out of the way. 'I have a new mission. A big one. I've proved myself now, and they want me to take part in an important mission.'

'What?'

He was silent for a moment, gazing into her eyes as though deciding whether to confide. At last he shook his head. 'No. I cannot tell you. It would put you in danger. What you don't know you can't confess to, should anything ever happen. You must understand this. I must do what I can to keep you safe.'

She leaned in close to him, breathing in his musky scent, relishing the feel of his strong, broad shoulder beneath her cheek. 'You want to keep me safe, yet you are pleased and proud that I carry messages for the Volunteers, that I put myself in danger every day passing the RIC roadblock?'

He put his arms around her and pulled her closer still, resting his chin on the top of her head. 'I am proud, and I am terrified. I love you so much. I want to tuck you away somewhere safe, away from all this, until the war is over. And I want you to play your part, understand the issues at first hand, so that in the future you can look at our proud, independent nation and say, *I helped to build that.* But I must weigh up every last detail, to work out what is for the best, which risks should be taken and which should be shied away from. In this case, telling you my next mission: my judgement is that it's too dangerous for you to know.' He kissed her lips. 'But I promise you, my darling Ellen, I will take no unnecessary risks. I will carry out my mission as best I can, and then I will return.'

'How long?'

'I don't know. A week. Two. Maybe more. We need to wait for the . . . for the right opportunity.'

'Where will you be?'

He smiled, and kissed her again. 'Ah, my sweet Ellen, that I also cannot tell you, for your own safety. Come on. I have about an hour before I must leave. Let's not waste a moment of it.'

And then there more whispers of love, and kisses, long and deep, with an urgency about them. Ellen wondered when she would see him next, and what he might have done by then.

★ ★ ★

Their time was over all too quickly. Jimmy glanced at the clock on the mantelpiece in his room and leapt to his feet, stuffing clothes and personal items into his kit bag. From under the bed he pulled out a gun and tucked that into his belt. Ellen made no comment, but shivered to think she'd been sitting on the bed while such a lethal weapon lurked beneath it. A weapon that Jimmy was trained to use, and probably would, to end someone's life.

When the bag was packed, he opened a drawer and pulled out a small box and handed it to Ellen. 'I want you to have this.'

She stared at him, and opened the box. Nestling inside was a chain on which hung his silver First Communion medallion, engraved on the back with his name and the date he took Holy Communion. 'I can't, this is your . . . '

He waved away her protests. 'I'd give you a ring, only I haven't one, so perhaps this can do instead. Tis the only thing I have of value.'

'A ring? Do you mean . . . '

He caught her and pulled her close. 'When this is all over, I hope we can be married, Ellen, my sweet, precious colleen. I want you to keep this as a sign of my love, and my commitment to you.' He kissed her, and she tucked the little box into the pocket of her skirt. It may not be of any significant value, but to her, it meant the world. It was the most personal thing he could have given her.

'Well,' he said, 'best go down now. It's time.'

She followed him downstairs and into the kitchen, where his family and another man were waiting.

Mrs Gallagher took him in her arms. 'Be careful, now,' she told him. 'Send me word when you are coming home and I'll roast a leg of mutton for you.'

'Will do, Mammy,' he replied.

He shook his father's hand, but then Mr Gallagher pulled him into a hug too, saying nothing. Ellen noticed tears in the old man's eyes.

'If I can borrow your bicycle, I can join the Fianna over at Navan,' Mickey said.

'You're too young, Mickey,' Mrs Gallagher cut in.

'Another year, kid,' said Jimmy, ruffling his brother's hair. 'Then you can join them, if Mammy and Daddy agree.'

'Ready?' asked the stranger.

Jimmy turned to Ellen and hugged her one last time. She tried to imprint every inch of him on her mind, knowing if she never saw him again this last embrace would be the one she'd remember him by. Tears came to her eyes at the thought. No. This would not, could not be the last one. He'd return, safe, triumphant, and ready, perhaps, to leave the Volunteers, settle down and take her as his wife.

'I'm ready,' he said. He picked up his kit bag, followed the man out of the house and climbed into the sidecar of a motorcycle that was parked in the farmyard. It sped off in a cloud of dust, the roar of its engine mingling with the roar of fear inside Ellen's head. Please Lord, let him come home safely, she prayed, silently.

15

Clare, May 2016

Janice insisted on staying with me until nine p.m., making sure I'd eaten, asking over and over if I'd like to go and stay with her for the night. 'I'd stay here with you if I could, but the kids . . . you know,' she said, with a grimace. 'I've only a blow-up bed to put in the sitting room but it's comfortable enough. I'm not sure you should be on your own tonight.'

I hugged her. 'I'll be fine. Thank you so much for everything. I guess I needed a little cry.' It had been, I realised, the first time I'd cried properly since coming to Ireland. Since leaving Paul, and our twenty-five-year marriage.

'Little cry? It was like a dam had burst! I'm drenched.' She laughed. 'Well, if you're sure, I should get off home now. I'll come and see you tomorrow afternoon after the school run.'

She was a good friend. I was glad to have met her.

★   ★   ★

The next day I awoke stiff and sore, with some impressive bruises blooming across my chest and shoulder where the seat-belt had restrained me. I hauled myself out of bed, made myself breakfast, then called the insurance company. I wasn't sure how these things worked, but at least I knew which company Paul had insured the car with, and was able to find a number for them online. I didn't have the paperwork or policy number, but they were able to look it up using the registration plate and Paul's name and address.

'You won't need to tell my husband, will you?' I said, once the insurance clerk had taken down all the details. 'Only . . . we are separated. The car's mine, even though the insurance is in his name.'

'Sorry, Mrs Farrell, we do have to inform the policy holder about this claim. However, if he agrees to go ahead with the claim, any insurance payout will come to you as the registered owner of the vehicle.'

'And if he doesn't agree?'

'Then I'm afraid we cannot progress with the claim. Perhaps you can talk to him about it, so he knows to expect to hear from us. I'm very sorry we cannot do it any other way, but be assured of our best attention at all times.'

He was reading from a script, I could tell, and beginning to annoy me. 'Very well. I will send evidence of the accident as you requested and let my husband know. Goodbye.'

I decided to leave talking to Paul until later, when I felt up to it. It wouldn't be an easy conversation.

Mid-morning a man from the local garage called by. They'd recovered my car from the field and he brought me a bag containing everything they'd retrieved from the glove compartment and door pockets. 'And these books were in the field nearby,' he said, handing me another bag containing Ryan's books on Irish history, all sodden as it had rained during the night. I'd have to pay Ryan for them. Maybe they'd dry out and still be readable if I put them in the airing cupboard.

The garage man also handed me a document confirming the car was a write-off. 'You'll need that for your insurance claim,' he said. 'You're lucky you weren't hurt.'

'I know,' I said, thinking about my bruises and the increasing stiffness in my back and shoulders. If I didn't keep moving today I felt I'd seize up completely.

⋆　⋆　⋆

Ryan was the next visitor. I guessed Janice must have popped across the road from the café and told him what had happened. He knocked on the back door and came straight in, not waiting for a reply, and took me straight into his arms. 'Oh my God, Clare. What a thing to happen. Janice says it was a cow in the road. Thank the good Lord you're not hurt.'

'Just a little bruised,' I said, wriggling out of his arms because he was hurting me, squeezing too tight.

'Arrgh, sorry,' he said, letting go. 'So, anything I can do? You've no car, so if you need shopping done, or a lift anywhere, you've only to call and ask me. Please. I want to help.'

'Thank you.' I smiled at him. To tell the truth I hadn't thought how I was going to manage, living here in the middle of the countryside, with no car. I supposed I'd have to buy another pretty quickly, probably before the insurance money came through. 'Ah, your books. Sorry. They got left in the field in the rain.' I showed him the pile of soggy books.

'Who cares about a few books? Main thing is you're not badly hurt.' He ran his hands through his hair and shook his head. 'If only my car hadn't been in the garage yesterday, then you wouldn't have been driving up the lane.'

'No, you would have, with me in the car, and the cow would still have been there, and we'd both have been in the accident,' I said.

'I guess so. Anyway, in happier news, I did a bit of digging around on that name that's on the communion medallion. Turns out that our James Gallagher was a Volunteer, fighting for Irish independence.'

'So maybe he had something to do with those guns we found?'

'Almost certainly, I'd say. I also had a look at the 1911 census to see who lived here back then, around the time of young James's First Communion.'

I frowned. 'I thought Ireland's census returns were all destroyed in a fire?' I was sure I'd read that somewhere.

'Most of the ones from the nineteenth century, yes. But the 1901 and 1911 and parts of others survived. So, it seems young James grew up here. In 1911 the farm was owned by his father, Michael Gallagher. Our James lived here with his parents and younger brother who was also called

Michael. It was probably James himself who hid the medallion in the chair.'

'But why? And why was it with a birth certificate for someone else?'

Ryan shook his head. 'I've not had a chance to look much into that yet. Anyways I think I should leave it for you! It'll be a good bit of research to do quietly, while you recuperate.'

'Thanks. I'm sure there must be some connection between the two. The certificate was folded around the medallion so I think they were put there at the same time, by the same person. Maybe it was even James Gallagher. My grandmother was also involved in the War of Independence. I found some notes my cousin made about her — I've been meaning to read them all but haven't had time yet, and I don't feel up to it today. I've a few things to do then I want to lie in the bath with a good book and try to soak away the aches and pains.'

'That sounds like a good plan,' Ryan said, his eyes full of sympathy. 'Well, I'd better make a move. Don't forget to let me know if you need anything.'

'I'm short of milk . . . ' I said, tentatively.

'I'll pick some up and bring it this afternoon. Anything else?'

'No, it's all right.'

'OK.' He stood in front of me for a moment, then bent forward and kissed my cheek, so gently it felt like a butterfly had brushed its wings against me. Then he was gone, and I was left touching my cheek, thinking what a good friend he was, and wondering if I could ever contemplate a time when there was another man in my life.

My friends had buoyed me up. I felt strong enough to call Paul and tell him. Not that it should matter to him, as it was my car, but as the insurance company had said, he had to be informed. Better that it came from me.

I pulled out my old phone, switched it on, and called him. Better to get it done quickly.

'Paul? It's me. Clare. I need to talk to you about someth — .'

'Clare?! About time you turned your phone on. I've left hundreds of messages. Have you listened to them all?'

'Not yet, but I need . . . '

'It's hell here. How I'm supposed to do the shopping as well as working I don't know. Had to buy a new car but all I could get quickly is a rubbish little Focus. I hate it.'

'About the car . . . '

'The bathroom needs cleaning. And the washing machine shrunk my T-shirts. When are you coming home?'

'Paul, I told you. I'm not coming home. This is my home now. Listen, I need to tell you something important.'

'What? You found another man? You can't have. Who'd want you?'

I closed my eyes and took a deep breath. Let that one go, Clare, I told myself. Just stick to the reason why you rang him. 'No. It's the car. I had a little accident. The insurance company will be in touch with you about it.'

'What? You've pranged the car? For God's

sake, Clare! How bad is it?'

'It's a write-off.'

'What? How on earth did you manage that?'

'There was a cow in the road. I swerved to avoid it, went through a hedge and the car flipped over.'

'For God's sake. That'll fuck up my no claims discount.'

I realised he hadn't asked whether I'd been hurt or not. I decided not to say anything unless he asked, but found tears springing to my eyes. This man had cared about me once. We'd had twenty-five years together, and at the beginning it had been good. But now he cared more about the car, which wasn't even his.

'Well anyway, the insurance company will need you to sign forms or something. I've already spoken to them.'

'Hope they pay out quickly. I'll be able to get something better than this crappy Focus.'

'Paul, the car was mine. The payout will come to me.'

'But the insurance is in my name.'

'Even so, the insurance clerk said any payout goes to the registered owner of the vehicle. That's me.' As I said it I knew he'd explode, and so was ready for the tirade when it came.

'For fuck's sake! You steal our car, trash it, and then take the money and leave me with nothing? Well thanks a lot, Clare. Don't expect me to sign anything if I'm not getting any of the money. Sort it out yourself. If you can. You never had a head for money or paperwork — I've always had to handle all that sort of thing. You'll have no chance. But don't come crying to me. You're insisting it's your car so you deal with the claim. I'll not lift a finger to help.'

And then he hung up. I was left open-mouthed, a rogue tear running down my face. 'It's all right, I wasn't hurt at all, though it could have killed me,' I said quietly to the wallpaper photo on my phone. Had Paul always been like this? He had loved me and cared about me, once. Surely though, even though we'd split up he'd still be concerned if I was hurt? I'd care if I heard he was injured in an accident — I know I would. I mean, you can't spend twenty-five years with someone and then just not care in the slightest if they're hurt. Not even ask.

Well if that's how he wanted to play it then fine. I hoped he'd change his mind about making things difficult for me regarding the insurance claim, once he'd calmed down. I could afford to buy a car using the money left to me by Uncle Pádraig but I'd rather keep that money to spend on doing up the farm, and to live on until I figured out some way of earning a living.

I called the boys next, to tell them what had happened before their father did. Predictably, the first thing each of them asked was whether I'd been hurt.

'Because if you need me, I can change my holiday and come over sooner. Tomorrow. Hell, this afternoon,' said Matt, sounding distressed. I could picture him pacing up and down, running his hand through his hair in that way he had when he was upset.

'No, I'm fine. Honestly. A little stiff today but it'll ease up soon. And I have made friends here,

Matt. I'm not alone.'

'Oh, Mum. I worry about you, you know?'

'Yes, I know. And I am truly grateful to have such a wonderful son.'

Jon, typically, made jokes about it, once he'd ascertained I was all right. 'Like, Mum, you know that cars can't actually fly, right? Chitty Chitty Bang Bang, the car in Harry Potter — that was all special effects, you know? Next time you want to go through a hedge, find a gate rather than try to fly over it.'

'I will, I promise,' I said, laughing.

'You sure you're OK? Like if I find you've got broken legs or something when I come over next week, I'm gonna be one seriously cross son, you get me?'

'Yes, darling. I promise I have no broken legs or anything else. Thanks for your concern. I appreciate it.'

'You told Dad yet?'

'Yes. Car insurance is in his name so he has to agree to the claim.'

'Uh-oh. There may be trouble ahead,' he sang, making me laugh again even though I suspected there was more than a little truth in his words.

★ ★ ★

I hated the way having to deal with anything 'official' like the car insurance made me feel so nervous and useless. It was, I knew, because I'd spent so many years not working, not handling the household finances, doing nothing more taxing than a bit of curtain-making. I'd given up

180

work when I was pregnant with Matt and never went back.

Well, that is apart from a very short-lived job as a lunchtime supervisor at my sons' primary school. I shuddered a little as I remembered. Both boys had started school, and I found myself with too much time on my hands. There was a vacancy for a lunchtime supervisor — not much money but just a couple of hours a day, term-time only — perfect for me! And I was excited about having a little money of my own that I could spend how I liked, rather than feeling guilty about buying something for myself out of the housekeeping allowance.

Paul grumbled a bit but then appeared to be happy about it, and I started work one Monday lunchtime feeling positive and excited. And I enjoyed the work — the children gathering around me, all wanting to tell me their news, wanting to hold my hands, wanting me to join in their games of tag.

But on the Wednesday of the second week, my eighth day at work, I came home after my shift to find Paul already home, in bed, sick. I say 'sick' but he seemed all right to me. No raised temperature, no physical signs.

'I feel terrible,' he said. 'Came home hoping to be looked after. Forgot you were at work.' He gave a hangdog look that was supposed to inspire my sympathy. Actually it made me feel a pang of annoyance. I only went to work for an hour and a half. Not that long to be left on your own, even if you were feeling awful. Not when you're a grown man.

181

'Well, I'm here now,' I said. 'I'll make you a hot lemon.'

He nodded feebly and turned his face away, sighing. I had the impression it was all an act.

For the next two days he phoned in sick, and insisted I stay home to look after him. So I had to make excuses with the school, and stay at home all day at his beck and call, apart from walking our kids to school and fetching them at home time. He could cope on his own for those two thirty-minute periods it seemed, but not for the ninety-minute period when I was supposed to be at work. When I argued with him about it he reminded me my priority was him and the kids, not my job.

And then he suggested he increase the housekeeping allowance to cover what I could earn from the school. On Sunday he emailed the school from my email address telling them I was resigning from the job as it didn't fit with my other responsibilities. There was a terse reply from them the next day — an email I opened after Paul had gone to work. He'd made a sudden amazing recovery once I reluctantly agreed to stay home and not work.

It's so easy to look back and see just how manipulative he was. But at the time I constantly made excuses for him, gave in to him and did whatever he wanted, to keep the peace. I told myself at the time it was better for the boys, and I needed to put them first. It all left me with such low self-esteem, and not a lot of knowledge of how the world operates. Or how to 'adult', as Jon would put it. I was no good at adulting, despite being almost 50.

I sighed, made myself yet another cup of tea, and to put the accident out of my mind I looked back on what I *had* achieved in the last couple of months. From opening my own bank account to dealing with a cache of guns found buried under my barn — look, Clare, I told myself, you've dealt with a lot. You've done all right so far.

16

Ellen, April 1920

Jimmy had been gone two weeks when the news came, reported in all the newspapers, of an attack on an RIC barracks in the county. There'd been an explosion in the night, and while the RIC were running around in confusion, half-dressed, trying to get out, a couple of Volunteer snipers had picked off a few of them. In all the RIC death toll was thought to be around ten men. One Volunteer had been injured but was expected to make a full recovery according to a report in *An Phoblacht*. Madame Carlton seemed jubilant about the news.

'With that barracks unusable that'll mean the RIC have to pull back to Dublin. They have no other barracks left in this county. It might mean they stop manning some of the roadblocks,' she told Ellen.

'Yes, Madame. Do you know who was injured?' Ellen was terrified this had been Jimmy's mission. What if it was he who'd been hurt?

Madame Carlton smiled. 'Not your young man, is all I can say.'

'Pity so many had to die,' said Ellen, half to herself. It was war, and people always died in wars, but she still felt pity for them. After all, they were someone's son, someone's husband, someone's brother. They'd been unlucky. And the RIC were mostly Irishmen, unlike the Black and Tans. Irishmen who'd been their friends before this conflict began and they found themselves separated from their neighbours by their duties. Like Siobhan's brother. He was stationed in a different county, so wouldn't have been hurt in this raid.

'War's harsh.' Madame Carlton said, gently. 'Ellen, there is one thing you should know. The men involved in that mission, and that does include your Jimmy, are now on the run.'

Ellen gasped. 'What does that mean?'

'It means Jimmy can't come home. The RIC and the Black and Tans will be looking for him, and the others. He will need to stay away, keep a low profile.'

'Where will he stay?'

'We have safe houses across the county. He's in one now, and may need to move on, to stay ahead of the authorities. He will be all right, Ellen, I promise. We have many men on the run. We have a good system of support for them.' Madame Carlton put her hand on Ellen's shoulder.

Ellen stifled a sob. 'Will I be able to see him?'

The older woman nodded. 'I think we can arrange something. You'll have to be very careful though.'

Ellen forced herself to smile. 'Thank you, Madame. I miss him, so.'

'Of course you do. Leave it with me. I'll see if I can't arrange for you to meet on your next day off.'

Ellen thanked the Lord that she had such a good and understanding mistress. To think she'd been in the job less than a year! A year ago she'd been living with her father, keeping house for him, wondering what her future might hold. The war had barely begun. And now here she was, a member of the Cumann na mBan, fighting for Ireland's freedom. And she was practically an engaged woman. She fingered the medallion that she'd worn around her neck ever since Jimmy had given it to her. All she could do now was wait to hear the arrangements for her to see Jimmy from Madame Carlton.

★   ★   ★

Her day off, two days later, arrived with no more news of Jimmy. Ellen left Carlton House with a heavy heart. On a whim she decided to call at Clonamurty Farm on her way home, to see if his parents had heard anything more. She knew she must not pass on what she had learned from Madame Carlton, however.

All was in uproar at the farm. Mrs Gallagher was in the kitchen, in tears. Cupboards were open, their doors torn off hinges, bags of flour and potatoes had been ripped open and the contents strewn across the room. Crockery lay broken on the floor and dented pans kicked under the table.

'What's happened?' Ellen said, rushing in to comfort Mrs Gallagher.

'RIC. Came in here looking for Jimmy, so they did. I told them he wasn't here. They turned the place upside down. As if he'd be hiding in a sack of flour!'

'Where's Mr Gallagher?'

186

'They took him for questioning. Thank the Lord it was the RIC and not the Black and Tans or I fear they'd've ... they'd have ... ' She dissolved into tears and Ellen pulled her close. She didn't need to hear the end of the sentence. She remembered all too well the fate of Jimmy's friend Gerry.

'And Mickey?'

'In the sitting room. Trying to make a start on tidying it. It'll take days.'

'I'll stay and help,' Ellen said. 'Have you heard anything from Jimmy?'

'Of course not. He's away with his Volunteers, the eejit, and we'll not see him till the war's over. Unless we see him before then in his coffin. Why'd he have to get involved, I just don't understand. And that one in there' — Mrs Gallagher pointed towards the sitting room — 'he only wants to go and do the same thing. Ran off last week, didn't he, and joined the Fianna. Came home full of tales of how he'd learned to clean a gun.' She cried again, and Ellen tried to hold her once more, but Mrs Gallagher shrugged her off. 'Don't mind me. I'm only the little woman in all this. Our job's just to support the men and boys, isn't it? Not to get involved ourselves. Just to suffer the consequences for what the men do.'

'Some women are involved,' Ellen said, stooping to pick up the larger pieces of broken crockery.

'Your Mrs Carlton and her Cumann na mBan? They'd do better to keep their noses out. War is men's work. If women ruled the world there'd be no war.' Mrs Gallagher brushed flour off a chair and sat at the kitchen table, head in hands.

Ellen was about to say something more, but decided against it. The best thing she could do for the Gallaghers now would be to help clear up this mess. She set to work, replacing anything unbroken in the cupboards, sweeping the floor, wiping the flour off all surfaces. It didn't take long to have the kitchen looking respectable again. She put a kettle on the range to make tea. Mrs Gallagher was still sitting at the table, sobbing quietly.

Ellen went in search of Mickey to see if he needed help. The living room was in as much of a mess as the kitchen had been. Books and papers were strewn everywhere. The basket of turf that sat beside the fireplace had been upended and the turf bricks kicked around the room. The chair where Jimmy had his hiding place was tipped on its back but, Ellen was relieved to see, not slashed open, though she doubted he'd have left anything incriminating in it.

It was clear that this was an attempt to make as much mess as possible. The RIC hadn't been looking for anything in particular. They just wanted to cause chaos. At least, Ellen thought, they hadn't hurt anyone. It was bad, but it could have been so much worse.

Mickey was lying stretched full length on the sofa, his forearm across his forehead, eyes fixed on a spot on the ceiling.

'Need some help clearing up?' Ellen said, as

cheerily as she could manage.

'Aye, I do,' Mickey said. 'Promised Mammy I'd sort this room, but I don't know where to start.' He swung his legs round and sat up. 'Ellen, this is after making me so cross. I don't know whether I'm more cross that Jimmy's actions made them do this to us, or that I can't be with him, fighting alongside him.'

She sat next to him and put a sisterly arm around his shoulders. 'You can support him here, by looking after your mammy. While your daddy's away being questioned you're the man of the house. To be sure it is all a big mess but the place to start is in your own head. Get yourself together, then come and help me clear up.'

Ellen stood and began picking up the debris, restoring order. Mickey roused himself and joined her a few moments later, and she was able to go and finish making the tea for Mrs Gallagher. It seemed to revive the older woman.

'Thanks for all you've done, love,' said Mrs Gallagher, catching her hand and squeezing it.

'You're welcome. I hope Mr Gallagher will be back soon.'

'Yes, and Jimmy too. If you hear anything, you will let us know?'

Ellen smiled. 'I know he's safe, that's all.' It couldn't hurt to tell her that much.

'Thanks be to God for that, at least.'

★ ★ ★

She stayed at Clonamurty Farm until Mr Gallagher returned, tired, stressed but unhurt.

'Just questions,' he said, in response to his wife's enquiries. 'Endless questions. When did I last see Jimmy? What was he planning? Who did he associate with? They knew nothing. They were just fishing.'

'What did you tell them, sir?' Ellen asked, wondering if he'd been forced into telling them about those guns she'd seen him hide under the floor of the barn. Even Mrs Gallagher didn't know about those.

Mr Gallagher shrugged. 'Told them I hadn't seen Jimmy for weeks, that he was his own man now, making his own decisions, and seeing his own friends. That I knew nothing of any plans, and had no idea why they were questioning me. Thankfully they let me go. I knew the officer — McMurphy — used to have a pint with him in the pub most weeks, before all this began. What's it come to, that he and I are on different sides, and all because his job forces him to be against us?' Mr Gallagher shook his head sadly. 'Jimmy's put us in danger. We were lucky this time. Next time it could be the Black and Tans. They wouldn't stop at just questions.'

His words played on Ellen's mind as she walked along the lane towards her father's cottage. She supported Jimmy, as did his family at heart, but his decisions were affecting them all. It was always this way — the ordinary people suffering due to the actions of a few. But it'd be worth it, in the long term, if Irish freedom was won, wouldn't it?

'There you are, girl. I'm after waiting hours for you. I'm in need of some dinner.' Her father was

190

as grumpy as ever, sitting in his chair by the kitchen range, empty bottles of beer at his feet. Digger was nosing despondently at his empty food bowl.

'I'll get something in the oven, then.' She hunted for some food, found rashers of bacon and potatoes, and began preparing a meal. She found the remains of last week's leg of lamb for Digger. As she worked her father kept up a steady stream of grumbles.

'Hear that Jimmy Gallagher's gone missing. The lad you're sweet on. Best keep away from him. If he's got himself caught up with this war, it'll do no one any good. I blame those eejits from 1916. The ones who tried to take over Dublin. They're the ones who started it all. Life was peaceful enough before then, and now look at us! Blackstown burned. The barracks blown up. Roadblocks everywhere. Men on the run. That Markievicz woman elected to Parliament, yet she was one of the rebels! Doesn't make any sense. They should have left her to rot in prison. We don't want women running the country, so we don't.' He grunted, shifting in his chair while Ellen bit her lip. There was no point arguing.

'Who knows where it'll all end?' Da went on. 'With the Volunteers dead or surrendered, and the Union flag flying again over Dublin castle, just as it always has, that's where. And people like us end up rebuilding the country. They've demolished the Boyne bridge — did you hear about that? Just to make it harder for the RIC to get around. Makes it harder for all of us, doesn't it? Did they think about that, this Irish

Republican Army or whatever they're calling themselves now? How're the farmers to get to market without that bridge? How're people to move around? Hmm?'

'I don't know, Da,' Ellen said, but he continued grumbling, obviously not caring for any response.

'When it's all over and the Volunteers are in prison, there'll only be people like me and you left to rebuild that bridge and put it all right. The RIC won't help us then, not after they've been shot at and blown up. We used to get along all right, people minding their own business, RIC keeping order. And now look. It's a shame, that's what it is. A crying shame.'

Ellen had stopped listening. She knew deep down he was in favour of Irish independence. It was just the inconvenience to himself that he was grumbling about. There were those who went out and fought for what they believed was right, and those who sat at home and grumbled. Well, she knew which type of people gained her respect.

With the dinner cooking she quickly mixed a soda-bread dough, formed it into a loaf and slashed the top of it to let the fairies out, as her mother had taught her. She put it onto a tray in the range oven.

'There, Da. Dinner's almost ready and there's bread in the oven. All's well with the world, so.' She smiled brightly at him. She'd have liked to talk about what had gone on at Clonamurty but it would only set him off grumbling again. Better to talk of inconsequential things when he was in this mood.

★　★　★

The next day, early in the morning while Ellen was still at her father's house making breakfast, a message arrived. A boy from Blackstown brought it. He was, he explained to Ellen, out of earshot of her father, a member of the Fianna but had been advised not to wear his uniform.

'I'd be a target for the Black and Tans, if I wore it,' he said, sounding almost proud. 'Anyways, I was asked to find you and bring you this. You weren't up at Madame Carlton's and they said to look for you here.'

'You've done well, thank you,' said Ellen, taking the grubby note from him with shaking hands. 'Have a slice of bread and butter before you go?'

'All right.' The boy took the bread she offered and ate it greedily. 'I'll be going now, miss. Got more errands to run, and the Black and Tans are on the Blackstown road, so I'll have to go through the fields.'

When he'd gone, she opened the note with shaking hands, and recognised at once Jimmy's handwriting.

Dearest Ellen. I hope this reaches you safely. Usual place, after school, if you're able. J.

He wanted to meet her! Today, under the old oak, after church! She completed making breakfast with a song in her heart. When her father rose and joined her she decided a small lie was the best way ahead.

'Da? I'm sorry but I will have to go back to Carlton House straight after church. I'll prepare

193

the dinner this morning before I go and all you'll have to do is put it in the oven. Wish I could stay longer but Madame Carlton said I'm needed. Siobhan, the other housemaid, is after being sick all week. I was lucky to get any time off at all.'

'Hmph. You could have said yesterday. You were late back to me and now leaving early. What kind of a daughter are you?'

'Da, it was you who wanted me to find a job, so it was.'

'Don't you be answering me back, girl! Where's your respect? You just make sure everything's done for my Sunday roast before you go. Another meal I have to eat alone.'

Today, his grumbling couldn't upset Ellen. She was going to meet Jimmy! She worked like a Trojan all morning to get everything done, the cottage cleaned and her father's dinners and pies for the week made.

★ ★ ★

At last it was time for church. At last Father O'Riordan stopped droning on in his sermon. At last it was time to meet Jimmy. Ellen kissed her father goodbye. 'Put the stew in the oven for an hour like I told you. Enjoy. I'll see you next weekend.'

'Aye, and don't be late next week.' Her father shuffled away, still grumbling to himself. When he was out of sight Ellen skipped happily to the old oak, their childhood meeting place. It was the perfect place. Just out of town and well secluded.

When she arrived he was not there yet. She had no idea which direction he'd be coming from. And, thinking about it, she realised he'd have to take extreme care. He was on the run, now. He was wanted by the RIC. If he was spotted and recognised he would be arrested, or worse. She hoped he'd keep hidden. There were ways of approaching the oak, across the fields, keeping close to hedgerows, which meant you couldn't be seen from any road. She stood leaning against the tree, prepared for a long wait if necessary. It was a fine, if breezy, day, and she had plenty of time before she was really due back at Carlton House. She sang quietly to herself as she waited.

'Ah, a pretty colleen! Why would you be standing here? Waiting for someone?'

She spun around to see who was talking. Two men, in the mismatched uniforms of the Black and Tans. She quickly replaced the look of horror on her face with a smile.

'Hello, sirs. Just my . . . sister. She's away delivering a basket of eggs, to, um, to Mrs O'Flanaghan. She said she'd meet me back here.'

'Eggs, hmm? And what've you got for the likes of us? Poor hard-working soldiers, we are, trying to keep the peace in this godforsaken country.' The man leered at her, standing so close she could smell his foul breath.

Ellen took a step away, praying that Jimmy wouldn't come now, not with these men here. If they spotted him . . . well, it didn't bear thinking about.

'What's the matter, pet? Don't you like me?' He turned to his friend, who was leaning against the tree, lighting a cigarette. 'She don't like me, Bert. What's wrong with me?'

'Too pug-ugly, ain't you?' the other one replied, and laughed at his own joke.

'Well, my sister doesn't look like she's turning up any time soon, so I'll be going home, now,' Ellen said, and took a step away. The man caught her arm.

'Not yet, you ain't. Give us a kiss, first.'

She pulled away from him and at that moment, across the field on the far side of the tree, she caught a glimpse of Jimmy approaching. He couldn't see the men from where he was — they were hidden by the enormous girth of the tree trunk. He'd spotted her, though, and lifted a hand to wave. Any moment now and he'd be visible to the Black and Tan men.

She thought quickly, and just as the man made a grab for her again she lifted a hand and made their old childhood sign for 'watch out, teacher's coming'. For anyone else, for these Black and Tan thugs, it would pass as an odd sort of wave, disguised by her pulling away from the man.

But out of the corner of her eye she saw Jimmy stop, then duck for cover beneath the hedgerow. He'd understood her warning. He was safe.

'Just leave me be,' she said, mustering as much force to her voice as possible. 'I've done nothing wrong. You've no right to hold me. I'll be on my way home now.'

'Ah, leave her. There are other girls in town more willing. Prettier, too,' said the second man. The first one let go, flinging her arm back at her harshly.

She offered up a quick silent prayer of thanks, held her head high, and marched away as quickly as possible. Part of her wanted to go after Jimmy, but she went in the opposite direction, in case the Black and Tans followed.

Their plans were ruined. She headed back to Carlton House, tears in her eyes, wondering when on earth she'd get the chance to see Jimmy again. Thank goodness she'd been able to warn him to stay away before the Black and Tans had seen him.

17

Clare, May 2016

It was six days since the accident and I had the most beautiful bruise across my right shoulder from the seatbelt. Every day it developed a new colour and I now had the full rainbow. But it didn't hurt unless I pressed it, and after a couple of days the stiffness in my back had faded and I'd been able to get back to working on the house. Just as well because Matt and Jon were due very soon and I needed to get a couple of bedrooms in a fit state for them to use. Matt was taking a week off work, and Jon's university term had finished for the summer. I'd hired a car to get me around until the insurance money came through.

I hadn't heard back from the insurance company, and had to pluck up the courage and mental strength to turn the Paul-phone back on, to ring him again and try to persuade him to let the insurance claim go ahead. But as soon as I'd turned the phone on, it rang, with a voicemail message from him.

'Clare, look, I over-reacted. Sorry I shouted at you. Awful news about your accident. Matt says you weren't too badly hurt and . . . well . . . I'm glad about that. Um . . . well. I've agreed the insurance claim. Shouldn't take too long to go through. Um . . . right. Ring me when you get this message. If you like. Not long till your birthday, is it? The big one. So, right. Yeah. Ring me. Bye.'

I was gobsmacked, to use one of Jon's words. Paul, apologising, agreeing to the insurance claim, being *reasonable* for once. Unbelievable. The message had been left only an hour before, so I rang him there and then, hoping that he'd still be in the same mood as when he left me the message.

He answered straight away. 'Clare! Good to hear your voice. I . . . miss you, you know?'

'Um, thanks for sorting out the insurance claim.' Of course he missed me. No one cooking his dinners, was there?

'No problem. It was a bit of a shock, hearing you'd had an accident. I think it was the shock that made me have a go at you. Sorry about that.'

Another apology. This was a different side of Paul, one I didn't remember ever seeing before. I just grunted in response.

'Boys are coming to see you for your birthday, aren't they?' he asked.

'Yes, they are. I'm looking forward to it.'

'It'd have been nice for us all to be together for it. But you do what you want. I'll send you over a card, if that's all right. We've been married twenty-five years, Clare. I can't just throw it all away, even if you can.'

I sighed. It was on the tip of my tongue to say I wasn't throwing our shared past away; I was just moving on, to my own future. But that would lead to a row, and I didn't want to spoil

199

this conversation. It was the first I'd had with Paul since telling him I was leaving, in which he hadn't ranted and raved at me. 'Send me a card. Yes, I'd like that. Sorry Paul, must go now, there's . . . so much I need to do today. Bye, then.'

I hung up before he had chance to say anything more. I sat there, at my kitchen table with a cold cup of tea in front of me, for a good ten minutes pondering that call and Paul's apparent conciliatory tone. If he could only continue being reasonable, the whole divorce proceedings would be a lot easier. Perhaps we'd even manage to stay in touch and be friends, of a kind, for the boys' sake.

Perhaps if he'd been like that throughout our marriage I wouldn't now be wanting to divorce him.

⋆ ⋆ ⋆

I'd bought some bed linen for the boys. Plain blue for Matt and one with Marvel comic heroes plastered all over it for Jon.

'Aw, for a wee grandson?' asked the woman at the Dunnes Stores till when I went to pay for it.

'Actually no, for my son. He's never quite grown up,' I'd told her. He'd love it, I knew.

I spent an exhausting day cleaning and shifting furniture in and out of bedrooms until I had two set up ready for the boys, with their new bed linen, the least offensive curtains I could find in the house, somewhere to put away their clothes and a chair. In Matt's I'd put a large geometric patterned rug on the floor — one I remembered had been Daithí's when he was a boy. I used to play a kind of hopscotch on it, while he lay on his bed reading and just about tolerating my presence.

I'd bought loads of food — rib of beef to roast, huge bags of pasta and jars of tomato and basil sauce for lunches, a kilo of cheese, a jumbo pack of chocolate mini rolls. All their old favourites. I planned to spoil them. And prove to them I could manage on my own. And show them I was happy here.

I also needed to prove to myself that being 50 was the start of a new, wonderful phase in my life. But to tell the truth, there was something about reaching that horrible half-century figure that terrified me. It felt like it'd be all downhill from here.

I'd had time to spend on my upholstery project, as well. I'd stripped it back completely, to just the wooden frame. I'd sanded and varnished the legs — the only wooden parts that would show when I'd finished. Next job was to add webbing, then tie the springs to that, knotting them through the webbing and then tying the tops down to form a rough dome shape.

I was reusing the original springs. It always felt right to reuse as much as possible. Even most of the stuffing was salvageable — it was all horse hair. I'd used an old trick — put the horse hair into an old duvet cover (of which I had plenty inherited from Uncle Pádraig), sew it up loosely, then put the whole lot in the washing machine. Once washed, I'd unpicked the stitching, removed the horsehair and spread it out in the sunshine to dry. It was good stuff and definitely worth saving.

The old barn was proving to be a good workshop, though eventually I wanted to fit it out properly with a cutting table and some better lighting and heating for the winter, if I was going to work on more projects out here. I also needed to buy a few new upholstery tools. I'd made do with what I could find among Uncle Pádraig's so far but soon I'd need a magnetic hammer, a large box of upholstery tacks, a set of curved needles in various sizes, some decent scissors and a double-ended mattress needle. Also hessian, webbing, calico, extra stuffing, upholsterer's twine, piping cord, not to mention fabric for the final cover. Oh, and I'd need a sewing machine.

I made a list and found a website where I could order most of the things I needed. The sewing machine and fabric would need to wait until I could go to Dublin for a day.

I'd read the rest of Daithí's notebooks in which he'd interviewed Granny Irish. It was odd hearing her words, across the decades, via the ghost of my cousin.

'*I liked working up at the big house,*' Daithí had written. '*There were two of us sharing a room at the top of the house. We called the mistress Madame. She was good to us. She ran the Cuman Na Barn (not sure of spelling). It was like the women's version of the old IRA. There was all sorts going on in that house during the war. I'm not sure even now I should tell you*

202

it all. It's hard, after keeping quiet all these years, so it is.'

There was a gap, and then Daithí had continued writing in a different pen.

'Granny told me she wasn't always sure if she was doing the right thing, supporting the Volunteers. She hated war, hated the idea that people got hurt, and wished the conflict could just end peacefully without bloodshed. I think that's wrong. I think if you believe something's right, it's worth fighting for. Only people who are on the wrong side get hurt. Or people who stand in your way.'

I sighed, reading that. You hurt people, and got hurt too, Daithí. You gave your life for what you believed in. And I don't know whether you were right to do that. I was with Granny on this. Why can't conflicts be resolved by negotiation? In the end, Daithí's conflict *was* resolved by talks rather than guns — by the Good Friday Agreement.

★ ★ ★

Matt and Jon had managed to arrange things so that they arrived on the same flight. I was like a kid at Christmas waiting until it was time to set off to the airport to collect them. It was about an hour's drive to Dublin airport and I left in the hire car far too early and had to spend thirty minutes sipping coffee in the arrivals hall before finally their flight showed as having landed.

At last, there they were, coming through from customs together, my two tall, handsome sons. I felt a surge of pride as I watched them walk through. Matt had obviously come straight from the office, as he was wearing a suit, although he'd removed his tie. Jon was in ripped jeans and a black hoodie. He'd obviously just made some sort of joke as Matt threw back his head laughing, then gave his brother a playful punch on the arm. At that moment they spotted me and marched over.

'Mum! Hey! Good to see you!' Matt hugged me, and Jon ruffled my hair as though I was a small child. To be fair, he is about a foot taller than me.

I hugged them back, and blinked away a tear. It was so good to see them and they were both staying for a full week. I was so excited. 'Well then, shall we get going? I can't wait to show you the farm.'

'Oooh arr, the farrrm,' said Jon in a British west-country accent, as we made our way out of the terminal and across the road to the short stay car park where I had left the hire car.

The journey passed quickly with all three of us talking at once and lots of laughter. It was the first time either of them had been to Ireland — a fact I felt a pang of guilt about. I'd never even brought them over when they were little to visit Uncle Pádraig and Aunt Lily. I suppose because Paul had never shown any interest in wanting to visit any members of my family. Or his own, for that matter. His parents had retired to Spain and his brother moved to Australia and Paul seemed content to never see or talk to them, and just send Christmas and birthday cards.

Finally we turned into the lane and I pointed

out the flattened hedge. 'That's where my car left the road. I ended up upside down in the field beyond.'

'Christ, Mum. A miracle you weren't badly hurt,' said Matt.

'I know.' We were quiet for a while pondering my lucky escape, until I turned into Clonamurty Farm's gateway and parked in front of the old barn. 'Well, here we are.'

'Wow, Mum. It's huge!' Matt said. 'I didn't realise there were all these outbuildings. Do you own loads of land as well? What will you do with it all?'

'Not much land, no. Just what you can see here, up to that fence, and a garden round the back. Uncle Pádraig sold most of it off when he retired from farming. But yes, the house is quite large. The main barn I'm using as an upholstery workshop.'

'You could run this place as a bed and breakfast. Or convert the barn into holiday cottages.'

'Or install a quad bike track, and use the barn for laser-quest,' Jon added, helpfully.

'Hmm, not sure about any of those ideas,' I replied, trying and failing to imagine myself cooking breakfast for a stream of holiday makers or organising teenage birthday parties. 'Come on. Let's get inside. It needs a lot of work as you'll see but I've sorted out a couple of bedrooms for you.'

I gave them the tour, showed them their bedrooms (Jon was delighted by the Marvel duvet cover while Matt rolled his eyes) and then

I ushered them back downstairs to sit in the kitchen and drink a beer while I got dinner on the go. Spaghetti Bolognese tonight — a staple while they were growing up, and a meal we'd all loved. Only Paul used to complain about having it every week and insist I cook something different just for him.

'So, Mum. Is the insurance claim going ahead? For the car?' Matt asked, as I stirred chopped onions and tomatoes in a frying pan.

'Seems to be, yes. Your dad had left me a message about it, and I rang him.'

'Brave? Or just stupid?' said Jon earning himself a thump from Matt.

'Funnily enough, he seemed quite reasonable on the phone. He was actually sorry for shouting. He was apologetic. Sympathetic, even.'

'Not words I associate with Dad,' Matt said, frowning.

'Who was he, and what had he done with my father?' Jon added.

I smiled. 'Well, that's how he was. Maybe my leaving him has made him grow up a little.'

'And realise what he's lost.' Matt looked thoughtful.

'There's another thing,' Jon said, looking from me to Matt. 'He's talking about coming over to see you. Says even you wouldn't turn him away if he's on the doorstep. Wants one last family get-together, for your birthday.'

I put down my wooden spoon and sat down heavily at the table. Paul turning up here just as I was beginning to feel settled and organised was the last thing I wanted. Though I knew we needed to talk, *properly* talk, about the way ahead for us, and the best way to do that would be face to face; the prospect of actually doing it made me sweat. Would I be able to cope having him here? I tried to imagine showing him into a spare room, making polite conversation over the breakfast table — no. It wouldn't work. If he did come he'd have to stay in a guest house somewhere else. There were a couple in Blackstown.

'Mum?' Jon stood, leaned over me and put his arms around my shoulders. 'I tried to tell him not to come but you know what he's like. He won't listen to anyone.'

'It's all right.' I patted Jon's comforting arm. 'I mean, we're grown-ups. We're going to have to talk to each other about getting a divorce sooner or later. May as well do it here, if he comes.'

'I just hope he doesn't cause any trouble,' Matt said.

There was silence for a moment. We were all lost in our own thoughts, each imagining the confrontation if or when Paul turned up here. At least, that's what I was doing. Eventually I shook the images out of my head and returned to the Bolognese sauce before it burned. I'd ring Paul again, tell him not to come over. But not today. Not when I had my lovely sons with me, and the promise of a laughter-filled day ahead.

18

Ellen, April 1920

It was over two weeks later before another note arrived for Ellen, this time delivered via the milk cans she carried regularly to the farmyard. She'd made the trip as usual, with no problems as the RIC roadblock was no longer in place. Back at Carlton House Madame had taken the empty can from her to look for messages, and a moment later called Ellen back to the housekeeper's room.

'This one's for you,' she said, handing over a scrap of paper with a smile.

Ellen took it and unfolded it immediately. *Message for E. Gatesend Barn. Your employer knows. Any time. J.*

'Madame? What does this mean, please?' Ellen handed it back.

'Your young man is telling you where he is hiding, and is asking you to visit him there. Gatesend Barn is our code name for a deserted farmhouse. I can show you a map and tell you how to get there. It's about ten miles from here. There is a bicycle you may borrow, though you will have to walk the last part over the fields.'

Ellen's excitement was growing steadily. There was another chance to see Jimmy! Memories of the close escape with the Black and Tans surfaced. 'But Madame, will it be safe? Not for me, I mean, is there a danger to Jimmy or anyone else if I go?'

Madame Carlton shook her head. 'No more danger than anything else we do. You've been carrying messages almost daily, haven't you, and have never been stopped or searched? They don't look at young girls going about their business in the countryside.'

Ellen shuffled her feet. But they did. They caught you by the arm, and made lewd suggestions. And there'd been that one time the RIC had searched her (thankfully empty) milk cans.

'What is it, Ellen? Has something happened?' Madame Carlton caught Ellen's chin and lifted it so she was able to look directly into her eyes.

'Yes, Madame. I'm scared of being caught.' She told the older woman then what had happened on her last day off, the day she had so nearly met with Jimmy.

'You did well to warn him away. That was good thinking. Now, do you want to go to see Jimmy? I have some messages I need delivering, which you can take to him. I can't spare you today, but tomorrow, perhaps?'

'Oh, Madame! Yes, I do want to see him. I miss him so much. Thank you!'

Madame Carlton smiled. 'I was young once. You deserve a chance. Now, work doubly hard today to get everything done, and I'll give you the letters tomorrow.'

★   ★   ★

The time flew by, as Ellen scurried around the house cleaning, scrubbing, making beds and

209

fires, carrying trays, filling coal scuttles. She did everything with a smile on her face, which appeared to annoy Siobhan.

'What have you to be so cheerful about? Sending me mad, so it is, your incessant grinning.' Siobhan picked up a pail of water angrily, so that it sloshed around and spilt. 'Now see what you've made me do? More work. Always work.'

'I'll mop that up,' Ellen offered, being careful not to smile. Even Siobhan's grumbling couldn't take the edge off her mood. She was going to see Jimmy tomorrow! She decided not to tell Siobhan. It would only antagonise her.

At last it was time to go. Madame had explained exactly how to get there, and showed her on a map. She wouldn't let Ellen take the map, just in case she was searched after all. But it wasn't a difficult route, and Ellen had repeated the instructions back to Madame several times.

'Now, here are the messages you're to take,' Madame said, and handed her a couple of envelopes. 'Tuck those somewhere safe in your clothing, and hand them to Captain Cunningham who is also hiding out at Gatesend. You know him, of course. You helped nurse him.'

Ellen's smile broadened at the thought of seeing Captain Cunningham again. She'd liked him, and enjoyed their quiet afternoons talking of books and poems while he was recuperating.

She picked up a small bag of belongings, laced her boots tight and went out via the kitchen door. Leaning against the wall there was a bicycle. Usually Madame Carlton used it to get around locally, and to scout areas where the Volunteers were considering some action. There was a basket tied to the handlebars, and Ellen dropped her bundle in it. She wheeled the bike out of the yard and onto the driveway, mounted it and she was off. It was a grey, overcast day but with no rain or wind, and inside her heart the sun was shining brightly.

It took about an hour and a half to reach the abandoned farm. There was a rusty iron gate across its entrance, chained and padlocked. Ellen hid her bicycle in the hedge on the opposite side of the lane, as she'd been instructed. Checking no one was around to see, she then climbed over the gate and ducked behind the hedge. Rather than walk straight up the track to the farmhouse, she followed the hedgerow around, keeping close, so that no one on the road would be able to see her. She approached the farmhouse via the back, again, exactly as Madame had told her to.

The door opened before she'd put a hand to it, and her heart leapt momentarily to her mouth. What if this safe place had been compromised, and the Black and Tans were here?

But it was Jimmy. Lovely, handsome Jimmy, who tugged her inside and wrapped his arms around her, pulling her into his embrace and kissing her soundly on the lips.

'Woo-hoo, put the young lady down!' came a familiar voice. Jimmy let her go and Ellen turned to see Captain Cunningham, now in his Volunteer's uniform and looking very well indeed, standing in a doorway opposite.

'Sir, it's good to see you,' she said, pulling out

the notes Madame had given her and handing them to him.

'And you too, Ellen. As you can see, your nursing paid off. I will be forever in your debt. Well, I will leave you young lovers alone, now. Keep away from the windows.'

'Of course, sir,' Ellen said, trying to sound as though she already knew she'd need to take this precaution.

'Come on. I'll make you tea in my room,' Jimmy said, taking her hand and pulling her towards the door Captain Cunningham had just left by. Was it right to go with him to his room? Ellen wondered. And then, just as quickly, she realised she didn't care what was right and proper. She only cared that she loved this man, and it was war time, and he was on the run. She had until midday the next day to stay with him. She determined to make the most of every moment.

Jimmy's room was upstairs, at the back of the house. There was a piece of sacking pinned over the window, which meant the room was gloomy. There was an old, stained mattress on the floor, with a couple of blankets thrown on it. A Primus stove and a tin mug stood on a small table. Beside the mug lay a revolver.

Jimmy picked up a small tin can and filled it with water from an old-fashioned cracked ewer. 'There's no running water here, but there's a pump in the yard. We fill the jugs after dark and make it last all day. I've some tea but no milk, and this evening we have potatoes and tinned fish. I think there's some apples left as well.'

He lit the stove and placed the pan on top, and put a spoonful of tea from a brown paper packet into the tin mug. He smiled wryly. 'We'll have to share the mug. I've only the one.'

'I don't mind. I'll share anything with you,' she said. She opened her bundle. 'I brought a loaf of bread, cheese, some fruit cake and two bottles of beer.' It was all she'd dared bring. It had to look no more than one person's picnic, in case she was stopped and searched.

Jimmy grinned. 'A feast! Let's have the cake now, save the beers for dinner, and the bread and cheese for breakfast. There may be eggs in the morning, too. Sit down, do. Sorry there's nowhere other than that mattress.'

'Where does your food come from?' Ellen asked, sitting down on the bed and leaning against the wall. She knew Jimmy had been here for at least five days.

He shrugged. 'Who knows? Some mornings we find a basket's been left on the back doorstep overnight. Or a side of ham, wrapped in a cloth, or a sack of potatoes. Some local people know we are here and are supporting us. We're very grateful, so we are. And there was a stock of coal and turf left in one of the barns, and we cook on an open fire downstairs, or on our primus stoves.'

Ellen stared at him. 'But if local people know you're here, are you not afraid some of them might report you to the RIC? Not everyone supports the Cause.'

'It's a risk we have to take. If we get wind of traitors in the area, we'll move on. This is the third place I've been in since that last mission.'

'The barracks?' She realised she wanted to know what his part in that mission had been.

'Yes.'

'Tell me so, what did you do?'

'Do you really want to know?'

'I do. I want to know everything about you, share in everything.' She moved closer to him on the old mattress, leaning sideways against him. He slipped an arm around her shoulders and kissed her hair.

'All right. I'll tell you.' He took a deep breath. 'We were targeting the Blackstown barracks, as you know. Trying to get the RIC out of the county. We set explosives in the night, by each of the doors. I'm a good shot; my job was as a sniper. Once the explosives went off, the idea was to pick off any men who tried to run for it.'

'You shot them, as they tried to escape?' It was not a picture Ellen wanted in her head. Those poor men, Irish men, whose only crime was to be on the other side in this conflict.

He did not look at her as he answered. 'Aye, I did. And they shot back. Two of our men were hit, but the RIC came off much worse. As more came out of the burning building we were outnumbered and had to pull back. That's when Cunningham and I were spotted, and that's why we're now on the run. Cunningham realised the danger first, and got me away safely. He's a good man. One of the very best; loyal and steady and I owe him my life.'

She was silent, trying to take it all in, trying to come to terms with the idea that her Jimmy had killed.

'Does it upset you?' Jimmy asked her, gently.

She realised a tear had run down her cheek. 'I'm after wishing it could all be resolved through talk. Why do people have to kill each other? It just seems so sad, such a waste of life.'

He nodded. 'I know what you mean. But the end justifies the means. Ireland unfree will never be at peace.'

'You said those words before.' She remembered his mutterings at Gerry's graveside, the previous autumn.

'I believe them, with all my heart. We must fight, Ellen, and surely swift attacks, targeting the military as we are, is better than a protracted war like the Great War was, when so many millions died?'

'But then they fight back, targeting the ordinary people.' She was thinking of the attacks on Blackstown pubs and businesses a few months earlier.

'Reprisals, aye, are a sad fact.' Jimmy fell silent. The pan on the stove was bubbling, so he jumped up, made the mug of tea and handed it to her, along with the cake she'd brought in her bundle. 'Let's talk no more of the struggle. We have so little time together. What time must you be back with Madame?'

She blushed. 'I have until midday tomorrow.'

'You can stay the night?'

'Yes.'

'You will have the mattress then, and the blankets. It's not much but you should be warm enough. I can . . . take a coat and sleep . . . somewhere else . . . '

215

This was the moment. She turned to face him and gazed into his eyes. 'You'll do no such thing, Jimmy. I want you here, with me. We will curl up together.'

He stared at her, and smiled slowly. 'I can think of nothing I would like more.' And then he pulled her close and kissed her, deep and warm, with more passion than ever before. She was panting when at last the kiss ended. How long until the evening, until they could lie down together, kiss some more, and see where it led them? She was ready for this. Jimmy was her love, her man, and she wanted no other. She would give herself to him, readily and joyfully.

The afternoon passed quickly. They talked and laughed and kissed, and grew closer and closer throughout. In the early evening they went downstairs where, in what was once the sitting room, Cunningham and another man were already preparing a meal. Ellen stepped forward and helped, and the two bottles of beer she'd brought were split four ways.

After they'd cleared up, and the men had completed some security checks outside, Jimmy took Ellen's hand and led her out of the room, back upstairs. She noticed Cunningham smile and wink at Jimmy as they left, but she found she didn't care. So what if they knew what was going to happen? The conflict made life precarious, and time was too precious to worry about social conventions. The Lord would forgive them, if what they did, they did for love.

And it was every bit as magical as she had hoped. They lay down together, with an oil lamp casting a warm glow in the room, pulled the blankets over themselves, and lay on their sides facing each other, kissing, gently at first and then more passionately. His hands began to explore her body, and after a while she got up, removed her dress and stockings, and lay down again in only her underclothes. She fumbled at his trouser fastenings, and he tugged them off. He pressed against her and she could feel his excitement. Gently, so carefully, he lifted her shift and rolled her onto her back, easing himself onto her. And then he was inside, murmuring words of love in her ear, and melting into her and she was melting into him, and she felt complete.

Afterwards Jimmy turned out the lamp and they lay in the dark, warm and snug under the blankets, holding each other.

'Jimmy?' Ellen said, quietly, 'will you do any more missions? Or just stay safe and on the run until it's all over?'

He paused before replying, and she wondered if he'd fallen asleep. At last he answered, 'One more, There's something big being planned, and I'm to be a part of it. Then I'll have done my bit, and I can retire from the Volunteers with my head held high. And we can be together. One more.'

One more. Could she bear the wait, the anxiety, the not knowing? Did she have any choice?

'It'll be over soon,' he whispered. 'We'll win, and it will all have been worth it. Wait for me, my love.'

She held him close, tears gently running down her cheeks, until he fell asleep in her arms, his slow, even breaths caressing her cheek. Eventually she too slept, and dreamed of a future, a magnificent, joyful future where they had their own farm, half a dozen children, and a country free from oppression.

19

Clare, May 2016

It was so good having Matt and Jon to stay. I'd filled them in about the guns found under the barn and the items found inside the old chair. Neither of them were very much into history and I suppose as it wasn't their home they weren't as fascinated by the mysteries as I was. I'd told them too what I'd found out about Granny Irish.

'Look, boys. Your great-grandmother's listed in this book.' It was one of the ones Ryan had given me on the day of the car crash, thankfully still readable after it dried out.

'She's in a book?' Matt looked vaguely impressed.

'*Volunteers from County Meath: the heroes of the War of Independence*. It lists anyone from the county who played a part, with a short paragraph describing what they did.'

'Let's see.' Matt took the book from me and scanned the brief paragraph. 'Wow, this says she worked as a spy! According to this she passed information about RIC movements to the Volunteers, and sent false information back.'

'Cool!' was Jon's only response, accompanied by a shrug. I supposed it meant less to the young, who were more interested in looking forward rather than backwards.

★　★　★

I took the boys to Tara, and also to the beach at Bettystown where we parked on the firm sand and went for a walk along by the dunes. It's one of those flat, hard-sand beaches that makes you want to run and skip and do cartwheels.

I remembered being there with Uncle Pádraig, Aunt Lily and my cousins when I was small. The boys had gone off running races along the sand and I could not keep up, so I'd practised gymnastics by myself. After a while David had come back and asked me to teach him how to do a handstand. He was useless at it — could not seem to get his weight over his arms right and his legs were bent at terrible angles. At that age I was obsessed by Nadia Comaneci and wanted to be just like her when I grew up. Cartwheels, handstands, walkovers and crabs were about as much as I could manage, but, hey, *I* could do it and David couldn't! I don't think I'd ever felt so proud of myself.

Being back there, now, at the grand old age of 49-very-nearly-50 left me with an obscene urge to try to do a cartwheel. To see if I still could. A little run, a skip up turning sideways with arms up, and over you go. Commit to it as your hands go down, get those legs up and in a good starfish shape, let the waist be loose and bend sideways . . . yes, I could remember how to do it. But could I? Was I flexible enough still? Would my arms take my weight; could my waist bend sideways enough?

And then I remembered my bruised shoulder, and thought better of it. I was too old for such things. I know there are people doing gymnastics in their eighties but they'd probably kept it up all their lives, whereas I'd done nothing more physically taxing than a spot of vacuum-cleaning and the occasional climb up a loft-ladder for the last twenty-five years.

'All right, Mum? You look a bit pensive.' Matt had come to walk beside me.

'Just remembering being here years ago, when I was a child.' I sighed, picturing again the child I'd been, chasing across the sands after her big cousins, longing to be noticed. 'Feeling the passage of time, I suppose. Something to do with that big birthday I've got coming up.'

'Ah, Mum. It's only a number.'

'Yeah, the number of times you've been around the sun,' Jon added. 'Who cares if you're getting old. You're still our lovely mum. Group hug!'

Good job they both wrapped their arms around me then as it meant I could bury my face against their shoulders until I got my emotions back under control.

When they released me, Jon sprinted off towards the dunes and came back with a piece of drift-wood and a badly chewed tennis ball. 'Anyone for cricket?' he asked, in a mock upper-class accent.

We played for ages, taking it in turns to bat (which soon morphed into catching the ball and then flinging it as far as you could, as the drift-wood made a lousy bat), bowl and field. I laughed till I cried, got out of breath running after the ball and loved every minute of it. Those boys were making me feel young again. I was middle-aged, but didn't have to act it.

★ ★ ★

We were sitting in a café near the beach, sipping huge mugs of milky tea, when Ryan phoned. I found myself blushing as I answered it, and did not miss the way Jon nudged Matt and raised his eyebrows when I said, 'Hi, Ryan.'

'Hey, Clare. I was thinking, it's your birthday soon, isn't it? Any chance you'd allow me to take you out for a meal to celebrate? I know your sons are coming to visit but perhaps you're free before they arrive?'

'They're actually already here,' I said, glancing at the boys across the table. Matt was pretending not to listen in, while Jon was not pretending at all, but cupping his hand behind his ear and leaning forward towards me. I slapped him away.

'Oh! Sorry. Well, perhaps . . . we could all go out?' Ryan said.

I tried to imagine the four of us out for a posh dinner. Although all the fellas would get on well, I suspected I'd feel a little awkward, trying to find common ground between my new friend and my sons. The waiting staff would assume we were a family. The boys would be wondering whether there was anything going on between Ryan and me — Matt would feel vaguely embarrassed and Jon would make excruciating jokes the whole time. No. I'd be happy for Ryan to call round for a cuppa while the boys were here, but not a birthday dinner out.

'Um, not sure when we'd all be free to go out . . . '

'Mum, if you want to go out it's fine — Jon

and I can go to the pub or just hang out and drink beer and watch TV,' Matt said, quietly. 'You don't have to spend every night with us.'

I smiled at him. He'd clearly guessed what was being said at the other end of the phone. 'Tuesday?' I said, raising my eyebrows at Matt, who nodded. Jon too nodded, mock solemnity on his face. I almost snorted with laughter at his expression but managed to hold it back.

'Tuesday?' Ryan said, sounding confused.

'I'll be free Tuesday. The boys have, um, got something else planned for that day.'

'Perfect! There's a great restaurant a few miles out of town — The Carlton. It's in an old country house hotel. I'll book a table and pick you up around seven, if that's OK?'

I grinned. 'Perfect for me, too.'

'Mum's got a date! Mum's got a date!' Jon sang, after I'd hung up. Matt thumped his arm, looking mortified on behalf of his brother.

'Not a date. Ryan's a friend. He runs the bookshop in town and lent me those books about Irish history. I'm sure you'll meet him while you're here. He's ... well he's just someone who's helped make me feel welcome here. Along with lovely Janice from the café. You'll meet her too.' Maybe I'd invite them both round for drinks on my birthday. Just a small party of five, but it'd be perfect. Janice's kids could come too — Jon would probably think of some wacky game they could play that would no doubt entail charging around the house, up and down the stairs, laughing noisily and generally doing what kids do best.

'Ah, but you're smiling a secret little smile, Mum,' said Matt. 'Methinks this Ryan's more than just a friend.'

I shook my head, still smiling. 'No, he really isn't. But he is a thoroughly nice bloke.'

'Thoroughly. Nice. Bloke. She means he's hot.' Jon translated my words into Millennial-speak, making me blush.

★ ★ ★

Tuesday came round quickly. But not before I'd agonised over what to wear, gone shopping for something new (with Jon, who'd always been a good shopping companion), bought a nice little dress in navy, white and pale blue that 'clung in all the right places', as Jon put it, and then panicked as I had no suitable shoes to wear with it.

'He won't look at your feet,' Jon said, but even so I ended up spending more than I should have on a pair of heeled strappy sandals. Paul had rarely let me spend much on clothes. If I needed an outfit for something, he'd come with me himself, picking out the kind of clothes he thought I should wear. Which weren't often what I would have picked out myself, but there was never any point arguing. I'd left all those clothes back with my old life.

'This is so different to what I've seen you in on nights out before,' Matt said, when I put the dress and shoes on to show him, back at the farm. 'It looks great. Really suits you.'

Matt wasn't the kind of person who often

complimented someone on their appearance, and he'd never say you looked good if he didn't genuinely think so. I was left glowing with pride and with a much-needed confidence boost. I found myself wondering what Paul would have thought of the new me, in that outfit. The new Paul, that is — the apologetic, contrite one I'd spoken to in our last phone call.

★   ★   ★

'So, you boys have a pizza for dinner, and if you want to make a salad please do . . . or shall I prepare one for you? You know how to work the oven. Is there enough beer in the fridge? I'll put some more in. The TV remote's on the mantelpiece, and do you want — '

'Mum, stop. We'll be fine. We've got this. We're grown men, not 12-year-olds being left home alone for the first time.' Matt took the tea towel I'd been twisting out of my hands.

'You'd leave beer for 12-year-olds?' commented Jon, handing me a glass of gin and tonic. 'Here, drink this. It'll loosen you up a little. You seem a bit nervous considering this is 'not a date'.' He made speech marks in the air.

'It's not a date. It's a dinner out. With a friend who happens to be a man. I'm not nervous.' I took a big gulp of the drink, and felt the alcohol rush straight into my veins, warming me and lending me a surge of courage. I was only meeting Ryan, after all. Kind, gentle Ryan. We'd probably spend the evening talking about Irish history and local landmarks.

Ryan arrived on the dot of seven o'clock. I invited him to come in and meet the boys for a few minutes before we set off. He did, and there were handshakes all round, smiles and polite conversation for a few minutes. I tried to gauge what the boys thought of him, but both had neutral, pleasant expressions on their faces and for once, even Jon did not make any kind of quip. Was that a good sign or a bad sign? Surely if he liked Ryan he'd have made some sort of joke . . .

I stopped myself before going too far down this train of thought. Ryan was only a friend and this was *not a date*, so why did it matter whether my sons liked him or not?

★ ★ ★

It took less than ten minutes to drive to the restaurant. It was a beautiful evening — warm and still, with the setting sun casting a yellow light across the landscape. The kind of spring evening that promises a fabulous summer to come, though I knew all too well that you can't rely on the weather in Ireland. Hot sunshine in December and freezing rain in July were equally possible.

The route took us further along the lane that Clonamurty Farm was on, then up a long driveway lined with elm trees. There were gaps where I guessed some trees had died, but it was still an impressive approach. The hotel itself was an imposing Georgian mansion set in stunning parkland. Probably once the home of English landowners.

'You look lovely,' Ryan said, as I got out of the

226

car in the restaurant car park. 'Fabulous dress.'

'Thanks. Jon helped me choose it.' As soon as I said this I cursed inwardly. Why had I let on that I'd bought something new especially for this occasion? 'A birthday present to myself,' I added, hastily.

'And why not? You deserve it,' Ryan said, as we went into the grand entrance hall, and from there into the restaurant, which I guessed had at one stage been a drawing room. There was a huge and beautiful fireplace, ornate coving and a fabulous vista through French doors across the parkland that swept down towards the River Boyne. With the sun just settling down into a vale between two hills the view was stunning.

'Lovely, isn't it?' Ryan said, noticing the direction of my gaze. 'A view that has barely changed for centuries.'

'It is wonderful. I love imagining my Irish ancestors gazing out at much the same view, hundreds of years ago.'

'Are they from Meath originally?' Ryan asked. 'I thought you'd said your grandparents were the first of your family to live at Clonamurty Farm.'

I nodded. 'Yes, they were. They moved into it in the late 1920s. But as far as I know the family were local before then. My grandmother definitely was. She was in service in a large house. Could even have been this one, for all I know! I did try to research my genealogy once, but didn't get far.'

I didn't want to add that Paul had found me digging around on an ancestry website and ranted for half an hour solid about what a waste of time that was, before changing the broadband password. It was a week before he would tell me the new password, and that was only because he needed me to do some online shopping for him. Yet again I wondered why on earth I had put up with him for so long.

'So many records were burned in a fire at the public records office during the civil war,' Ryan said. 'A tragedy for us history buffs.'

The waitress arrived then, and we ordered our food. It looked like an intriguing blend of modern cuisine but with nods to traditional Irish fare. 'Posh colcannon and deconstructed Irish stew,' Ryan said with a laugh, when I made this comment to him. 'But yes, it's very tasty and that's what matters. Anyway, we were talking about ancestry. Have you had any chance to research the names on the birth certificate and medallion?'

For once I had news to share on this score. 'Yes, in fact. One of those books you gave me, that unfortunately had to spend a night in the field, was a listing of all those from County Meath who'd fought in the War of Independence.'

He nodded. 'Oh yes. It gives a paragraph on what each person did. Bought mostly by people whose fathers or grandfathers were involved.'

'Well, our James Gallagher is listed there. You'd already told me he was a Volunteer and there are some more details about him in that book. He signed up young, at about 19, and took part in a number of missions. And my grandmother is listed — she was some kind of double agent, passing information about RIC activities to the Volunteers, and feeding false information back. I'd love to know more about exactly what she did. I wonder if she perhaps knew James Gallagher. I mean, if she'd worked here, and he lived at Clonamurty Farm — it's not far away at all.'

'Intriguing!' Ryan smiled.

'It's all so sad, though. It all happened so soon after the First World War, and didn't many Irish fight in that war for the UK? Then just a couple of years later they were fighting the War of Independence against the UK.'

Ryan nodded, and we were both quiet for a moment contemplating this, before our first courses arrived. The rest of the meal was spent chatting about anything and everything. Just like on our visit to the Hill of Tara, I felt as though Ryan was an old friend who I could talk to about anything. He told me about his past — he was a widower with one daughter who was working in Australia and whom he missed immensely.

In response I found myself touching on details about my marriage and the reasons I'd walked out. Not too much detail, of course. I was having a lovely evening out and didn't want to spoil it by thinking too much about Paul.

'So he was abusive?' Ryan asked at one point, with a frown.

'Not physically, no. Actually he could be very charming, and would often buy me little gifts and take me on amazing trips away. But he tried to control me. Leaving him was my way of wresting back control of my own life.' I sighed.

'He still doesn't see it. He still thinks I'll go running back as soon as I hit some difficulty or other. Although he did seem more reasonable the last time I spoke to him. I had a little glimpse of the man I married.'

Ryan didn't answer that, but I noticed him bite his bottom lip as though he'd thought of a response but stopped himself from saying anything. I changed the subject quickly, on to my plans for the farmhouse renovations, and we spent the rest of the evening chatting companionably. He really was an easy man to get along with, and despite telling myself 'this is not a date' and 'it's too soon after Paul to be looking for anyone else' I found myself wishing it was a date, and the first of many.

We went for a drink in a pub after the meal, and then Ryan drove me home. I did not want the evening to end. As he parked outside my farmhouse, he switched the car engine off.

I gathered my handbag from the foot-well and turned towards him. 'I've had a lovely evening. Thank you, so much.'

'Thank you for being such lovely company. And happy birthday.' He reached out a hand and brushed the back of it against the side of my face. I felt a flutter of excitement.

And then he leaned towards me, his eyes questioning, his hand gently cupping my chin, and his lips were on mine, soft, warm, teasing. I kissed him back, oh, how I kissed him back! When we parted I rested my forehead against his for a moment, wondering where we were going with this, excited that he clearly felt for me what

I was beginning to feel for him, but scared, so scared.

It had been over twenty-five years since I'd been with anyone other than Paul. How did it all work when you were in middle age? What were expectations these days? Was he going to want to come inside? He'd switched the engine off, he'd kissed me — that all meant he was expecting to be invited in, and then . . . Oh God. What happened next? Last time I was in this situation, aged about 18, it led to snogging in the kitchen while my parents sat watching TV next door.

'I'd ask you in . . . for coffee . . . but actually . . . ' I stammered, feeling myself blushing furiously.

'It's all right. Your sons . . . I mean . . . ' He tailed off and shrugged.

I felt a churn of both disappointment and relief, and a sudden urge to be out of the car, in my own home, sitting somewhere alone where I could work out what just happened and how I felt about it. 'Another time, I guess. When we've . . . '

' . . . had more time to get to know each other,' he finished for me, smiling. Yes. That was exactly what I wanted to say. There was no point rushing this. We had plenty of time to let things develop.

'Well, thanks again, and goodnight,' I said, as I climbed out of the car.

I had the most stupid grin on my face as I approached the kitchen door. Had to fight hard to get my face under control before going inside and facing a barrage of questioning and innuendo from my sons. Had I really just kissed a man who was not my husband?

20

Ellen, summer 1920

The weeks after Ellen's visit to Jimmy at Gatesend Farm dragged slowly on. About two weeks later, Madame told Ellen that Jimmy and the others had moved on, but she did not know where. 'Further up county, I believe, but I'm not privy to the details of operations in that area.' She'd patted Ellen kindly. 'We'd hear if anything bad happened. No news is good news, Ellen dear.'

But it was hard. Now that they'd become so close, now that she'd become a real woman, not being with him or having news of him seemed harder than ever.

And then came the day when she realised with a start that her monthly was overdue. Very overdue. Her breasts seemed a little tender, too. She knew immediately what it meant. She was carrying Jimmy's child. Now she longed even more for news of him, news that his final mission, whatever it was, had been successful and that he was returning to her, to marry her, so they could begin that idyllic future she'd dreamed of.

But the news never came. The weeks passed, and her condition began to show. She tried to hide it by tying her apron badly, by letting out her dress, hunching her shoulders over a little as she walked. Sooner or later, she realised, she was going to have to tell someone. She'd lose her job. Her father would be furious. Who knew what the Gallagher family would say. She'd kept away from Clonamurty Farm once she'd realised she was pregnant. If only Jimmy was here! If only this damned war had never begun!

By her reckoning she was five months gone when she decided she could keep the secret no longer. She'd already had questioning looks from Siobhan and Madame, but neither had said anything to her face.

Until one day when she stood up from having been kneeling at a fireplace, brushing out the grate. Her back pained her and she stretched as she rose, arching her back a little to ease her aching muscles. At that moment Madame walked in. Her bump, Ellen knew, was unmistakeable while she stood in that pose. She tried to hunch over, but it was too late. Madame had definitely noticed, and there could be no more pretending. She felt a blush rise to her cheeks, and she put a protective hand on her midriff.

'How far gone?' Madame's voice was gentle.

'F-five months, I think,' she replied.

'Jimmy?'

She nodded. 'He doesn't know. Oh, Madame, do you know where he is? I need to get word to him!'

Madame shook her head. 'No, Ellen, dear. I have no idea where he is. The last I heard, his company had headed north, into Cavan. Beyond the reach of my little pocket of influence. But, as I said to you before, no news is good news. If

234

anything had happened to him, we would have heard.' She sighed. 'I will hate to lose you. You've been a real asset to the Cause.'

'Madame, will I have to leave here?' Ellen held her breath awaiting an answer. She'd rather stay here, work for as long as she could, hope for news of Jimmy and never go home to face her father's anger.

Madame Carlton nodded. 'You will. I'm sorry. We have to keep this household appearing as 'normal' as possible. I can't have an unmarried pregnant girl living here. I'm sorry, it would draw too much attention to us. I fear my influence is less than it was. Someone has been passing information to the RIC about our activities here.'

Ellen clapped a hand to her mouth. 'It's not me, Madame! Don't suspect me!'

'Of course I don't suspect you! But you will have to go home to your father, at least until your young man returns.'

Ellen must have looked crestfallen, for Madame took a step towards her and put a comforting arm around her shoulders. 'I can understand you wanting to send a message to him. I shall see what I can do. There may be a way. Don't give up hope.'

Ellen forced herself to smile. 'Thank you, Madame. I would be very grateful, so I would.'

'You should go today to tell your father. Let's not put it off. Take your day off early. Come back here tomorrow and work another week or two, until I can find a replacement. You will soon find the work too hard as your baby grows, in any case.'

'May I come back, after the baby is born?' Ellen felt at home in Carlton House. The thought of leaving it was unbearable.

'You will have your baby to care for. But if some arrangement is made that means you are free, then yes, you will be welcome to return.' Mrs Carlton smiled kindly. 'I imagine, however, that you will find you want to stay at home with your child. It is a mother's place.'

Ellen smiled through her tears in return. Yes, she could imagine wanting to be with her child, Jimmy's child, at all times. Would it be a boy with Jimmy's dark eyes and cheeky grin, or a girl with his curly hair and long fingers? She placed a hand on her midriff, feeling the baby kick as though it knew what she was thinking. She could not wait to meet this child. The first of a new generation, proof of her love for Jimmy and his love for her. There were exciting times ahead.

'So,' Madame Carlton went on, 'finish up here, go and change, and then go to tell your father. Come back tomorrow for another week's work. At the end of the week I shall pay you what you are owed, plus a little more for the baby, and you will pack up your room and return to live with your father. But we will stay in touch, of course, and if I hear any news of Jimmy or his company I will let you know.'

There was nothing more to be said or done. Ellen did as Madame had bid, and an hour later she was ready to leave Carlton House, a few things she needed for an overnight stay at her father's cottage in a bag. She bumped into Siobhan on the way out.

'Are you after getting another day off?' the other girl asked, glaring at Ellen.

'Madame brought it forward. I'll be back tomorrow,' Ellen replied. She did not want to tell Siobhan about the baby yet. Not before she'd told her father.

'She favours you,' Siobhan grumbled. 'She always has. And you think you're a cut above the rest of us, because she trusts you and gives you stupid little jobs to do, telling you it's all for Ireland. It's all a load of rubbish. All of it. Ireland will never be free of Britain, and why would we want to be anyway? Won't do us any good. No good will come to the mistress. She's heading for a fall, so she is. You'll see.'

Ellen stared at her. It was the first time she'd heard Siobhan say anything against the Cause. A shiver ran down her spine. Could Siobhan be a danger to all at Carlton Hall? No, surely not. She'd worked there longer than Ellen herself had. She might not be involved with the Cumann na mBan and her brother might be in the RIC, but she was sympathetic to the Cause. She'd said so, many times. This was probably just jealousy talking.

Before Ellen could think of a reply Siobhan had turned on her heel and flounced off. Ellen determined that as soon as she came back the next day, she'd tell Madame about Siobhan's brother. Let Madame herself decide whether Siobhan was a danger or not. Right now all Ellen could think about was how she was going to break her news to her father. That moment was only about an hour away.

★ ★ ★

'You've brought shame on the O'Brien family, girl! Thank the good Lord your mammy isn't here to see this day. She'll be turning in her grave, so she will.' There were flecks of spittle at the corners of her father's mouth. Ellen stood in the kitchen, her hands clasped in front of her, her head bowed. She had no choice but to endure his rage. He'd need to rant for a while. He'd probably want to punish her in some way — make her clean out the chicken coop for the next month, or sleep on the floor, or say ten Hail Marys every day for a week. She would have to go along with whatever he said. She'd been sinful — falling pregnant outside of marriage. God made no allowances for the fact there was a war on.

'You'll go away to have this baby. There's a place run by nuns just outside Dublin. You'll go there, where they don't know us.'

'But, Da, how can we afford for me to stay away? I won't be earning . . . '

'You work for the nuns. They take in laundry or some such. You work for your keep, and when your time comes they'll attend the birth.'

Ellen was horrified. She'd thought she would stay at home with her father, with Blackstown's midwife and doctor attending the birth. Not sent away among strangers. 'Please, Da. Let me stay here with you. I can cook, and clean, and do all my old jobs. I can keep away from town, so no one need know. And when Jimmy comes home — '

238

'That no-good piece of junk. He won't be coming round here if he knows what's good for him. I'll knock him into next week if ever I see him again.'

'Da, I love him! And he loves me. He'll marry me, I'm sure of it, as soon as he knows about the baby and is able to come back to Blackstown.'

'Are you after telling me he doesn't know?'

'Not yet. He's away somewhere with his company. I've sent word, but I don't know when it'll reach him.'

'Where is he?' Her father looked apoplectic. His fists were clenched at his sides and his face was red.

'I . . . I don't exactly know. Cavan, somewhere. He'll come as soon as he can, I'm sure of it.'

'He'll run in the other direction, I've no doubt,' sneered her father. 'Young lad like that won't want to be saddled with a wife and child. That's if he doesn't get himself shot by the Black and Tans first. No, lass. You're off to the Merciful Sisters. I'd send you right now only it's too late in the day to arrange it.'

'I've to go back to Carlton House tomorrow, and work another week, Madame says,' sniffed Ellen. She could not believe what was happening.

'Aye, you'll go back there, get what you're owed, give it to me as I'll have to make a donation to the Sisters, and then you'll be off on the bus. I'll take you, make sure you go in and don't run off somewhere. The shame of it.' He shook his head.

The rage was dying down, but in its place Ellen could see a grim determination. She realised she had no choice. She would have to do as he said. Go to this place, the Merciful Sisters whoever they were, have her baby there, and hold on to the hope that Jimmy would hear what had happened, and would come for her. She'd be safe with the Sisters. As would her child. And when he or she was born, she'd find a way to be with Jimmy, if he hadn't already come for her. Maybe the war would be over by then, and their baby would be born in peacetime. That would be something worth praying for.

★　★　★

It was an uncomfortable evening. Ellen's father had a joint of ham, which Ellen cooked, along with some potatoes and turnips. She made soda bread too, cleaned the cottage, and did some laundry. All to try to prove she'd be an asset if she was allowed to stay. But her father grumbled and ignored her protests, and made it clear his mind was made up and could not be changed.

At last, when there were no more jobs she could do, Ellen bid her father goodnight. As she leaned over to kiss his cheek he turned his face away, muttering something about shame. She left the room before he could see the tears that had sprung to her eyes, and went to her old bedroom. Thank goodness tomorrow she'd be back at Carlton House, with Madame who'd been sympathetic to her plight. Madame was more of a parent to her, more supportive of her, than her father had ever been.

Ellen resolved to ask her about the Merciful Sisters. Maybe she knew of them. Maybe she'd be able to reassure Ellen that it was the right place for her to go.

Next morning her father said very little to Ellen as she prepared breakfast, ate, and cleared up afterwards. At last it was time to leave.

'I'll be back next week,' she said, as she stepped out of the cottage.

'Aye, and then it's off to the Sisters with you,' he replied, gruffly, not raising his eyes to hers.

'Goodbye, then,' she said, but he'd closed the cottage door behind her. She sighed, and set off on the familiar route back to Carlton House. One more week, that's all she had. Her dress was tight and there was no more room to let out the seams. She'd have to keep some money back to get a new one, or make one. Or would the Merciful Sisters provide something she could wear until the baby came? She knew very little about the institution. It sounded all right, she supposed, but it was away from home, away from Blackstown. If Jimmy came back looking for her — well she'd just have to hope that someone, her father perhaps, or Madame, would tell him where she was.

She was lost in thought as she turned in to the long drive leading up to Carlton House. So much so that she didn't immediately spot the motorcar parked in front of the building, or the uniformed men standing guard at the door. She was a few yards up the drive before she saw them, and ducked behind one of the majestic elms that flanked the lane. Thankfully they did not seem to have spotted her. She peered around the tree trunk. The uniforms were those of the RIC. What were they doing here?

Someone was being led out of the house in handcuffs, and roughly pushed into the motor-car. It was Madame Carlton! Ellen gasped. She'd thought that being a woman, Madame would be safe from the authorities, no matter what she did. Wasn't that the reason Madame had asked her, Ellen, to carry all those messages up to the farm-yard? How could they arrest Madame? What would happen to her? It didn't bear thinking about.

Someone else was standing outside the house. Another woman. Siobhan. Was she being arrested too? No, she was standing with her hands clasped, and one of the RIC officers was talking to her, handing her a package.

It was Siobhan's doing, Ellen realised. Siobhan had betrayed Madame.

The horror of the situation made Ellen gasp. She'd known Siobhan might be a risk. She'd meant to warn Madame — she'd been going to, as soon as she got back today! But it was too late. Oh why hadn't she said something yesterday, when Madame had said they were being watched? Madame could have got away, gone into hiding up at Gatesend Farm or somewhere else. If only she, Ellen, had warned her of what she knew about Siobhan. It was all her fault. She'd failed Madame.

The car's engine started. Ellen realised it was about to come down the drive, past where she was hiding. She had seconds to react, running back to the gate and throwing herself behind the hedge on the opposite side of the lane. She kept her head down as the car roared past, then gingerly got to her feet.

There was no way she could go back to the house now. With Madame gone the household would disperse. She could only return to her father's, but via the fields rather than the roads. Would they be out looking for her? Siobhan might have mentioned her as being a member of the Cumann na mBan, or maybe she hadn't. Ellen was only a simple housemaid, after all. Was she safe? Would her father be safe, if he harboured her? With Madame arrested, Ellen had never felt more alone. How could Siobhan have done such a thing? For money, presumably. Or to find favour with her brother.

By the time she was back at her father's cottage she'd realised the safest thing for everyone was for her to go today to this institution, if she could. Surely a religious institution like the Merciful Sisters would be safe from any raids by the RIC? She couldn't risk staying at home, in case the authorities were looking for her. She was on the run, just like Jimmy. If only she was actually with Jimmy — how much easier it would all be!

*　*　*

'Sure and what are you doing back here so soon?' her father asked, as Ellen hurried into the kitchen and collapsed in the nearest chair. 'I was after thinking you had another week to work.'

'There's been a raid, on Carlton House.

243

Madame's been arrested. I saw them put her in a motorcar. The RIC. They have her.'

'Always knew there was some dodgy dealings up at Carlton's,' her father grumbled. 'That woman, that *Madame* as you call her, she should have known her place and kept out of it. Fighting's a man's job. So is politics. No call for a woman to be involved.'

Ellen bit her lip. No point responding to this. Nothing she could say would change her father's mind. Thankfully, now that older women had the vote, and women could be elected to Parliament, and women like the Countess Markievicz and Madame Carlton were proving that women did indeed have a part to play in war and politics, things were beginning to change. But for now, she had her own predicament to worry about. And she did not want to put her father in danger.

'Da, I need to get away. I'm scared they'll come looking for me, because I worked at Carlton House and I was . . . ' She stopped herself in time. No need to tell him any more detail. The less he knew the safer he was. 'If they come for me, they might hurt you. That place you said, the Merciful Sisters, I should go there today, so I should.'

Her father nodded. 'Aye, you should. You've brought enough shame on us. You'll bring no more. I'll borrow Mickey Flanagan's pony and trap and take you there myself. Stay here and pack your things while I fetch it.' He hauled himself out of his chair, shoved a hat on his head, and left the cottage immediately.

Ellen stood staring after him for a minute. She

was grateful for the lift, but at the same time horrified that he seemed so desperate to get rid of her as quickly as possible. But the sooner she was gone the safer he would be. She climbed the steps to her old bedroom and looked around it. There was hardly anything here for her to pack. All her possessions were at Carlton House. Thankfully Jimmy's medallion was around her neck, not left in the bedroom she'd shared with Siobhan. It was the only thing she truly valued. There was only her overnight bag, which she'd brought from Carlton House the previous day, and that was already packed. Nothing else to add to it.

She wondered when she would see this room again. She'd be a mother, then. Would she be returning here with a babe in her arms? Would her father welcome her back? Somehow she doubted it. There were hard times ahead for her as an unmarried mother. Her only hope was that Jimmy would come for her.

Back downstairs, Ellen picked up her bag, sat on a chair at the kitchen table, and awaited her father's return. It wasn't long before she heard the sound of hooves and cart wheels clattering on the cobbles outside.

'Hop up then,' her father said, without meeting her eye.

She did as she was bid, and bade a silent goodbye to the cottage, Carlton House, Clonamurty Farm, Blackstown, the area where she'd spent her whole life. The Merciful Sisters institution was across the border into Dublin county, on the edge of the big city. It was as far

245

away as she'd ever been. In different circumstances she'd have been excited about the
journey, curious about the new country she was
travelling through. But all she could think about
was that she was travelling further away from
Jimmy. He was in hiding further north, in Cavan,
Madame had said, so travelling south towards
Dublin was putting more miles between them
with every minute that passed.

'Da?' she said, as they crossed the county
border. 'If Jimmy comes looking for me, promise
me you'll tell him where I am? It's his baby too.
He'll marry me, I'm sure of it.'

'Aye, if I see him I'll tell him.'

She gave him a weak smile. It was enough. It
was all she could ask of him, and it gave her at
least a little hope that things would work out for
them, in the end.

21

Clare, May 2016

The boys took a trip into Dublin the day after my not-date with Ryan. I dropped them off in Blackstown where there was a good bus service running into the city centre, and then went back home to the farmhouse. I had the whole day to myself, to prep dinner for the three of us that evening, to do a bit of work on the old chair, and finally, to do some research into the person whose birth certificate had been shoved inside that old chair for decades.

It was a day for me, at least until the boys came home in the evening, so I decided to start with a cup of coffee and my laptop and try that research. I took out the birth certificate, spread it on the kitchen table and weighted down the ends with a couple of clean mugs to stop it rolling up. Despite finding it weeks ago this was the first time I had looked closely at it. The writing was in a sloping copperplate script, hard to read, and I had to stare at it for some time before I could decipher the details.

The child's name was James O'Brien and there was no father listed. 'Born out of wedlock, little James,' I said, typing the names into a document on my PC. Date of birth 25th December 1920. A little Christmas baby! Place of birth: the Merciful Sisters Charitable Refuge for Penitent Females, Dublin. 'What on earth kind of place is that?' I muttered.

Well, there was one way to find out, so I typed the phrase into Google, clicked on a likely looking response, followed a few links and before long found myself reading a Wikipedia article about Magdalene Laundries. I'd heard of them, and vaguely recalled there was some sort of scandal surrounding them that was uncovered twenty years or so back, but knew no detail.

These places seemed to have started out with good intent, as a place where 'fallen women' could take shelter and be fed and housed and cared for in return for working in the laundry. Usually run by some religious order or other, some of them had still been active right up until the last decade of the twentieth century. Often the families of disgraced women would send their daughters to the laundry. It wouldn't be only pregnant girls ending up there; the institutions would also take those of 'low morals' — prostitutes or anyone caught having sex outside marriage, even if they'd been seduced or raped — as well as girls of limited mental capacity who, I assumed, the family just wanted to hide away somewhere.

Some women would enter a laundry and never again live outside, although others would just be there for a short stay. Presumably to have their babies. I wondered what happened to the babies afterwards — did the girls keep them? The articles I read suggested some babies were forcibly adopted against their mothers' wishes. Others were brought up in the laundries if their mothers stayed on. What a life. It was clear that conditions for the inmates were very harsh, with many reports of cruelty and abuse.

Following links on Google I came to a report from a few years previously — the scandal I'd vaguely recalled — about how a large number of children's remains had been excavated from the grounds of one Magdalene Laundry. Many small children had died there, it seemed, and been buried. There were no records of who they were. The last Magdalene Laundry had closed as late as 1996.

So unmarried Mary-Ellen O'Brien had got herself pregnant, ended up giving birth in a Magdalene Laundry, and then what? What had happened to the child? How had her baby's birth certificate ended up inside a chair in this farmhouse? She must have had a connection to this place. Perhaps she worked here, as a kitchen maid or dairy maid. Or did she know someone here? Maybe the child's father lived here . . .

A thought occurred to me. I retrieved the communion medallion from the mantelpiece and put it on the table beside the birth certificate. James Gallagher would have been around 20 when James O'Brien was born. I already knew from Ryan's research that a family named Gallagher owned Clonamurty Farm in the 1920s. Given the name Mary-Ellen chose for her baby, and the fact I'd found the birth certificate and medallion together, I felt it was almost certain that James Gallagher was the child's father.

I felt delighted with this bit of amateur sleuthing, and wrote some quick notes with relevant links in a document on my laptop. I couldn't wait to talk it all through with Ryan, and actually picked up my phone to call him. But then I stopped myself. Two reasons: firstly, he'd be at work and I didn't like to disturb him in the shop, and secondly, calling him the morning after our date and our kiss felt a bit pushy.

What would I say about last night? What would *he* say? What if he was regretting it? I wasn't sure how I felt about it — the kiss was lovely, but it was so soon after leaving Paul. Twenty-five years of marriage had left me with absolutely no idea how to handle starting a new relationship, if that's what we were doing here.

And what if Ryan had woken up this morning vowing never to see me again? If I called him, what if he took that as meaning I wanted to repeat our date on a night when my sons weren't in the house, and he could come in, and we could . . . Oh God. No. Not yet, anyway. I couldn't . . . it had been so long. Anyway, I decided not to call Ryan.

Which didn't mean I didn't sit there hoping he'd call me.

★ ★ ★

By mid-afternoon, I'd finished making notes on my research, eaten a bowl of soup for lunch, tidied up a bit and prepared a lasagne for dinner. I'd also re-webbed the chair and attached the springs. It was so satisfying rebuilding it. Just as I was rebuilding my life, here in Ireland.

I was in the kitchen, making a cup of tea, when I heard the front door, which I never used, rattle. Odd time for the post to arrive, I thought, and went to check. But there was no post on the doormat. The door rattled again. Someone was out there, trying to get in. I dithered for a moment, torn between wanting to run to the back door and lock it, or grabbing a poker from the sitting-room fireplace to use as a weapon against the intruder.

'Clare? Open the door, would you? It's raining out here.'

That voice. I froze. How could it be? Oh God.

'Paul?' I called out. 'What are you doing here?'

'Getting wet! Let me in,' he yelled. 'Please!'

'You have to come round the back.' Even as I said it, I wished I hadn't but what else could I do? I'd been putting off phoning him, and this was the result. Obviously he wanted to talk to me, face to face. And to be fair, we needed to do that. I couldn't turn him away. I remembered the kiss with Ryan the previous night, with a pang of guilt. Good job that had gone no further. I imagined what might have happened if Ryan had been here when Paul turned up. Not a pretty image.

'Still not fixed this door then?' I heard him grumble. A minute later he entered by the back door, his raincoat dripping on my doormat. He removed it, hung it on top of my leather jacket on the pegs by the door, and walked through to the sitting room leaving muddy footprints along the hall passage that I had just mopped.

I gritted my teeth and reminded myself to be

civilised. 'Hello, Paul. Tea?'

'Something stronger. Got any whiskey?'

'Sorry, no.' Why was I saying sorry?

'Wine? You must have some wine somewhere.'

I said nothing, but fetched a bottle of Rioja from the kitchen, a corkscrew and a single glass. I put them in front of him. 'Help yourself.'

He was silent as he uncorked the bottle, sat on the sofa and poured himself a large glass He drank half of it, grimacing. 'Shit wine, but it'll do. You never were any good at choosing decent wine, were you?'

'Well, I like it.'

'An uneducated palate. I failed to teach you what's decent and what's not.'

'Paul, I'm not a child to be taught. Now, would you tell me why you've come here?'

He stared at me, took another swig of wine, then composed his features into a sad kind of smile. 'OK, let's start again. It's been a long, tough journey, I got soaking wet outside your door, and snapped. Sorry.' His voice was softer now.

I just stared back. Paul saying sorry? Again? This would take some getting used to.

'So anyway, why I'm here . . . it's your birthday on Friday. Isn't it?'

'Ye-es.' He knew that. In all our years together he'd never forgotten my birthday. That was one thing I couldn't complain about.

'And it's a big one. And the boys are visiting you, aren't they? Matt told me.'

'They are.'

'Here, now?'

252

'Gone to Dublin for the day.'

He nodded. 'So I thought, we should all be together for your big day.'

It was the last thing I wanted. My visions of a little party with Janice and Ryan evaporated like smoke on the wind. 'Couldn't you have called and asked if it was all right to come?'

He shrugged and smiled. 'You'd have said no.'

'Yes, I would have.'

'So I wanted to just turn up. And I wanted to talk to you. Like grown-ups.' He took another sip of wine, then patted the sofa beside him. 'Listen, Clare. Sit down with me. Have a glass of wine — it's not bad. I'm sorry I said it was shit.'

I stared at him for a moment, then perched on the edge of the sofa, as far from him as I could. 'I don't want any wine. Go on. What do you want to talk about?'

'Us. What we had. Look, I realise we had problems. I get that you wanted more to do. A job, or whatever. I get that we needed to move on from how we'd lived when the kids were at home. I get that I probably didn't recognise this in time.

'But, Clare — we've been married twenty-five years. That's incredible. So many people I know of our generation are divorced or on their second or third marriages. We were strong. We had a great partnership — at least I always thought so. It's hard for me, realising that you didn't see it that way.' He sighed, and sipped more wine. I decided not to respond yet. I'd let him say all that he wanted to.

'I miss you, Clare. I miss the family life we

had. I miss having someone there to talk to, to share my life with. Is there any chance we could . . . try again?' He raised his eyes to mine. His expression was sad but hopeful. I half expected to see tears in his eyes after such an impassioned speech, but there weren't any.

How to respond to all that? I took a moment to think. Maybe I should have had that glass of wine after all. He was right that we'd lasted longer than so many of our contemporaries. I missed the family life too, but then, the boys were grown-up now. I took a deep breath and tried to answer.

'Paul, I don't know. I like it here, in Ireland. I'm beginning to make a life for myself. If I came back to England I think you'd . . . we'd soon slip back into our old ways and I'd be unhappy again. We had twenty-five years. A lot of it was good. But I don't want to go back to that.'

I didn't want to, did I? Even as I said it, I was unsure of myself. If Paul was really recognising that things needed to change, was there some way back for us?

'You could split your time, between here and home,' he said. 'Don't cut me off as completely as you have done. I wouldn't stand in your way. Just . . . come home now and again. For a couple of weeks each month, perhaps.

'What do you say, Clare? We could stay married, just living apart for some of the time. You come home to me now and again, and we'll have the boys to visit as well. Perhaps you'll allow me to come back here as well.' He glanced around the living room, with its threadbare carpet, peeling wallpaper and battered furniture. 'When you've

254

made the place more liveable, anyway.'

'I don't know,' I said, again. 'I really don't. Let's just see how we get on for the next couple of days. I assume you're in Ireland till after my birthday? Where are you staying? There's a couple of decent small hotels in Blackstown — .'

'Can I stay here?' he interrupted.

Paul asking permission rather than assuming was a novelty in itself. He did seem different. It'd be OK, I thought, as the boys were here too. An image of Ryan, cupping my face as he kissed me, flitted through my mind. I quickly suppressed it, before Paul noticed my flushed face.

'I'll go and make up a bed for you, then,' I said, and went off to do that. I had no more new linen. He'd have to have one of the ancient orange floral duvet covers. The only remaining spare bedroom was the smallest, tucked under the eaves, half filled with boxes as I had been using it as storage. It'd have to do.

★ ★ ★

I was still upstairs trying to make the little room respectable when I heard a car pull up outside. I peered out of the bedroom window and noticed Paul's Focus parked next to my hire car. The noise I'd heard was a taxi, and Matt and Jon were climbing out. They'd saved me a journey into Blackstown to collect them from the Dublin bus. I hurried downstairs to warn them Paul had come, and arrived at the foot of the stairs just in time to hear Matt say, 'Dad! What on earth are you doing here?'

'Aren't you pleased to see me, Matt? I'm here for your mum's big birthday, same as you. Isn't it nice that we're all together again? First time since last Christmas, isn't it? Jon! Good to see you, buddy.' Paul gave each son a manly hug, which they each reciprocated rather awkwardly.

'Hey, Mum. Got you a little present in Dublin,' Jon said, once he'd extricated himself from his father's embrace. He pulled a box of Bewley's chocolates from a carrier bag and handed them over.

'Thanks, love. Did you have a good day? Go on inside and I'll put the kettle on. Or is it beer o'clock yet?'

'Beer o'clock,' Matt said firmly, with a glance at his father.

'OK. I'll bring them through.'

⋆　⋆　⋆

It was an odd sort of evening. I'd made a lasagne and salad, another of the boys' old favourites. We sat around the battered old table in the kitchen. Paul kept up an air of jollity, making jokes and bantering with the boys. They played along, but threw me some questioning sideways glances at times.

Halfway through, my phone rang. It was Ryan.

'Hey!' I said, as I pushed my chair back to leave the room. Paul frowned, watching me go.

'Just checking how you are,' Ryan said, as I went out to the hallway. 'You know, after last night . . .'

'I'm fine. No regrets, if that's what you're

256

asking. It was a lovely evening.'

'Having fun with the boys?'

'Yes, it's great having them here. Although . . . '

'What?'

I'd always felt I could say anything to Ryan. I wanted to tell him what had happened. 'Paul turned up. It was totally unexpected. He . . . wants to talk. I think he's going to stay for a couple of days . . . '

'Ah. All right, so. Well, you have a full house. I'll let you get back to them. Bye, then.'

'I'll ring again in a couple of days,' I said.

'Sure. Speak to you later, then. Bye, now.' It was odd, hearing his voice, with Paul the other side of the kitchen door. I hadn't time to analyse my feelings about it all. There'd be a sleepless night or two ahead of me, I suspected.

I took a deep breath and went back into the kitchen, where Paul was telling the boys some long, involved anecdote about someone he worked with. The boys were laughing. Perhaps we could play happy families for a few days. Perhaps we'd even enjoy doing it. And then I'd make it clear once again to Paul that our marriage was over, though if we could stay on good terms, that would be a bonus for all of us. If that was how I still felt.

22

Ellen, Christmas 1920

Ellen had lived with the Merciful Sisters for four months now. Sometimes it seemed hard to imagine any other life, as she hauled a basket of wet laundry out of the wash room to hang on the lines outside, or the inside lines if it was raining. It was back-breaking work, and now that she was nearly full-term and as round as a bale of hay, it was getting harder and harder. She'd asked to be given lighter duties but the sister had scowled at her and told her she was lucky to have somewhere warm and safe to sleep and regular food, and not be out in the fields, and what more did she want?

There'd been no news of Jimmy. In all these months she'd had no visitors. Even her father had not come. He was too ashamed, she supposed. But it was Jimmy she'd been longing for. Surely, she told herself, if there was bad news of Jimmy her father would have come to tell her, or written to tell her. She wrote weekly letters to him, and had the occasional brief reply back. Da wasn't much of a letter-writer. She'd dared not ask for news of Jimmy or Madame Carlton directly, but surely her words, *Please let me know any news you hear of my friends, especially those closest to my heart*, were clear enough. All Da ever wrote was that the farm was still standing, the 'big house' was still closed, and that he'd not heard from her brothers in America and England.

Ellen often thought of Siobhan. She still had not forgiven herself for not warning Madame Carlton. Was Siobhan proud of her actions? Or had she come to regret what she'd done? Ellen supposed she'd never see her old room-mate again. That was for the best.

She did get some news from the outside world, from occasional newspapers that were passed around and read from cover to cover. Like the atrocity at Croke Park, when the RIC had opened fire on the crowd during a football game, in retaliation for the assassination of several under-cover British intelligence agents. Ellen had wept for those innocent people, enjoying their day of rest, who'd lost their lives just by being unlucky.

The one thing that kept her going was her friendship with one of the other girls. Mairead slept in the next bed to hers, in the dormitory they shared with six other women. Mairead had been living at the Merciful Sisters for two years. She'd been living in a room in Dublin where the rent was paid by her lover, who kept saying he was going to marry her as soon as he'd saved enough, but who'd turned out to be already married. When his wife found out, he stopped visiting, stopped paying the rent, and Mairead found herself out on the streets. She'd been arrested and charged with soliciting, although in truth she'd been simply begging, and sent to the Merciful Sisters, where she was admitted as a 'fallen woman'.

'Not fallen as far as you though,' Mairead had said, eyeing up Ellen's bump, with a twinkle in her eye.

Ellen had laughed. 'Awful expression, so it is. Why is it the women who've fallen? What about the men? I mean, it takes two . . . '

'Ah, tis the world we live in, Ellen, A man's world. They make the rules and we can only follow them.'

Her days since entering the Merciful Sisters had followed a pattern. A bell woke them at six o'clock, and they had to rise immediately, wash in cold water and dress in drab grey with a white apron, their hair covered with a white cap. Breakfast was a bowl of thin porridge and a cup of weak tea. From then until midday they worked in the laundry, opening the sacks of dirty laundry that came in daily — mostly sheets and uniforms from prisons and hospitals — leaning over huge tubs of steamy water, pummelling the laundry with huge wooden paddles, hauling it out, putting it through massive mangles and hanging it out to dry.

Lunch was a bowl of soup and a few ounces of gritty bread. More laundry work in the afternoon, from one till six. Often she'd be put to ironing sheets, then folding them ready for return. Her hands were red raw from the washing and there were several burn marks on her wrists from the irons.

The evening meal would be a slice of pie and a hot potato, with another cup of weak tea. There were daily church services, where the nuns would preach about penance and humility. If anyone stepped out of line or appeared to be slacking in their work, the punishment was a week of floor-scrubbing. And because the floors needed scrubbing every week, there was always someone being punished, whether they'd transgressed or not. Ellen had been set to do the floors twice. Her knees had been so sore by the end of each day she'd been barely able to stand.

Today it was Christmas Eve, but that meant no let-up in their chores. 'Sheets still get dirty at Christmas,' Sister Anthony said. 'Get to it. You have an extra hour for your lunch break tomorrow, when we will celebrate the birth of Our Lord, and for which you will be grateful.'

Ellen sighed, and stretched her back as she reached up to peg a sheet on the line in the yard outside. At that moment she felt a spot of rain. She glanced up at the darkening sky, put the sheet back in her basket and went over to speak to Sister Anthony, who was overseeing the day's work.

'Mother, I'm fearing it's about to rain. Will I peg these inside instead, save bringing them in later?'

The sister's face was thunderous. 'You'll peg them outside as you've been told. And if the good Lord sees fit to make it rain, you'll then fetch them in, put them back through the mangle, and hang them inside.'

'But Mother, I was only trying to save us the bother, if they get wet . . . ' As she spoke, the rain began to fall. Ellen picked up her basket of laundry and hurried towards the door that led back to the laundry room.

'Where do you think you are going? Get back here, and hang those sheets *outside* as you've been told!' Sister Anthony was standing under the eaves of the building, sheltered. As she spoke, two other girls, including Mairead, came running out to bring in the other laundry that was already hanging outside.

Ellen stared at the nun. It was ridiculous, hanging this set out only to give them all more work. But Sister Anthony was glaring at her, and there was no choice. She hoisted the heavy basket onto her hip, ignored the feeling of a tightening band around her bump that she'd been experiencing all day, and went back to the washing line. Mairead ran over to her.

'This is madness, so it is,' whispered Mairead. 'Let me help.'

Ellen shook her head. 'You'll only get in trouble yourself. I'll do it.'

Mairead pressed her lips together but ignored her, pulling the sheets out of the basket and helping hang them up, while the rain grew steadily heavier. As soon as they were all pegged up they looked over to Sister Anthony, who nodded her approval for them to be taken down again. The basket was too heavy for Ellen to carry in by herself, now that the sheets were soaking, but Mairead helped. The two of them were drenched, rain water dripping from their hair and noses, their aprons and dresses soaked through, their shoes muddy.

'Look at the state of you,' Sister Anthony grumbled as they went indoors. 'Clean yourselves up. Then report to me for your punishments.'

'Yes, Mother,' the girls said, and hurried off to their dormitory. They had two uniforms each, so could change into the other set and hang the wet clothes on the bentwood chairs each woman had beside her bed, to dry.

Ellen felt that tightening again, as she bent to remove her wet stockings. She put a hand on her midriff and tried to suppress a groan.

'Are you all right? Is it — is it your time coming?' Mairead put a hand on her shoulder.

'Ah no. I'm grand. No, I don't think it's my time till the middle of January, as far as I can work out. Just the baby moving, I suppose.' Ellen smiled, hoping to reassure her friend. No need for Mairead to be worrying about her. She'd heard from other women in the laundry, that the body sometimes 'practised' contractions, a month or even more before the due date. That was all that was happening, she was sure.

In dry clothes, they reported back to Sister Anthony as ordered, and stood before her with hands clasped in front, heads lowered.

'Mairead, you'll miss your dinner tonight and instead will spend the time praying for forgiveness in the chapel. I'm being lenient on you as I know you did what you did only out of concern for your friend. But I'll not have disobedience. The work was Ellen's to complete and she should have been left to do it alone.'

Out of the corner of her eye Ellen saw Mairead open her mouth as if to speak. She nudged her friend gently with her elbow. Don't say anything, she thought, it'll only make it worse. One missed dinner wasn't too bad a punishment. One of the girls would smuggle a piece of bread up to the dormitory for Mairead to eat later.

'And as for you, Mary-Ellen, you're on floor-cleaning duty for the next fortnight. Starting this afternoon.'

'Ah, but Mother,' Mairead blurted out, 'Ellen's baby is almost due, and sure isn't scrubbing the floors hard enough without having the weight of a baby pulling you down too? May I do the floors instead of her? Maybe Ellen could take her turn later, after her baby's come?'

Ellen held her breath awaiting the nun's response to this. While she hated the idea of Mairead doing floors for two weeks, she knew her friend was right — in her condition she'd never manage to spend two weeks on her knees, scrubbing. How she'd ever make it up to Mairead she didn't know, but she'd find a way.

'And another harlot tries to tell me how to run this place! My word is law here, not yours. How dare you try to tell me who'll scrub the floors and when. Mary-Ellen will do them for the next fortnight. And you, Mairead, will do them the fortnight after that, for your insolence. Away with you both. Back to your duties. Mary-Ellen, the first-floor corridor today, for you.'

There was no point saying anything more. Mairead squeezed Ellen's hand as they left. 'Take it easy,' she whispered. 'They won't even notice how well it's scrubbed. I'll come past as often as I can to check you're all right.'

Ellen smiled her thanks and went to collect a bucket of water and scrubbing brush. If only there was something she could kneel on while she worked, but there was nothing, other than taking her shoes off and kneeling on those. She tried this, but the buckles on her shoes hurt her knees as much as the floor would, and her toes were cold. The baby seemed heavy as she knelt and stretched and scrubbed. Her back began aching, so much so she could only scrub a small patch before she needed to sit up and arch backwards to ease the pain.

And those tightenings continued, growing stronger and more insistent, more frequent and longer. Were they still those practice contractions the other girls who'd given birth had talked about? Or were they — she hardly dared even think the words to herself — were they the real thing? Was it starting?

She kept going, scrubbing, stretching, trying to breathe deeply through the contractions, trying to keep an image of Jimmy at the forefront of her mind. It was Christmas tomorrow. What she would give to be able to spend it with him! Next year. Ireland would be independent, Jimmy would be home, they would be married and the two of them, no, the *three* of them, would be living in a little cottage somewhere near Blackstown, keeping their own chickens, farming their own few acres. Or maybe Jimmy would be at college, training to be a lawyer, and they'd be renting rooms in Dublin. Either way, she'd be there, alongside him, raising his child.

Another contraction hit, this one fiercer than all the others, and Ellen could not stop herself from letting out a long, low moan. She lay on the

265

floor, curled up, her arms around her bump. She became aware there was something wet between her legs — was it what the other mothers had called her waters breaking? When the contraction eased off she hauled herself to her feet and staggered along the corridor towards the hospital wing. Coming the other way was Sister Anthony.

'Shirking your job, Mary-Ellen O'Brien? Get back to it at once!' The nun caught hold of Ellen's arm and pushed her backwards.

'Mother, I can't, the baby . . . ' and at that moment, another contraction hit. Ellen leaned against the wall, doubled over, moaning in pain. The pain became everything, her whole world, and it was only as it tailed off that she realised the sister was still standing beside her. 'I'll get on . . . ' she began to say, but Sister Anthony's expression had changed.

'No. You need to be in the hospital wing. That baby of yours will be here any moment now, so it will. Come on.'

The nun took hold of Ellen's arm again, but not roughly this time, more supportive. Ellen allowed herself to be led along. It was the first time she'd experienced anything approaching kindness from this nun, although some of the others weren't as bad. The next contraction hit just as they entered the hospital wing, and another sister rushed over to help Ellen onto a bed.

'Stop your yelling now, you'll upset the other girls and wake the babies,' this new sister, who Ellen didn't know, scolded. ''Tis only natural — it doesn't hurt, so stop making such a fuss about it all. To be sure, tis your own fault you've a baby in you anyway.'

'I'll be leaving you to it,' Sister Anthony said, giving a curt nod in the general direction of Ellen's bed.

'Mother, will you tell Mairead where I am? Please, if it's not too much bother . . . '

The nun regarded her with cold eyes for a moment, and then nodded once more, before leaving the room.

'Now then, let me have a look at you,' the new sister said, and she forced Ellen's knees apart and tore at her underclothes. Ellen tried to stop her, but the nun scowled. 'How am I to see how far gone you are if I can't have a look? Down there's where the baby comes out, so you'll have to take your bloomers off sooner or later.'

There was a logic to what she was saying, so Ellen lay back, let her remaining dignity dissolve around her, and tried to mentally prepare herself for the next contraction. There were two other girls in the room. Not mothers, but sick inmates. They at least had the decency to turn onto their sides, facing away from Ellen, while the nun examined her. She winced as the nun's fingers swooped around inside her.

'Hmph. Barely dilated at all. You've hours to go, so you have. You should still be at work, not lying here idle. I suppose I could put you to work in here . . . ' The sister broke off speaking as another contraction hit. Ellen clamped her lips together to stop herself from groaning, and curled on her side on the bed. When it subsided, the sister carried on speaking as though nothing had happened. 'You could fold some linens

267

between the pains. And when the pains hit, breathe through them, girl. Don't be holding your breath — it makes them worse. All right so, I'll bring you a basket of clean laundry to fold. There's darning needs doing, too.' The hours passed slowly, with contractions coming every few minutes, and baskets of clean laundry for folding or woollen stockings for mending appearing regularly. The sanatorium smelled of carbolic soap — a scent Ellen had never liked and which seemed more offensive than ever now. The other girls spent the day asleep, or lying quietly watching her. Ellen tried to smile and make friends but neither of them responded. Either they were too sick or too scared of the nun in charge to open their mouths. Mairead managed to look in on her once, arriving with a made-up message for the sister in charge of the sanatorium.

'I can't believe they're making you work,' she whispered.

'Ah, it's all right. Takes my mind off things. I may as well be useful while I'm here,' Ellen replied.

'You're an angel, so you are. Your reward's in heaven.'

Mairead couldn't stay long, but Ellen appreciated the visit.

It was a long, sleepless night. The sister would not allow Ellen to eat anything, other than sips of weak tea. 'You'll only throw it up, and then we'll be having more work to do,' she said. Ellen didn't feel much like eating anyway. The pains were still coming, gradually stronger, wearing her down. The sister had examined her again and said she was still in the early stages.

'Will it hurt more as the time goes on?' Ellen asked.

'I'm after telling you, it doesn't hurt, aren't I? You girls make such a fuss.'

It's all right for you, Ellen thought, you've never had a baby. She completed a darning job the sister had given her and collapsed onto the bed assigned to her, grateful for the opportunity to sleep at last.

But there was no sleep for her that night. She'd be on the point of dozing off when the next contraction hit, and then she'd lie, twisting the sheets in her fists, clamping her teeth together to try to stop herself crying out. She discovered if she disappeared into her imagination with each contraction, dreaming of a country cottage, with roses around the door and Jimmy tending to their fields, the pain was more bearable.

When her baby came Ellen knew she'd have to return to work, visiting the baby in the nursery wing a few times a day just to feed him or her. Once babies were weaned they were cared for by a group of Sisters, and their mothers would be allowed to see them for a few minutes once a day. Ellen had not let herself think about life with the Merciful Sisters after the birth of her child, or the prospect of being kept apart from her baby. She'd been so sure Jimmy would come for her before that happened. Or perhaps she could leave, with the baby, and return to her father — if he would only have her back, with the shame of her infant in her arms.

As another contraction hit she decided not to think on it now. There was no point. She needed all her strength, both physical and mental, for the next few hours or however long it took for the baby to come.

At last, as the weak December dawn brought light into the room, and another nun — Sister Mary Magdalene — came to check on her progress, a contraction that felt different to the previous ones began. This one felt as though it had purpose. Rather than just a tightening band, making her gasp with pain, this one brought with it a different quality — an urge to push. The sister grasped her hand as Ellen yelled out.

As the contraction subsided Ellen stared at the nun. 'I'm sorry sister, for calling out, I couldn't help myself.'

'Ah, tis to be expected. You're into the last stage now, I'd say. The baby will be here in an hour, or less. We'll get you ready. Can you kneel up, turn round, hold on to the top end of the bed? And you two' — she turned to the other girls in the room — 'can stop staring. Mary-Ellen's going to be making some noise now, and it's only natural.'

Ellen gave her a weak, grateful smile. This sister was much kinder and more sympathetic than the one who'd been here the previous day. 'Mother, will you stay with me, please?'

'Aye, I will. You've not so long to go. Now come on, move position before your next pain comes.'

Ellen did as she was told, moving onto her

knees facing the wall at the head of her bed. She gripped the bedstead tightly as each contraction came, and found that being upright helped — as though gravity was helping push the baby out.

'That's good, now, push with the pain, Mary-Ellen, good girl,' encouraged Sister Mary Magdalene.

The pain was excruciating. Ellen felt as though she was being torn in half. During one contraction the nun gripped her arm. 'I can see the head; we're nearly there. Need to slow it down — pant a little, like a dog, try not to push for a moment.'

Ellen did what she was told, and the contraction ended, but still that burning, searing pain in her most intimate area went on. She was both longing for and dreading the next contraction — the sooner it came the sooner it would be over, but would she be able to bear the pain? A thought of Jimmy came into her head — Jimmy's face when he met their child, his expression of pure love and wonder — yes, it would all be worth it for that moment, and surely that moment would not be far away. She'd have the baby and find a way out of here, back to Da, back to Blackstown where she'd find a way to discover where Jimmy was . . .

When the contraction came it was the strongest yet, and the burning, tearing feeling was unbearable. Someone was screaming, an animal noise like a fox in a trap, and it was a moment before she realised the sound was coming from her . . . and then there was a rush, an unbelievable gushing slithering rush of relief as the baby slid out of her, into the sister's hands . . . and her legs began to shake uncontrollably. No longer able to kneel she tried to sit back but the nun pushed her upright. 'Don't want to be sitting on your little boy now, do you?'

A boy! It was a boy! Jimmy's son! Ellen was gasping and panting and desperate to turn to see the child, but the nun was busy doing something there behind her, wiping, folding, putting something on the bed. There was a whimpering noise, a sound like a newborn puppy nuzzling its mother for milk, and she realised that was him. That was her baby. Her son. Her Christmas present to Jimmy.

'All right, so, you can sit back now. Turn yourself around. I'll put a pillow behind you. Still got the afterbirth to come, so there'll be more contractions, you know, but you can hold him now.'

Once she was in position Sister Mary Magdalene placed a bundle wrapped tightly in cloths in her arms. Only a small, red face, eyes tightly closed, mouth puckering into a tiny cry, forehead wrinkled as though with worry about the world he'd been born into, was exposed.

'Oh, my boy, my darling boy!' Ellen whispered, kissing the child and holding him close. He immediately tried to turn his head towards her, mouth open wide.

'He's looking to feed. He can wait a little, mind. You've the afterbirth to get out of you first. Lie back on that pillow.'

As she said this, a contraction came, much weaker than before but still with that urge to push. Ellen heaved, and there was another slithering rush, and then the nun was taking something away in a covered bowl.

She was back a moment later, and helped Ellen get the baby latched on and suckling. 'There. He's a hungry little lad, after all that. I'll leave you to it. I'll be back when he's finished and sleeping, and then we can see about cleaning you up and making the bed, and you can have a sleep.'

But Ellen felt so alive, all her senses alert, as though she'd never need to sleep again. As the baby fed, she gazed down at his perfect, soft little head and felt the most profound sense of love and completeness she'd ever experienced. He opened his eyes and stared at her with deep blue eyes, looking like an old soul in the youngest of bodies.

She smiled at him. 'Ah, son. I'm very pleased to meet you, so I am. And so will your father be. He'll be delighted to make your acquaintance. Oh yes, young man, we're going to be a very happy family, when we're all together at last.'

23

Clare

The morning after Paul arrived, Thursday — the day before my birthday — we all set off into Blackstown. Despite the size of the farmhouse, ever since Paul's arrival it had begun to feel claustrophobic. A trip into town would be a relief. I'd raved about the cakes in Janice's café, and was looking forward to choosing the biggest, most calorie-laden cake and enjoying eating every crumb of it in front of Paul. It was hard to believe that the first time I'd visited that café I'd allowed him to bully me out of having cake. No more. The old Clare, giving in to everything Paul said, allowing herself to be walked over, sat upon and bullied, was gone. Whatever happened between us in the future, I was not going to let that happen again.

We did a spot of shopping first; the boys and Paul good-naturedly joshing and joking as we trawled the aisles for supplies for the next couple of days. Paul, thankfully, had said he was booked on the car ferry for Saturday, the day after my birthday. Today, while we were out, he was behaving, and the old, fun, charming Paul I'd originally fallen in love with, was on show.

'Let's all eat out tomorrow,' I said, as we walked along Blackstown High Street towards the café. I'd given up on the idea of inviting

Ryan and Janice round and had planned on cooking for myself and the boys, but since Paul seemed easier to get along with out of the house, it made sense to go out for dinner instead.

'Great idea,' Matt said. 'You shouldn't have to cook on your birthday.'

'Yes, very good idea. I'll treat us all.' Paul smiled beneficently at me.

'No need, I can ... ' I began, and then stopped. Why not let him pay? It's what he liked best — being the Great Benefactor, the man with the wallet, the generous husband. And to be fair, he had always been generous when it came to treating me and the boys. Just a shame I'd never been allowed any money of my own, beyond what he'd given me for housekeeping.

On the side of a bus stop there was a poster advertising The Carlton, the restaurant I'd been to with Ryan. Paul stopped in front of it.

'This looks nice,' he said.

'It is,' I agreed automatically, then cursed myself. I'd wanted to keep this place as somewhere special for Ryan and me. But then, tomorrow was my fiftieth birthday, I had my sons with me, and it deserved to be a special occasion. As long as Paul continued to act reasonably and respectfully towards me, as he had done this morning, we'd be all right.

Paul pulled out his mobile and punched in the number displayed at the foot of the billboard.

'Yeah, table for four tomorrow evening please. Eight o'clock. Name's Farrell. Perfect, cheers.' He turned to face us all looking pleased with himself. 'Right, that's all sorted. I'm surprised you didn't have something planned and booked already, Clare.'

I gritted my teeth. Seemed he couldn't keep the snarky comments to himself for long, then. 'OK, great. Come on, chaps, let's get to the café before they run out of my favourite chocolate fudge cake.' I linked arms with both Matt and Jon and marched off before Paul could say anything more.

As we approached the café I glanced over at Ryan's bookshop opposite, but couldn't see him inside, as the sun was reflecting off the windows. Paul darted in front of me and held the café door open for the rest of us, as Jon made some wisecrack about how if it had been a pub rather than a café Paul would have been the first through the door not the last, that had us all guffawing as we entered.

'Hey there!' Janice greeted me with a grin as we chose a table near the window. 'These your boys, are they? Fine lads. And this is . . . ?'

'Um, this is Paul. And my sons, Matt, Jon,' I said, pointing to the boys. 'Guys, this is my friend Janice.'

There were a number of hellos and hand-shakes, between which she glanced quizzically at me, and I shrugged in reply. I'd never told her all the detail about what had gone wrong in our marriage, but she certainly knew my husband's name was Paul, and she'd be wondering why he was here now. She'd have to wait to hear the full story.

We ordered coffees and cakes, and thankfully Paul did not make any comments about my choices or my weight. He even ordered carrot cake for himself, and made a point of praising Janice on its moistness and flavour.

'So, your birthday tomorrow, is it?' Janice asked. I nodded and she darted into the café's kitchen and emerged with a large cake box. 'Made you a little something as a present, to help celebrate it. Oh, and here's your card.' She pulled an envelope out of her apron pocket and put it on top of the box, on the table.

'Aw, thanks, you shouldn't have!' I felt tears pricking my eyes. I'd only known this woman five minutes yet here she was baking me birthday cakes.

'Yes I should. And when you've got more time, you and I are having a girls' night out to celebrate it. Deal?'

'Deal!' I laughed, and she clapped me on the back as she returned to her work.

'She's nice,' Matt said.

'Go on, open the cake box!' Jon started picking at the sticky tape that held it closed.

'No, not till tomorrow,' I said, feeling suddenly protective of my cake. When had anyone last made me a birthday cake? I'd baked my own, or had shop-bought ones, other than that time when Jon was 10 and had made me a chocolate cake from a packet mix as a surprise. (The main surprise had been the state of the kitchen afterwards.) This felt truly special.

When we left the café I suggested Matt, Jon and Paul should go ahead with the shopping and the cake, as I needed to pick up a few more things in Dunnes Stores — a couple of towels and a set of wine glasses as I'd realised there were only three in the house. 'I'll be five minutes,' I told them.

'Be as long as you like,' Paul said. 'We'll drop the stuff off in the car and then go for a pint. Been ages since I had a drink with my sons. All right, boys?'

'Sure!' they both said, and off the three of them went. I was pleased. Whatever happened between Paul and me I wanted to make sure the boys still had a good relationship with their father.

As I passed by the bookshop again, I glanced through the window. Ryan was there, looking out, and when he saw me he beckoned me inside. Paul and the boys had already turned a corner towards the car park, so I went in.

'Hey, Clare. I thought I saw you earlier, going into Janice's café.' He seemed tense, and did not move to kiss or even hug me.

'Yes, we had coffee and a cake,' I replied. So he had seen us. All of us.

'You, your two sons, and Paul.' Ryan looked at me, a question in his eyes. 'That's nice. All of you together for your birthday, then.'

'Yes, but . . . he won't stay long and then . . . '

Ryan held up a hand. 'It's all right. I understand. I'll keep out of the way. You enjoy yourselves. Thanks for the other night. It was . . . lovely.'

'Yes, I enjoyed it too,' I said, but Ryan had turned away to serve a customer. I gave him a little wave and left the shop.

Seeing Ryan again, being with Paul today

when he was being charming and fun — it all felt so confusing. My past on the one hand, and was it my future on the other? Or was Ryan destined to be only ever a friend, with whom I'd shared a single, ill-advised kiss while going through a bad patch with my husband? Who knew. I couldn't see what the future held.

★   ★   ★

I did the rest of the shopping, found the fellas in the pub having an in-depth conversation about the likelihood of Leicester beating Munster in a forthcoming rugby match, and dragged them back home to help unpack the shopping. No one needed lunch after our huge portions of cake in Janice's café. I suggested a walk through the fields behind the house — there was a bridleway that led towards a small copse and beyond that, to the banks of the Boyne and I'd long since been meaning to explore it.

'Think I'll have a snooze in the sitting room,' Paul said. 'I didn't sleep all that well in that tiny bedroom. You three go for the walk, leave me here with a cup of tea and the TV remote.'

It seemed odd to leave him alone in *my* house — I fleetingly wondered what he'd get up to on his own. Would he rummage through my possessions, looking for evidence of . . . what? Another man? Was there anything to make him suspicious, make him guess at the existence of Ryan? No, nothing I could think of. For goodness' sake, I'd only had one evening out with Ryan, and shared one kiss. There was nothing incriminating in the house; nothing I would care about Paul finding.

Except perhaps the birth certificate, communion medallion, and my research notes. I could imagine Paul's scathing tones if I tried to explain why I was researching who lived here a hundred years ago. He'd dismiss it as an utter waste of time — at least the old Paul would have. Maybe now he'd be more interested, or at least pretend he was. Either way, I didn't want to have that conversation. Before we left, I tucked my laptop and the items from the old chair away in a drawer in my bedroom.

Matt, Jon and I donned walking boots and macs — the day was fine but clouds on the horizon and a stiff breeze threatened sudden change. The track was muddy and churned by horses' hooves. We set off, walking three abreast on the wide bridleway.

'Hey, slow down a little,' I said. 'You forget that I only have little legs compared to you two.'

'Aw, Midget Mummy,' said Jon, using a nickname he'd given me from the moment, aged 14, he'd discovered he was taller than me. But they slowed down anyway.

We chatted about this and that. I told them what I knew of the history of the area, repeating some of what Ryan had told me about the Battle of the Boyne, the United Irishmen's 1798 rebellion, and the twentieth-century War of Independence. I told them the latest news of my research into the medallion and birth certificate, and about the notes on Granny Irish that I'd found in Daithi's exercise books.

We reached the banks of the Boyne, and turned onto a footpath that ran alongside it. There was a bench overlooking a pretty spot, so we decided to sit down and rest for a moment.

'Should have brought a picnic,' I commented.

'Could have brought your birthday cake,' Jon said.

'Here, have a fruit pastille.' Matt pulled a packet out of his pocket and offered them round. 'Actually, Mum, while we sit here, away from . . . well . . . away from Dad, there's something I wanted to ask you.'

'Ooh er, that sounds ominous,' I joked, but he was looking serious. So was Jon.

'I'll come straight out with it. Hope you don't mind. It's this — are you planning on getting back together with Dad?'

'Because we don't think you should,' added Jon.

'Well, I only — '

'In the pub today,' Matt interrupted, 'there was something Dad said that made me worried. He said if he played his cards right, you'd go back to him. And that he was pretty sure you would. He said he reckoned he'd get you to do what he wanted, one way or another.'

'He's manipulating you, Mum,' Jon added. 'Don't let him. You've done the right thing coming here.'

'Yeah, I reckon you'll love it here, once you're settled. The people are so friendly. The farm is amazing — or will be once it's had the Clare Farrell treatment top to bottom. And you seem — or did seem, until Dad turned up — so much happier than you were.' Matt put another fruit pastille into his mouth and chewed it thoughtfully. 'So what I'm saying is, I hope you'll give it serious consideration before you agree to go back to him.'

Jon took another pastille from the packet. 'Just don't do it. And if you're thinking you should for our benefit, stop thinking that. It's all about you.'

I smiled. Here they were again, my lovely sons, counselling me. And they were right. There was no way I wanted to lose the bit of independence I'd fought for and won. 'It's all right. I don't intend moving back to England to your dad. At least not permanently. I want to stay here. I don't know if we'll stay married or not. But if we can be amicable about it, and somehow manage to stay friends, of a kind — surely that's better? Your dad seems to be making an effort. I think I should do the same. But whatever happens, I won't let him manipulate me. Not any more.'

Matt grinned and hugged me. 'Attagirl!'

'*Attagirl*?' Jon laughed. 'What century are you even in, Matt? But yeah. Way to go, Mum, way to go.'

24

Ellen, March 1921

Life had settled into a new routine at the Merciful Sisters. Little James was now three months old, but there'd still not been any sign of Jimmy. Letters from Ellen's father were as sparse and uninformative as ever. He'd written to say he was glad she'd survived the birth of the child, but had not congratulated her in any way or made any suggestion that she might go home. When she'd written to ask him directly if he'd take her back, he'd ignored the question. Ellen had been out of the institution just once since the baby's birth, to the registry office to register little James's birth, accompanied by Sister Anthony.

'You'll be leaving the father's name blank, no doubt,' the nun said, her face showing even more disapproval than ever.

'No I won't. I'm proud of this baby's father, so I am, and I know he'll be proud of his son too.' Ellen glared at Sister Anthony.

'If you're not married and the father isn't here to register the birth, then you cannot put his name on the certificate,' the nun said. 'And that's all there is to it.'

Ellen had not been able to get her way about naming Jimmy; however, she had managed to keep hold of the birth certificate. They were usually kept by the nuns, locked away in a filing cabinet in an office, but Sister Anthony seemed distracted as they returned to the institution, and hurried away without taking the certificate from Ellen. She'd tucked it away, under her mattress, along with Jimmy's communion medallion. Precious things, which reminded her there was another life waiting for her, outside of this place, with Jimmy by her side.

★ ★ ★

But there seemed no way out. The outer doors were kept locked at all times. 'May as well be in a prison,' Ellen said to Mairead. 'At least then you'd be allowed out when your sentence was over.'

Mairead nodded. The two of them were side by side in the laundry room, up to their elbows in soapy water, their hands red and raw, as they scrubbed at mounds of dirty linen. 'I'm after thinking those in prison aren't worked as hard as we are, too. I wonder what the food's like.'

'No worse than here, I'd reckon,' Ellen said. She glanced at the clock on the wall, and smiled. 'Time for me to go and feed my little James.' She dried her hands and went off to the nursery wing. It was her favourite part of the day. When James was born, she'd been allowed to hold him and feed him six times a day at strict four-hourly intervals.

Gradually the timings had changed and many feeds were now administered by bottle by the nuns, but she was still feeding him twice a day,

284

early morning and late afternoon. Those precious moments, holding him in her arms that ached whenever she was not with him, gazing at his blue eyes as he fed, tickling him to make him smile while she changed his nappy, holding him over her shoulder to wind him when he'd finished feeding and then rocking him to sleep, were all that kept her going.

As time went on her fears for Jimmy grew. Why hadn't he come to find her? Why was there no news? She could only hope that Madame Carlton's words were true — that no news was good news.

'If only your daddy could see you now,' she whispered to little James, as she got him latched on and suckling. 'I'm going to have to find a way to get us both out of here, and go to look for him. Would you like that, hmm? Would you like to meet your daddy?'

As if he understood and agreed with every word, little James broke off from feeding for a moment and gave her a wide, toothless grin. She smiled back. 'I'll take that as a yes, then. All right. I'll make a plan. Don't you go saying anything to the nuns, now. They wouldn't like it, so they wouldn't.'

Her mind was made up. She had to find a way out. She spent the next couple of weeks thinking of nothing else, discussing possibilities in whispers with Mairead. But no plans presented themselves. She wrote to her Da begging him once more to come and fetch them, promising she'd find somewhere to live away from Blackstown if he was concerned about the shame she'd bring, but had no reply. That worried her. He'd never written much but he'd always replied to her letters. What had happened to him?

Not for the first time she wished that Madame Carlton was still at Carlton House, so she could write to her for help. But Madame was probably in prison somewhere, with enough troubles of her own to deal with.

The weather was improving, and sheets from the laundry could be hung outside most days, on the lines in the yard. There was an eight-foot-high brick wall all around the yard, but Ellen knew at the far end it backed onto a road. You could hear the traffic passing — horses' hooves, carriage wheels, occasional motorcars and buses. There was a blue-painted gate set into the wall, but Ellen had never seen it used. To the side, another gate led through to a second yard. This was also kept locked. The girls weren't allowed into the second yard, and no one knew what it was used for.

'A pleasure garden, for the nuns to sit in and sip their coffee,' Mairead had suggested.

'A vegetable patch?' Ellen said.

'No. If it was that, we'd be the ones out there tending it, wouldn't we, so?' Mairead replied. She had a point. Ellen had not seen the nuns do any real work at all, except for Sister Mary Magdalene in the sanatorium.

*　*　*

A plan began to formulate itself in her mind a couple of days later. Ellen was hanging out washing, when a nun came out into the yard and opened the gate in the side wall, went through to the second yard leaving the gate ajar.

Ellen checked no one was watching and tiptoed over to peek through. She was shocked to see the nun was digging — but not a vegetable patch. It looked more like a grave. Had someone died? She'd heard nothing about any tragedies. The grave wasn't very big. Just three feet or so in length. Elsewhere in that second yard there were other patches of ground that looked as though they'd been dug, small mounds here and there. It was very clearly a graveyard, but there were no grave markers. Ellen shivered. More than ever she felt she had to get herself and little James out from under the control of the Merciful Sisters.

That's when she noticed another gate, in the end wall of that second yard. It must open onto the road, like the one in the end wall of the drying yard. But this one seemed to be secured only by bolts on the inside, with no lock. So anyone in that graveyard, if that's what it was, would easily be able to get out onto the street. She glanced up at the building. There were no windows directly overlooking that yard. The question was, how would she gain access to it? The gate between the two yards was always kept locked.

Maybe she'd be able to slip through, when the nun's back was turned. But no, it was too far across the yard, and the bolts might be stiff or squeak, and in any case, how could she collect little James first?

A few minutes later the nun came out of the

second yard and locked the gate behind her. Ellen noticed that she had to pull hard on the gate to make it latch, before turning the key in the lock.

That night, in bed, she held a whispered conversation with Mairead.

'All I'm saying, is if I disappear, will you look after James for me? See if you can check in on him each day. I'd only be gone a couple of days at most, then I'll be back, with either Jimmy or my father, or someone else who'd sponsor me, and then I'd take James away.'

'Of course I'll do it, so, but how will you get out?'

Ellen told her about the second yard, and the gate to the road. 'I'm going to watch for my chance, and get out that way when I can. I can't say when it'll happen, but one day the chance will be there, and if I can rely on you to look after James I'll be able to go.'

Mairead reached out a hand in the darkness to Ellen. 'You can rely on me. I promise. You'd do the same for me if I had a little one, I know.'

'When I've somewhere to live, I'll come back again for you.'

They held hands in silence for a moment, and then Mairead whispered again. 'Who do you think is buried in that yard?'

Ellen brushed away the tear that had formed at Mairead's question. 'Children. Babies. Those graves are too small for it to be anything else.'

It was another week before the chance Ellen had been looking for arose. She'd made a point of volunteering to be on washing-line duty

— not a popular job as the baskets of wet sheets were heavy and it was back-breaking work. She'd taken to carrying her most precious possessions — James's birth certificate and Jimmy's medallion — with her at all times, in a hidden pocket she'd sewn into her skirt, so she was ready to go at any time.

And then one day as she pegged another load of sheets on the lines, she noticed a nun coming out of the second yard. Ellen watched from the corner of her eye as the sister pulled the gate closed. Just then the nun was summoned from the main building by Sister Anthony, and had to hurry locking the gate. Ellen could see it had failed to latch properly.

This was it. This was her chance. She took a quick look around. No one else was outside or near the door. She darted across the yard, through the gate and pushed it closed behind her, then ran to the gate in the end wall. Her heart was breaking at the thought of leaving little James, but it was only for a couple of days at most, and Mairead would do her best to keep an eye on him.

The bolts were rusty as she'd feared, but with a bit of jiggling she got them free, and pulled open the gate. It opened directly onto the street. She slipped through, and pulled the gate closed behind her. The hinges were rusty too, so that the gate stayed in its shut position, although of course she knew it wouldn't be long before her absence was noted.

Now, she needed to get to Blackstown. She had no money. She'd walk if she had to, but maybe once she was far enough away from the laundry she could try to get a lift from someone. She hurried down the street. No one had noticed her slip out, and once she turned the corner onto a busier road she felt she could blend in with the crowd. She walked, heading northwards, following road signs pointing to towns she knew were in the right direction — in County Meath — for hours. Her feet were sore and blistered, she was hungry and exhausted, but every step led her closer to finding Jimmy, closer to freedom and a future for her, Jimmy and little James.

She soon left Dublin and the road she was following began to be flanked by fields and farms. Would she come across any road-blocks? How she would get past RIC or Black and Tans she did not know. She prayed she was passing through areas controlled by the Volunteers. She wondered if she'd dare ask any Volunteers she came across if they had news of Jimmy. Maybe they'd help her. She'd done her part for them in the past, hadn't she? But how could she prove she was on their side?

She was some distance out of town when a farm cart passed her, and then stopped. The farmer jumped down and approached her.

'What's a young colleen like yourself doing walking alone on this road? There was fighting here last week. Tis not safe.'

'I'm . . . heading to Blackstown. My Da lives near there,' Ellen replied, thinking it was probably best to stick as close to the truth as possible.

'Aye. Well you'd best jump up then. I'm going that way.'

Ellen smiled her thanks and climbed up onto the box. The farmer sat alongside her, but thankfully he didn't question her further, except to ask where she'd been.

'Staying with a friend,' she replied, thinking that Mairead was her friend, and she'd been living in the same room as her, so actually her answer hadn't been too far from the truth.

'Hmph. A long walk back,' was the farmer's only reply, before he lapsed into silence.

★　★　★

It was dark before they neared the edge of Blackstown. The farmer stopped the cart at a junction. 'I'm after wanting to go this way,' he said, 'but Blackstown's just a half-mile in that direction. You'd best be finding yourself somewhere safe to sleep tonight. Black and Tans have been raiding houses round here every night. Under a hedge is your best bet. Tis what I do, along with my wife.'

Ellen stared at him, wide-eyed. People sleeping in the fields for safety! This was a new development since she'd left home. She thanked the farmer and climbed down from the cart, continuing along the road to Blackstown, then away down the lane that led to her father's cottage. She kept a sharp lookout for militia from both sides. It would be best not to run into anyone.

Thankfully she saw no one, and reached the cottage safely. There was no one about. No Digger to greet her with his wet nose and wagging tail. Had her father been hurt, or turned out of his home? She went into the kitchen. The range was not lit, and was cold. A jug of milk stood on the table, long since curdled. On the front doormat lay her last two letters, unopened. She picked them up and put them on the table, in her father's usual place. Where was he?

She went about the house, looking for clues. Had he taken anything with him? There seemed to be no signs of a raid, though why either side would want to raid this cottage she couldn't think. Her father had remained neutral throughout.

She went into her father's bedroom, feeling strangely as though she was violating him by being in there. He had a drawer, she knew, in which he kept his money, tucked into an old sock. If that was gone it'd mean he'd taken it and left the cottage of his own accord. She held her breath as she opened the drawer. The sock was still there, but seemed to be empty. She picked it up and felt the rustle of paper within it. There was a note — addressed to her.

Mary-Ellen, if you are reading this then somehow you have come home and found me gone. It's not safe to stay here any more. Nor is it safe in the fields, with them Black and Tans at us all day and night. I have gone to Dublin to take a boat to Liverpool. I'll look for work in England. The dog died. There's nothing left for me in Ireland. The cottage is yours to use but when peace comes I'll be wanting to sell it. There's no news of that Gallagher boy. Your Da.

She read it twice. At least he was safe, but

— nothing left for him in Ireland? What about *her*? she wanted to scream across the Irish Sea to him. What about his only daughter, who he'd abandoned to live in an institution that was little different to a prison? What about his grandson, who he'd never even met? She brushed away a tear for loyal Digger, and hoped his end had been peaceful.

And no news of Jimmy. How could she find him? She could go to Clonamurty Farm. But if the Gallaghers had any news of him, surely they would have told Da who would have written to her. An idea came to her. She needed to contact Madame Carlton. She would know something, or be able to put Ellen in touch with someone who'd know. And surely Madame would be easy to track down. Someone in town would know what had happened to her after the raid on Carlton House, after she'd been taken away in handcuffs.

Maybe Ellen could find Siobhan and find out what she knew, though she'd be fearful Siobhan would betray her too. If Madame was in prison, perhaps Ellen could visit her, or write to her, and glean whatever information she might have. Perhaps too, she could help her old friend somehow, to make amends for not warning her about Siobhan.

But it was late now, and getting dark, and she needed to decide where to spend the night. The farmer's words had worried her, but surely if this cottage had been empty for weeks there'd be no raid on it, so she may as well stay there, as long as she was sure not to let any light show at the windows. Just like that night, almost a year ago now, when she'd stayed with Jimmy in the safe house. The last time she'd seen him. The night when little James had been conceived. It felt like another lifetime.

25

Clare

The day dawned bright and clear for my birthday. One of those gorgeous late spring mornings where everything is vivid and blue, and you feel full of energy from the moment you wake up. I woke, yawned, stretched, pulled back the curtains to let the sunshine flood in and smiled. And then I remembered two things. Firstly that I was now 50. Half a century! But I didn't feel any different, and as Jon had said, it was only the number of times I've been round the sun. Why did it matter?

The second thing I remembered was rather more sobering. Paul was still here. Well, there were just over twenty-four hours until he was due to leave. I was determined to enjoy my birthday despite his presence. If he carried on being charming and pleasant, maybe he'd even help me enjoy it. All of us together, as he'd said. But first things first — I'd bought sausages, bacon and eggs for breakfast. I don't normally have a cooked breakfast, but it was my birthday so why not? I slipped on a dressing gown and slippers and went downstairs to start cooking.

The boys had beaten me to it. The sausages were in the oven, bacon under the grill, bread being toasted two by two and stacked on the rack, and eggs ready to fry. Tea was in the pot and the table set.

'Aw, Mum! You're not supposed to catch us in the act!' Jon said. 'We were going to call you when it was all ready.'

'Oh, you darlings,' I said. 'I wasn't expecting this. Do you need a hand with those eggs? Let me put the coffee machine on.'

'Mum, sit down,' Matt said firmly, waving an egg turner at me. 'Just sit at the table and we'll do everything. Jon, can you give Dad a five-minute warning?'

'Sure.' Jon disappeared upstairs while I sat at the table, enjoying being waited on. I allowed myself to imagine, just for a moment, what it might have been like if Paul wasn't here and if my relationship with Ryan had moved a little further on. I suppose I must have had a soppy smile on my face because Matt nudged me with his egg turner.

'What are you thinking about, Mum?'

'Oh, nothing much. How lovely it is to have such wonderful sons cooking me a birthday breakfast. What a lovely day it's shaping up to be.'

'As long as Dad behaves.' Matt gave a wry smile then returned to his egg pan as he heard Jon and Paul coming down the stairs.

★ ★ ★

Breakfast passed without incident. Later, once we were all showered and dressed and I'd opened my cards and presents — a gorgeous carved wooden sewing box from Matt and a silk scarf covered with pictures of cute kittens from Jon — I made another pot of tea and we discussed plans for the day.

'The meal this evening is at eight,' Paul said, 'but before then I have a little surprise for you, Clare. Your birthday present. We need to leave in thirty minutes to collect it. Just you and me. The boys can stay here and amuse themselves.'

'Just us?' I said, and couldn't help but frown.

'I'm still your husband, Clare. Still fighting to keep you. It's your birthday, and I want to treat you to something. Don't look so worried.'

I glanced at Matt and Jon, to see if they had any idea what this might be about. Both shrugged, but said nothing.

'It's the reason I came over,' he went on.

So now I was stuck. I didn't trust him, but what could he possibly be planning that could hurt me? It would be some little treat. Maybe a trip to a jeweller's to pick out something — I wouldn't put it past Paul to try to get me to choose an eternity ring despite my attempts to end our marriage.

I forced a smile onto my face, remembering my decision yesterday to give Paul a chance. If he was making an effort to be amicable so would I. I'd make the best of it. If he tried to force too extravagant a present on me, I could always refuse, or take it back later and transfer the money back to him. 'OK, sounds intriguing. Half an hour?' I glanced down at my jeans and sweatshirt. 'Do I need to change?'

'You're just fine as you are,' he replied.

I noticed raised eyebrows from Matt and Jon. Normally Paul would not miss an occasion to criticise my too-casual dress sense.

I decided to take him at his word and didn't so much as daub a smear of lipstick on.

⋆　⋆　⋆

We went out to the car, where Paul opened the passenger door for me, always the perfect gentleman.

'Door's a bit stiff,' he said, as I climbed in. 'I'll probably need to open it from the outside to let you out, too. Something's wrong with the handle.'

As we left, the boys were standing by the open front door. They each raised a hand to wave but neither was smiling. I felt a flutter of worry about what Paul was planning. Ridiculous, really. I'd been married to him for twenty-five years. I knew him, inside and out. I had no reason to fear him or think he might do anything to harm me. Other than his usual taunts and jibes and general criticism of me, of course, but he'd done less of that here in Ireland. The worst that could happen on this little trip out would be a row. But I would try to avoid that happening if I could. And maybe we'd even have a pleasant trip out, wherever we were going.

Paul drove along the lane, through Blackstown and out onto the old Dublin road, making small talk about the weather, the scenery, the differences he noted between Ireland and England as we went.

★ ★ ★

We headed south of Blackstown, but not on the motorway to Dublin. 'Where are we going?' I asked. 'This is the old road to Dublin, isn't it?'

'It is. I thought it'd be more scenic than the motorway.'

'We're going to Dublin, then?'

'Uh-huh.' The reply was non-committal. I tried to imagine what we'd be doing there. Jewellery shopping was still a possibility. Or a lunch out — perhaps Blackstown wasn't good enough for two meals out in one day. Or to catch a matinee show. But he hadn't wanted me to dress up.

A few minutes later Paul pulled off the road, up a narrow lane and into a tiny, gravel car park beside a small copse.

'Pretty spot,' I said, wondering what we were doing there.

'Yes. I thought we'd have a little break from driving, and toast your birthday.' Paul reached behind him, into the rear seat foot-well, and pulled out a small rucksack. Inside was a small bottle of whiskey — twelve-year-old Jameson.

'Still your favourite?' he asked, with a smile.

It'd been years since I drank any Jameson, but yes, back in the day when we first met, I'd been partial to a drop of Jemmy, as I'd affectionately termed it.

'Sure!' I said. 'But only a tiny sip now. It's a bit early to be drinking.'

'It's your birthday. Your fiftieth. If you can't let your hair down then, when can you?' He pulled a

299

shot glass out of the rucksack pocket and poured a generous measure. 'Here. Want to sit outside to drink it?'

There was a bench on the edge of the car park, sited so that it overlooked the rolling farmland to the left of the copse. It looked a little uncared for — grimy, slightly wet.

'I'm all right here,' I said, taking the glass from him and sipping the fiery amber liquid. It slipped down wonderfully, warming as it went. I'd forgotten how much I enjoyed an occasional whiskey.

He reached out a hand to take mine. 'Clare, listen. I miss you. I miss you so much. I wish you'd come back to me.'

I pulled my hand away. 'I . . . like I said, I'm not sure it'd work . . . '

But Paul wasn't listening to my objections. He had a speech prepared, it seemed, and he was going to say it.

'It's hard, being on my own. I think about you all day at work, and then I get home and you're not there. No one's there. I cook my own dinner, clear up, and sit on my own in the living room, wondering what you're doing. I'm exhausted by the weekend, and I end up spending it cleaning the house. We used to go out for walks, or have lunch out at the weekend. I miss all that.'

I didn't remember many walks and lunches out. What I did remember, however, is cooking his tea every night, clearing up, cleaning — I hadn't minded it, because that was the way our marriage had been.

I took another sip of my whiskey and realised

he wasn't drinking. 'Are you not having any?' I asked.

'Me? No, of course not. We've got quite a way to drive, yet.'

'Well, we can get a taxi to the restaurant and back this evening, if you want to have a drink then,' I said, taking another sip.

'Sure, that's a good idea. More?' he said, holding out the bottle to top up my glass.

'Why not?' It was my birthday after all. I twisted round in my seat so he could pour, and banged my elbow on the car window.

'Sorry about the poky little car. But of course, you took the decent car, and then wrote it off,' he said, that old snide tone back in his voice.

'It was mine and I didn't exactly write it off on purpose,' I said, quietly. And that was all it took. His comment reminded me that however charming he appeared to be, underneath he was still the controlling, manipulative man I'd made myself leave. He didn't want me back — he wanted a cook and a cleaner. I suddenly realised the boys were right — he had not really changed. He'd been putting on an act these last few days, and I *must not* let myself be fooled by it. I had a new life here in Ireland. A good one. I'd made my decision months ago, and it was the right one. *Arise and go now*, I reminded myself.

'Whatever,' he said. 'Good whiskey?' He began to top my glass up again.

I held up a hand to stop him. 'Whoa! I can't have too much. It's not even midday!'

'OK. Just finish that then, and perhaps you can have another later.' He watched, as I sipped the drink. I've never been able to knock spirits back in one, so it took me ten minutes or more to drink. By the end, I was feeling quite tipsy.

'I think that'sh enough,' I said, surprised to hear myself slurring. This wasn't like me. OK so it was whiskey but I hadn't had all that much, had I? I peered at the glass trying to decide if it was a pub measure, a double, or what.

'We'd better crack on, then. Here, have some water.' Paul pulled out a bottle of water and handed it to me. I glugged down a few mouthfuls, but felt more drunk, not less, as a result.

Paul started the car, reversed out of the car park and onto the lane, back onto the route to Dublin.

'I feel so shleepy,' I said, and giggled. Why was it affecting me so much? I thought I could hold my drink. God knows I drank enough wine to build up a tolerance, but maybe whiskey had a different effect. It'd been a long time since I was drunk on spirits.

'Put your head back,' Paul said. 'Have a little nap. We've a way to go yet. I'll wake you up when we're there.'

'K. Thanksh,' I said, leaning back and closing my eyes. The car was spinning around me. I hoped I wasn't going to be sick, all over Paul's new-not-new car. No, I wasn't going to be sick. I was just going to sleep. I could feel myself falling, falling, drifting away, down, deeper and down, into a peaceful, dark oblivion.

26

Ellen, March 1921

Ellen barely slept. The cottage felt strange and unfamiliar without her father in it, and she startled at every little sound, every creak of the old house, wondering if it signalled a raid by the Black and Tans. She missed the gentle snores of Mairead sleeping in the next bed. Her arms ached, longing to hold little James again, and her breasts were engorged and sore from missing the usual feeds. The nuns would give James bottles when she failed to turn up to feed him, she knew. He would not go hungry, and she hoped she would be able to resume feeding him as soon as they were reunited. Tomorrow if all went well.

In the morning, her stomach groaning with hunger, she scoured the kitchen looking for food. There was nothing, not so much as a withered potato in the back of a cupboard. But outside a couple of hens were pecking around the yard, and in the henhouse there were dozens of eggs. She picked out three that seemed freshest, still warm from having been just laid, and took them back inside. It would take too long to get the range going, but she made a small fire in the sitting-room grate and fried the eggs there.

Feeling better with something inside her, she made her plans for the day. First step had to be Clonamurty Farm. The Gallaghers might know something of where Jimmy was. The Merciful Sisters had only allowed her to write to her father, or she'd have written to them long ago to ask.

She tidied up a little, though to what end she didn't know, and set off up the lane towards Clonamurty Farm. It was early morning, a fine spring day, full of birdsong and apple blossom and promise for the future, and it buoyed her spirits, making her feel ever more hopeful with each step she took towards the farm. Perhaps Jimmy was even there. Perhaps he'd come home and was hiding with his parents, and wondering where *she* was, now that her father was not there to inform him.

The more she thought of it the more she almost convinced herself that this was the truth, and it was all she could do not to start running up the lane. But she did not want to draw attention to herself. In the fields were whole families, rousing themselves from the hedgerows in which they'd slept, mothers folding blankets and pulling twigs from their children's hair, fathers stretching and yawning, picking up the little ones to carry them back to their homes for breakfast. What a terrible thing to happen — all these people, these good, hard-working, law-abiding people, being too scared to spend the night in their own homes!

She wondered whether the Gallaghers would be at home. Or would they be out under a hedgerow still. She could wait, she supposed, or go around the nearest fields looking for them. Young Mickey would no doubt think it all a grand adventure, camping out under the stars. She smiled at the thought, but then quickly stopped herself, remembering how terrifying it must be.

Turning the corner she could see Clonamurty Farm at last. It felt like coming home, more so than it had felt going to her father's cottage. There was no smoke rising from the chimney, but that didn't worry her, perhaps they were still out in the fields, or letting the range go out at nights to let the Black and Tans know the place was empty, no point in them looking for Volunteers there.

The barns were empty; there was no one about. A scrawny cat mewed at her approach, and a couple of chickens pecked listlessly in the dirt. The back door stood open, and Ellen tapped on it. 'Mrs Gallagher? It's me, Ellen. May I come in?'

There was no answer. A feeling of foreboding was beginning to rise up in Ellen, and she went inside, her heart pounding.

Someone had been here. Someone had turned the place over. Again. Everything in Mrs Gallagher's kitchen had been pulled out of her cupboards, strewn around the floor. All her crockery lay broken, her pans dented. The living room was as bad — the sofa had been knifed open, its stuffing spilling out. Newspapers were torn and scattered, the curtains had been slashed and the windows smashed. The damage was much worse than last time.

It was the same story upstairs, in every room. Devastation everywhere, and no sign of any member of the family. And on the wall, near the foot of the stairs, there was a bloodstain — a handprint, as though someone had put their hand out to steady themselves on the way down. Ellen gasped, and went around the house again, looking for more bloodstains. In the kitchen, on the floor under a jumble of pans there was blood, and more in the sitting room. Someone had been hurt; whatever had happened here, that much was clear.

They'd come looking for Jimmy. The Black and Tans. That must be it. He wouldn't have been here — she knew now that her hopes he'd be happily living here with his family were ridiculously naive. Of course he would not have come back and put them in any danger. But if the Black and Tans had come looking for him, and he wasn't here, whose blood was it?

She went back to the kitchen, picked up a chair and sat down heavily. There was so much she should do — go into Blackstown, try to find out what had happened here, and if anyone had news of Jimmy or Madame Carlton. She could clear up the farmhouse, she supposed. If Jimmy or anyone came back, they'd hate to see it like this. She'd spent so much time here it felt like a second home, and she felt a sense of responsibility. But should she touch anything? Were there some authorities she should notify?

Before the fighting, it'd have been the RIC she'd have talked to, to report such a crime. But for all she knew it might have been them who turned the house over. And if she went asking questions in the shops and pubs in Blackstown, she might be overheard by the wrong ears, and put herself in danger. But how else to find out what had happened? She felt paralysed by indecision. If only Madame Carlton was still in Carlton House!

A thought occurred to her then. Perhaps Madame was back in her home. Perhaps she'd been merely questioned and released, or even imprisoned for a while and released. It had been months since Ellen had seen her taken away. She should go to Carlton House and see what was happening there.

Feeling energised now that she had a plan of sorts, Ellen jumped to her feet, left the farm, and headed off along the familiar lane towards Carlton House. She was walking so fast, excited by the idea that Madame might be back in residence and able to give her news of Jimmy or his family, that she didn't bother to take any precautions, didn't look over the hedges into the fields, didn't keep an eye out for any sign of trouble. She was out of practice, having been shut away with the Merciful Sisters for so long.

And so it was that she jumped out of her skin when a figure emerged from the hedge and caught hold of her arm as she passed.

'What are you doing here? It's not safe.' He pulled her through the gap in the hedge from which he'd emerged.

'Get off me!' she tried to shout, but he'd clamped a hand over her mouth.

'Be quiet. The Tans are around the corner. They're on the move,' he whispered urgently.

So he must be a Volunteer, she guessed, as he

was hiding from the Black and Tans. She twisted her head to look at his face, and gasped in recognition.

'Captain Cunningham!' It was the Volunteer she'd helped nurse back to health, who she'd last seen hiding out in Gatesend Farm with Jimmy.

'Aye. And I remember you, Ellen O'Brien. But hush now, till the danger has passed.' He tugged her down, into the ditch behind the hedge, and bade her lie flat. They were well hidden from the lane, here. No one would spot them unless they came through the gap and then turned back around.

A moment later Ellen heard the sound of ragged marching, men talking and laughing as they walked up the lane. She made her breath as shallow and quiet as possible. Surely they couldn't hear the thumping of her heart? Beside her, Cunningham lay just as still, but beneath his greatcoat he moved his arm slightly, caught hold of her hand and squeezed it. His hand was warm and strong, and she drew strength from the gesture.

They stayed in the ditch for minutes after the band of Tans had passed by, until eventually Captain Cunningham rolled away from her and crawled back to the gap in the hedge. She watched him cautiously peer through, and then at last, with a grunt, he stood up and beckoned to her. 'It's safe. They've gone.'

She got to her feet and went to join him. 'Thank you. I'd have walked straight into them, so I would.'

'They'd not have harmed you. But better not

to take any chances.' He regarded her curiously. 'Where were you going, anyway?'

'To Carlton House. I've . . . been away. I was wondering whether Madame was back there.' She clapped a hand over her mouth. Did he even know Madame had been arrested? He could be trusted, she was sure of that, but Madame had always taught her not to tell anyone anything they didn't need to know.

He shook his head. 'Madame Carlton is in Mountjoy Prison. She won't be released while this conflict goes on, sadly.'

'Oh. Poor Madame. I'll try to visit her, will I? Or write to her?'

'They won't let you see her. She's a political prisoner so can receive no visitors. You may be able to write but her mail will be read and censored, so be careful.'

Madame in prison, and all Ellen's fault. It was too much. She needed to confide her guilt to someone. 'That Siobhan. Sir, I have a confession. I knew Siobhan's brother was in the RIC. But, honest to God, I never thought she'd betray Madame. I was going to tell Madame, but I was too late. Sir, I've been eaten up with guilt, that it was all my fault. I should have warned her . . . '

Captain Cunningham twisted his mouth and stared into the distance for a moment before answering.

'You weren't to know what she'd do. It's unfortunate, but Ellen, you must not blame yourself.'

Ellen nodded and bit her lip. 'Sir, may I ask you something else?'

He smiled. 'Certainly. And no need to call me sir. My name is Jack.'

'Jack, do you know anything of Jimmy? Where he is, what he's doing, or even . . . ' she could barely say the words ' . . . if he's still alive?'

He regarded her solemnly for a moment and she thought he was about to say that Jimmy had died, been shot in some incident. She steeled herself to hear whatever he was going to say.

But it was not bad news. It was no news. 'I'm sorry, Ellen. I wouldn't be knowing what's become of him. A few days after you visited us in Gatesend Farm we moved on, and split up. Jimmy went north with another company on a big mission. The mission was successful, I know that much, but I don't know what became of him. There were . . . some Volunteer casualties. I think I would have heard if it had been him, so I'm hoping it wasn't, but I don't know for certain either way.'

'Who would know? How can I find out?'

'I'll ask around for you. There are some local companies. They might know.'

She nodded her thanks. 'Jack, I'm after having been to Clonamurty Farm. Tis Jimmy's parents' farm. They're not there. Someone's been in and . . . turned it over. There's . . . blood . . . '

He sighed heavily and lowered his head. When he raised his eyes to hers again she saw a deep sadness within. 'It'll be the Black and Tans. A reprisal action. They must have heard that Jimmy's a Volunteer and went there to put pressure on his parents. I'll find out what's happened to them. With luck, they might be . . . '

He tailed off, and looked away, gazing across the fields.

Ellen frowned, pondering what he might have been about to say. With luck, what? With luck they were still alive? 'I'll be grateful for whatever you can find out.'

'I'll do what I can. Where are you staying?'

An image of little James came into her head, and she realised she missed him more than anything. 'I have to go . . . back to Dublin. Today. There's . . . something I left there, that I must fetch. I'll be back in Blackstown in a couple of days. I can stay at my father's cottage.' She explained how he could find the house.

'Very well. I'll see what I can find out, and then I'll come to find you.' Jack took a step away as if to go, but then turned back to her. 'How will you get to Dublin?'

'I'll walk, or perhaps some farmer will give me a lift in his cart,' she replied.

'Would a bicycle help?' he asked. 'I know where there's one you can use.'

'It would.' She smiled at him.

'Aye well then, you may as well take it.' He explained where it was — in a barn in a farm that was now uninhabited. Ellen did not dare ask what had happened to its owners.

'I'll leave it back when I'm done with it,' she said, but Cunningham just shrugged.

'Keep it as long as you need it. And you'll be needing some money. Here. I haven't much, but this'll buy you a meal at least.' He handed her a few coins.

She shook her head, even as he pushed the

coins into her hand. 'I can't take your money!'

'Ah, you can and you will. Well, I must be off myself, into town. I'll see what I can find out about Jimmy. I'll look for you at your father's cottage at noon in two days' time.' He reached out to her and touched her arm. 'Be careful, Ellen. I'll see you soon.'

'Thank you. For everything.'

She set off towards the abandoned farm where the bicycle was stowed. After a few steps she turned to look back, and Cunningham was still standing there, gazing after her. She raised a hand to wave, and he waved back.

★　★　★

The bicycle was exactly where he said it would be. Ellen felt almost as though she was stealing it, but Jack had said the farm was empty. And she'd only keep it for a day or two. Perhaps she could even get back today now that she had a bicycle. She could use a shawl to tie little James tightly to her back, and she'd be able to cycle like that. It was a plan. She was excited now — she would be back at the Merciful Sisters by mid-afternoon and reunited with little James. One way or another she'd leave the laundry with him. Her breasts ached at the thought of her baby — it had been well over a day since she'd fed him.

She cycled first back to Clonamurty Farm. On the off-chance that Jimmy might return there, she wanted to leave some sign, something to show she'd been there. She leaned the bike against the wall by the back door and went inside. It was just as she'd left it earlier. She averted her eyes from the bloodstains, not daring to think whose it was or what had become of the family. She walked through to the sitting room, wondering where she could leave a note, or a token of some sort. Anything to tell him she was safe, to give him a message, to inform him that he had a son — oh, there was so much she needed to tell him!

The chair, the one where Jimmy had once shown her his childhood hiding place for things he wanted to keep secret from his brother, was still in the sitting room, more or less untouched by the devastation. It had been kicked over but not slashed and torn like the sofa was. She hauled it upright, and slipped her hand into the gap in the upholstery. Yes, this was a good place. If Jimmy came back, maybe he'd remember he'd shown her this, and would put his hand in here too . . .

She took his communion medallion out of the pocket where she'd kept it safe. Yes, that would tell him she'd been here. But how to tell him about his son? There was only one way. She pulled out little James's birth certificate, kissed it, folded it around the medallion and slipped them both into the chair's depths. Then she placed the chair in front of the fireplace, facing the door. Not in its usual spot. That, she hoped, would alert Jimmy, if he came here, that the chair was significant and there was something hidden in it.

'Aye, tis all I can do,' she told herself, 'though I hope we'll be returning here together, with little James in his father's arms while I retrieve the certificate.' One day. One day soon, if Jack Cunningham could only find out where Jimmy was, and what had become of his family. She had to keep believing they'd be reunited. Hope was all she had.

She left the farm, got back on the bicycle heading to Blackstown and out onto the Dublin road, all the while her mind whirling with plans of how to get little James out of the laundry. Could she sneak in by the same way she'd come out, if the Sisters had not noticed the gate was closed? Or should she simply ring the doorbell, walk in at the front door and demand her son? She could say she was taking him to stay with her father, the child's grandfather, the person who'd sent her into the institution in the first place. They surely wouldn't check. If she was assertive enough, it'd work. She had to be brave, and insist on her rights. For her son.

The miles passed quickly, although her legs were soon tired. Realising she was starving hungry and there were still twenty miles or so to go, she stopped at an inn for something to eat, silently thanking the Lord for Jack Cunningham's generosity. She ordered a mutton pie and a mug of tea and sat in a corner of the pub relishing the feel of a good meal filling her belly. She'd almost finished when it happened.

A half-dozen Black and Tans came crashing through the door of the pub, brandishing guns. As soon as they came in, a young man who'd been sitting on a bar stool chatting to the publican ran out of the back door, which led to the outside toilets. Two other men tried to follow but were caught by the patrol and wrestled to the ground at gunpoint. One of the Black and Tans closed and locked the door, then stood guard, while two others went out the back after the young man. Ellen heard gunshots fired, and sent up a silent prayer that the man had got away, as she cowered in her corner.

'Youse all is under arrest,' shouted the man guarding the door. 'No one goes anywhere.'

'Excuse me, I'm a doctor and have patients awaiting calls this afternoon,' said one man who'd been sitting at a table near Ellen.

He was pushed roughly back to his seat by the guard. 'You don't go anywhere, not till we've questioned youse all.'

The two men who'd been wrestled to the floor were hauled upright and taken to a back room of the pub. Ellen presumed they were first to be questioned. She heard raised voices and sounds of a scuffle, and eventually the two men were let back into the main part of the pub, their faces bloodied. The doctor was taken through next, but released unharmed, and allowed to go on his way.

All Ellen could do was wait until it was her turn, and pray she'd then be allowed to leave. Two hours of waiting in silence while the Black and Tans questioned other customers, beating up some of them, all the while keeping their guns at the ready and the pub doors locked. The barman was badly beaten, and when he emerged from the back room he was shoved into a seat next to Ellen. He was clutching a bloody handkerchief to his nose. Ellen took the chance to whisper a question to him.

'The man who ran, did he get away?'

The barman shook his head. 'They shot him, God rest his soul. He was a Volunteer. Someone must have informed on us.'

'Can I do anything to help you?' she asked.

'No, lass. Keep your distance or they'll suspect you. I'm all right, so I am. Managed to convince them I know nothing.'

The guard on the door turned to face them as if he'd heard something, and Ellen shuffled a little bit away from the barman. Her instincts were to tend to his wounds but he was right, it'd land her in trouble, and that might mean she'd be unable to get back to little James. She was a mother now, and needed to think of her son first.

At last they called her through, pushing her roughly into the back room where one of their gang, a rough-looking man with a scar across his cheek and untidy black hair, bade her sit down at a table opposite him.

'Name?' he demanded.

A thought crossed her mind that maybe she should give a false name, in case somehow her name was linked to Jimmy's. But she knew she wouldn't be able to lie convincingly. Better to say as little as possible, but stay near to the truth. 'Mary O'Brien,' she replied.

'Your business here?'

'I'm after eating some lunch. I was hungry.'

'Why not eat at home?'

'I'm on my way to Dublin.'

'Why?'

316

'To fetch my baby son.'

'Where's the child now?'

'Being looked after by a friend.'

'Do you know Éamonn Rafferty?'

She shook her head.

'The publican?'

'I never saw him before today. I've never been here before today.'

'You're after speaking to him, in the bar.'

'I asked if he needed help with . . . his injuries.'

She felt a trickle of sweat run down her chest, and clasped her hands together in her lap in an attempt to stop them trembling. She forced herself to look her interrogator in the eye. She had done nothing wrong, and had nothing to hide, but knew that did not mean she was safe.

'Know any members of the Republican Army?' he asked suddenly.

'No, sir, I do not,' she replied.

'No one you suspect?'

She shook her head.

The man was quiet for a moment and Ellen began to relax, thinking the questioning was over and she'd soon be released. But then he spoke again. 'Why did you leave your baby in Dublin? You're a long way from there.'

'I went to visit my father.'

'Why not take the child with you?'

'He . . . he was a little unwell. I did not want him to travel.'

'You left a sick baby with a friend? Why not wait till he was better before going to your father?'

'My father was ill. I wanted to see him before . . . ' She let the words trail away, and allowed a tear to run down her cheek. 'He's gone now.' To Liverpool, but why not let them think he'd gone to his grave.

The man stared at her for what seemed like hours before finally nodding slowly. 'All right. But you will stay here until we are done.'

Ellen opened her mouth to plead with him to let her go, but stopped herself. Better to go along with what they said. Besides, the afternoon was well advanced now, and she would not be able to reach Dublin while it was still light. If they let her go, it'd be better to set off in the morning. One more night away from little James. It would make no difference, in the long run.

27

Clare

My head was pounding. There was a crick in my neck. I straightened up in my seat, groaning, remembering. Paul had given me whiskey. How had it had such an effect? I forced my eyes open. I was still in the car. We were — where were we?

'Wha — what's going on?' I tried to say, though my mouth didn't seem to want to form words. What had been in that whiskey?

'Ssh, it's OK, go back to sleep,' Paul murmured.

But I was awake, trying to focus on what I could see through the windscreen. A white van, close in front. We were parked, no, not parked, the engine was running. The van moved forward and Paul inched after it. A traffic jam? No. A queue. As the van moved I saw a booth in front. The van driver leaned out of the window to pass over a document. I looked out of the side window — another queue of vehicles approaching another booth. With a start I realised where we were.

'Paul, what the fuck? Why are we here? We're not getting a ferry!'

'Ssh, It's all right.'

'No it's not! I'm not getting on the ferry!'

The van had moved on, and Paul pulled up by the booth and wound his window down. He handed over a printed sheet and two passports. He must have rummaged through my drawers and stolen mine, I realised.

'Mr and Mrs Farrell?' confirmed the man in the check-in booth, with a smile.

'Not me!' I yelled. 'Just him. I'm not travelling!' I tugged at the door handle but the door would not open. I recalled he'd said something about the passenger door being stiff.

The check-in clerk was looking concerned, but handed back the two passports, and as he did, Paul closed the window. 'Stop shouting. You're drawing attention to us,' he snarled at me.

Draw attention — that's exactly what I needed to do. 'Help!' I yelled. 'I can't get out of the car!' I unclipped my seatbelt and tried to climb over into the back seat. 'Help!'

Paul pulled me back down, but I could see the check-in clerk looked even more worried. He'd lifted a phone and was talking to someone. Security, I hoped.

'Let me go!' I screamed. 'Paul, you can't do this!'

'I'm taking you home with me,' he said. 'I've done my part, coming over to this godforsaken country. Now you're coming back with me.'

'No! No I'm not! Let me go!'

He was gripping my upper arms tightly, but I was struggling, trying to free myself. A man in uniform was outside — a security officer. He was trying to open the passenger door but Paul must have activated the central locking.

'Unlock the car, sir!' he was shouting, banging on the window.

'Let me go! This is abduction. They'll arrest you,' I hissed at Paul. Finally, somehow I managed to twist enough to free my left arm, and unlocked my door. The security officer opened it immediately and reached in to haul me out.

Paul opened his own door, almost fell out of the car and began running. God knows where he thought he was running to. The security officer shouted something into his radio and gave chase.

'Are you hurt at all? Sit down, now.' The check-in clerk had come out and was leading me to a chair in his booth. He was young, with a kind face, and a name badge that read 'Gabriel'. My guardian angel. Cars behind Paul's in the queue were manoeuvring across to join the other check-in line.

'I'm all right, just a bit, shocked, you know.'

'Is he your husband?'

'Yes, but we're separated. I was . . . asleep. Woke up here. I've no intention of getting on the ferry.' My head felt fuzzy; it was spinning and aching. That whiskey . . .

'You're booked on,' Gabriel said.

'He must have planned this. I live in Ireland now.'

'How could he know you'd be asleep at check-in?'

I didn't want to voice my suspicions, that there was something other than just whiskey in that flask. He'd spiked it. I was pretty certain of it. But if I mentioned this, Gabriel would call the Gardaí and Paul would be arrested. I'd have to give a statement. It would all take ages, and all I really wanted was him gone. Gone from my house, gone from Blackstown, gone from Ireland. In answer to Gabriel's question I just shrugged.

Over his shoulder I could see a couple of security guards had caught up with Paul and were frog-marching him back over to his car. 'They've caught him,' I said, and Gabriel looked around. 'I want a quick word with him.'

'You sure?' Paul and the security guards had almost reached us. 'I can call the Gardaí if you want to press charges. He more or less tried to abduct you, so he did.'

'No, thanks. I'd rather he just got on that ferry and left me alone.'

I went out of the booth as Paul and the guards approached. He at least managed to look contrite, mortified by what he'd done.

'Paul. I told you our marriage is over. Why on earth did you think pulling a stunt like this would make me change my mind?'

He shook his head. He was still being restrained by the guards. His shirt was untucked, jacket half off his shoulders where they'd caught hold of him. 'I don't know. Desperation. A mad moment.' He sighed. 'I've fucked it all up, haven't I?'

I nodded. 'There's no way back from here. But, Paul, there never really was, anyway. You need to accept that. Our marriage is over.'

'Are you pressing charges, ma'am?' asked the guard who'd helped me out of the car.

Paul stared at me. 'Please don't. Just let me go.'

I regarded him carefully for a moment. He was

sweating, terrified he was going to end up in an Irish police cell. 'All right. But you must let me go, too.'

He nodded. Just slightly, but enough that I knew he understood.

I turned to the guard and shook my head. 'No. Just let him get in his car and on the ferry. Away from me.'

'Clare, I'm sorry. Really.' And for once, I believed his apology was genuine.

I turned my back, retrieved my handbag and passport from Paul's car, and went back to Gabriel's check-in booth. The security guards then allowed Paul back into his car, and waved him on to the ferry.

'Can I get a bus from anywhere near here?' I asked Gabriel. 'I need to go to Blackstown.'

'Sure. Just in front of the ticket office building. You going to divorce that fella?'

'I most certainly am,' I replied. And I suspected after this, he wouldn't try to contest it.

Gabriel smiled in approval, and waved as I set off towards the bus terminal. My head was still pounding, so I bought a bottle of water from a vending machine to drink on the journey home. Once on the bus, I called home and told Jon I was on my way back, on my own.

* * *

I was so glad to get back to the farmhouse. The boys were waiting for me, with a pot of tea on the table.

'Mum, sit down. Drink tea. Tell us what

happened. I only got a garbled message from Jon that Dad tried to force you onto the ferry or something.' Matt pulled out a chair, gently pushed me into it and sat beside me.

Jon took a seat opposite. 'Yes, tell us everything. Don't try to defend him.'

I took a deep breath and told them all that had happened. The boys' jaws dropped open.

'And where is he now?' Matt asked.

'Halfway across the Irish Sea.'

'Dickhead,' Jon commented, summing up what we all thought of Paul right there, in one word.

'It's still your birthday. We should go out, and actually celebrate it properly, if you feel up to it, Mum?'

I considered his question. Actually, I did want to go out. There was a table booked at The Carlton for four — now, who could fill that fourth place? 'Boys, mind if I invite Ryan along to make up the numbers?'

'I think that sounds perfect,' Matt said, smiling. 'Ring him now.'

I did. But I took the phone into the sitting room, away from my well-meaning but nosy sons.

Ryan's tone sounded guarded. 'Happy birthday. Hope it's all going well, with your boys and your husband.'

I couldn't help it. I snorted.

'What?' Ryan said.

'It's not exactly going well. I will tell you all the details later. But for now, I wanted to invite you out to dinner tonight at The Carlton. With Matt and Jon.'

'And Paul?' Ryan sounded confused.

'Paul's, um, not available.'

'He had to leave, and you have a spare place? Listen, Clare, for a while I thought I was in with a chance with you. But I'm not someone who you can call to just step in whenever your husband is not available. I'm sorry, but sure I don't work like that.'

'Ryan, that's not how it is at all. I am separated from Paul, will divorce him as soon as I can. There is no way I want him back in my life.'

'Then why was he staying with you? I saw you in the café, all happy families . . .'

'He turned up, out of the blue. I felt I owed it to the boys to try to be civil when he's around. But not any more. Never again.'

Ryan was silent for a moment. 'Not if he turns up again charming you?'

I laughed. 'He's burned his bridges. He's . . .' I took a deep breath. May as well tell him now and get it out of the way. 'He's on his way back to England, after having tried to abduct me. Believe me, Ryan, after what he's done to me today there is no way on earth he could ever charm me again. Not that he charmed me this time, either.'

'What? What on earth did he do?'

'It's a long story.' But I told him. Matt brought a cup of tea in to me part way through the conversation and I nodded my thanks.

'Jesus, Mary and Joseph,' Ryan said quietly, when I'd finished. 'That's unbelievable, so it is. Thanks be to God you're all right. Look, I'm so

325

sorry I went off on one there. Just seeing you with him, I jumped to conclusions. Thought you were trying to restart your marriage, and I should back off. I'm sorry.'

'It's OK — it's totally understandable. Anyway, are you free this evening? As I said, we do have a spare place at the table tonight, and I would very much like you to be there. We're booked in for eight o'clock.'

'I would love to come. See you there at eight, then.'

I could tell he was smiling as we said goodbye and hung up. I was grinning too. It had been a hell of a day, but it was going to get much, much better before it ended. One thing was for certain — I'd had a fiftieth birthday I would never forget.

28

Ellen, March 1921

The Black and Tans allowed no one else to leave the pub until after dark. The local people then filtered out, grumbling. Two men were arrested and taken away by the gang, and the dead man's body retrieved by a local undertaker. Ellen left when she could, fetched her bicycle, which thankfully was still where she'd left it, and debated her options. She could not cycle to the Merciful Sisters in the dark. She would need to find somewhere to spend the night, but it would have to be away from here.

She was shaking as she pedalled a little further along the road, out of town, and into the countryside. As soon as she was away from all buildings she turned into a field, dismounted from her bike to open the gate and hauled the bike through. There was a good thick hedge, and for the second time that day she crawled into a ditch, thankful for the recent spell of dry weather, and lay down to sleep.

It was a long, cold and sleepless night. Ellen had no blanket, or even a coat. Just a thin shawl she'd collected from home. She wondered if she should move on; perhaps try to find a barn somewhere, or a farm that might take her in, or another person sleeping in a field who might share a blanket — but the thought of venturing further in the dark, in an area she was not familiar with, where companies of Black and Tans raided pubs and shot at anyone who ran, made her decide that her best bet was to stay put until dawn, then get going.

At long last the eastern sky lightened and turned pink. Ellen hauled herself to her feet, feeling stiff and cold, her clothes damp from dew. Once the sun was above the horizon it would warm her, and cycling would help. She comforted herself with the thought that she would be reunited with little James today, brushed herself down, and wheeled her bicycle out to the lane. There was no one about, thankfully.

She was hungry and thirsty but there was no hope of finding anything to eat this early. Perhaps when she arrived on the outskirts of Dublin she'd find a shop and buy herself an apple or a bread roll. She still had a few pence left from the money Jack Cunningham had given her.

It wasn't a straightforward cycle ride. She took a wrong turning somewhere, and found herself on a road that one side or the other had sabotaged. A bridge had been blown up, and there was no way to cross a small river. She retraced her route and tried another lane. This one had ditches dug across it — she knew this was a tactic the Volunteers had used to prevent the RIC and Black and Tans from being able to move around as easily in their motor vehicles. At least with a bicycle you could dismount and lift the bike across.

Finally the lane emerged onto a main road, and a signpost informed her there were just six more miles to Dublin. The Merciful Sisters institution was on the north side of the city, so perhaps just four more miles. With renewed energy she pedalled faster, stopping for a few minutes to buy something to eat and to ask directions.

It was midday by the time she reached the Merciful Sisters. Her heart beat faster as she approached the entrance. Within those walls was her son, and he could be in her arms in minutes. She only had to hold her nerve, demand he be brought to her, and then leave with him. They couldn't stop her. It wasn't a prison. She had every right to take her son and go back to her father's cottage. She'd find a way to make some money to keep them both, until Jimmy returned to her. It would all work out. It had to.

She leaned her bike against the wall to one side of the laundry's main entrance, and tugged on the bell pull. It seemed like another lifetime when she'd stood in this very spot with her father, on the day he'd brought her here. She pressed her lips together at the memory. Had Da known what kind of place this was? He'd persuaded her it was the best option, but had he any idea of how the Sisters treated the inmates? Well, she was outside now, but her son was inside, and she needed him.

The huge oak door opened with a creak, and Sister Anthony peered around its edge, her face hardening when she saw Ellen.

'You've come back,' she stated. 'You had better come in.'

'I've come for my son. My father is taking me back. We can live in his cottage now, and trouble you no more.'

The sister just stared at her and frowned, then stood aside, gesturing for her to enter. As the heavy door clanged shut behind her Ellen felt a shiver of dread run down her spine. What if they refused to let her leave? What if they forced her back to the laundry, and kept her away from her son?

'Mary-Ellen, go into the office and take a seat,' Sister Anthony told her.

'Will someone fetch my baby, please, Sister?' Ellen could not bring herself to call the nun 'Mother' as the inmates were instructed to.

Sister Anthony did not answer, but instead gestured to a chair for Ellen, and walked around the desk to sit behind it. She regarded Ellen in silence for a moment.

Ellen tried to read the nun's expression. She looked as though she was trying to find the right words for something. 'Sister? May I see Mairead?' Perhaps Mairead would be able to bring little James to her.

'Mairead is at work and you may not disturb her. I understand that you do not wish to return to live here and it is good that your father will take you back. You are a lucky girl. Perhaps you have learned from your experiences and will go on to live a good, Christian life.'

'Yes, Sister.' Ellen could hardly believe what she was hearing. She had not thought it would be this easy. 'May I fetch my son now, please?'

The nun sighed and shook her head, glancing

330

down at the desk. When she raised her head there was some new emotion in her eyes. Sadness, but with something else behind it, something that made Ellen feel Sister Anthony was enjoying this moment, relishing wielding her power. Ellen could do nothing but wait patiently, and try not to antagonise the nun.

At last Sister Anthony spoke. 'When you disappeared, Mary-Ellen, we were left rather at a loss as to where you had gone and whether you were ever coming back. You abandoned your baby son. He was already showing signs of ailing on the day you ran away, and I'm afraid the poor little mite deteriorated rather rapidly.'

Ellen gasped. 'What do you mean? He was perfectly well when I left, and Mairead had promised to keep an eye . . . '

Sister Anthony shook her head. 'Mairead is not allowed anywhere near the nursery, as she is not a mother. Your poor child became seriously ill, and only this morning he passed away and is now in the arms of Our Lord in Heaven.'

'What? No! He can't be!' Ellen leapt to her feet, pushing the chair back hard so that it fell over, and leaned over the desk. She wanted to grab the nun, shake her, and have her admit that she was lying, and that James was perfectly well and she could take him home now.

'I'm afraid so. He didn't suffer and is in a better place now. Tis a blessing, really. A child born to one such as you has no chance in this world. And without him, just maybe you will be able to move on and make something of yourself.' Sister Anthony rose to her feet and

331

opened the door to the office to show Ellen out.

'I can't go . . . I need to see him. Please, let me see him and hold him one last time?' Ellen clasped her hands together, pleading with the nun.

'The babe has already been buried,' Sister Anthony said.

'Already? You said he . . . d-died only this morning?'

'Indeed he did. But we cannot let a dead child lie around. The priest blessed him and he was buried.'

'May I at least see his grave, then?' His grave. Her darling James's grave. How could those two words belong together? It was all wrong, so very wrong!

Sister Anthony sighed heavily. 'I suppose so. It might help you to accept what I'm telling you. Follow me.' She led Ellen along a corridor and out through a door. It led into the second courtyard, the one through which Ellen had escaped just two days earlier. There was a patch of recently dug earth beside the wall, and the sister led her to it, and gestured at the ground. 'Your son's body lies here. His spirit is with Jesus. Be thankful.'

Ellen sank to her knees and laid her hands flat on the muddy earth, as if somehow she could feel little James's body through the ground, as if her love could penetrate through and comfort him. But it was too late. She would never hold him again, never kiss his soft head or smell that wonderful milky scent of him. She should never have left him. This would not have happened if she'd stayed. She'd have held him and loved him and somehow she'd have healed him.

'Sister, what did he die of? Did he see a doctor? Was there . . . was there really nothing to be-done?' She fought hard to hold back her sobs as she spoke.

'We sent for a doctor, but the child died before he came. It was . . . a fever. Sudden and unstoppable. It happens, sometimes, with very young children. Do not mourn him, Ellen. Jesus wanted him, and who are we to question Our Lord and Saviour?'

'I wanted him too! I loved him, I'd have done anything for him!'

'You left him, all alone here, without a mother's love in his final hours. Come, it's time for you to leave now. Go back to your father. Pray for your son and pray for your own salvation.' Sister Anthony bent and caught hold of Ellen's arm, hauling her to her feet.

Ellen was numb. It was too much to take in. Tears were streaming down her face and she could barely see. She glanced back once at the unmarked grave, and let herself be led back through the building to the main door. 'We won't expect to see you again, Mary-Ellen. Lead a good and humble Christian life and you will soon forget this unfortunate baby.'

'I will never forget him,' Ellen whispered. Sister Anthony was holding the door open for her. Ellen was torn between wanting to stay close to little James's remains and wanting to get as far away as possible from the Merciful Sisters.

'I suspect you will in time, child.' Sister

333

Anthony pushed her gently but firmly outside, and closed the door behind her. It sounded so final. The ending of a chapter of her life, a chapter in which she had all too briefly been a mother. Ellen walked numbly back to where she had left the bicycle, and sank down to the ground beside it, her face resting on her knees, arms folded around her head, huge sobs racking her body as she tried to come to terms with the shock of her loss.

★　★　★

How long she stayed there, crouched sobbing on the roadside, she had no idea, but at some point she became aware that a woman was kneeling beside her, tapping her shoulder. 'Are you all right, love? Is there anything I can do? Is there someone I can fetch for you?'

Ellen raised her head to look at her companion — a middle-aged woman with a kind face and a shawl tied tightly around her head.

'Ah, you poor love. You're after having a proper cry, aren't you? Come with me. I've a few pennies — enough to buy us both a cup of tea. It won't put everything right, but it'll make a start, won't it?' The woman gently pulled Ellen upright. 'This your bicycle? Let's not leave it here or it'll be gone when you come back to it.' She took hold of the bicycle and began wheeling it along the street. Ellen followed numbly.

There was a café around the corner. The woman left the bike in a side alley and took Ellen inside, seating her in a corner before ordering two cups of tea and a plate of soda bread with butter and jam. 'There now. This will help, believe me. My name's Angela. Will it help to talk about your troubles? Or if you don't want to, just sit, drink your tea. I'm here for you.'

Ellen sipped her tea. Its warmth spread through her, although it could not reach the cold, dead space where little James had been. 'Thank you,' she croaked. 'My name's Ellen. The tea is helping, you were right.'

Angela was kind, but Ellen did not feel she wanted to talk. There was too much to tell. And there was still Jimmy to find. As she nibbled the bread and butter she felt strength and resolve return to her. She had to go back to Blackstown, back to her father's cottage, meet Jack Cunningham, get news of Jimmy and then find him. She would not be able to present him with his son, but she could tell him about their baby, and he would mourn little James with her, and in time, perhaps, there would be more children. There was still something to live for, still a future ahead of her.

She forced a weak smile to her face. 'Angela, you have saved me. Thank you. I was in the depths, back there.'

'You're welcome, love. Come on, eat up the bread. It's for you.'

'I can't pay you back, I'm sorry.'

Angela shook her head. 'I don't want paying back. We women have to help each other out, don't we? One day you'll help some other poor lass, and that'll be you paying me back, in a way. So you don't want to tell me what upset you, so.

That's all right. Some things are best left unsaid.'

By the time Ellen left the café she felt composed and ready to face the journey back to Blackstown. To be in an area she knew, with people she knew and trusted nearby — Jack Cunningham, at least. To be far away from the Merciful Sisters and all that they represented. She felt a pang of guilt at leaving without having seen Mairead, and of course, to be distancing herself from little James's grave, but there was nothing she could do about that. She would write to Mairead. Perhaps the nuns would allow Mairead to write back.

★　★　★

She parted from Angela a little while later, hugging the older woman before she left.

'You sure you'll be all right, on that bicycle?' Angela asked. 'Have you far to go, now?'

'Ah, not far,' Ellen replied, not wanting to explain why she was so far from home. 'Thank you once again.'

She set off, determined to make it back to Blackstown before nightfall. Could it really have been only last night that she slept in a field, and yesterday that she met with Jack Cunningham and then was detained in a pub for hours? It all seemed like a lifetime ago, as though it had happened to a different person. It had — she'd been a mother then. Now she was a bereaved parent. She took a hand off the handlebars to dash away a tear, and wobbled around a pothole. It wouldn't do to fall off and hurt herself. She still had Jimmy to live for. She must concentrate and put all her thoughts and efforts into getting home.

It was a tough ride, but she knew the way now, and knew which roads to avoid. She didn't dare stop to rest, and besides, she had no money to spend on any food. It was after dark by the time she neared Blackstown, but there was a nearly full moon and she was on familiar roads, so she pushed on and finally reached her father's cottage, exhausted. It was just as she'd left it. The chickens had laid fresh eggs, so she fed them from a sack of grain stored in a shed, and scrambled the eggs for her dinner.

'Should I sleep in the fields, I wonder?' she asked herself. 'Would the Black and Tans raid this cottage?'

But she knew she was too exhausted to leave, and too devastated by the loss of her son to care. She curled up in her old bed, and fell asleep almost immediately, dreaming of little James lying alone in the cold, dark earth.

★   ★   ★

In the morning there were, thankfully, more eggs for breakfast, and then she set about cleaning the cottage and making it fit for habitation. If, or when, she found Jimmy, they had to live somewhere. Clonamurty Farm was in no state for anyone to live in, and until she knew what had happened to Jimmy's family she did not want to venture there. Concentrating on her tasks took her mind off what had happened yesterday, although every now and again her grief washed over her like a tidal wave, sending her crumpling to the floor, sobbing.

Jack Cunningham arrived at midday, just as he'd promised. Ellen invited him in to sit at the kitchen table. She'd washed her face, tidied her clothing, managed to get the range lit, and had a kettle set to boil before he came. There was tea she'd found in the larder, but no milk.

'I'm pleased to find you back here,' Jack said, as he sat down. His face was grave. 'Did you fetch whatever it was you'd gone to Dublin for?'

She shook her head and whispered her reply. 'No. It was not possible.'

Jack frowned, and looked as though he was about to ask her more about it, but she pinched her lips together. Maybe one day she'd tell him about her baby, but not before she'd told Jimmy.

'Any news, Jack? I'm so desperate to find Jimmy, so I am. I need him so much. Please tell me.'

He sighed and looked down at the table for a moment. It was the same movement Sister Anthony had made, before telling her about little James. Ellen sank down into a chair. 'Jack, you're not about to give me bad news, are you? I don't think I can . . . '

He raised his eyes to hers and she read anguish and deep sorrow within. 'Ellen, I am so sorry. So very sorry.'

'How? When?' she whispered.

'Two months ago. He took part in an ambush, up near the Cavan border. A company of Black and Tans were on the move. Somehow word had

338

got to them, and they'd placed snipers in the woods nearby. As soon as the Volunteers launched their action, the snipers fired, and three were killed. I'm so sorry, Ellen. Jimmy was one of the men killed. He was a good man. Loyal and brave, and far too young.'

Ellen stared at him. She could find no words, nothing she could say, nothing she could do. There were no tears. Only a cold, dark hole inside her. She'd lost them both. Jimmy and their son.

'Ellen, there's something else. I hate to be the one . . . but you have to know. You told me Jimmy's parents' farm had been raided. It was a reprisal attack, it seems. Once again, I'm sorry. They were shot. His parents and brother — all gone. They were buried in Blackstown cemetery. Jimmy's somewhere in Cavan. I'm not sure where, but I will find out, so you can pay your respects.'

'They shot them? Even little Mickey? He was only a child.'

Jack nodded. 'Aye. All of them.' He was silent for a moment while she stared at him, unable to comprehend what she had heard. 'Ellen, listen. I've arranged somewhere for you to stay for a while. Just until . . . things get better. You'll be looked after, and in a while maybe you can work a little to earn your keep. I'll be able to look in on you from time to time. We owe you. Ireland owes you, and we'll look after you.' He reached across the table and took her hand. 'It's been a tremendous shock, I know, but I need you to come with me now. You can't stay here on your own.'

Ellen stood and followed him out of the cottage. She could not take in what she had heard. Jack had told her Jimmy and all his family were dead. Sister Anthony had told her little James was dead. It was one of those glorious blue and yellow days, with the scent of spring in the air and the promise of warm days to come, but for Ellen there was no future, nothing to live for, nothing at all.

She felt hardened, numb, unfeeling, as though it was someone else walking across the yard after Jack, not her. Her ghost perhaps. Maybe she was dead, too, for she could feel nothing. She could not cry. She could not think. Only the caress of a breeze on her skin reminded her that she was alive. She was alive, but all those she loved were gone.

29

Clare, May 2016

It was a fortnight after my birthday. I was getting used to the idea that I was now 50, and that I lived in Ireland in my own farmhouse. Matt and Jon had both visited Paul after they returned to England, and had reported back that he was remorseful, blaming momentary madness, and begging them to forgive him. They'd each told him what they thought of him in no uncertain terms and had refused to take his side, pointing out it can't have been 'momentary madness' as he'd booked me onto the ferry and stolen my passport.

I had no intention of having any further dealings with Paul, except via solicitors. I'd begun divorce proceedings and my solicitor had informed me Paul had agreed to everything and was not contesting a thing. Perhaps being drugged and abducted had been worth it, if it made the divorce easier to achieve.

With the boys having returned to England I had time to get on with my various projects. Before they'd left they'd helped me shift the junk out of the barn and Ryan's scrap-dealer friend had called by and collected it all. I'd installed a large workbench and had an electrician fit sockets and lights. I'd taken the old sitting-room carpet up and put that down in the barn, and all the upholstery and sewing tools had arrived.

I'd done a lot of work on my old chair — rebuilding it alongside rebuilding my life. It now had webbing, springs, hessian over the springs as a base for the stuffing, cotton-fibre stuffing, calico covers. I'd done the arms, wings, seat and most of the back. The arms and wings had their final cover on — a heavy cotton twill in a rich deep red colour. The colour of revolution, I thought. It seemed fitting somehow.

And I'd had time to make those curtains Janice had asked me for. She'd picked out a blue striped fabric for her youngest boy's bedroom. Something fresh and simple that he wouldn't grow out of. I'd used triple pinch-pleat heading tape, lined the curtains with a good quality lining fabric and made matching tie-backs. Janice had been delighted, treated me to a night out as a thank-you and showed the curtains to all her friends. I had a couple more commissions already — for another pair of curtains and to re-cover a set of dining-room chairs.

I'd set up a simple website with contact details and pictures of my work, and had ordered a pack of business cards, which Janice and Ryan were displaying in their respective shops. My little business was beginning to pick up. I'd soon have an income of my own, for the first time since that doomed job as a school lunchtime supervisor all those years ago. And this time there was no Paul to scupper it. Imagine — just a couple of months earlier I didn't even have my own bank account. Now I had my own business.

I'd also emailed Sarah, Jess and Lynne, my old

school friends. I'd told them my news, apologised for my years of silence, and invited them to come to stay. Maybe we could pick up our old friendship. I hoped so. It was worth a try.

Piece by piece I was building myself a life.

* * *

As well as all the upholstery, I'd finally had time to do more research into James O'Brien, the child whose birth certificate had been tucked inside the chair. I'd already discovered his birthplace was a Magdalene Laundry, situated on the north side of Dublin. The place had closed down long ago, back in the 1960s After a fair amount of searching online I discovered the records from the laundry had been stored for years by the Catholic Church, with very little access granted to them.

But now, at last, some records were being made available online. Details of deaths in the laundries, and details of births and adoptions of children, were gradually being released. I sat down in the kitchen with my laptop one Sunday after lunch, with a cup of tea and packet of biscuits to hand, and began searching.

I had James O'Brien's birth certificate, and so it was easy enough to find the Merciful Sisters' record of his birth, with details matching those I already knew. The only addition was to note the name of the nun who'd acted as midwife — a Sister Mary Magdalene. But what had happened to the child? I searched for details of his death, both in the laundry records and in the wider internet. Nothing. Back to the laundry records, I trawled through but found nothing.

Eventually I leaned back in my chair and sighed. Perhaps I'd never find out what had become of the child. Maybe he'd left the laundry with his mother and been brought up somewhere outside. I hoped so. Everything I knew about the Magdalene Laundries told me they were unpleasant places to live or grow up in. For some reason, despite my only connection to little James being that his birth certificate had been found in my house, I wanted to think he'd thrived, and lived a happy life. But there were those terrible reports, of mass children's graves, discovered in one or two laundries. I fervently hoped that had not been this child's fate.

Buried on one page of the website was a contact form. The website owner, it seemed, had access to more records that were not available online. It was worth a shot. I filled in the form, asking for any details of what had become of James, giving his date of birth and his mother's name. Maybe I'd get no response. Or maybe I'd solve the mystery.

I clicked Send on the form, then on a whim, put Granny Irish's maiden name into Google. Would there be any more details on her career as a Volunteers' spy?

There was. A website dedicated to female Volunteers contained a paragraph about her.

At the start of the War of Independence, Siobhan O'Malley's loyalties were torn. Her brother Seán was a member of the RIC in Leitrim. Desperate to win favour with him, and also possibly for monetary gain, she passed information about her employer, Emily Carlton, who was a prominent member of the Cumann na mBan, to the RIC. This action led to Mrs Carlton being incarcerated in Mountjoy Prison for the remainder of the war, though afterwards she was to play a major part in Irish politics for many years.

O'Malley, it seems, rapidly came to regret her actions, and offered her services to the Blackstown Volunteers, as a spy or double agent. She spent the remainder of the war feeding false information to the RIC, and passing details of RIC movements to the Volunteers. It was on receipt of a tip-off from her that a company of Volunteers were able to avoid a major ambush that had been planned around Christmas 1920.

So she'd been both villain and hero, at different times, depending on which side you were on. I could understand why she'd kept quiet about her involvement, even in such a Republican family as hers was. Only Daithí had ever got her to talk about it. I guessed her betrayal of this Emily Carlton may have been the one thing she'd done that she regretted, as I'd read in Daithí's notebooks. I'd just finished noting down all the details when there was a tap at the back door, and in came Ryan.

'Hey, Clare,' he said, as he entered the kitchen. He leaned over and kissed my cheek. 'Good to catch you at home. I was wondering if you'd like a little trip out, this afternoon. Weather's brightening up. Perhaps we could go to the site of the Battle of the Boyne? I never did get to show you that. Or we could just have a walk? That's if you've got time?'

'Always got time for you, mate,' I said. 'I fancy a walk. Let's just walk to the Boyne from here, shall we?'

'Sure!'

It was the same walk I'd done with Matt and Jon, and was fast becoming a favourite. Down the bridleway to the river, along its banks to a place where there was a great view of The Carlton, then onto a lane that looped around and back to Clonamurty Farm. As we walked, Ryan took my hand and it felt like the most natural thing in the world to walk hand in hand, discussing this and that, laughing at each other's jokes.

I told him where I'd got to with the search for James O'Brien, and he nodded. 'Good progress. Hope you hear back soon from the archivist.'

We sat side by side on the bench overlooking the river, and Ryan draped an arm casually around my shoulders. I looked at him and he raised an eyebrow. 'Sorry, does it bother you? Should I . . . '

'No, it's fine,' I replied, and then we sat quietly, me leaning slightly in to him, wondering whether this was right or not, whether I wanted this closeness, a relationship, to be part of a couple again. Or was it too soon? Should I have a few months, a year or two of independence first? Could I be in a relationship and still be independent? I liked Ryan, a lot. I was definitely attracted to him. But was it the right thing to do? Too many questions, too many decisions. I sighed, without meaning to, and Ryan removed his arm.

'You all right?' he asked.

I smiled back at him. 'Yes. I'm fine. Shall we walk on?' Easier to walk alongside him than sit snuggled up to him, wondering whether I should even be there.

We walked on in companionable silence, along the river, out onto the lane, and looped back to my house. I invited Ryan in for a cup of tea, and while the kettle was boiling checked my laptop for any emails.

'Hey, I've had a reply already, from the Magdalene archivist,' I said, with some excitement.

'That was quick! What does it say?'

I scanned the email. 'Says a lot of records are still protected but that he can tell me that a child named James O'Brien with the birth date I'd stated was adopted in March 1921, by a family named Haggerty, from Cavan.'

'She gave him up, then. So many did, after having a child out of wedlock. It was hard back then to be a single parent, and she'd have had less chance of finding a husband. She probably had no choice.'

He was right, I knew, but still. I'd kind of hoped that somehow Mary-Ellen O'Brien had kept her child, taken him out of the laundry and managed to bring him up herself. 'I wonder if he was happy with his adoptive family.'

'You could try to trace him. He'll be in his nineties now if he's still alive but maybe he had children who could tell you more about him.'

347

'That's a thought,' I said. I'd love to know what kind of life he led. And perhaps I could pass James Gallagher's communion medallion on to James O'Brien's children. Maybe they'd like to know who their birth grandfather and mother were.

I made the tea, then sat down at my laptop and began searching online, this time for James Haggerty. There were several hits for that name. But some links looked promising — in particular a motor workshop in County Cavan called Haggerty's, whose 'About Us' page stated the garage had been founded in 1942 by James Haggerty and was still a family-run business. There was a picture of a trio of middle-aged men in grimy blue overalls, holding spanners and grinning, standing around a white-haired man in a wheelchair.

'Look at this,' I said to Ryan, who'd been running searches himself using his smartphone connected to my Wi-Fi. 'Could that be him?'

'Right name, looks old enough,' Ryan said. 'Give them a ring.'

I stared at him. 'And say what?'

'That you think you have something that belongs to the old man?'

'But' — I could think of a million problems here — 'what if he never knew he was adopted? What if he knew but never wanted to know who his birth parents were? What if he knew but his children didn't know . . . '

Ryan frowned. 'I see what you mean. Tricky. Perhaps send an email first then, not giving too much away, that they can ignore if they prefer.'

We sat side by side and spent the rest of the afternoon composing that email, writing a few words, deleting them, and starting again, over and over. Eventually we came up with:

Hello, I am researching some people who have historical links with my home and the name of James Haggerty came up, who I believe is the founder of your garage. Would it be possible to come to meet you to explain the links and find out more about Mr Haggerty?

'Suitably vague, gives nothing away, and if they say yes we can feel our way when we go to meet them,' Ryan said, when we'd finally written the email.

'We?' I said, raising my eyebrows, although I loved the idea he wanted to come too.

'If you'll let me come with you,' he responded.

'Sure, why not?'

He leaned over and kissed me.

The laptop pinged alerting us to an incoming email, and we broke apart.

'That was quick,' I said, opening it. Ryan leaned over to read it at the same time.

Dear Ms Farrell,

My father-in-law is 95 so I am typing this email for him. He says he would love to meet you and is intrigued to know about your research and his possible links to your home. He was adopted as a baby but knows very little of the circumstances of his birth. He is too frail to travel far, but if you are able to come to visit us,

he will see you at any time.
  Yours,
  Noreen Haggerty

'Oh my God he's still alive!' we said, pretty much in unison. This was beyond my wildest dreams. I'd be able to hand him his original birth certificate and his father's communion medallion in person. That could be a very special moment!

'When?' I said, grinning at Ryan.

'Tomorrow afternoon? I can get someone to cover the shop from about two.'

'Great!' I emailed Noreen back straight away.

When I'd finished I turned to Ryan. 'You know what else is in Cavan? The grave of Jimmy Gallagher, according to the book about Volunteers from Meath County.' I nipped into the sitting room to fetch the book, and opened it at the page I'd marked that listed Jimmy Gallagher's part in the war. 'Yes, look here. He's buried at a cemetery near Blacklion. He was only 20 when he died, the poor lad.'

'That's only a few miles from Haggerty's garage. We can visit both tomorrow. It's only about an hour's drive up there.'

We soon had it all arranged. I was so excited I had no idea how I'd sleep that night. I had the feeling Ryan would have stayed the night with me, if I'd given him even a tiny hint of encouragement. Half of me wanted him to stay. But the more cautious half said no, and that side won the debate.

30

Ellen, August 1921

It had been over five months since Jack Cunningham had taken Ellen to live with his sister, in a tidy, two-storey house near the beach in Bettystown. Aisling Cunningham was unmarried and worked as a journalist for the local newspaper. She had several spare rooms and had welcomed Ellen with open arms. 'Any friend of my brother is a friend of mine,' she'd said, when Jack had brought a grief-stricken, numb Ellen to her. 'And I know how well you nursed him when he was injured. I am forever in your debt for that.'

Ellen had barely got out of bed for the first week, and Aisling had taken time off work to nurse her, coaxing her to eat bowls of nourishing soup, sitting quietly beside her, reading to her, being ready to listen if she wanted to talk, providing a comforting arm about her shoulders when Ellen needed to cry.

At last when Ellen had felt able to function again, able to get up, prepare her own meals, venture to the nearby shops for groceries, Aisling had returned to work. Little by little Ellen had begun taking over the management of the household, and the easy and repetitive work of cleaning and cooking had gradually numbed the pain of her losses. She'd written to the Merciful

Sisters, who had forwarded a brief letter from her father that simply stated he'd left Liverpool and was moving to London in search of work. He'd given no address, and had not written again.

As the season moved from spring to summer Ellen had taken to walking for long periods on the beach, paddling in the shallows if it was warm enough, following the line of sand dunes that stretched as far as the eye could see. She would imagine Jimmy walking alongside her, little James as a toddler splashing in the waves, giggling and laughing.

Somehow these visions of what might have been comforted her. Maybe somewhere, out there in another life, another universe, Jimmy and James were still alive and they were all living the life together that she'd always dreamed of. For as long as she drew breath they would live on, in her thoughts, in her memories. No one is truly dead until there's no one left to remember them, she told herself. And Jimmy had played an important part in the war for Ireland's freedom. He would never be forgotten. His name would be in the history books for ever.

Ireland's freedom, that elusive goal, had, in July, become so much closer. A reality in fact, when a truce was declared between the British and Irish. The two sides still needed to negotiate a treaty, but, Aisling said, the feeling was that Britain was impoverished and in recession after the Great War and in no mood to continue fighting. Meanwhile, the Irish Republican Army could use the time to regroup, so if the war did resume, they'd be ready for it.

'Will it come to that?' Ellen asked Aisling, over breakfast one morning.

'No, I don't think so. Our problem is that there are many in the north who don't want independence. They want to stay part of the union with Great Britain. That's where the sticking point will be. And there are too many Republicans who won't accept a divided Ireland. Well, we shall see. Meanwhile, we can enjoy our summer of peace.'

And Ellen was beginning to enjoy it. With the cessation of hostilities, Jack was no longer on the run, and able to live with them openly. He was returning to his peacetime job as a solicitor, and beginning to build up his business, run from an office in Bettystown. At the weekends he would accompany Ellen on her walks along the beach, and they'd talk of Jimmy and of Madame Carlton. Ellen had tentatively opened up to Jack, and told him of the loss of her child.

'I can't believe your father sent you to that laundry,' Jack said, with a sad shake of his head. 'If only I'd found you then. Aisling would have taken you in, and maybe . . . '

'Ssh. I can't bear to think of what might have been. It was God's will that little James should be taken so young. It would have happened even if I'd been living with Aisling.' Would it? Ellen was less sure than she might once have been. But it was no good dwelling on the past. She'd never forget Jimmy or James, but she was young and there were many years ahead of her.

After the truce came the welcome news that

353

political prisoners were to be freed. That meant Madame Carlton would be released, and Ellen asked Jack to take her to Blackstown and to Carlton House.

It was an emotional reunion. Madame, looking a little older and thinner than when Ellen had last seen her, pulled Ellen into a tight embrace.

'I am so sorry, my dear, for your losses. So terrible for one so young to have suffered so much. Your father . . . ' Madame Carlton broke off and shook her head. 'I can't believe he sent you away to that terrible place. If only you'd come to me rather than go there.'

'I did, Madame. But it was the day you were arrested. I saw them take you away.'

'What terrible timing. I am so sorry I was not able to help you.'

'I'm sorry too that I wasn't able to visit you in prison,' Ellen replied. She'd written to Madame since moving in with Aisling, but had not been able to make the journey to Mountjoy Prison to see her.

'Don't worry. They wouldn't have let you in anyway, I suspect. It's so good to see you now.' Madame Carlton ushered Ellen through to the drawing room of Carlton House, a room Ellen knew so well from all the times she'd cleaned it, set the fire, and brought refreshments to Madame's guests. To now be asked in, to sit on the sofa, while Madame herself served tea — there being no servants left to do it — felt very strange, yet Madame made her feel at her ease.

With an effort, Ellen composed herself to

finally say to Madame what she should have told her so long ago, on the day Madame had discovered Ellen's pregnancy. How differently things might have worked out, if she'd confided in her then, before going to see her father.

It was not easy, but Madame listened quietly, intently, while Ellen spoke.

'You must not blame yourself, Ellen, dear. I have a confession of my own — I knew about Siobhan's brother. He'd written to her, and I was checking all incoming mail. But I was giving her the benefit of the doubt. She'd done nothing to that point, and I trusted her.' There was a bitter edge to Madame's voice. 'I was wrong to trust her, as it turned out. But what's done is done. The war split so many families. Later on, Siobhan redeemed herself. I'm told she saved a lot of Volunteer lives through her actions.'

Ellen was astonished. 'Redeemed herself? But Madame, how?'

Madame smiled. 'Siobhan became a spy, a sort of double agent. It seems she regretted betraying me, and so offered her services to the Volunteers in recompense. She passed false information to the RIC, and fed information back. The RIC trusted her, after what happened with me.'

'That's . . . incredible, so it is,' Ellen said. She remembered how Siobhan had felt her loyalties were divided, all along.

'Information from Siobhan helped prevent a whole company of Volunteers being wiped out in an ambush the RIC had planned for them, around December 1920,' Madame continued. 'So maybe my imprisonment was a small price to pay, for those lives to be saved by Siobhan's actions. She wrote to me recently, to explain and apologise. I have accepted that apology. Ellen, you must not blame yourself for not telling me about her brother. As I said, I already knew.'

'Thank you, Madame.' Ellen sighed with relief. At last she felt she could live with herself again.

'I'm going into politics,' Madame went on. 'I've quite a taste for it, after my efforts in the war. Now that women at last have the right to stand for election, I shall do so, and if I'm elected I can continue to fight to make Ireland a better place for all.'

Ellen smiled. Madame was an inspiration. She'd played an active part in the war and was now going to enter another traditionally male arena. Times were changing. Women could do anything nowadays, if they put their mind to it. What would she, Ellen, do with her life? Something worthwhile. Something that would have made Jimmy proud.

★   ★   ★

Increasingly on their beach walks, Jack and Ellen would talk of the future, what it might hold for Ireland, and for themselves.

'Aisling has been offered a job on a Dublin newspaper,' Jack told her, on one fine but breezy day, when the sea was being whipped into froth that lined the beach. 'It's quite a step up, so it is. She will need to find lodgings in the city.'

'Will I go with her?' Ellen asked, trying to

356

imagine what it might be like, living in Dublin again, although this time in much more comfort and freedom than with the Merciful Sisters.

Jack frowned slightly. 'If you want to, of course you must. Aisling has taken a great liking to you. Alternatively . . . if you prefer . . . you could stay here, in Bettystown.' He cleared his throat. 'With me.'

Ellen gasped. 'But it wouldn't be right, Jack. Not without your sister. I mean, if you and I were alone in the house . . . your reputation . . . people would gossip.'

He stopped walking and turned to face her. The wind blew his hair back from his face as he gazed at her. 'Not if you were my wife. I'm not Jimmy, I'll never be able to replace Jimmy in your heart, I know it, but do you think . . . Might we . . . ' He broke off, as she stared at him, a million emotions rushing through her. 'What I am after trying to say, Ellen, is that I have grown to love you, with all my heart. And I'm wondering if you think you might, one day, grow to love me a little, too.'

She could see the truth of his words in his eyes, and searched her heart for an answer. She didn't love him — not the way she'd loved Jimmy and would always love Jimmy, but she did like him very much, and cared about him, and enjoyed his company. It was a start, and who knew if one day it might grow into something more? Was it enough?

She turned away and gazed out to sea, the wind whipping her hair around her face and whispering in her ear. If Jimmy could speak to her, what would he advise?

'He's a good man, Cunningham,' Jimmy had said, back at Gatesend Farm. 'One of the very best; loyal and steady and I owe him my life.' Jimmy's words came back to her, clear as if he was standing beside her speaking them now.

Shall I say yes? she asked Jimmy, silently, then she waited for an answer, a sign, anything to tell her which direction her life should now take. But nothing came.

With a smile she realised that meant she was empowered to make her own decision. There was no one, no man or anyone else, to tell her what to do. Just her own mind. She knew what she needed to do.

She took Jack's hands, and faced him. 'Jack, I like and respect you, and care for you very much. And one day I might love you too — I don't know. I can't tell. But I can't marry you until I feel love for you. It wouldn't be right. So, Jack, I think I should go with Aisling to Dublin. I'm thinking I'd like to get a job there if I can, and be independent for a while. And you must visit us — every week, if you can. It's not so very far. Then, one day in the future, if that love has grown and you still feel the same — *then* I think we should marry.'

He listened quietly to her words and then smiled broadly, pulling her into an embrace. 'Ah, Ellen my love, so it's not a no and it's not a yes. It's a maybe, one day. It's a hope for the future, and that's more than I dared wish for.'

She breathed a sigh of relief that he had not been offended or upset by her answer. 'Thank you for understanding, Jack.'

'Thank you for your honesty, Ellen. And you know, with honesty and understanding under-pinning our relationship, there's hope for us yet.'

She linked arms with him and they turned to walk back along the beach, skipping away from the waves that chased at their feet, laughing when they misjudged one and wet their toes, relishing the feel of the wind at their backs and the sun on their faces, and dreaming of a hundred possible wonderful futures.

31

Clare, May 2016

I spent the evening after Ryan had gone working on my chair, to keep myself busy and stop me spending hours fretting about what the next day would bring. There were only a few bits to complete. First I cut a piece for the outside back, back-tacked it at the top, tacked it underneath and then hand-sewed down the sides with a curved needle. I flipped the chair over and tacked a piece of black-lining on the underside to cover the webbing. Finally I dipped a cloth in Danish oil and rubbed at the wooden legs until they shone.

'You're finished,' I said to the chair, and then realised I'd been working on it so long it was past dark. I carried the chair out to the yard, switched off the barn lights and closed it up, then took the chair inside and placed it beside the fireplace in the living room. It looked somehow both totally at home there, and also out of place, being the only smart piece of furniture in the room. But it was a start. I was making my home here.

Next job was to decorate this sitting room. The floorboards I'd uncovered when I'd removed the old carpet and taken it out to the barn were solid, and I'd been thinking they'd look good sanded and polished, with a thick red rug in front of the fireplace to match the armchair upholstery. I poured a glass of wine and sat in my beautiful new chair, relaxing and wondering what the next day would bring.

It was so exciting to think I'd very soon be meeting the person whose birth certificate I'd found in this very chair. I ran through a hundred and one possible ways the conversation might go, in my head. I was glad Ryan would be there too, to step in if I clammed up or said the wrong thing.

Ryan. Dear old Ryan, who already felt like someone I'd known a thousand years. Someone I was fond of, comfortable with, and whose company I very much enjoyed. Where were we headed with our relationship? Where did I *want* us to head? Pondering those questions took me through a second glass of wine, but by bedtime I had made a decision.

★　★　★

The next day I was up with the larks and then remembered I had the whole morning to get through before meeting Ryan for our drive up to Cavan. I needed something to do to take my mind off it all, and found myself regretting finishing the chair yesterday. Should have left myself something to do on it today.

There was always the internet. I could waste a couple of hours online. I opened my laptop and then remembered I'd wanted to research more about Mary-Ellen O'Brien. What had become of her after her baby was adopted? I began running some searches.

After some time and several cups of tea I found a newspaper archive that contained a report of a marriage in 1930 between a Mary-Ellen O'Brien and a Jack Cunningham. The wedding took place in Bettystown. The groom was described as being a veteran of the War of Independence, now a solicitor with a thriving practice in Bettystown. The bride was 29 — quite an advanced age to marry in those days, I thought — and described as having worked as a companion and housekeeper to the groom's sister, the well-respected journalist Aisling Cunningham, for many years.

'Is this you, Mary-Ellen?' I whispered. I did a quick calculation — 29 in 1930 put her at about the same age as Jimmy Gallagher, in 1920. Perhaps, heart-broken from Jimmy Gallagher's death she'd given up her child for adoption, and then taken years to feel ready for another relationship.

I pulled out my book of Meath Volunteers and looked up Jack Cunningham. Yes, there he was. He'd been a captain, involved in many operations. Three-quarters of a page was dedicated to him. Cross-checking with Jimmy Gallagher I saw that they'd both been involved in the same successful mission, early in 1920, in which an RIC barracks had been attacked. Was it possible Mary-Ellen had met Jack through Jimmy? And maybe Jack had helped her after Jimmy's death, putting her in touch with his sister and giving her a home . . .

I searched through the archives of the paper that had reported their wedding a little more, and found several birth announcements in later years. Mary-Ellen and Jack had five children

362

together over the following decade. They would be half-siblings to James Haggerty, and at ten or more years younger than him might well be still alive.

It was good to think that Mary-Ellen appeared to have had a happy life in the end, after losing her lover in the war and having to give up her first child for adoption. Did she ever think of her first-born, wondering what kind of life he was living with his adoptive family? Or was she content knowing that she'd done the right thing giving him up when she'd been so young, unable to bring him up herself? I'd never know. You can research ancestry all you like, but how people actually felt and what they thought is lost in the mists of time.

★　★　★

I had a quick lunch, dithered over what to wear and settled on my only pair of trousers that were not jeans and a long-sleeved floral print top. I brushed my hair and even put a bit of make-up on. Not because I was meeting Ryan, I told myself, but because I was meeting an old man who I didn't know, but on whom I wanted to make a good impression.

At last it was time to drive to Blackstown and pick up Ryan from the bookshop as we'd arranged. My hands were sweaty on the steering wheel. I had to switch on the air conditioning for the first time since I moved to Ireland. Another thing I still had to do. Buy myself a car and give back this rental.

'Hey,' Ryan said, as he got in the car and leaned over to kiss me. 'All set?'

'Kind of,' I said, with a grimace. 'Not too sure how today will go, though.'

'Play it by ear. We'll be fine, so.'

As we drove north I filled him in on what I'd found out about Mary-Ellen O'Brien.

'Aw, I'm glad she had a happy ending,' Ryan said, and I nodded.

'She had a good few years on her own though,' I said carefully, 'between having her baby and marrying Jack Cunningham. Yet she must have known him if she was his sister's housekeeper and companion for years. He was also in the same company of Volunteers as Jimmy Gallagher, so she might have known him back then.'

'Good for her to make a life of her own, and not just rely on a man,' Ryan said, and I saw my chance.

'Mm-hm. I'm glad she did, too. Ryan, I've been thinking.'

'Uh-oh, what about?' he said, and I stole a quick sideways glance at him before continuing.

'About you and me. Us. Our . . . relationship.'

'OK . . . '

I took a deep breath. 'I really like you. A lot. Really.'

'I can feel a 'but' coming?'

I sighed. 'I'm only just free of a long, abusive — emotionally if not physically — relationship. I'm not sure . . . I don't think I should go straight into another one. I don't mean another abusive relationship, oh God, of course not, I mean, you're not abusive, you're lovely, but . . . '

364

I stole another glance. He was grinning.

'You're right there. I'm not abusive.'

'I know. You're . . . you and Janice . . . you're the best friends I've made in Ireland.'

'Only friends?' There was a pang of regret in his voice.

'Ryan, I'm sorry. For now, friends only. I need to . . . take things slowly. Find my feet. Establish my independence, before I . . . '

'I wouldn't take away your independence, Clare. I'm not like Paul. I wouldn't try to control you, believe me.'

'I know you wouldn't. But even so, I just feel I need some time. To find myself, I suppose. Work out who I am, when I'm not with Paul.'

Ryan reached across and covered my hand where it rested on my thigh with his. 'It's OK. I understand. I guess, as I've been on my own a few years and am ready for someone new, I forget what it's like. I needed time after my wife died, too.'

'We'll be friends, we'll see each other often, go out now and again.'

'I'd like that.'

'And I reckon in a few months, a year or so . . . if you're still here . . . still available . . . '

He chuckled. 'I'll still be here. I'll still be available. It's not a problem, Clare. I'll wait, until you're ready.'

'Thank you.' In that moment I realised I had probably met the most perfect man in all the world, and yet here I was pushing him away. But he was OK with that, and I knew it was the right thing to do. I had to do it, for myself. I'd broken free of Paul, made a start at building my own life, and had to complete that rebuild before I could move on. He understood and he'd wait, and that's what made him perfect.

He squeezed my hand and then let go. I smiled at him, and then we travelled in a comfortable silence for a while, until we were approaching Blacklion, a village right on the border with Northern Ireland.

'Across the border there is Belcoo, County Fermanagh,' Ryan said. 'Before the Good Friday Agreement there used to be a watchtower, right there, and a checkpoint on the road. Hard to imagine now, isn't it?'

I nodded. It had taken a long time, but peace had finally been won.

We'd decided to take a quick look at Jimmy Gallagher's grave first, and take a photo of it. Perhaps James Haggerty would like to see it.

★　★　★

It took a while going up and down the neat rows of the cemetery before we found the right headstone. It bore a simple engraving: *James Gallagher November 1900 — January 1921. Fuair sé bás ag troid ar son saoirse na hÉireann.*

'What does that mean?' I asked, pointing to the Irish.

'He died fighting for the freedom of Ireland,' Ryan replied.

An image of Daithí crossed my mind. He'd basically been fighting for the same thing, sixty years later. But most people, especially in

Britain, would consider him a terrorist rather than a hero.

We stood a moment in silence, paying our respects to a young man who'd died for what he believed in, far too young. A young man I'd never known but who'd been brought up in my house and who'd touched my life. 'Glad to meet you at last,' I whispered to him. In my pocket I clutched his communion medallion. If James Haggerty didn't want it, I'd bring it back here and bury it with its original owner.

* * *

And then it was time to meet his son. It was a short distance to the Haggerty garage, sited on the edge of the village with a smart two-storey house behind. The garage was a hive of activity with around a half-dozen mechanics in blue overalls working on three cars.

'Looks like a thriving business,' Ryan said, as we approached the office where a middle-aged woman with a friendly face was sitting behind a desk, stuffing invoices into envelopes. A bell rang as we opened the door and she looked up, smiling.

'Can I help you? Oh, you would be Clare Farrell, here to see my father-in-law? I'm Noreen Haggerty.' She held out a hand and we both shook it.

'Yes, I'm Clare, this is my friend Ryan.'

'Well, come on through! He can't wait to meet you, you know. He's talked of nothing else since your email arrived.' She led us through the workshop to a back door, across a yard and into the house behind.

'Dad? Clare's here, with a friend,' she called, as we walked through the hallway and sitting room and into a conservatory at the back of the house, which overlooked a well-maintained garden. An old man with a shock of white hair was sitting in a wheelchair facing out across the lawn. As we entered he spun the chair around to face us, and his face broke into a broad grin. I liked him instantly.

'Well now, Miss Farrell, is it? Or Mrs?'

'Please, just call me Clare,' I said, and shook his hand.

'And I'm James,' he replied. I introduced Ryan.

'I'll put the kettle on, so,' Noreen said, as she gestured to a sofa for Ryan and me to sit on.

'Now. Tell me the whole story, would you? How has an Englishwoman such as yourself come to be in Ireland, tracking down an old man such as me?' James said, and I did as he'd asked, telling him how I'd inherited the farm, stripped back the old chair and discovered his birth certificate inside it.

With Ryan commenting now and again I outlined the research that had led us to James. Halfway through Noreen brought in tea, poured it, but then left us to return to her work in the office. 'I'll hear it all later, so I will,' she said with a smile as she left.

'Quite a story!' James said, when I'd finished. His eyes were sparkling.

'So this,' I said, pulling out the birth certificate, 'is your original birth certificate. It shows your mother's name but no father's name.'

'As they were unmarried and presumably your father wasn't present when the birth was registered — the father's name was left blank,' Ryan explained.

James took the certificate, pulled out a large pair of spectacles, which he perched on the end of his nose, and peered at the details.

'O'Brien, eh? I know a few O'Briens. Would be odd if they were relatives, but sure it's a common enough name.'

I told him then about the research I'd done into Mary-Ellen O'Brien's later life. 'So you see, you do have some relatives out there. Half-brothers and sisters.'

'That's incredible, so it is.' He shook his head slowly. Ryan and I stayed quiet for a moment, giving him time to get to grips with this new knowledge. 'So, I could find them, could I? And tell them I'm their long-lost brother?'

I smiled. 'If you wanted to, yes. Might be a shock to them though, if their — your — mother never mentioned an earlier baby.'

He nodded. 'Aye. It'd be a delicate conversation to have. I was lucky — I always knew I'd been adopted from a Magdalene Laundry. I was one of the lucky ones, not having to grow up in that institution. When it all came out, in the news, about what went on in those places and how harsh it was for the poor girls, I was horrified. It was a lucky escape, I think.'

'Yes, I think so, too.'

'And lots of children in those places died and were just buried in the grounds. That's one of

369

the most shocking things. Well, I got out, and you're after telling me my mother got out too and had a happy life after. That's something. A real comfort. Now, tell me what you know of my father.'

'His name was Jimmy Gallagher. He was a Volunteer, fighting for Ireland's independence, and sadly he died during a mission around the time you were born. There's a short write-up of his actions during the war in this book.' I pulled out the Meath Volunteers book and opened it at Jimmy Gallagher's page.

James scanned it and smiled. 'Ah, I'm a chip off the old block, it seems. I'm a Republican all through. I've been refusing to die until Ireland's united. Now I see I've been only wanting to see my father's work finished. Buried near Blacklion, was he?'

'Yes.' I showed him the photo of Jimmy Gallagher's grave and told him where it was.

'Aye. I know that cemetery well. My parents — adoptive parents, of course — are buried there. And some friends. To think, I've been walking past my birth father's grave all these times, without ever knowing it! Noreen and my boy Martin will have to take me there soon, so I can pay my respects. Look at him. A Volunteer! Makes me very proud.'

'You might like to have this,' I said, taking the medallion out of my pocket.

He took it, pushed his spectacles further up his nose and gasped as he read the inscription. 'This was his?'

'Yes. It was tucked inside the old chair,

370

folded inside the birth certificate. Whoever put them there — Mary-Ellen, I'm guessing — meant the two things to stay together. It's yours by rights.'

'It's something they both would have touched,' he whispered, and I watched as his gnarled old hands closed tightly around it. He closed his eyes and leaned back in his wheelchair, as though trying to connect with his birth parents through the medallion.

I turned to Ryan and smiled. He held out a hand to me, and I took it and squeezed it. I was glad to be sharing this moment with him. In time, we'd share a lot more together, I was certain.

James had opened his eyes and was smiling at us, his eyes watering a little, or was that a tear pooling against his eyelashes? 'This means such a lot,' he said. 'Such a lot. Thank you so much for tracking me down. I had a good childhood, but now I know where I came from. It makes my life feel complete. These people, Jimmy and Mary-Ellen, I think they were good people. I'd have liked them.'

'I think you're right, James. I'm glad to have found you.' In a strange kind of way, it felt as though I'd completed Jimmy and Mary-Ellen's story, and brought them closure. In restarting my own life, I'd managed to tie up the loose ends of theirs. The forgotten secret, buried in the depths of that old chair, now revealed and resolved.

James was gazing at the medallion again. An old man, near the end of his life, happy to finally know where he'd come from. And here was I, comfortable at last in my mid-life, looking forward to a future that promised so much.

Acknowledgements

Firstly, thanks to my editor Celia Lomas for helping me shape this book. It wasn't an easy one to write, so I assume it wasn't an easy one to edit either, but Celia's insightful comments really helped me find the right story to tell.

Thanks too to my beta readers — my husband Ignatius McGurl, son Fionn McGurl and friend Lor Bingham. Your comments helped massively, and your encouragement helped boost my confidence in this book.

As always the team at HQ deserve a mention for the cover design, copy-editing, proofing and marketing. Thank you all!

Finally, thanks to my mother-in-law Jane McGurl, whose throwaway comment many years ago about how her father had a stash of weapons from the War of Independence buried under his cowshed was the seed that grew, eventually, into this novel. Be careful what you say around writers — it could all end up in a novel some day.

We do hope that you have enjoyed reading this large print book.

Did you know that all of our titles are available for purchase?

We publish a wide range of high quality large print books including:
Romances, Mysteries, Classics
General Fiction
Non Fiction and Westerns

Special interest titles available in large print are:
The Little Oxford Dictionary
Music Book
Song Book
Hymn Book
Service Book

Also available from us courtesy of Oxford University Press:
Young Readers' Dictionary
(large print edition)
Young Readers' Thesaurus
(large print edition)

For further information or a free brochure, please contact us at:
Ulverscroft Large Print Books Ltd.,
The Green, Bradgate Road, Anstey,
Leicester, LE7 7FU, England.
Tel: (00 44) 0116 236 4325
Fax: (00 44) 0116 234 0205

THE DROWNED VILLAGE

Kathleen McGurl

It's the summer of 1935, and eleven-year-old Stella Walker is preparing to leave her home forever. Forced to evacuate to make way for a new reservoir, the village of Brackendale Green will soon be lost. But before the water has even reached them, a dreadful event threatens to tear Stella's family apart . . . In the present day, Stella is living with her granddaughter Laura, who helps to care for her as she attempts to leave double heartache behind. A fierce summer has dried up the lake and revealed the remnants of the deserted village, and Stella is sure the place still holds answers for her. With only days until the rain returns, she begs Laura to make the journey for her — and to finally solve the mysteries of the almost forgotten past.

THE GIRL FROM BALLYMOR

Kathleen McGurl

Ballymor, Ireland, 1847: As famine grips the country, Kitty McCarthy is left widowed and alone. Fighting to keep her two remaining children alive against all odds, she must decide how far she will go to save her family . . . Present day: Arriving in Ballymor, Maria is researching her ancestor, Victorian artist Michael McCarthy, and his beloved mother, the mysterious Kitty who disappeared without a trace. Running from her future, it's not only answers about the past that Maria hopes to find in Ireland. As her search brings her closer to the truth about Kitty's fate, Maria must make the biggest decision of her life . . .